STRANGER MAGICS

STRANGER MAGICS

ASH FITZSIMMONS

HARPER

VOYAGER
IMPULSE

An Imprint of HarperCollinsPublishers

This is a work of fiction. Names, characters, places, and incidents are products of the author's imagination or are used fictitiously and are not to be construed as real. Any resemblance to actual events, locales, organizations, or persons, living or dead, is entirely coincidental.

STRANGER MAGICS. Copyright © 2017 by Ash Fitzsimmons. All rights reserved. Printed in the United States of America. No part of this book may be used or reproduced in any manner whatsoever without written permission except in the case of brief quotations embodied in critical articles and reviews. For information, address HarperCollins Publishers, 195 Broadway, New York, NY 10007.

Digital Edition NOVEMBER 2017 ISBN: 978-0-06-268672-5
Print Edition ISBN: 978-0-06-268673-2

Cover design by Alicia Tatone
Cover photos by © Michael Steden/Shutterstock (book); © MrVander/
Shutterstock (star burst)

Harper Voyager, the Harper Voyager logo, and Harper Voyager Impulse are trademarks of HarperCollins Publishers.

HarperCollins is a registered trademark of HarperCollins Publishers in the United States of America and other countries.

FIRST EDITION

17 18 19 20 21   HDC   10 9 8 7 6 5 4 3 2 1

To Jennifer

STRANGER MAGICS

CHAPTER 1

Shortly after ten on a windy March evening, I parked my Honda midway up the semicircular dirt driveway of a well-tended farmhouse and surveyed the place, ignoring the panicked sounds of my passenger as he attempted to unbuckle with shaking hands. Father Paul's trusty white Volvo sat a few yards ahead of me, unattended, and beyond that, a pair of BMW sedans— the homeowners' vehicles, no doubt—aimed toward the road in case a sudden escape was warranted. Paul had told me nothing about the clients, but then again, understanding people was the priest's job, not mine.

I stepped out, listened to the rustling of the nearby pines, and breathed deeply as I stretched my legs after the drive.

Perfect night for an exorcism.

Well, an exorcism of sorts.

In an unusual change of pace, Paul had also told me virtually nothing about the job when he called Slim's that night to find me. As usual, I'd left my cell phone back at Ex Libris, my bookstore, when I closed up for the day. But Paul knew me as well as any mortal did, and so he'd put the bar's number on speed-dial. Slim, the proprietor and sole bartender, also knew me well enough to hand over the phone, a notepad, and the stub of a golf pencil as soon as the caller identified himself.

"The situation's in Harrow," Paul had said. "It's a wide patch of dirt with a stop sign about an hour northwest of you. Can't be completely sure, but I think I'm dealing with a friend of yours."

I'd offered to leave immediately, but Paul had asked me to wait. "I can hold the fort for now," he'd said as a screen door squealed and slammed behind him. "Maybe an hour or two. Give me time to do a proper house blessing, at least. But, uh . . . I've called Joseph in to help, and he's on his way to you now."

That had piqued my interest. "You've told him about me?" I'd asked.

"Very little. Told him to find a dark-haired, green-eyed guy about his age." Paul had hesitated, then added, "I like this one, Colin. He's doing well at Immaculate Conception, hard worker, good kid. Go easy on him, huh?"

Young Joey might have been a fine seminarian, but he had a long way to go before he'd make a decent shotgun passenger. The kid had climbed out of my car on fawn's legs, clutching the door for support. Seeing him sway in the light of the driveway's security lamp, I had a flash of guilt for taking the winding, two-lane roads at a hundred miles an hour. I mean, there was no reason *not* to—I'd built a fine enchantment around my car that made it invisible to police radar, and another that warned away the deer that plague Virginia like overgrown rats—but I knew that no amount of reassurance would have helped the situation. I'm simply not one to follow speed laws.

And so I busied myself with the kit in my trunk as Joey retched in the tall grass along the driveway. All seemed to be as I'd left it, but still, I patted the contents with my gloved hands until I felt the warning tingle of the iron through the protective leather. By the time Joey came up for air, I had slipped into my usual brown hooded robe and was cinching the rope belt. He looked at me strangely—and a touch queasily, if we're being honest—and I shrugged. "Fewer questions this way," I explained as I fastened an oversized wooden cross around my neck. "Exorcists call for backup all the time."

One eyebrow rose. I'd told him I was a seller of used books, but I'd left the matter at that. "What are you supposed to be, anyway?" he asked.

"Monk. Mendicant friar. Whatever, it doesn't matter. Those people in there just want the problem resolved," I said, nodding toward the farmhouse, "and they're not going to ask too many doctrinal questions if I tell them that I can make the bogeyman go away. Here, be of use." I shoved my kit into his arms, and Joey followed me toward the front door.

There was no need to knock—Father Paul had been watching us through the dining-room windows. "You made good time," he began, stepping onto the stoop. "I hadn't expected to see you before eleven."

"Good traffic," I replied.

The old priest cut his eyes to his green-faced protégé, then back to me. "I see you're breaking him in gently."

"I do my best." I raised my hood, throwing my face into shadow, and glanced around him into the foyer. "They're here?"

"Kitchen," he murmured. "Back of the house. It started throwing furniture around, and I thought it best if they went somewhere safer."

I nodded. There was enough steel in the average kitchen to keep anyone temporarily safe, if they were smart enough to stay close to the appliances or the knife block. "You told them I was coming, Paul?"

He grunted. "Said I was calling in an expert."

"Nothing more?" He shook his head, and I briefly considered the situation before throwing together a glamour that wrinkled my face to late middle age. "They're scared," I said, seeing the question in his expression. "They want an older priest, not a green boy. Come, Joey," I ordered, pushing past Paul before slowing my walk to match my appearance.

Hearing our footsteps, a young couple peeked around the corner, then crept into the foyer to join us. I sized them up quickly enough: the tiny crocodile on his shirt marked him as a probable NOVA escapee, while her navy sweatpants, deceptively plain, were branded with a small whale. Moneyed, obviously, a professional couple trying their hand with a fixer-upper in the country, commuting north as necessary. Lawyers, maybe, or young politicos.

In other words, completely out of their element.

I clasped my hands together and muttered, "Peace be unto this house."

They nodded frantically, looking to Paul for a cue, and he cleared his throat. "Simone, Martin, this is, uh . . . Brother Colin. He's the expert I told you about."

Their relief was almost palpable. "He can get rid of it?" the one I assumed to be Martin asked. "For good?"

His wife watched with red-rimmed eyes, clinging to his arm, and I nodded again. "Father Paul and I need to discuss the particulars of your case," I said, taking care that my voice cracked to match my apparent age. "You two would be safest in the kitchen. My things," I told Joey, and beckoned for my kit.

He dutifully brought the plastic tackle box over and placed it on the hallway table. Fortunately, the homeowners were too interested in me to see his double-take upon catching my new look. A twitch of my mouth forbade questions, and Joey, though wide-eyed, stepped back without a word.

Quick study, that one. I made a note to commend Paul for his choice.

I opened the kit and rummaged around until my gloves touched a wooden cylinder, then lifted it free and passed it to Joey. "Salt," I told him, "mixed with holy water. Take these two into the kitchen and pour a circle around them for protection." Martin seemed poised to protest, and so I held up a hand to cut him off. "I take no chances. There are dangerous forces at work, and I'll work better knowing that you're protected."

They seemed skeptical, but Joey had coaxed them away inside a minute, and I sighed. "So what can you tell me?" I murmured to Paul.

He waited until their voices faded. "Holy water?"

"Nope, just Morton's and tap. Does the trick." I pushed back my hood and folded my arms. "What led you to fetch me?"

Paul reached into the pocket of his trousers and pulled out a slim digital recorder, incongruous in his liver-spotted hand. "Aside from the poltergeist activity, they said they'd been hearing a deep voice. Satanic, they told me. I thought I would try to coax it out, see what I was dealing with."

"And?"

"I called to it. It answered in Latin." He hit the play button, and a voice that sounded like a garbage disposal full of glass shards roared a response to the priest's question. When he cut the recorder off, I snorted. "You heard that, did you?" he muttered.

"Heard what?" Joey whispered, returning from the kitchen.

"Play it again," I said, and Paul and I watched the seminarian as he tried to make sense of the recording. When it ended, I tapped the little machine. "Did you understand that, Joey?"

His brow had creased into deep valleys. "Father asked the spirit his name . . . and . . . um . . ."

"Stumped on the Latin?" I asked.

He flushed, and I said, "Loosely translated, 'Two all-beef patties, special sauce,' et cetera, et cetera."

"Huh?"

"It's the old Big Mac jingle," Paul explained.

"He's fucking with you," I added. "And he's in the living room. Keep the yuppies out of the way, I'll have him out in no time."

With that, I left them in the foyer and strode into the next room, all pretense of infirmity abandoned. I dropped my kit on the floor and bellowed for the homeowners' benefit, "Unclean spirit! I command you to show yourself."

"Lord Coileán," a quiet voice said from the empty space beside a dying ficus. "When my lord hears of this—"

"When your lord hears of this," I replied in Fae, "you can tell him that I invite him to screw himself. Now, *what* is the meaning of this? And show yourself before I make you," I snapped.

The empty space shimmered like a heat mirage, and then a small, messy-haired boy appeared beside the plant, hugging himself as he glared up at me. "I'm doing no harm," he whined.

"You've got those two scared out of their minds," I retorted, keeping my voice down as I pointed toward the kitchen. "And I thought I told you not to try this again."

His lower lip jutted. "I'm just having a little fun."

The glamour of youth that he wore only served to annoy me. I simply didn't know what to do with a two-hundred-year-old man who preferred to look like a schoolboy. "You're trying my patience, Benatin. *Again.*"

"My lord gave me leave."

"Your lord's orders are second to mine," I said, and crossed the room before he could slip away. Grabbing him by the shirt, I hoisted him to my eye level and stared until he looked down. "I told you to let the mortals be. We've been having this talk over and over for the last forty years, haven't we?"

"Lord Robin—"

"Damn him!" I hissed, shaking Benatin until he quieted. "And damn you for dragging me out here tonight, you little bastard!"

His dark eyes widened as he sensed the depth of my anger. "Let me go," he begged, "I'll leave them alone, I promise, you have my word, even if my lord . . ."

As he continued to spout pleas, I carried him over to my kit, reached in, and pulled the iron bar out of the bottom. He tried to jerk out of my grasp when he saw it, but my fist was tight, even gloved. I pinned his left arm to the floor with my knee, ignored his cries for mercy, and pressed the bar against the back of his hand.

He screamed as his flesh began to smoke, but I held the bar firm for five seconds, letting it sear its way into his skin. When I released him, Benatin leapt across the room, still wailing in pain, then shattered the front window in his haste to escape.

"And stay out," I muttered, flicking bits of cooked faerie off my bar before I put it away.

The couple had been shepherded back into the foyer by the time I had my kit packed. I limped out to greet them, the very picture of the aged warrior, and placed my covered hands on their shoulders. "Bless you, my children," I wheezed. "The evil one has departed. Go with God."

Their grateful words of thanks followed me out into the night, and I let Paul tend to them as I loaded my car. Before I could slip away, however, Joey jogged up and whispered, "What *was* that?"

"Faerie," I grunted, slamming the trunk. With the homeowners watching, the robe had to stay in place, but at least it was dark enough in the driveway to drop the glamour.

Joey took a step back as my face changed. "What do you mean, *faerie*?"

"They had a faerie problem," I muttered, casting my glance on the broken front window. "Nothing demonic, just annoying as hell."

"The furniture flew around! I saw it!"

I shrugged. "Not a difficult trick. I've had dealings with that one before," I added, opening the car door, "and he shouldn't bother them again. Benatin knows I'm serious."

Joey held the door open against my tug on the inside handle. "Who the hell *are* you?"

"Another time, kid." A tiny flicker of will was all it took to heat the door frame to an uncomfortable temperature, and Joey released it with a cry of surprise. Before he could recover, I slammed it closed, tucked my robe up over my knees, and headed home.

As I climbed the stairs into the apartment above my bookstore, I heard the kitchen phone ring and picked up my pace. I knew it could only be Paul; no one else would call me at midnight. I grabbed the handset and flopped onto my couch. "This couldn't wait until morning?"

"What took you?" Paul asked. "I've been trying to reach you. Dropped Joseph off half an hour ago."

"I got caught behind a semi."

"Why'd you bother to drive, anyway? There's nothing scenic about switchbacks in the dark."

"Eh," I yawned, "clearing my mind."

"Colin, if I could open a gate straight into my garage from anywhere, I wouldn't be shy about using it."

I chuckled and tucked my free arm behind my head as I kicked my loafers off and onto the rug. "Fair point. Is it debriefing time? We couldn't do this tomorrow?"

"Depends on how early you wanted to chat," he replied. "I've got a conference call with the bishop at eight, and he's going to ask about Harrow."

"My condolences, and since when are you telling the bishop anything about me?"

"He knows the bare minimum. Satisfy my curiosity, and then I'll make up something vague to give him."

"Atta boy." A select few of the Church higher-ups knew of my existence, but in general, the less that was spoken of me, the better everyone slept. "Benatin again. One of Oberon's miscreants. I wouldn't be too concerned about a repeat performance."

I listened to the sound of Paul's pen scratching against his battered notebook. "Yeah," he murmured as he wrote, "I saw the window. He put up a fight?"

"Not much. I gave him a little souvenir, and he ran."

"Mm. Did he say *why* he was messing with those two?"

"No, but he's full-blooded. That's explanation enough, yes?"

"Indeed," he sighed. "Psychopathy's such a delight."

"You're preaching to the choir." Propping my feet on the armrest, I said, "Tell me about the kid."

"Why, did he pass his audition?"

"*Audition?* You're saying I get a vote in this now?"

The priest laughed. "Input, at least. Think you could work with him?"

I mulled the question over, considering his performance that night. "Perhaps. More importantly, do you think he could work with *me*? And does this mean retirement is imminent?" I asked, hoping to be mistaken.

To my relief, Paul said, "Not imminent, but it's past time that I started training a proper replacement. The boy's done well academically, and the bishop signed off on it. I think he has promise."

"Then I suppose I'll trust your judgment." I pulled a pillow under my head to free my arm. As I held out my hand, a tumbler of single malt materialized in my grip. "So really, what have you told him?"

"That we've been working together for a while, and that you're not to be trifled with. But if you don't hate him, I'll start giving him a fuller picture."

I paused for a sip of scotch. "Sure, enlighten him. See if he runs for the hills."

"You see, now, that's the outcome I'm trying to avoid." Paul groaned softly, and I could imagine him wincing as he shifted in his desk chair. "Any suggestions?"

"Whatever Father Mark told you back in the day seemed to work. What was his preliminary spiel?"

"The basics," said Paul. "A bit about the courts—Mab got kicked out and went MIA, Oberon's gallivanting around in the human world somewhere, and Titania's playing king of the hill back in Faerie, more or less. He told me you were generally on our side, but"—his voice modulated to mimic Mark's wavering tenor—"I was never to forget that I was consorting with a high lord. Take precautions, carry iron."

I rolled my eyes and finished my drink as I thought of Paul's eternally dour predecessor. "Mark never trusted me."

"Bit of an understatement. What are you drinking?"

The glass refilled, and I sipped again. "It's peaty, you wouldn't like it. Look, Paul, tell the boy whatever you think best. You're the best judge of how much he can take."

His chair squealed its familiar protest, and I knew Paul was heading for his modest liquor cabinet. "Maybe I won't tell him about Mommy Dearest right away."

"She hasn't left that realm in centuries. Oberon's court is the bigger problem."

"Granted, but that's beside the point. Colin . . ." He hesitated. "You have to understand that it's somewhat nerve-wracking to know you're running around with the heir to Faerie. It takes . . . adjustment."

"The *half-fae* heir," I protested. "That counts for something, right?"

"Yes, but all things considered . . ."

"Paul." The priest had a point, but it was a point that hurt coming from him. As far as I knew, he was the one person in the mortal realm who was aware of the whole truth about me, yet still considered me a friend.

A roar of air heralded the opening of his freezer, followed by the clink of ice on glass. "I thought I'd start with broad strokes, then get to the nitty-gritty if he can hack it. Try not to overwhelm him, you know?"

"I suppose this *is* all slightly overwhelming," I muttered.

"By now, I would imagine that you've dealt with enough mundanes to know the answer to that," he replied. "Now, I've been working from the assumption that you're not getting out of this game anytime soon, but have I been hasty?"

I snorted. "No. What else am I going to do? Take up golf?"

"Well, personally, I've given some thought to

requesting a transfer to a place that doesn't get blizzards—"

"Not Arizona again," I interrupted as my stomach clenched with sudden unease.

"Not Arizona," he assured me. "And anyway, by that point, it'll be you and Joseph. Maybe you two can start fresh somewhere more exciting."

The idea of a move, though an unavoidable eventuality, always left me a little depressed. I'd been following priests across the country for nearly two centuries, and seaside Rigby wasn't the worst place I'd landed, not by a long shot. There were always new and distant backwaters where a priest on the outs with his superiors might wind up, and since the ones who worked with me leaned toward the rogue end of the spectrum, I'd seen my share of charming one-horse towns. But more important, the transfers prevented me from giving in to the temptation to put down roots.

I couldn't stay anywhere permanently due to one tiny complication: mortals age and die. Even if I glamoured myself to look older than my natural mid-twenties appearance, I'd have to fake my death eventually if I stayed in one place long enough. So, sooner or later, I *always* started over. Getting the timing right just meant less paperwork.

"I'll put in a list of transfer suggestions with the bishop," I joked.

"Good luck with that." Paul's chair creaked as he

returned to his desk. "You said the culprit tonight was one of Oberon's, yes?"

"Yeah." My liquor level was getting low again, and I topped up my glass. "Benatin likes pushing buttons. Mortals are amusing."

"Sounds about par for the course. Uh . . ." He paused, and I waited in silence while he collected his thoughts. "Listen, Colin, before I bring the boy in on this, there's something that's been worrying me for a while."

I sipped again, watching the amber liquid slosh in the glass and feeling slightly ashamed of myself for drinking decent scotch like it was nothing more than soda. "What's on your mind?"

"Well, to be blunt, when's Oberon going to tell you to knock it off, and how forceful is he going to be when he delivers the message?"

"He's not going to get involved. His court's been in this realm since the eighteenth century. If he were going to do something about me, he would have done so at the start." With a final slurp, I finished my drink and sent the leavings into the ether. "I've put the two of them in a tough position. Oberon can't come after me directly because that would be stepping on Mother's toes. Regardless of her feelings toward me, an attack on one of her own would be an attack on her. He's not about to start that fight. You can tell Joey not to lose any sleep over that possibility."

"All right. In that case, when is *she* going to tell you to cease and desist?"

I smiled to myself in the dark apartment. "We haven't spoken in seven hundred years—why ruin a good thing?"

"That's not a real answer."

"Then let me put your mind at ease. Mother hasn't left Faerie in ages, and she's not going anywhere now that she rules it alone. She won't risk giving Oberon a chance to sidle back home. Besides, she has her own ways of making my life miserable," I said, closing my eyes as the liquor did its job. "You've seen that."

Paul hesitated. "You haven't had to mercy-kill anyone in a few years."

"Maybe not, but she'll send someone my way again soon enough. I'm sure she knows where I am—she'll rectify the oversight, trust me. So, no, she's not going to stop me from helping you. I think she has more fun making me suffer than she would in killing me outright."

"Mm. And if my seminarian asks me whether he's going to be murdered in his sleep by one of the Three?"

"Occupational hazard, but unlikely."

"Then I suppose I'll take what I can get," he said with a sigh. "And you, get some rest. Go to bed. There's no sense in passing out on the couch again."

My smile returned for a moment. "Have you been hiding cameras in here, Paul?"

"Don't need them. I know you too well, old boy."

We said our brief good nights, and I dropped the handset onto the coffee table as I peeled myself off the couch and headed for my bedroom. Surely, I thought, I'd had enough to drink that night to keep the worst of the dreams at bay. But as I lay there, staring at the ceiling and listening to the feral cats yowl in the alley, I couldn't seem to turn my mind off.

I remembered my first meeting alone with Paul when he was still wet behind the ears, a seminarian with a conspiracy theorist's thirst for hidden knowledge and a pocketknife up his sleeve, just in case. He'd been nervous sitting in my study, and he'd drunk the bourbon I offered him like it was apple juice. I'd told him the full truth of the courts that night. How the Three had partitioned their followers and Faerie eons ago to stop their endless war for power. How Mab had then risen against the others, lost, and been exiled a millennium before Paul was born, cast out with her court. How Oberon and Titania had split the spoils until Oberon—whether from spite or ennui, I couldn't say—took his court on forced walkabout in the mortal realm, leading to the bulk of my clients' faerie problems.

"There are forces in this universe beyond my ken," I'd told Paul, "but nine times out of ten, if you're called to cleanse a house or stop a haunting, it's nothing but a faerie making a nuisance of himself."

"But *why*?" he'd pressed. "What's the point?"

I could only shrug. "Entertainment. You're fun because you're incomprehensible. Faeries are amoral—they recognize *power*, and they'll act when their pride is on the line because suffering insults makes them look weaker. You, now, you act out of altruism, duty, love. They can't understand your motivations, so you're interesting. And when you prove inscrutable, they can always provoke you to blind terror and have a good laugh."

Unsettled, Paul had knocked back his drink in one burning shot, and I'd poured again while he coughed and caught his breath. "So, what are you gaining, then?" he'd managed to choke out. "You keep saying *they* and *you*—where do you fall in all of this?"

"I'm half fae. We get the perks—magic, immortality, youth—but with mortal sensibilities like guilt thrown in. Makes us unpopular over there because we're killjoys. I'm not the first to flee the asylum, if you follow."

"So . . . there are others like you? Here?"

"Some, but not many. The fae population is low to begin with, and the half fae don't always last that long. We don't play well at court politics." I smirked. "Plus, think about the ones born in this realm. What do you do if the furniture flies around every time your child throws a tantrum? Call a priest? Worse?"

Paul had grimaced and raised his tumbler. "I get the picture."

"You're beginning to. Listen closely." I'd leaned toward him, and Paul, emboldened by the bourbon, met me in the middle. "Forget everything you think you know about us. Most of it is wrong, if not dangerously wrong. I'll do my best to protect you, but you'll have to trust me."

He'd nodded. "So, hypothetically speaking, the odds of my being kidnapped into Faerie and returned in a hundred years' time are what, exactly?"

"Low."

"*Low?*" His voice had cracked as he'd leaned back into his chair. "It's *possible?*"

I'd held out my hand and willed a blue fireball into being in my palm. "You're dealing with magic, boy. Almost everything is possible. Focus on probability." The flame vanished as quickly as it had appeared, and I'd looked into his wide, worried eyes. "Yes, changelings are still taken. Not as often these days, so you're probably safe. And if you *were* to be taken and kept for a hundred years, you wouldn't want to leave."

"I'd like the place that much?"

"No. Coming home would be suicide. There's enough magic in Faerie to keep mortals from aging past a certain point, but once you're dropped on this side of the border again, the years you've postponed hit you at once. Take a two-hundred-year-old changeling and push him through a gate, and he'll be dust before he hits the ground. I've seen it happen," I'd told him, refilling my glass. "A group of faeries having fun with their longtime servants. They made a dinner party out of the affair."

"My God," he'd whispered.

"It was horrifying," I said grimly. "So, this is what I do, in a nutshell: I try to protect people like you from people like me. Are you in?"

And Paul, scared and slightly drunk as he had been, had nodded.

I hadn't told him everything that night, of course. I'd neglected to mention that I had by then become Mother's eldest living child, her heir, and quite probably a target. I could have discussed with him the *third* realm, the Gray Lands, where even I feared to tread. And I could have told him the real reason why I'd left Faerie, and why I was in no rush to see Mother again. Paul had a right to know who and what he was trusting with his life. But he was barely twenty-four, and I've done so much more than I care to remember.

Still, as I stepped outside into the fog to get my newspaper the morning after my visit to Harrow, the only thing on my mind was the coffee percolating back on the kitchen counter. It was going to turn into a lovely day, I thought, warm for March, with the promise of several hours of uninterrupted sunshine against the eternal sea breeze. I ran through my mental checklist, making a note to call a few book dealers once I opened the store, but otherwise began to settle in to another routine day.

And then Mrs. Cooper called my name.

CHAPTER 2

"**M**r. Leffee! Oh, Mr. *Leffee!*"

I groaned internally before straightening, mist-damp newspaper in one hand, and tightened my robe against the chill. "Morning, Mrs. Cooper," I replied, keeping my voice low even as the echoes of her call rang down the deserted street. We weren't the only two people who lived above our shops in this town, and most of the others didn't open until late morning. Since our nearest neighbor ran a tattoo parlor and answered to "Spike," I tried to stay on his good side and keep quiet before ten. "Everything all right?"

She fluttered across the street, her quilted pink housecoat flapping in her wake, and clasped my free hand. "I'm so glad you're up," she rushed, crushing my fingers in her moist fist. "I didn't want to wake you—I know how *late* you got in last night . . ."

Her surveillance was nothing new. She was notorious for spying on the neighborhood through her yellow lace curtains, but at least that made her a reliable source of information. "What's going on?"

Her lips, pale and lined with age, briefly thinned into a tight, nearly white line. "You'd better come across and see," she replied, then half dragged me into her shop.

It wasn't the first time that I'd darkened the doorway of Tea for Two, not by a long shot, but it was certainly the first time I'd done so less than fully dressed. That alone gave me cause for concern, even without my host's nervous sweating.

Eunice Cooper was the closest thing to a friend I had in Rigby, though the casual observer would see nothing in common between us. Mrs. Cooper—there was no longer a Mr. Cooper, though she spoke of him frequently enough, and never by his first name—had to be close to eighty. Her manners were quite nearly Victorian. She was the kind of person who stops by, finds that you're away, and leaves a calling card—then gets miffed if you don't return the courtesy.

But she liked me because I was quiet, kept to myself, and never attracted the wrong sort of customers. Once a week or so, when custom was low—in other words, when Rigby's senior population was either at bridge or Bunco—she invited me into her tea house, poured a pot of Lipton, and, between telling me stories about dear Mr. Cooper, tried to figure out why I hadn't found a nice young lady yet.

Mrs. Cooper believed I was gay, but she was too polite to ask, and I wasn't about to disabuse her of the notion. Weak tea I could handle, off-brand cookies and slightly stale tea sandwiches I could stomach, but the thought of Mrs. Cooper trying to set me up was beyond imagining.

The thing is, though, despite her frumpiness and love of doilies, Mrs. Cooper was still remarkably sharp. And as far as I could have said before that day, she had only two moods: prim and grandmotherly, and prim and displeased. But that morning, I noticed that her face was naked but for a greenish film. Her nightly face cream, I realized after a second's contemplation—which meant she had yet to fix herself up with her usual shellacking of heavy cosmetics and was anxious enough that she wasn't giving it a second thought.

My guts knotted.

Mrs. Cooper guided me into a corner of the tea room, and we hunched together beneath a cinnamon broom that had long ago given off its final whiff of spice. "Last night," she whispered, "about midnight, I woke up. I won't bore you with the details—"

I nodded, relieved to be spared another trip through her gastrointestinal maladies.

"—and I looked outside to see if you were back

yet. You took off in such a hurry . . ." She paused,
waiting for an explanation.

"Seminarian. Works with a priest I know—you've
seen him, the one who comes by every few weeks.
The kid was in town and got word of a family emergency, but his car's in the shop, and he needed a lift."

Her grip on my hand momentarily relaxed into a
soft pat, and she offered me a strained smile. "You're
a nice young man, Mr. Leffee. But I'm pretty sure you
were speeding." She clucked twice, then cut her eyes
toward the back wall and the closed door to her apartment. "Anyway, I was up, and I happened to look
outside, and there was this young thing wandering
around in the street, crying her eyes out. Well, I went
out to see what the matter was—"

I tried to imagine the poor kid having her private
moment interrupted by Mrs. Cooper and her green
rejuvenating masque.

"—and she wouldn't tell me!" she concluded, seemingly befuddled. "Not a word!"

"Is she from around here?"

"I have no idea, the little thing won't talk to me.
Maybe she's foreign?"

I shrugged. "Where is she now?"

Mrs. Cooper pointed to the door. "I gave her a cup
of tea and put her to bed, but she was up an hour ago.
Won't eat. Still won't talk to me," she huffed, then
squeezed my hand again. "Won't you go up and try
to talk to her?"

"Well, sure, if you like," I replied, slightly confused. I carefully freed myself from her grip once the pressure abated. "But I'm not really sure how I can help . . ."

Mrs. Cooper was already leading the way toward the door. "She's about your age, I think," she said over her shoulder. "Maybe she'll be more willing to talk to you. I just don't *understand* young people, Mr. Leffee," she added, almost muttering. "So *rude* these days. Present company excluded, naturally."

"Likewise," I said, following her up the staircase. She turned around with a look of bemusement, and I explained, "Young people these days. You're all impossible."

"Oh, you *flirt*," she replied, beaming, and tramped upstairs in a blaze of pink.

Those of us sensitive to magic sense it in different ways. Most perceive it as a swirling, colorful mass. Some hear it, usually a high tone like a television in a distant room. We can all feel it to one extent, either as a pressure or a tingle along the skin. And then there are a few of us unlucky ones who smell it. For me, the scent is difficult to describe—the only thing magic really smells like is *magic*—but if I were approximating, I'd say it smells like charred citronella, the odor of a lit mosquito candle. And the girl huddled on Mrs. Cooper's antique love seat reeked like a midsummer evening picnic.

From what I could tell in the dimness of the shaded sitting room, she was pale, thin framed, and either brunette or unwashed blonde. When Mrs. Cooper turned on the faux Tiffany sitting on the end table, I could see that she was dressed like a Ren Faire reject, her bodiced gown slightly ragged and, in a punkish touch, solid black. She had tucked her feet up on the cushions and hugged her knees, regarding the two of us with suspicion. Her pale blue eyes, puffy and black-smudged, squinted against the sudden illumination, and her full lips remained pressed closed.

It didn't take a genius to see that we were dealing with a changeling, though oddly enough, a teenager. Mrs. Cooper's guess about her age had been off by perhaps a decade, but then again, she regarded anyone under forty as a child.

I thought quickly, then patted Mrs. Cooper's shoulder and whispered, "Let me try something. I might have an idea." She nodded and stepped back to the wall, and I approached the girl with my palms outstretched and empty.

"Don't show any emotional reaction," I began in Fae, keeping my voice low. "I know you understand me. Nod."

Her eyes widened, and her mouth began to open.

"What did I just say?"

It snapped shut, and she nodded frantically.

"Good." I sighed. "Just do as I say, and I'll get you out of here. Agreed?"

She nodded again, even more emphatically, and I pulled Mrs. Cooper into the kitchen. "Okay, then," I told her, "it's as I thought."

Her hands had clasped above her chest in her agitation. "What did you—"

"She's a cult member," I lied. "Harmless, but somewhat brainwashed. I guess they just kicked her out," I continued, cocking my head toward the sitting room. "It's going to take some time—she may be a little traumatized."

"But *what* did you say to her?"

"Standard greeting for that particular cult," I said, willing the lie to hold, and pressing a touch of suggestion into play for good measure. "I used to do some mentoring—the priest I know, that's how we met— and he saw these people every so often. Told me what to do to gain their trust."

She still seemed unconvinced. "What sort of cult?"

"Something vaguely pagan. Lot of bonfires, some running naked in the woods, but they don't kill anything. And since I've seen this sort of thing before, I'd like to take the girl back to my place and try to figure out where she belongs."

Mrs. Cooper still seemed doubtful. "Are you sure that's safe? Do you want some help? I mean, if she starts to take her clothes—"

"We'll manage," I interrupted, pushing the enchantment until I saw the concern fade from my neighbor's eyes.

"Well, all right then," she said. "I'll just get the door for you."

While she headed for the stairs, I returned to the sitting room and beckoned for the girl to follow. "We're going across the street," I muttered when Mrs. Cooper was out of earshot. "My place. No commentary until we're inside."

It took only a matter of seconds to shepherd my charge into my store, but the seconds stretched into worry-inducing minutes every time she slowed or turned her head to gawk at the scenery. I could only imagine what might happen if someone chanced to drive by and saw me half-pulling an adolescent Goth into my home at an odd hour. We made it without incident, however, and I relaxed slightly once I stepped through the network of protective magic flowing around my building.

The girl wrinkled her upturned nose at my shop, pivoting slowly to take in the tall shelves and dusty books, and folded her thin arms across her bodice. "What *is* this place?" she asked with a disdainful sniff.

"My store," I replied, turning the locks behind us. "Go on upstairs—there's a door in the back, and my apartment is up a floor."

She regarded me with unease. "How do I know I can trust you?"

"You don't have much of a choice, kid," I snapped, pulling down the shades against Mrs. Cooper's binoculars. "If you're not happy here, you're free to go back across the way."

She shuddered. "No. But how did you come to learn the high tongue? We seldom have dealings with wizards."

I rolled my eyes. "Do you always insult your hosts?" I asked, taking her elbow and steering her toward the stairs.

Her brow creased into deep furrows. "You . . . are not a wizard?"

"Moon and stars," I sighed, and pushed open the apartment door. "What on earth would give you that ridiculous idea?"

"Well, um . . . the spells around this place—"

"That's not spellcraft," I replied, unsure of whether to be proud of the technicality of my work or insulted by the insinuation. "Probably not the sort of enchantment you're accustomed to seeing, but far from spellcraft. Do they teach nothing of magic in Faerie these days?"

Her eyes flew open wide, scanning me up and down. "You're *fae*?"

I glanced at my terry robe and fraying sweatpants and shrugged. "Again, probably not what you're accustomed to seeing."

The girl slipped from my grasp, then retreated to my kitchen, putting the short wall dividing the two rooms between us. "I am Lady Moyna, daughter of the queen," she said, attempting to sound intimidating. "I order you to keep your distance and state your liege."

I leaned against the wall and folded my arms, watching as the girl's jaw clenched. "Coileán," I said quietly. "The old bitch's eldest. And if you are who you claim to be, your half brother."

Her façade fell. "You . . . you . . ." She pointed at me over my dusty panini press, trying to formulate a response of more than one syllable.

"Lord Coileán, if you prefer. But don't tell Mrs. Cooper. She worries enough about me as it is without thinking I've lost my mind."

Her mouth opened and closed a few times.

"I'm not going to hurt you," I said, suspecting that she was ready to bolt. "I'm just trying to help. Relax."

She floundered for a moment more, casting her eyes toward the door and windows for escape routes. "What are you doing here?" she finally asked, realizing there was no easy way out.

"You may have noticed the store directly beneath your feet. I sell books. A little freelance pest removal on the side, but I assume you've heard about that."

"You rebelled for *this*?" she asked incredulously.

"Believe me, dear lady, it was far rougher when I first came, though I believe Faerie is still the more barbarous place. Speaking of which, let's talk about you." I felt her shield begin to go up as I stepped closer—I smelled it long before I walked into it—and paused. "So, you did learn *something* about magic, then."

Her stare was defiant and cold, and I probed her defenses, gauging their strength and limit. "If you mean me ill," she warned, "I will protect myself, hospitality or no."

"Really, I don't," I replied, and felt the shield fade. "Though I *am* surprised that you managed so complicated a shield."

"I told you, I am the daughter of—"

"No, you're not."

The words hung between us, sudden and silencing. "Yes, I am," she whispered.

"She tired of you, didn't she?" I murmured. "When did she send you away? Last night?" The girl gave no reply, and I planted my hands on the counter, a few feet away from her trembling chin. "You're a changeling. Let me help you."

That was, on reflection, the worst thing I could have said.

Half an hour later, once Moyna stopped sobbing, I crouched beside her on the kitchen floor and offered her a box of Kleenex. She yanked a handful free and honked, then balled the tissues up in her fists and stared at the white refrigerator, which hummed on, oblivious to her sorrow. "She threw me out," she mumbled, then hiccupped. "She threw me out."

Little pieces of blue tissue clung to her bodice, but she didn't move to brush them off.

"Want to tell me what happened?" I ventured.

Moyna briefly turned her puffy eyes to me, then pulled her knees to her chin and resumed staring into space.

"If you tell me," I pressed, keeping my distance for fear of setting her off again, "maybe I can do something about it. You're welcome to sit here and keep crying, but that's not going to change anything."

I tensed, awaiting the next explosion as she took a hitching breath, but she managed to swallow the tears before they could erupt again and steadied herself enough to speak. "Yesterday was my birthday. Sixteenth." Her voice had flattened to a low monotone. "Mother asked me to come to court at sunset. Wouldn't tell me why. I thought she was going to have a party, you know, a . . . a surprise ball or . . . something. For me."

I waited silently as she swiped at her black-smeared eyes with the back of her hand.

"So I dressed for it. Every trick I knew. Every bit of glamour. New dress, fixed my hair . . ." She waved her hand in the vicinity of her wrinkled skirt. "It was going to be a night affair, I thought, so I decided a black dress would be nice, and I made it twinkle like stars . . ."

Nothing original there—*every* girl I had ever known in Faerie, and most of the boys, went through a twinkly star phase—but I refrained from saying so. "Sounds pretty."

Moyna sniffed. "I was beautiful. And I walked into the throne room, played dumb." She paused, swallowing hard. "There was no ball."

"Uh-huh."

"Just Mother and some of her ladies. She . . . she didn't even say anything about my dress . . ."

Again, I proffered the Kleenex once the newest flood slowed. "She told you the truth?"

She nodded as she absently ripped a tissue into shreds. "Announced it in front of *everyone*. The ladies all . . . they laughed. They *laughed*." The ripping increased in tempo. "And Mo . . . Mother, she said that because . . . because it was my buh . . . birthday, she was going to give me a present . . ."

The tears were becoming tiresome, but I waited them out. "Here," I said once she came up for air, "why don't you just take the whole box?"

She squeezed it into the space between her chin and knees. "She gave me some piece of trash. Said I'd been wearing it when she took me," she mumbled. "And gave me the tongue of this hellish place. And . . ." Moyna finally turned to look at me again, her face splotchy and streaked, her eyes red and watery. "She said I could only come back if I brought something she really wanted. But she wouldn't tell me what it was!"

"That sounds like her. Listen, you've had a hard

night," I said, pushing myself from the floor. "I'm sure you didn't get any rest across the street. Why don't you wash your face and go to sleep?"

She wiped her runny nose on her sleeve, leaving a glistening stain on the black silk. "Here?"

"Yeah. I'll go fix the bed. Rest, and we'll deal with this later."

I pulled her off the floor and escorted her to the bathroom, then stood outside the closed door, mulling over what she had said as I listened to the water run. "Hey, Moyna?"

"Yes?" she called from the other side.

"That thing she gave you, can I see it?"

The water stopped. "Why?"

"Because it might help me figure out where you belong."

"I belong in *Faerie*," she snapped.

"Please don't be difficult," I sighed. "Just let me see it, all right?"

The door opened a crack, and two thin fingers appeared in the space, pinching a tiny gold chain from which dangled a baby locket. "Whatever amuses you," she muttered. "Where's my bed?"

It didn't make sense. It just didn't make *sense*.

Within thirty seconds of Moyna stepping into my bedroom, the hunter green blanket had become pale pink and fluffy, the light-blocking curtains had been exchanged for creamy gauze that somehow still did the trick, and Moyna was hidden from view by coordinating bed drapes that hung from new canopy rails. I cut the lights when the drapes slid closed, then saw myself back into the kitchen, disturbed by more than the locket in my hand.

I didn't mind the changes she had made to my décor—it's expected among the fae that one will always change one's surroundings to best suit one's tastes, and besides, I could put my room back to rights in under a minute. Hell, I mused, reheating my coffee, I might even keep the canopy, or at least the headboard. Her taste wasn't entirely terrible. No, what perplexed me was how she had managed the transformation in the first place.

It's no secret that changelings who dwell long term in Faerie often develop rudimentary magical skills of their own. If you stand in the sea long enough, you're going to get wet, and you may eventually learn to swim. But take changelings out of Faerie—assuming that they don't instantly die of extreme old age—and ask them to manipulate magic, and they're almost certain to fail. There simply isn't as much magic on the other side of the border, after all, and it's harder to control. A changeling brought back into the mortal realm usually can't even work a personal glamour, which for a faerie is as easy as breathing.

But the girl—as far as I could tell, a changeling for certain—had redecorated with hardly a thought. Her control of magic appeared effortless.

It was impossible, unless . . .

No. She didn't *feel* like a wizard. I had been wrong before, granted, but what she had done wasn't spell-craft.

I fixed my coffee, holding the mug with one hand while the other flipped the locket in all directions. Gold. But then, surely Titania wouldn't have taken silver into Faerie. My thumb found the clasp, and I popped the locket open with a little *snick*.

Olive, the engraving read. *March 7, 1997*.

The date was accurate, I thought, comparing it to what little information Moyna had given me. But I needed more.

"**D**o you have an originating state?"

"No," I replied, sipping my drink and twirling the locket at the end of its chain. "The first name and the birth date. Is that enough?"

"Maybe."

I could hear Paul's laborious two-fingered typing on the other end of the line. Calling on him to do my research wasn't fair, but I hadn't owned a computer since a poorly aimed enchantment turned my IBM into an expensive hunk of melted plastic and twisted metal. "She's blonde," I told him. "Sandy blonde, really, sort of close to brown. Blue eyes, very light blue. No weird birthmarks that I can see. Five and a half feet, perhaps."

"That's meaningless if she was abducted as an infant," he muttered. "Hang on, it's loading . . ."

His voice faded, and I frowned at the locket. "Yes?"

"I've got a hit."

"You sound surprised."

"I wasn't expecting only one." Paul cleared his throat and tapped a few more keys. "Okay, let's see . . . Olive Marie Horn, born on the right date, taken from . . ." He paused, then muttered, "Coleridge."

Ice ran through my veins. "Does it list her next of kin?"

Paul hesitated. "Just the mother."

I closed my eyes. "Is it . . . it's Meggy?" I asked, my voice hoarse.

There was silence on the other end for a long moment. "Yeah, I think so."

"Can you send me her address?"

"Sure," he said slowly. "She moved, actually— looks like she's in Virginia now."

I felt a dull pain in my hand and realized that I had been crushing the locket against my palm. "Really."

"Maybe an hour's drive from you. But look, Colin, I've got a bad feeling about this. Nothing good is going to come out of you revisiting everything that happened in Phoenix. You know that. If you want help, I'm willing. Say the word."

"I've got it," I said shortly. "Just . . . the address. Please."

Paul hung up a moment later, but I barely registered his farewell or the subsequent text message on my phone with the address. The tightness in my chest was unbearable.

My mother had done this to Meggy.

And I hadn't stopped her.

Perhaps it was irresponsible of me to sneak out while Moyna slept, but my once-cozy apartment's walls were pressing in on me. In times of stress, it's only natural to seek out comforting surroundings, and for me, that meant a brisk walk through the sleeping town to Slim's.

Rigby offered two options for social imbibing. The kids who wanted to be seen and didn't mind paying exorbitant sums for spiked fruit juice frequented the tiki-themed bar on the beach, which offered a deck with a view of the rolling Atlantic. My ilk, on the other hand, found refuge at Slim's, a dingy hole with a decent selection and a grimy television tuned to ESPN. When I slunk in shortly after midnight, the place was deserted but for Slim himself, who leaned his bulk against the bar to watch a highlight reel.

My bartender was not a conventionally handsome man. Though middle-aged, pasty, and bulbous, Slim had retained most of his dark hair, but there was little else to commend him from an aesthetic standpoint. That night, he sported his typical uniform: straining black T-shirt, matching sweatpants, and black Crocs. "You're late," he said by way of greeting as I threaded my way between the tables to my usual bar stool. "Everything all right?"

"No," I muttered, and made myself comfortable.

"Cup of coffee? Maybe lace it?"

As I'd been a patron of Slim's for some years, he didn't bat an eye at the request. "Something to do with that priest guy?" he asked, heading for the kitchen at the back.

"No."

A few minutes later, after he slid a full mug in front of me, I looked up to find Slim regarding me with his arms folded and his brown eyes narrowed in thought. "Really, the priest is fine," I told him. "Needed me to give his trainee a ride, that's all."

"What's bothering you, then?"

I sipped, stalling while I thought of what to tell him. Slim wasn't stupid, and I'd been in his orbit long enough for him to know my moods. Still, I couldn't simply tell him the truth. "I, uh . . . I've got to go see someone tomorrow," I finally said. "Someone I haven't seen in a long time."

"A female someone?" he enquired.

"Yes."

"Things ended badly, I take it?"

I sighed and raised my mug. "You could say that."

"Mm." He watched me drink for a moment, then said, "Well, last call's at two. Holler if you need something," he added, and returned to his program.

I needed many things—a time machine, to start—but there was nothing Slim could do to improve the situation. And so, I drank in silence, letting the television wash over me like white noise, and wondered what the hell I was going to say to Meggy in the morning.

CHAPTER 3

In 1995, I'd been enjoying all Boston had to offer for a decade—making the most of a city that was the perfect compromise between the energy of New York and the relative safety and reasonable pricing of anywhere else—but in April, Paul gave me notice that he'd been transferred out west. "There's an opening near Phoenix," he'd explained over pizza at the rectory. "I volunteered."

"*Why?*" I'd whined around a mouthful of crust.

"My asthma keeps flaring, and the doctor said the desert climate might help. And besides," he'd added, helping himself to a soda from the old green refrigerator, "these winters are the pits. I'm not getting any younger, you know."

I'd pointed what remained of my crust at him in accusation. "You're forty-nine. Stop complaining."

"Says the one of us who can't get arthritis," he'd retorted. "Look, my transfer's not up for discussion. You're welcome to come with me, but I understand if you'd rather stay on the coast. Your call."

I'd studied the vestiges of my dinner for a moment, then sighed. "I suppose it's time to press on, but really, *Phoenix*? You couldn't have pushed for LA or something?"

Paul's reply had been a shrug. "I go where the Lord wills and the allergist directs."

And that had been that. Sure, I could have lingered in Boston, aging my glamour as necessary, but by then, I'd been working with Paul for fifteen years, and a good exorcist was hard to find.

The move went off without incident. Paul drove out in early June, and I followed a few weeks later, silently cursing him every time I stopped for a rest and felt myself broil just a little more in the sun. He'd helped me make the arrangements for my new life— "If anyone asks, you're my nephew," he'd instructed over the phone—and located a modest house and empty storefront in the suburb where he'd been stationed, Coleridge. Unfortunately, as I soon learned, Coleridge was light on all vegetation that wasn't cacti or succulents, and my new store had bad western exposure. But there was nothing to do for it, and so I parked my new black pickup truck on the street that Saturday morning, grabbed two duffel bags, and headed for the door. At least I had been able to drop the age-disguising glamour, one less thing to think about while I adjusted to a new city.

Moving is seldom fun, but it's slightly easier if one is fae. With the shades drawn and the door locked, I undertook a few minutes of enchantment-aided renovation, staining the hardwood floor, painting the walls an inoffensive beige, and removing the cobwebs the realtor had overlooked. With the basics completed, I opened one bag and pulled out my stock—entire shelves, shrunk to the size of dollhouse furniture and plastic-wrapped to keep the books in place during transit. I carefully unbound and resized each and directed it into position, stuck the cardboard box of bargain paperbacks by the door, and turned to the second bag.

The store had a stockroom tucked behind the office, into which I carried the portion of my wares that wasn't marketed to the general public. For these books, in lieu of a shelving unit, I opted for a lockable cabinet with solid doors and wards against fire, water, and theft. Here, I kept my better editions and signed copies, treasures I'd accrued over time and carried from city to city. True, most of my customers weren't in the market for a first printing of Dante, but that didn't bother me.

It wasn't as if I needed to actually *sell* books when I could produce cash from thin air.

My move-in was complete within half an hour, and as I stepped outside to hang my wooden sign, I

noticed a young woman sitting at a plastic table outside the café next door. Much of what I saw at first
glance was hair, a tied-back mass of fiery curls that
bounced as their owner nodded in time to the music
coming through her headphones. She appeared to
be working—she had a notebook in front of her,
at least—but her pencil beat a drum solo against
the tabletop, giving the true object of her attention
away. Smiling to myself, I leaned my ladder against
the brick, then climbed up with my sign and a decoy
screwdriver. I had no desire to procure a proper ma-
sonry drill, and I'd found that as long as I seemed to
know what I was doing and was quick with the enchantment, passersby never gave me a second glance.

I was three-quarters of the way up and double-
checking my protective gloves before going for the
screwdriver when I felt the ladder twitch. Looking
down, I saw the redhead standing between the ladder
and the building, her pale blue eyes staring incredulously up at me. "Are you *nuts?*" she said, clinging
to the sides of the ladder. "This thing isn't properly
braced. One bump, and you'll have a broken arm or
worse."

I gaped for a few seconds, surprised at the chastise-
ment. "Uh . . . thank you?"

"Go ahead, I've got you," she said. Hastily, I affixed
my sign to the building and climbed down, and she
released the ladder with a grunt of disapproval. "If
you want a real ladder, my dad could hook you up.

Bellamy Hardware, it's a few blocks that way." She pointed down the cross street, then stuck out her hand. "I'm Meggy."

"Colin," I replied, and shook it.

She looked curiously at my leather gloves. "Dad could show you some real work gloves, too. You're going to ruin those if you're rough on them."

"I have extra. Skin condition," I said, resorting to my customary half-truth, which was usually enough to end the matter.

But Meggy was intrigued. "Ooh." She grimaced. "Psoriasis?"

"Contact dermatitis."

Her eyes flew wide open. "Me, too!" she exclaimed, surprising me for the second time. "What triggers it for you? I'm sensitive to metals—so is my mom, but not as badly as me. See?" Taking a closer look at her hands, I noticed the network of old scars like hatch marks across her fingers and palm, even her wrists. "Benadryl doesn't work. Got any tips?"

Startled by her enthusiastic reaction, I could only manage, "Gloves."

"Well, *yeah*"—she sighed—"but it's going to one-ten here next week. Leather and Arizona don't necessarily mix."

I stared at Meggy, momentarily convinced that I'd stumbled upon another half faerie, and decided to take the risk of revealing myself by glancing at her mind. A mundane would never suspect—I'd grown skilled enough that my touch no longer left the target with even the slightest headache. But anyone with sensitivity to magic would notice the intrusion.

With a flicker of will, I was in . . . but there was nothing on the surface of her thoughts to suggest that she was anything but mundane. The young woman was genuinely excited to meet someone with whom she could commiserate about her condition—and, I saw with amusement, she thought I was cute.

When I retreated a few seconds later, Meggy seemed unperturbed, and so I chalked the matter up to an unfortunate coincidence. "Want to come in?" I asked, pulling the ladder from the wall. "The air-conditioning works, at least."

"Sure," she said, and held the door for me while I wrangled the ladder back inside.

Returning from the stockroom, I caught Meggy staring about the store with her hands on her hips, taking in my recent modifications. "Decent start?" I said.

"Totally. I didn't even know anyone was working in here, and I come downtown all the time. But you could use some chairs, you know? Something cushy. Maybe there, by the window," she suggested, pointing to an open spot of floor.

I began checking the laminated paper flags demarcating the various sections. "Good idea. And since you were so kind as to keep me from breaking my neck, how about an opening-day special? Pick something on the house."

"Really?" She beamed a megawatt smile that dimpled her sun-freckled cheeks my way.

"Yeah, sure," I replied, trying to keep my cool but finding myself grinning back at her.

"Thanks!" she exclaimed, and immediately bounced away among the shelves.

While she browsed through the romance novels, I caught myself sneaking glances at her as I worked. She was moderately tall—the hair added at least an inch—and of a healthy build, somewhere in the soft spot between thin and athletic. Her oversized blue and white linen blouse hid most of her curves, but I caught hints when it slid away from the navy tank top beneath. Her cutoff denim shorts and white Keds certainly did nothing to disguise her toned legs. All in all, she cut a striking figure, her aesthetic lodged at the intersection of grunge, prep, and Saturday casual, and I decided that I wouldn't mind if she had a nice, long browse.

All too soon, however, she had made her selection and squirreled it away in her canvas messenger bag. "Thanks again, Colin," she said, catching me at the end of the aisle. "This is your place, huh?"

Having anticipated that line of enquiry—I did look rather young for a business owner—I nodded and continued straightening the shelf. "Orphaned. Took my inheritance and tried to make something of it. I recently joined my uncle out here," I lied.

I wasn't expecting to feel her hand on my shoulder. "I am *so* sorry," she said in a rush.

"Nothing to be sorry about," I said, and flashed a smile. "It's been a while. Your family lives in town, I take it?"

"Yeah. Dad's the third generation to run the hardware store." She paused, and her hand tightened around her bag's strap. "Uh . . . by any chance, are you looking to hire help?"

"Help?" I echoed.

"Like, you know, salespeople, stock assistants, janitors, whatever. I'll be honest," she said, cutting her eyes to the floor, "I need a job. Anything. So if you could use someone, or . . ."

In general, *anything* is a dangerous word to throw around when bargaining with a faerie, but I had no intention of upsetting Meggy, who seemed to be growing comelier by the minute. "I suppose I could do with some help," I said, and she flashed that dazzling smile again. "There's nothing glamorous to do here, but if you don't mind retail . . . sure, why not?"

She squealed, then threw her arms around me. "Oh, thank you!" she cried as she squeezed. "This is *so* great. I've been working on my stupid résumé for two days, and I'm about ready to shred it." Releasing me from her exuberant hug, she took off her bag and straightened her shirts. "I finished my associate's in accounting last month, but no one seems to be hiring. Anyway, I can definitely handle money. When can I start?"

I glanced around the otherwise empty store. "How about today? You hold down the register in case anyone slips in, and I'll see about those chairs."

"You've got it," she said, and hurried to the front of the building to raise the shades. "And you won't regret this, Colin. I promise."

My unheralded grand opening was a total bust in terms of customers, so Meggy and I passed the time in the pair of purple armchairs I'd conjured up and lugged in, drinking coffee and chatting. She was twenty, she informed me, an Aries, and hoped to be leaving town in two years' time, once her fiancé graduated from Clemson. Jack Horn—the original owner of the gold class ring that Meggy wore as a necklace—was across the country on a football scholarship and working on campus over the summer, but he'd promised that she'd have a real ring from him as soon as he had his degree. She had wanted to go east with him, but her parents had refused to bankroll it, and so she had opted for community college in Phoenix. "I may go back and finish a four-year degree someday," she explained, "but it'll depend on where Jack gets a job. He's hoping to do well in the NFL draft."

I kept the conversation going with half-truths and

questions that turned the focus back on Meggy, and before I knew it, it was five o'clock, and Coleridge was beginning to roll up its sidewalks. "Give you a ride home?" I offered as I locked up.

Meggy took me up on it, but instead of directing me into one of the little neighborhoods around the downtown district, she guided us out of town and almost to I-10, into the parking lot of an extended-stay motel. "This is me," she said, smiling as she collected her bag. "Thanks for the lift."

I considered the establishment—midcentury in construction and largely untouched since—its parking lot half empty and its neon sign half lit. I caught Meggy's wrist before she could slide out of my truck, hardly realizing what I was doing. "I thought you said your parents live in town."

"They do. Kicked me out last week. Dad said it's time I got my own place, so I'm living here until I can get an apartment."

"Is this . . . *safe*?" I gave the motel another dubious glance.

"Eh," she shrugged, "I guess so. And I've got a hot plate and a TV, so I'm set for the essentials."

Having wandered through more unsavory properties than I cared to remember, I knew well enough the look of a good place to get into trouble. The young men lurking in the parking lot, far from the security lights, only heightened my suspicion. "You're wasting your money," I heard myself tell her before I knew what I was going to say. "I have a spare bedroom. Stay with me for now, save up for rent, get yourself a place that doesn't scream 'narcotics raid.'" When she hesitated, I said, "How about we grab dinner first, and you think it over? Did you have any plans tonight?"

She looked sheepish. "It was going to be peanut butter or Taco Bell."

"Do you like Chinese? And if so, is there a decent place anywhere near here? I haven't had a chance to go scouting."

Meggy glanced once more at the dilapidated motel, then grinned at me. "I might be able to help you."

Two hours later, having swung by the motel with our Bamboo Garden takeout so that Meggy could retrieve her belongings and surrender her key, we lounged on my leather couch in a post-dinner coma, staring at the television in comfortable quiet. Eventually, I looked at my new roommate—I still couldn't quite believe that I'd managed to acquire one—and found her asleep against the cushion. I threw an afghan over her and settled back into my spot, telling myself that I'd go to bed after another half hour.

Instead, I woke with a crick in my neck and the sun in my eyes when Meggy muttered, "Oh, *shit*," and climbed off the couch. Blinking sleep away, I watched her rummage through her suitcase and extract a wrinkled blue dress and a toiletry bag. "Bathroom?" she asked.

"Upstairs, second door on the left," I said between

yawns, and followed her to the staircase. "What's your rush? It's Sunday."

"And Mass is at ten," she replied, hurrying up the steps. "Which means I have half an hour, assuming the bus runs close by—"

"Are you going to Our Lady of Sorrows, by chance?" When she nodded, I asked, "Want company?"

And so I soon found myself stuffed into the lightest suit I owned and flipping through the bulletin while Meggy glanced around at the church's modest crowd. I was lapsed, I confessed to Meggy, but she didn't mind, and I remembered enough of the choreography to avoid embarrassing myself. Finally, we joined the press heading out of the sanctuary, and Meggy pulled me aside to speak to the priest. "Father," she began, nudging me closer, "this is Colin, he's new to town—"

Paul just smiled. "Yes, it's about time he stopped by," he replied, and patted my shoulder. "Are you keeping my nephew out of trouble, Ms. Bellamy?"

"Neph—*oh*," she said, looking back and forth between us as the realization dawned. "Colin, you didn't say—"

"Because he has a reputation to uphold," Paul interrupted, and winked. "Stop by the rectory sometime, bud. We should catch up."

"**I** understand you're living in sin with Meggy Bellamy." Paul eyed me over the rim of his beer. We had just finished an especially brutal extraction of several faeries who had decided to encamp in the old theater, and though I was sore, the alcohol was helping.

I rolled my eyes and swigged. "It's perfectly chaste. She needs funds to get an apartment, so she's staying in my guest bedroom for a few months. And she's a pretty good cook, so this isn't entirely a charity case." I picked at the label on the bottle. "Made lasagna to die for last weekend." I drank again, then frowned. "Lousy of her folks to throw her out with nothing. She doesn't even have a mattress."

Paul made no reply for a long moment, though he worried his lip with his teeth, a sure sign he was agitated. Finally, he said, "This is in strict confidence, and should the subject ever arise, it's news to you. Understood?" I motioned him on, and he rose from the table and disappeared into his study. On his return, he held a spiral-bound book—a parish photo directory. "In all of my placements, I've found that the most helpful person is the church gossip," he said, wincing as he took his seat. "If you want to know why your people behave the way they do, you have to have some idea of what they're hiding. Luckily for me, Mildred Anne Winthrop has a big mouth."

He flipped through the first pages, then turned the book around and pointed to the Bellamy family portrait. "What do you see?"

The height of the hair and width of Mrs. Bellamy's shoulder pads gave away the picture's age, even before I looked closely enough to see that Meggy couldn't have been in high school when the book was made. There were five of them in the picture: the seated mother, the father standing behind her right shoulder, the pair of sons flanking them, and Meggy, shortest of the lot, squeezed in between her mother and brother. Aside from the decade-old fashion, nothing seemed out of place . . . and then I realized what Paul was trying to show me. The Bellamy men were broad-shouldered, dark-haired, and brown-eyed. Mrs. Bellamy also had brown eyes, but she wore her honey-blonde hair in an updo. And then there was Meggy—blue eyes, red ringlets, abundant freckles, and gapped front teeth.

"She's adopted," I murmured.

"Not exactly." Paul took the book back and closed it. "As Mildred tells it, Charlie and Sandra had their boys, Justin and Mike, and then Sandra went down to Florida on a girls' trip, got plastered, and had a quickie with a bartender."

I frowned at that. "She talks about her affair?"

"No. Mildred just happened to be polishing the altar silver when Sandra went to confession, and the booth isn't soundproof. Apparently, Charlie almost left her when Meggy was born looking like that and Sandra told him the truth. But they went through counseling and stuck it out for the boys' sake. I don't think he has much to do with Meggy, to be honest."

With that, the picture began to come into focus—why Meggy wasn't in school with her fiancé, why she'd been pushed from the nest with a couple suitcases to her name, why she called Jack long-distance every other night but never seemed to phone home.

"All I'm saying," Paul continued, "is that Meggy already has a taint on her through no fault of her own. She's kept her nose clean, and she's engaged to a fellow who is, by all accounts, a nice boy. Don't give her a reputation."

"I assure you," I said, lifting my beer again, "there's nothing untoward about it. We're sharing common areas, nothing more."

Though he seemed unconvinced, Paul resumed drinking. He even chuckled after a moment, "Well anyway, she's too young for you, am I right?" When I didn't answer immediately, he caught my gaze and held it. "*Right?*"

"She's . . . very pretty," I admitted. "Vivacious. Has a good head for business—"

"And you're *forty times* her age," he retorted.

"That doesn't make me blind," I snapped. "And since I can't stand most of the women in the multi-century club . . ."

The priest sighed and shook his head. "Do right by her," he warned, and took a pull of his beer. "That's all I'm saying."

As usual, Paul was absolutely right. Had I been wiser, I'd have fronted Meggy the money and helped her move into her own place. But by the end of our first month together—and between work and home, we were together nearly all of the time—I found myself dreading the day that she would move out.

Meggy was effervescent in a way I had never known another person to be. When she laughed, it was childlike in its lack of restraint, but when she was in a contemplative mood, she seemed the more mature of us. As the summer passed, she showed me Coleridge from the passenger seat of my pickup truck, then her favorite places in and around Phoenix. Under her tutelage, I ate salsa so hot that my eyes streamed, learned which movie theater was least likely to catch patrons who stuck around for a second film, and followed her into the desert to stare up at the stars. In turn, I introduced her to the oldest books in my locked collection and showed her how they were made. I taught her to swing dance. She taught me her mother's secret Guinness chocolate cake recipe.

By the time the inferno of the southwestern summer began to cool, I knew I was falling for her in a serious way—and I hadn't the faintest idea of what to do about it. The foundation of any relationship should be trust, but how could I tell her that most of what she knew about me was a lie? How could I tell her the truth without losing her? If I tried, surely she'd think I was utterly insane and run as fast as she could.

Really, though, I told myself, it wasn't as if I *had* her. Meggy still wore Jack's class ring, after all, and she spoke of him fondly. But I'd noticed that her calls to South Carolina had become less frequent with the start of the semester, and part of me—a part that I tried in vain to silence—rejoiced at this development.

Still, as little as I liked it, Meggy was excited about renting her own apartment. I paid her handsomely, and by Thanksgiving, she had a comfortable cushion in her savings account. That Saturday, after she'd recovered from the holiday at her parents' house, I drove her to her new place, then braved Walmart and the furniture store with her to buy the essentials. Late that night, after Chinese takeout at her new kitchen table, I reluctantly took my leave and drove home to my too quiet house, then flopped onto the couch to distract myself with the television. But even the leather seemed to have absorbed the scent of her shampoo and drugstore perfume, and so I stared at the ceiling and tried to come to terms with the fact that after nearly eight centuries alone, I was in love.

I could make it work, I mused. If I never told her, if I stopped hunting bothersome faeries and settled down to a mundane existence, then she would never suspect. I'd use glamour to age myself as needed, and we . . .

The pleasant dream popped like an overinflated

balloon. If we were lucky, we'd be together for sixty or seventy years, and then Meggy, her hair white, her vision dim, and perhaps even her memory fading, would slip away. I'd be alone again, but bereaved this time, forever spotting her from the corner of my eye or hearing an echo of her laughter in another's throat.

And Meggy deserved better than the illusion I could give her. She would marry Jack in another couple of years, she would leave Coleridge at his side for greener pastures . . . and I would be a memory, just the harmless, friendly loner who'd given her a job. Maybe I'd cross her mind one day and she'd idly wonder about whatever happened to me, but that would be the extent of it.

And that was as it should be, I decided, ignoring the protestation of my heart.

By March, Jack had once again become a regular topic of conversation. He was coming home that summer, Meggy informed me, and the two of them were going on vacation. "He promised me we'd go to California," she said one Friday evening as she dusted the hold shelf behind the counter. "I've never seen the ocean, and Jack says I'll love it. You'll have to meet him," she added, grinning at me as she worked. "We'll hang out. I bet you two will hit it off."

I was saved from having to offer a noncommittal response by the jingle of the bell over the door. A short man in a tan mackintosh and dark sunglasses shuffled in, and I appraised the stranger quickly—the raincoat was enough to set off my internal alarm, especially in Arizona. But then I detected the unmistakable stench of magic about him. "Hey, Meggy, why don't you go see about Monday's shipping, okay?" I said, keeping my voice light. "And sir, what can I do for you?"

He looked around at the nearest shelves of paperbacks until she had disappeared into the back, then stood straighter and slipped off the glasses. "Your servant?"

"My employee," I said quietly. "What are you doing here?"

His smile was thin, little more than a twitch of the lips. "Aren't you going to ask me who I am?"

"You're a wizard. I don't need further specifics."

"Surely you'll want my name if we're to do business."

"I don't deal with your kind."

"Oh?" He reached into his coat and extracted a long, fat wallet. "Perhaps this will change your mind," he murmured, and opened it on the counter. A stack of hundred-dollar bills peeked out from the slit. "I'm looking for a book."

"Tempting, but I'm set for the moment."

He put the wallet away. "Perhaps something else, then? What's the price for your services?"

"I'm not for hire."

The little man's dark eyes narrowed. "The Arcanum doesn't take no for an answer."

"It does now," I replied. "And you have nothing that I need, so really, unless you're interested in a first-edition Fitzgerald or Twain, I suggest you leave before you exhaust my patience."

His glance shifted toward the door separating the stockroom from the front of the store. "Pity that you're uninterested in my proposition. It would be a shame if something happened to that pretty face, wouldn't it?"

Those who have never had occasion to fight a faerie and try to do so unprepared learn, to their peril, that we don't play by mundane rules. Two mortals, even two wizards, standing a few yards apart will generally either rush each other or pull out weapons and go to work. But as I can manipulate reality in an environment sufficiently saturated with magic, nine times out of ten, I can be pummeling my opponent's face before he remembers that I don't have to walk across the room—and I've had a few centuries to cultivate a decent right hook.

I broke his nose with the first blow. By the fourth, I had knocked him to the floor and was straddling him, punching with one hand while my other groped in his coat for his wand. My searching fingers felt something hard moving beneath them, and I paused in the beating to rip his button-down open, exposing the chain mail beneath. "Clever boy," I muttered.

I never noticed when Meggy returned from the back, but as I yanked his wand out of his inside pocket, I heard her call my name. "What the hell?!" she yelped. "Colin! What's going on?"

"Get out of here!" I barked, then grabbed the wizard by the raincoat collar and slammed his head against the floor. As Meggy's running footsteps receded, I snapped his wand in two and let its powdery core run into my hand. "Unicorn horn?" I asked after giving it a test sniff. "And you thought you could best *me* with that? Now you're just being insulting."

There was blood in his eyes, but not so much that he couldn't see when I set his wand on fire. It burned to ashes in a matter of seconds, and I brushed the debris from my palms as Meggy returned with the office telephone. "Cops are on their way," she announced. "Don't try any—*hey*!"

I looked over my shoulder to see the wizard limping toward the door. "Let him go," I told Meggy, and locked the door behind him.

Uncertain, she clutched the handset like an amulet. "What did he want?"

"Nothing good," I said, beginning to feel the ache in my fingers from the unaccustomed beating. "I think I got through to him, but there's a chance that he might come back with friends. Meggy, uh . . . how would you feel about spending the night at my place?"

Her gaze landed on the bloody floor, and she murmured, "Yeah. Okay."

I stood at the front window, feeling the house's wards and testing their strength. There was nothing getting in without my blessing, but I was too wired to rest, and too paranoid to take the risk. I was mulling over my options when I caught the quick flash in the street, like the afterimage of lightning on the inside of the eyes. In the glow of the streetlight, I noticed the twinkle of glass, then spotted the middle-aged man in a navy polo and khakis standing by my mailbox. He saw me at the window and held up his empty hands.

I nodded.

He walked up the little stone path I'd made through the cactus garden of the front yard and knocked quietly. When I opened the door, he again held out his hands. "I came to offer an apology," he murmured. "Will you hear me?"

His face, dark as mahogany and gently lined under his thick glasses, showed no flicker of deceit, but still I hesitated, trying to sense a trap. When no gang of wizards appeared, however, I stepped to the side and pointed toward the den. "Grand Magus."

"Lord Coileán," he replied, nodding, and took an armchair. As I sank onto the sofa, he looked toward the ceiling. "We're not alone, I take it." He must have seen me bristle, because he quickly added, "I mean neither of you ill—I just don't want to wake her."

"Appreciated," I muttered. "Your purpose, then?"

"As I said, to apologize." He folded his long fingers together. "What happened today was unauthorized in every sense of the word. I *sincerely* regret the affront—"

"That little shit threatened my employee."

"He told me as much. I thank you for showing such restraint."

I paused, trying to read him. "He's going to need a new wand."

"It'll be a while before anyone's willing to make it. The Arcanum doesn't tolerate rogues." He glanced at my swollen hands and frowned. "You know, I've got a really good salve that might fix you up . . ."

"I don't deal in spellcraft."

"It's not," he replied, standing briefly to pull an unmarked tube from his pocket. "Got this from an old school friend who compounds. It's basically Vaseline and capsaicin—helps with the arthritis pain." I shook my head, and he put it away. "You still don't trust me, do you?"

"It's nothing personal, Greg."

He shrugged. "Understood. But really, I mean you no harm."

His lack of a wand did nothing to set my mind at ease. One does not become the head of a worldwide organization of wizards without high inborn skill with magic and the knowledge to wield it effectively. Most magi barely need a wand, and I hadn't seen a grand magus in centuries who relied on one. Greg

Harrison had assumed the title young, sometime in his mid-thirties, and he'd remained unfailingly polite in our occasional dealings, deferential and unthreatening, a Harvard man who used the occasional bit of Nashville charm to win over his opponents.

I sat back and folded my arms. "Anything else?"

"That's all." He pushed himself to his feet and tucked his salve back into his pocket. "Just an official, 'We're sorry, and we had nothing to do with this.'"

"And her safety?"

"Assured," he replied as one eyebrow twitched upward. "We have no quarrel with her, last I checked. Well," he nodded, "you have a nice evening. I can see myself out—"

"What are you searching for?"

Greg paused and smiled faintly. "I thought you didn't deal with my kind."

"I don't, but as long as you're here . . ."

He resumed his seat. "We're looking for a book."

"Yes, I'd gathered that. More specifically?"

"The diary of Simon Magus. The Younger," he hastily added, seeing my eyes widen. "Grand magus during the Great War—"

"Yes, I know the name." I chuckled. "You don't think it's scrap by now?"

"With the number of spells protecting it, I figure it's fine, wherever it is." He leaned forward, resting his arms on his knees. "And that's the problem—we have no idea where that might be."

I studied his face for a moment, seeing a flash of hunger beneath the impassive mask. "You don't want this for purely historical reasons, I take it."

He didn't try to deny it. "Simon Magus was the creator of a range of magic-storing devices. That's how we won the war, you know. Anyway, rumor has it that he hid his creations before he died, and we're guessing there might be clues to their whereabouts in the diary."

I shrugged. "Forgotten your locating spells?"

"If it were that easy, we'd have found the damn book years ago. The Magus went religious in his later years, changed his name, took orders, broke his wand—I suppose you know the rest," he said as I nodded. "But before he did, he put a particularly nasty little spell on his diary: you can only find it if you don't plan to use it. And that's our problem— Simon may have become a pacifist, but I'm from more pragmatic stock."

"And the rest of the Arcanum sees things your way?"

"Council was having a meeting a few days ago to brainstorm ways to find the diary. Someone mentioned you—given how long you've been in this business, I assume you know just about every rare book dealer out there."

"More or less," I allowed.

"Yeah, well, I told the Council you wouldn't get involved. The fellow you saw today, Jimmy Lamma . . ."

Greg removed his glasses and began polishing the lenses clean. "He's an aide. Smart kid, gifted, not a lick of common sense. He suggested that we could strong-arm you into finding it. I told him he was nuts. And then this evening, he came back licking his wounds and vowing revenge, and when I found out what he'd done, I smacked him upside the head. Guess I probably shouldn't have done that."

"Is he concussed?"

"No, but that boy can *yelp*." He paused to put his glasses back on. "So . . . because we're having this conversation, I guess it couldn't hurt to ask you properly if you'd be interested in this venture, huh?"

"Couldn't hurt," I agreed, "but my answer's unchanged."

He smirked. "Can't blame an old man for trying."

I sat in the living room for several minutes after Greg muttered a spell and closed the gate he'd opened into his office, waiting for the fug of magic to dissipate. When I was sure that I was alone, I crept upstairs to check on Meggy. She had fallen asleep in her clothes and was curled on her side with one hand tucked under her pillow.

I closed the door, telling myself that I didn't need to keep watch outside her room.

Meggy turned twenty-one that April, and we celebrated with a bottle of champagne and a Monday night of stargazing. By the time I dropped her off, Jack had left a message, and she hurried to call him back while I saw myself out.

The next morning, she was ebullient. "Jack's coach wants him to train at school this summer, but he's going to sneak home after finals," she confided as she readied the register. "We have to make plans. Have you ever been to California?"

I made a few suggestions, relieved for her sake that he'd be making the trip. The least he could do after missing the holidays was see the woman who'd been waiting for him for more than a year.

Finally, the end of the semester arrived, and Meggy grew more excited by the day. Jack would be home in a fortnight, in a week, in two days . . .

And then, on the Wednesday morning in early June on which he was due to make his grand arrival, I woke to the chime of my doorbell at six. When I shuffled downstairs to answer it, I found Meggy on the porch, her eyes red and swollen. "He's not coming," she managed, and burst into tears.

Between crying jags, Meggy told me what had transpired. Jack had called the night before with bad news—training was to begin immediately, and he needed to be there to support the rest of the team. His coach was adamant that he not take off for a week until later that summer, perhaps early August. "A delay, then," I told her, handing her a cup of coffee. "He'll be here as soon as he can, I'm sure."

She sniffed and stared into her mug, then mumbled, "Do you think he's really training?"

"What do you mean?"

"What if he's met someone?" she whispered. "What if he's staying at school to hang out with her this summer?" She raised her eyes to mine, blinking back fresh tears. "He promised me we'd go to California. He *promised*. And now . . ." She bit her lip. "Do you think he even loves me, Colin?"

Yes, of course he does, I should have said. *And he's missing you terribly right now, whatever he's doing.*

Instead, I pulled her to her feet. "Get in the truck."

We drove through the morning and into the afternoon, piloting west to the coast. Meggy still cried at first, but soon she began to smile again, and then to laugh as the road spread out before us. Her eyes brightened, her face beamed, and she rolled down the window to let the desert wind blow through her hair.

I stopped near the state line to pick up provisions. While I bought sandwiches, beer, and beach towels, Meggy tried on a dozen bathing suits, finally selecting a simple black two-piece that hugged every curve to perfection. With a giant soda in hand, she hopped back into my truck, propped her feet on the dashboard, and pointed toward the horizon.

Mid-afternoon, I found a secluded stretch of coast north of San Diego and parked at the public beach.

The day was perfect, partly cloudy and breezy, the temperature hovering on the cusp of eighty, and the midweek beach was nearly deserted. At her first glimpse of the ocean, Meggy squealed and jumped from the truck, dashed into the shelter to change her clothes, and before I had made camp on the sand, she was racing for the sea. I watched her run into the surf and laughed to myself as she shrieked at the cold water.

She soon trekked back up the beach, covered in goosebumps, and wrapped herself in a towel while she warmed up. We sat on the sand in comfortable silence, listening to the waves roll in and the birds squawk, and then I opened my case of Heineken. We cracked open a pair and drank them quickly, and then Meggy was back in the water again for a second go-around, fortified by the alcohol in her system.

The cycle repeated over and over as the light reddened and faded: down to the water and back for a bite or a beer. I pretended to read a book so that Meggy wouldn't suspect I was watching for sharks, but the shallows remained clear, and she returned unscathed each time, stomping out of the surf like a black-clad Venus with the beginnings of a sunburn.

We briefly discussed getting a hotel room once the stars came out, but the idea fizzled quickly. The beer was still relatively cold, the sandwiches relatively decent, and the waves continued their hypnotic advance and retreat. I could have sat there for hours, waiting for dawn, but Meggy was beside me, wrapped in her damp towel, and she leaned her head against my shoulder and sighed. When I looked down at her, she smiled up at me, and even in the darkness, I could see those eyes . . .

I don't often think about what happened next. It's painful and embarrassing now, and when I try to justify my behavior, I blame the beer. We were both pleasantly buzzed by that time, still able to control our bodies but lacking the good sense to warn us away from the situation. Many of the details of that night are lost, anyway, if I ever noticed them to begin with. All I'll say is that when she looked at me with that teasing smile, I kissed her, hard and properly, in ways Jack never had. She stiffened, then yielded to my touch, and when I guided her onto my towel, she didn't resist. She was beautiful in the darkness, my Meggy, young and strong, and she moved and tasted like the sea.

I woke at first light, alone. Meggy was standing on the shore, dressed in her shorts once more, hugging herself as the waves bathed her sunburned feet. I dressed and joined her, and we stood there for a long moment, neither of us speaking. She had been crying, and I was out of words.

We let the radio fill the silence on the long drive back, and I pulled into her apartment complex's parking lot that afternoon without managing to break the wall between us. "See you tomorrow," was all she said before she closed the door, and then she walked inside without glancing back.

I knew what I had to do.

My furniture was easily waved out of existence. I packed my few permanent possessions into three cardboard boxes, then drove to my shop that night. The street was deserted, and so no one saw my shelves shrink and my hanging sign fly off the brick and stow itself in the back of my truck. I tucked my inventory into my old duffel bags, cleaned out my desk, and locked up for the last time.

The rectory was quiet when I arrived around midnight. I put my house and store keys into an envelope, then scribbled a quick note to Paul: *Need to leave town. Heading east. I'll call.* I put the envelope into his mailbox, then turned my taillights on Coleridge.

I loved Meggy. Meggy loved Jack. And so I left.

"Last call," said Slim, pulling me from my reverie. I glanced around the quiet bar, considered my empty glass, then headed out into the night.

Paul had faxed me the rest of the story. The wedding write-up in the *Coleridge Reporter* four months after I skipped town. Meggy in a gown with puffy sleeves, with Jack Horn beside her, holding her hands and grinning like a fool in his rented tux. He'd looked thinner than a linebacker should have. Then the April paper, the front-page story about the missing baby, the tearful mother and somber father, the grandparents holding them up. The columns from the *Arizona Republic*. The one-year anniversary, now a cold case, the family exonerated of wrongdoing, the kidnapper still unknown, the baby vanished without a trace. And six months after that, Jack's obituary. Colon cancer, a swiftly moving surprise caught too late. Twenty-two years old, and dead of an old man's affliction.

All I really wanted to do was drive through the night, hold Meggy, and tell her I was so sorry, so very sorry. But dawn was only a few hours away, and so I made myself walk home.

CHAPTER 4

The drive had been slower than I would have liked—it was late Saturday morning, but seemingly every trooper in the eastern half of the state was lying in wait along I-64, and so I kept an eye on my speedometer. Under ordinary circumstances, I would have trusted my car's defenses to keep me safe from tickets, but I didn't want to chance getting stopped with Moyna in the car. The picture the two of us made—a somewhat haggard young man and a cosplaying female companion of questionable age—wouldn't sit well with any officer more than two days on the job.

When she finally woke, Moyna had changed her black dress for a lilac one with a neckline that scooped far too low for her years, and now she leaned against the passenger-side window, glowering at the road, twirling her hair around her middle finger.

I caught the gesture out of the corner of my eye, and my gut twisted once again. Meggy had pulled on a lock and twisted it in exactly the same fashion—same finger, same spot beside her left ear, a sign of boredom or deep thought. True, Moyna's hair was closer in color to Titania's, but I realized her eyes were Meggy's, especially when she cried. So much of her profile was her mother's, too—pert nose, full lips, thin brows. I shoved that image from my mind and concentrated on the two-lane road.

Moyna sighed again beside me, far more dramatically than the hour or the scenery warranted. "Yes?" I said.

"Do we *have* to do this?" she griped for the third time. "Can't we just—"

"We are doing this," I interrupted, gritting my teeth to hold my temper, "and you're going to behave, damn it."

Her body stiffened as her petulance switched to caution. "You don't have to be mean."

"I'm not. You're being a brat."

"I don't even *know* this woman."

"She's your mother. I'm sure you'll find something in common."

"She is *not* my mother," Moyna shot back. "She's just some stupid mortal—"

Moyna's rant ended in a little scream as I whipped the car onto the berm, slammed it into park, then grabbed her chin hard enough to make her flinch and spun her around to face me. "You listen to me, and you listen carefully," I murmured. "That woman has been searching for you for almost sixteen years. She is your *blood*. The least you can do is acknowledge that she was robbed by that whore you insist on calling your mother, understand?" Her chin trembled, but I ignored the theatrics and released her. "Meggy Bellamy is a special woman."

Moyna rubbed her face where I had grabbed it. "I thought you said her name was Meggy Horn."

"It is now."

"Why'd she change it?"

"She got married," I replied, hoping Moyna wouldn't press the issue.

A few silent minutes later, I wondered if I was being too hard on the girl. The last two days had been difficult for her, and I knew I was doing little to ease her stress. She had made it quite clear that she wanted to go home, and I had made it equally clear that I wasn't about to open a gate. "It could be suicide for you to go now," I had explained over dinner the night before, as she scowled at her chicken. "Titania told you not to come back without something she wants. If you disobey, she's likely to kill you."

"But she's my *mother* . . ."

I had bent down across the table then and stared at her until she met my gaze. "Speaking as one who is truly of her blood," I said quietly, "that doesn't make a damn bit of difference when she's upset."

As far as I could deduce, the something Mother wanted was *me*, but I saw no sense in sharing that fact with Moyna. Mother's intent couldn't have been more obvious: dump a scared changeling at my feet, make it easy for me to help the kid out, and Mother would have me to torture in person for as long as she liked. But as there was no way in hell I was going back to Faerie by my own will, I didn't see the need to crush Moyna's dream. Besides, once Titania had what she wanted, she would probably kill the kid as a nuisance.

What bothered me were the lengths to which she had gone to make her desire clear. Moyna wasn't just some random child plucked off the street or out of the woods—she was *Meggy's* baby. I hadn't realized that Mother had known about Meggy, but as I watched Moyna push carrots around her plate, I wasn't surprised. Mother's spies were everywhere, and it was no secret that she kept a tail on me.

Far too soon, I turned down a quarter-mile-long wooded driveway and parked in front of a tidy two-story brick house, its lawn winter brown now, but promising magazine-quality beauty as spring set in. A thick row of daffodils snaked around the front, softening the holly hedge behind it, while the old oaks that dotted the yard stretched bare branches toward each other like the scaffolding of a patchwork canopy. The place was neat without being immaculate, but everything hinted at the lushness of the summer to come—quite a change from Coleridge.

I shut the car off and sighed. "This is the place."

Moyna flicked her eyes toward me, then pointed to the yellow front door. "I go in?"

"No," I replied, fighting my nerves, "you stay here. Let me do the talking for the moment." I paused with my hands on the steering wheel, trying to come up with the proper face. Closing my eyes, I attempted to capture an image of early middle age, then made myself slightly heavier and softer, my hair flecked with threads of gray, my eyes marked with the beginnings of tiny crow's-feet. My blue windbreaker shifted into a brown crewneck cardigan with a partial zipper, my scuffed Reeboks to well-worn loafers. The jeans, I decided, were inoffensive enough to stay.

I flipped open the visor mirror for a quick check, then turned to Moyna. "How do I look?"

She rolled her eyes. "Hideous."

"That'll do." I pushed the door open and pocketed the keys. "Let me handle this, and I'll come and get you when it's time." Moyna merely shrugged, and so I closed the door and headed for the house like a man on his way to the executioner's block.

The front walkway was red brick, a perfect match to the house and nearly free of weeds. As I walked its length, I tried to think of opening lines—*Hiya, Meggy, long time no see! Hey, I was in the neighborhood, and I think I found your kid!*—but before I knew it, I had climbed the two wooden steps and was standing on a cheery green welcome mat. I glanced around and noticed a tiny camera mounted in the corner of the porch, but before I could ponder the security situation or even ring the doorbell, the front door flew open, and there she was.

Her red curls, still vibrant, were pulled back into a loose ponytail that hung below her neck. She wore an oversized white blouse over blue leggings, belted with a green braid, and matching ballet flats. Most of my attention was reserved for her eyes, which were indeed a perfect match for Moyna's, pale blue and saucer round.

We stared at each other across the threshold, Meggy holding the door open, me drinking in every detail of her face.

"Oh, my *God*," she finally whispered.

"Hi, Meggy," I mumbled, forcing myself to break my stare. "I, um . . . nice place you have here. Nice . . . uh . . . flowers."

"Colin."

"You remember me?" I said lamely, trying for a joke.

Meggy folded her arms and glared up at me with a petulant look I knew too well. "Where the *hell* have you been? And how did you find me?"

"Rigby, most recently. And I have an associate with an Internet connection."

Her face creased. "Rigby?"

"Yeah, up the coast. It's not so bad."

She stared back at me, momentarily flummoxed, then shook her head. "Colin Leffee."

I nodded. "Guilty."

"I never thought I'd see you again."

"I thought that's what you wanted. That's why I skipped town. I . . ." I floundered, trying to gauge her reaction, but all I could read from her was shock. "I'm sorry about Jack," I offered. "Truly, I am. I just found out last night."

Meggy shrugged, her thin arms still crossed. "That was a long time ago." She paused, then bit her lip, a flash of white against the red stain. "So why are you stalking me?"

"I'm not."

"I'm on Facebook, you know, you didn't have to drive all this way to let me know you're alive."

I had no idea what she was talking about, but I let it pass. "I'm not here to upset you . . ."

"I'm not upset," she retorted. "Confused, maybe."

And lying, but that wasn't the time to let her know that I was analyzing her emotions even as she tried to sort them out. "There's something that I need to tell you in person," I said in a low rush. "It's about Olive."

Her mood changed instantly, swinging from surprise and anger to anxiety and fear. "What about her? I can tell you there's nothing online but junk leads and fake psychics—"

"I found her," I said bluntly. "She's sitting in my car, right there." I pointed to the Accord. "She has her baby locket, the gold one . . ."

That was as far as I got before Meggy fainted. I

barely managed to catch her before she hit the hardwood floor of the foyer, and by the time I had her on the living-room couch, Moyna had joined me and was watching us with a little smirk. "*That* seemed to go well," she said with feigned cheer.

I looked up from arranging pillows under Meggy's head and glowered. "Be useful. Go get a wet rag or something—"

Before I could finish, the requested item materialized in Moyna's hand, a white cloth on the brink of saturation. "This?"

"Wring it out in the sink," I muttered. When she returned a moment later, I covered Meggy's eyes and stepped back from the couch, then took a seat in a chair across the room. "Get ready," I told Moyna.

I barely noticed the faint beeping that had just begun in the foyer.

She eyed Meggy warily. "For what?"

"As soon as she wakes, she's going to be all over you. Might want to back away."

"How bad—" she began, but the rest of her response was drowned out by the roar of an engine screaming down the driveway like a Harrier coming in for a landing.

"The hell?" I muttered, rising from my seat. "Stay with her. I'll handle this."

I headed for the front door in anticipation of the visitor, then noticed the panel in the foyer wall, a white plastic box with a little monitor embedded in the center, which was clearly the source of the beeping. The door camera, I realized. There had to be a sensor somewhere, perhaps an early warning system at the top of the driveway . . .

I pushed the flashing red button to silence the noise and scanned the monitor. The porch was as yet empty, but I saw the left half of a motorcycle parked in the grass and suspected that the rider would make his presence known momentarily.

It had to be a male. No self-respecting lady I'd ever known would ride a black Harley with chrome skull accents and decorative flames in the shape of cavorting naked women.

I heard him stomp up the stairs as I watched his approach on the monitor and sighed. The kid was scrawny, maybe my height but thirty pounds lighter. His acne scars stood out against his pale face, even in black and white, while his piggish eyes and oversized beak turned up at the camera and scowled. But it wasn't the face, or even the unkempt mop of black hair, that made me shake my head. No, it was the boy's wardrobe selection—a black turtleneck over skinny black jeans tucked into black boots that jingled at every step with their decorative chains. He had thrown an oversized black duster over the whole sad affair, but the *pièce de résistance* was the dragon pendant, a six-inch die-cast serpent with raised wings and red glass eyes.

"Bellamy!" he shouted at the camera, his voice too

high-pitched for his garb. "I'm giving you to the count of five to open the goddamned door!"

I noticed the yellow button marked *Intercom* in the viewing panel and depressed it. "Ms. Bellamy is unavailable at the moment," I replied in my best tone of placation. "If you'll give me your name and message, I'll tell her you dropped by."

The boy snarled back at me, exposing teeth far too straight and white to have come about by accident. "You listen to me, you little piece of shit," he snapped. "*Drago*, the Dark Lord of the fucking *Storm*, doesn't leave *messages!*"

Before I could tell the Dark Lord to shove off, I heard a gasp from the living room. "*Shit!*" Meggy hissed as the washcloth hit the floor with a wet plop. "Colin, *get over here!*"

"Just a minute," I sang into the intercom, then hurried back to her side and caught her as she tried to stand. "Meggy, you fainted, take it easy . . ."

She shrugged my arm off and shook her head. "No, no, it's not . . . it's not safe, you've got to get to the basement, there's a shelter in the basement, the wards . . . how did he get past the *wards?* Damn it, she said—"

"Five!" Drago yelled from the porch.

I jostled her shoulders until she focused and her eyes snapped back to mine. "What are you talking about? What wards?"

"Four!"

Meggy stared at me in panic. "I know this is going to sound crazy, but that guy out there is really dangerous. You need to get to my safe room downstairs, he can't get in, it's protected. I'll tell you about it later, but *get down there—*"

"Three!"

She paused, suddenly remembering the reason for my presence in her living room, then whipped around to find Moyna standing behind her. Her face went white. "Oh, my goodness, baby girl, you've got to get out of here!" She pushed Moyna toward me and snapped, "Basement! I'll hold him off!"

"*Two!*"

"What the hell is going on?" I cried, but before Meggy could respond, the door exploded in a shower of yellow splinters, and in strode Drago, clutching a foot-long wooden rod in his outstretched right hand.

"Oh, *fuck*," I snapped, then shoved Moyna back toward Meggy. "Keep her safe. I'll take care of it," I told Moyna, and closed the distance between us as the newcomer lifted his wand. "Kid, you really don't want to do that," I began, raising my voice to be heard over his boot chains.

He glared at me, then mumbled under his breath and flicked his wrist.

I anticipated the attack and threw up a shield around me, which deflected a portion of his shot back at him. It hit him hard enough to make him take two steps back, more surprised than hurt, but he stared at me like a wolf who's just realized that the sheep it's after is packing a rocket launcher.

The air between us shimmered until I lowered the shield, but the room still smelled like mosquito coils. "Okay, let's drop the act and be reasonable about this," I said, advancing while he was disoriented. "Starting with your name . . . your mother doesn't call you Drago, does she, *Stevie?*" He cringed, too bewildered to fight the mental attack, and I smiled to myself. "Right, then, Steve. Now, you want to tell me what this is all about?"

His lips moved for a few seconds before his voice caught up. "Who are you?" he squeaked, cracking on the last syllable.

I gave him an exaggerated shrug. "I answer to a lot of names. You can call me Colin. Now drop the stick."

His fingers tightened, the one part of him that had seemed to rediscover its courage.

"Drop the stick," I warned, "or you won't like what happens next."

The little wizard's stare was momentarily defiant until I threw a very thin, very *focused* bolt at his right wrist, shattering every bone. He screamed and grabbed his wounded hand, dropping the wand in the process. With a little touch of will, it was in my grip, and I broke it in half over my knee as he watched through streaming eyes. I held the halves of the wand toward him in my palm, then set the mess on fire and smiled with satisfaction as the blue flames consumed it. "So," I said, dusting the ash out of my gloved palm with a slow swipe, "let's talk about what you're doing here, shall we?" I kept my voice deceptively calm. "Because something tells me that Ms. Bellamy didn't invite you, Stevie boy."

He whimpered, all bravado replaced by pain and terror. "Nothing! I'll go!" he shouted. "Just don't hurt me, don't hurt—"

"You're a pathetic child, but maybe you've learned something here today," I said, then grabbed the front of his shirt and pulled his face within inches of mine. "What would that be?"

His jaw quivered. "St . . . stay away . . . don't bother . . . Bellamy?"

I released him. "Uh-huh. Smarter than you look, Drago. *Drago*," I repeated with a snort. "Is that your little game character's name, Stevie? Drago the Dark . . . what was it?"

My eye caught his left hand's motion toward his pocket, and I seized it. "What's hiding in your coat?" I murmured. "Silver? Iron? Backup stick?" Before he could twitch, I had set his duster's pocket on fire, and I ignored his shrieks and let the flames lick at his coat until the little bar inside fell onto the floor. He batted out the last of the spectral fire and stared at me, mouth hanging open.

I dropped my mask of age, the better to freak him

out. "Really," I tutted, "did you think this was my first fight? I'm guessing it's yours. Now, want to tell me what you're doing here?"

"B-book," he stuttered. "Need a . . . a book—"

"Not today. Get the hell off of this property."

I'll give him some credit—he managed to get the motorcycle up and racing away with only one functional hand. When the roar of his engine faded, I stepped back from the hole where the door had been, then waved the pieces into position and sealed them into place before I turned to face Meggy. "So," I said, crossing my arms, "what about that explanation?"

Her face seemed almost bloodless as she opened and closed her mouth, searching for her voice, before she finally managed to whisper, "You're fae."

I nodded, though I kicked myself for letting the glamour go. With the illusion gone, Meggy looked a decade my senior, and I was trying to keep the upper hand. "What the hell are you doing with wizards? Those people are dangerous!"

"You're *fae*!"

"Yes, we've established that," I muttered. Moyna's eyebrow quirked as Meggy sputtered, and I beckoned the girl closer. "Know anything about wards?" I asked her. She nodded, and I pointed to the driveway. "Did you feel anything when we came through?"

"Nothing at all."

"Go back to the road and see if you can't find a ward system. It may be in pieces, if it exists at all.

Please," I added before she could protest. "I need a few minutes with your mother, okay?"

Moyna rolled her eyes, sighed, and headed for the door.

"And put on something more appropriate, why don't you?"

That earned me a withering look, but the corseted dress she had chosen for the occasion shifted into a rough copy of Meggy's ensemble, albeit all in shades of rose. "Better?"

"It'll do. Go on, take your time. Thorough inspection."

She took the hint and slipped out the repaired front door, but I waited until the latch caught to release my breath. Feeling the weight of Meggy's eyes on me, I turned and forced myself to face her.

CHAPTER 5

We stood there in the foyer like idiots, staring at each other until long after Moyna's footsteps had ceased to echo off the walkway. Suddenly, Meggy's shocked paralysis broke, and she lunged for the door. I grabbed her arm and tugged her back, nearly pulling her off her feet as she swung around. "Let her go," I insisted as Meggy continued to strain for the doorknob. "She doesn't need drama. Just let her go for a few minutes, okay? It's only the edge of the property."

"That's my *baby*, you bastard!" she shouted, nearly dislocating her shoulder in an effort to free herself.

"She doesn't want to be!"

She wheeled on me as if struck, eyes wide and cheeks scarlet, and I took her by the shoulders and lowered my voice. "Meggy, listen to me. It's like Stockholm syndrome or something. All I know is that my mother abducted her and apparently raised her as her own, and then dumped her on my doorstep Thursday night. She wants to go home—to Faerie. She wants her . . . well, the person she thinks of as her mother, and she's none too pleased with me for dragging her down here. Let her go for a little while, calm down, and we'll figure out what's to be done."

Her eyes began to fill as she choked out, "She . . . she doesn't want to be with m-me?"

"It's going to take time . . ." Meggy's tears began to fall, and I squeezed her arms more tightly, wishing I could embrace her. "If I'd known for one second that your daughter had been taken, I'd have done everything in my power to get her back. You've got to believe me, Meggy, I didn't know. I'm sorry, I'm *so* sorry, but I had no idea your daughter was kidnapped."

Her streaming eyes met mine for a long moment. "Our daughter," she finally murmured. "Olive is . . . she's . . ."

I know that Meggy must have broken down then, but all I could focus on was the rushing in my ears like a hurricane and the faint pinpricks of light out of the corners of my eyes.

It couldn't be. I'd only been with Meggy for one night, and then only a few times . . .

But then I remembered everything the little changeling had done. Her clothes. My room. The washcloth on the living room floor, dampening the carpet where it had fallen.

Things she couldn't have done without having fae blood.

My blood.

"Oh, my God," I muttered, releasing Meggy abruptly. "Are you sure?"

"Yeah," she sniffed. "Olive's hair was fair like Jack's . . . still is, I guess," she amended, "but I knew she couldn't be his." She saw my confusion and wiped her eyes. "Jack came home about a month after you ran off. Finally told me the truth. He was diagnosed with cancer at the end of the season, and he'd been going to oncologists and specialists and the like since Christmas. He didn't want to scare me, so he pretended like everything was okay until he was pretty sure it *wasn't*. Then he came home and told me what was going on, and he asked if I still wanted to get married."

"Well, of course you did."

"Wrong," she snapped. "I'd thought about breaking off the engagement for months at that point, but what sort of bitch would throw her terminally ill fiancé to the curb, huh? And besides," she added, glaring at me through red-rimmed eyes, "it's not like I had an excuse anymore."

I felt my stomach begin to twist. "What are you saying?"

"I'm saying that I wanted to be with you. Or with the man I thought you were. Guess he doesn't exist, does he?" she replied, and began to cry once more.

I made coffee while Meggy tried to pull herself together. Under the circumstances, it seemed to be the only thing left that made sense.

"What do you want to know?" I asked her once she'd taken a few sips. "I'll tell you whatever I can, Meggy—about Olive, me, whatever. Name it."

She regarded me over the rim of her cup, her jaw set. "First thing, I wish you'd stop looking like that."

"Like what?" I said, taken aback.

"Like you're my kid brother or something."

I shifted back into the glamour I'd used at the door. "Better?"

Meggy gave me a quick up-and-down and frowned, but nodded. "Yeah. I guess that's better." She hesitated, then asked, "How old *are* you, anyway?"

I thought for a moment, running the math. "Eight hundred and . . . twelve? Maybe?"

"*Maybe?*"

"I was born in Faerie! That's the best I can do. They haven't exactly adopted the Gregorian calendar."

She leaned back into the couch and cupped her hands around her mug. "And you're really Colin? My Colin?"

I nodded. "I would have told you a long time ago, but you didn't need to know—"

"Didn't need to *know?*" she echoed, jabbing the mug toward my face. "I had *sex* with you! How was this something I didn't need to know?"

"And that was a terrible thing I did to you," I replied, reddening with the memory. "I'm sorry, Meggy—I betrayed your trust in the basest way possible, and I don't know how to make it right—"

"You didn't betray my trust," she interrupted, and took a sip of coffee. "Honestly, I was wondering what took you so long."

I sputtered for a moment before managing, "You were *engaged*."

"I loved you!" she blurted, then looked away, embarrassed.

Cautiously, trying to avoid a face covered in hot coffee, I took her free hand. "And I loved you, too, Meggy. I still do. That's why I left." Her angry eyes snapped back to mine. "I thought you wanted to be with Jack, and that what . . . happened with us was just a terrible, drunken mistake. You couldn't even speak to me—"

"I was trying to process everything. Deciding how I was going to break it off with Jack, and what my parents were going to say, and—"

"I thought I was doing the right thing," I said lamely. "That's all. I . . . you were with him, I didn't want to get in the way . . ."

"You could have talked to me about it like an adult!"

I started to counter that, gave up, tried again, and finally realized that it was futile. "You're right. I'm sorry."

The hurt had begun to overpower her anger. "Do

you have any idea how many times I called Father Paul, trying to find you? And then he left, too, and that was it, no note, no number, no way to track you down. And I was stuck." She looked away. "Don't get me wrong, I liked Jack. He was a sweet guy, and we . . . well, we made the best of the time he had left. We got married that September—poor thing had to wear a wig, but he was hopeful that the treatment would work. And Jack was thrilled when I told him I was pregnant. He thought we were having a miracle baby, and I didn't have it in me to tell him otherwise." Meggy's eyes softened. "But he loved Olive so much. Did everything he could for her, at least for those two weeks we had her. And then we woke up one morning, and she was gone. Not a trace. *Nothing*. He tried so hard to live long enough to see her home, but he didn't make it. And I . . ." She sighed. "I couldn't stay in Coleridge once Jack was gone. Moved east, dropped his name, tried to find my daughter, tried to move on."

Meggy looked back at me, her lip trembling. "I used to imagine that she'd come home, just turn up one day, and everything would be wonderful. And that you'd find me, and we'd . . . you know, be a family." She blushed even as she said it, and the tears began to fall. "Stupid, huh?"

"No, that's not stupid . . ."

I tried to pull her to me, but she stiffened and freed herself from my grasp, then set her mug on the coffee table and wiped her face with her sleeve. "It was stupid," she insisted. "I loved a lie, and you . . ." Her lip began to work in spite of her best efforts. "I don't even know your real name."

"Coileán," I said quietly. "It's just an older version of Colin. I . . . it was easier, with the spelling . . ."

She nodded. "Leffee. Le Fay."

I glanced at the ceiling to avoid her stare. "Needed something in a pinch, and it worked. I'd spent a lot of time in Ireland, and it sounded plausible to anyone who didn't know better."

Her face screwed up. "Why Ireland?"

"My father was Irish. It . . . seemed as good a place as any. Like Coleridge."

"Wait, are you saying your dad was—"

"Mortal, yeah. *Normal*, if you prefer. I'm only half fae."

"And he hooked up with a faerie?" she pressed.

I grimaced. "Not knowingly. It's complicated."

"Huh. Like mother, like son, I guess."

The comment stung, but I tried not to show it. "Meggy, I'm sorry—"

"Because, speaking as the mortal in this relationship, that's something I would have liked to know up front."

"I swear to you, I didn't take you to California to get in your pants."

Her smirk proved the lie. "Maybe not, but you didn't seem to mind once we started."

"That's . . . fair, I suppose," I muttered, my face burning more than I thought possible.

"Oh, come on, I was young, not blind. But all that's history, I guess." She picked up her coffee again and stared into its depths. "You said your mother kidnapped Olive. Why would she do that?"

"She's trying to get to me. There's a lot of bad blood between us. I think she's using Olive as a pawn."

Meggy frowned at that. "But now she's returned her. What's that supposed to mean, she got tired of the whole plan and gave up?"

"No. She took a spoiled little girl who grew up with anything she could possibly want, tossed her out on the streets of Rigby, and told her not to come back unless she brought something Mother wants—which I can only suppose is me. And Olive is desperate to go home."

"I don't understand . . ."

"Mother raised her as her own. Olive wants to go back there, where everything is lovely and fluffy and pink."

Meggy put the mug back on its coaster and pushed it away, then folded her arms. "I want justice. That bitch stole my child. I want her to suffer."

"I don't think that's possible—"

"She stole *your* child, too!" she protested. "You're not just going to let her get away with it, are you?" She stood and began to pace across the living room.

"I mean, she's your mom, I understand that, but it doesn't seem like the two of you are close—"

"Believe me, we're not."

"All the better. So she's of Titania's court, yes? If she was hiding Olive in Faerie, she'd have to be." Meggy glanced at my face, mistook my expression for surprise, and said, "You deal with enough wizards, you begin to pick a few things up. I know a bit about the courts. So I guess the next step would be . . . go to Titania? Drag your mom in and get a confession out of her? Help me out, here."

"You'd be right, except for one problem," I said, trying to ignore the look of hope in her eyes. "My mother *is* Titania. There's no one who can hold her in check."

Meggy stared at me, mouth slightly agape, then shouted, "Your mother is the fucking faerie queen? Christ, Colin, I did *not* sign up for . . ." She suddenly paused in her rant, looked at me queerly, then headed for the bookcase on the far side of the room. Squatting down, she rummaged through the detritus of the bottom shelf, then pulled out a scuffed black binder and began to flip through the pages.

"What's that?" I asked, standing for a better look and seeing nothing but tabs.

"Guide," she muttered. "My friend put it together for me . . . people to avoid in my work . . ."

"Which is?"

"Magical books," she replied absently, continuing

to hunt in her binder. "Picked up the gist of the book-selling thing from you, and my friend set me up with this niche market. Ah, here." She paused, then turned the binder around to show me a copy of a manuscript page with a sketch I had seen many times before, usually in the hands of an irate wizard. "Recognize this?"

I made a face. "It was the fifteenth century, and he couldn't draw for shit."

"That's you, though?" I nodded, and she took the binder back, avoiding the steel rings in the spine. Time, apparently, hadn't made Meggy's allergy any less severe. "Coileán Ironhand," she said, glancing at the next page of typed notes. "'Fae—son of Tita-nia and unknown father. Very dangerous. Can be deadly if provoked. Do not attempt'—and that bit's underlined—'do not attempt to use him as an agent, no matter how difficult the search. Does not deal with wizards, will probably know if you try to hide it. Best avoided. Unknown motives.'" She closed the binder and met my stare. "Well? Care to rebut?"

The fear in Meggy's eyes was new, and it made my heart twist. "*Ironhand*," I said quietly, "is a slightly more poetic way of saying *traitor*." And with that, I let myself out.

Meggy's tidy house came equipped with an immacu-lately swept covered porch in the back, which over-looked her yard and several acres of woods. I hadn't seen any sign of Moyna tramping through the trees, but given the size of the property, I wasn't yet concerned that she'd fled.

Meggy found me on her wooden porch swing, staring into space. "You're not going to run on me again, are you?" she asked, settling onto the empty cushion beside me.

I couldn't look at her. "Do you want me to go?"

"Not yet."

"Okay, then." I pushed back against the green rug, sending the swing into a slow rock. "Whoever your friend is," I said, staring out at the brown lawn, "he's right about me, I'm not going to deny it. But I would *never* hurt you. Not intentionally, at least," I mumbled.

For a long moment, the only sound between us was the squeak of the swing's chains.

"Faeries can't lie, can they?" she finally murmured. "You can bend the truth and twist it, but you can't actually lie, right?"

I risked a glance at Meggy and found her also contemplating the grass. "Wishful thinking. *Dangerous* wishful thinking. I know plenty who don't, but it's because they don't see the point in it. That doesn't mean they can't."

She turned to look at me. "But my friend said—"

"Your friend was misinformed."

"You just said she was right about you," she pointed out.

"I've been a known quantity for a while," I replied,

taking momentary comfort in the fact that Meggy's confidante was female. "There's probably a file on me at Arcanum HQ, and if so, it's bound to be thick by now. But really," I said, meeting her eyes, "you shouldn't just believe everything wizards tell you. Those people aren't stable."

"Says the faerie," she retorted.

"*Half.*"

She sniffed. "Same difference."

"Not exactly. The full-blooded ones are nuts, but—"

Meggy held up her hands, cutting off my explanation. "Just let me get this straight, okay? You're telling me my daughter's what, a quarter fae?"

"Yeah."

"Meaning?"

I shrugged. "Difficult to say right now. I've seen them on both ends of the spectrum, but they're usually not immortal. Some can be long-lived, but, uh . . ."

"Not like you?" she offered.

"No," I agreed, rubbing the back of my neck. "She has some inborn ability—I can't tell how much, but far more than any changeling should. It's not like I tested her last night. She was dumped on my street . . ." Meggy's face began to work again, and I said, "My neighbor found her Thursday night and took care of her. She handed her off in the morning, Father Paul helped me track her locket to you, and here we are. And, uh . . . for the record, Paul's not my uncle. Don't blame him."

Meggy shook her head. "How could your mother be so cruel? It's bad enough that she took her in the first place, but then to hurt her . . ." She sighed and looked away.

"Olive's home now," I assured her. "Maybe it'll take a while for her to accept that, but she will eventually. For the moment . . . give her time. Leaving Faerie can be something of a shock to the system."

"You seem to have managed."

"I was fifty, more or less, and I'd seen enough to know that I wanted out. She's sixteen and . . . you know, sixteen."

"Teenagers are idiots, right?"

"I'm sure you weren't."

Meggy chuckled softly. "Okay, consider the 'no lying' myth thoroughly debunked." She thought for a moment, then said, "Maybe it would be better if you took her back. If she's going to be miserable here . . . I mean," she said in a rush, "I want her here, I want her with me, but if she's going to be depressed—Colin, I don't want to hurt her. She's been through so much already."

"I understand. But sending her back might be a death sentence."

"*What?*"

I nodded, having been over it and over it in my mind. "I see this happening one of two ways. First, I open a gate and send Olive back. Easy enough, but if the kid goes through without bringing me along,

Mother would be extraordinarily pissed, and you don't want to see how creative she can be when she's angry."

"Olive's her granddaughter!" Meggy protested. "She wouldn't hurt—"

"She's killed her own children." Meggy's jaw dropped, and I took her hands. "If you're dealing with one of the Three—or pretty much any full-blooded faerie, for that matter—you have to set aside any possible outcome involving empathy. I assure you that Mother has no special affection for Olive merely because she's . . . mine."

"And option two?" Meggy asked once she found her voice again.

"Option two is that I go with her. If that happens . . . well, if the past is any clue to the present, that could mean that I wouldn't be able to escape Faerie for decades. But that's just me—I don't know what she'd do to Olive. I mean, once the girl's served her purpose, what further use would Mother have for her?"

"Surely she feels *something* for Olive."

I squeezed her hands. "The fae don't love." I thought briefly, then said, "If I were to ask you to describe the sound of the color green, could you?"

"Huh?"

"My point. Love doesn't compute with them. They might have some understanding of the concept, and they might be able to pull off a passable impression, but actually *feeling* love for another being? Never."

Meggy looked down at our entwined hands, hers bonier than I'd remembered, mine gloved in brown leather. "I thought you said you loved me."

"I do," I said softly. "You can thank my mortal father for that. Or blame him, if it's easier."

"I guess I'll thank him, then," she said, and gently freed her hands. "So why does she hate you?"

"Who, Mother?" Meggy nodded, and I let out a long breath. "We haven't seen eye to eye in quite some time. About seven and a half centuries, actually." I cut my eyes to Meggy, but she seemed nonplussed. "I, uh . . . I killed one of my brothers. Didn't mean to, but I got carried away. She didn't take it well."

Shock dropped back down over her features. "You did *what*?"

"He was attacking a girl," I said in a rush, hurrying to explain myself. "I tried to defend her. I grabbed the closest thing I could get my hands on, and it was a dagger. Beautiful weapon. Steel blade, nice craftsmanship. I kept it for years after that, sort of a reminder—"

"I thought you people were immortal."

"Immune to natural causes, let's say. But iron and silver are very effective." I held up my covered hands. "Just a little precaution. Hit a faerie with iron, and you may as well have splashed him with acid. I ran my brother through. He couldn't heal quickly enough, and that was it."

"Hence the name?"

"Hence the name. And it probably doesn't help matters that I've been doing more of the same for the last few hundred years." I looked around the porch, hoping to spot a cooler, but saw nothing but Meggy's neat pots of flowers. "Do you mind if I drink?"

"I've probably got a beer or two in the house," she said, beginning to rise from the swing, but I pulled her back down and produced a bottle of Johnnie from the air.

"No need, I bring my own," I said, seeing her eyes widen. "Do you want some?"

She took the bottle from my hands, held it up to the light, then opened the top and sniffed deeply. "It's whisky," she finally declared, surprised.

"I do a halfway decent mojito, too, if that's more your taste."

Meggy examined the bottle a moment longer, then passed it back to me and shrugged. "You know what? Sure. Mojito it is."

The drink appeared on the floor beside her, and she bent to pick it up on the next pass of the swing. "Okay?" I asked as she tasted it.

"Better than okay," she replied. "*Strong.* You're not trying to get me drunk again, are you?"

"Not you," I said, producing a straw, then stuck it down the neck of the bottle and took a long sip.

She watched for a moment, either concerned for

my liver or horrified by my manners. "You want a glass or something?"

"Nope."

"Suit yourself," she said, and we drank in silence, watching the trees wave in the wind.

The rum seemed to smooth over Meggy's shot nerves, and the whisky had its desired effect on my mind as well. By the time she'd finished and I'd downed a quarter of the bottle, she finally began to smile. "I can't believe you're actually here," she said, tossing her empty highball glass into the yard. It vanished before it could shatter, and she grinned. "Show-off."

"Come on, let me have my party trick," I replied, and laughed at her mock pout. "Fine, here," I said, and produced another glass. "Knock yourself out, kid."

She pitched it underhand into the yard, but the glass held together through the bounce. Before Meggy could protest, it exploded into a blue fireball and disappeared. "My grass!" she cried, but I'd left the yard unsinged, and she settled back into the swing, relieved. "Do me a favor and don't burn my stuff up, okay?" she said. "It's all I have, and the basement stock is highly flammable."

"Not a problem." I sent the whisky away and turned to Meggy, who had tucked one knee onto the swing and was halfway facing me. "So how did you get into magic books, anyway? That can't be an easy field to break into."

"Like I said, my friend got me started," she replied, resting her arm on the back of the swing. "Orders started coming in. I made connections. Kind of organic, really—one dealer leads to another, you know?"

I nodded. "Are you going to tell me who the cretin with the bike is?"

Meggy smirked. "Drago? Kid named Steve Brownfield. Lives somewhere around Richmond in his mom's house. He's a twerp, but he probably wouldn't hurt anyone. Maybe a little property damage . . ."

"That wasn't what I saw today. And that's not what you were telling me when he came to the door."

She faltered, stuttering with the lie, then sighed again. "Like I said, he's a twerp. Barely even Arcanum. He's a wizard, but not a particularly good one, and I don't like selling to him. He comes out here, he loses his temper, my friend puts it all back together, the end. And I wasn't *scared*," she protested, "I was caught off guard. There's a protective space in the basement, tight spellcraft, very safe. I usually go down there when he's in one of his moods, and . . . well, you two were there today, and I didn't have time to explain, you know, *magic* . . ."

"And then I broke his wrist for him," I finished.

Meggy rolled her eyes. "Was that really necessary, Colin? He wasn't going to hurt you."

"But he was going to hurt you, if he could. You know that, right? Please tell me that was obvious."

She gave up and leaned her head against the back of the swing. "My shelter's strong. I've dealt with him plenty of times before without your help."

"This shelter—was it built by the same person who put the wards around your property? The ones he broke through today? The ones Olive is still trying to locate?"

Her face tightened. "Those were experimental."

"Any trained wizard should have been able to construct a ward system to keep him out. Whoever you're trusting isn't Arcanum, is she?"

"It's not her fault," Meggy snapped.

"It is if you end up dead!"

"Don't worry, I've made it this long," she said, rising from the swing. "Come on, I'll show you."

People who know nothing of magic think that in order to keep evil forces at bay, you need to construct a circle of some kind, maybe something fancy with runes and unidentifiable powders and a pentacle. That's not entirely true. You *do* need a barrier—either enchantment or spellcraft will suffice—but you can make it in any shape you desire. A circle is simply easiest.

The steps down to Meggy's basement ended in a fence of wards. I couldn't see them, but I could smell the magic running like a current around the walls of the room, trapping every inch of floor space in a vaguely cuboid bubble. I pushed against the ward across the door, testing its strength, then stepped through with only a mild tingle. "Complex job," I said, pulling a glove off to touch the concrete wall. "Definitely spellcraft. Active, and . . . yeah." I covered my hand again and shook my head. "Running down. This is a pretty piece of work, but it's a junk ward."

"I felt it," she protested, pointing to the staircase. "Coming through, it opened for me . . ."

"Well, it didn't open for me, and yet here we are." I touched the invisible barrier in the doorway, then stuck my arm through, back and forth. "Something like this is designed to keep out all but its maker and his chosen exceptions. I assume your friend made this to keep you safe. Can she get in, too?"

Meggy nodded glumly. "Just her, though."

"Mm. I'm guessing it was designed to keep out anyone else bearing traces of magic—which should include me."

"You guess, or you know?"

"I guess," I said, giving the wards a last pat. "I can't see the spells used to build this, and even if I could, I can't really read them. It's spellcraft, it's not my forte."

"Spellcraft and enchantment, analog and digital, I know."

"Exactly. Your friend learned something from the Arcanum, at least." I looked around, taking in the homemade bookshelves that lined the walls, each neatly labeled in Meggy's steady hand, each only half-filled and stacked from the bottom for stability. "Keeping your inventory safe?"

"I *thought* it was," she replied, perching on the plastic card table in the middle of the room. Seeing a pair of wooden folding chairs on one side and an old wingback chair on the other, I assumed the setup was her office. "But yeah, this is my shop, more or less."

I crossed the room, scanning the spines and boxes for titles, breathing in the scent of musty paper, old parchment, and citronella. "I know some of these," I told her, pulling a slim box from one shelf. "This one predates me. How'd you get your hands on it?"

"Looking for a source swap?" she asked, faintly grinning.

"Just curious." I put the manuscript away and continued to examine her wares. "What was Drago looking to buy?"

Meggy joined me, passing over the boxes with her index finger until she settled on a squat brown book tucked between two much thicker volumes. "This," she said, holding it out for my inspection. "It's an old diary, a special order for my friend. She says it has historical value, and she's something of a collector. We were looking through some estate-sale catalogues a few weeks ago, and she asked me to buy it for her. Biddy up in Maryland. You wouldn't believe how many book collectors end up with a legitimate magical text or two." Meggy shrugged. "I don't know why Steve wanted it so badly. But the last time he was in, he saw it on the counter, asked me about it, and I told him it wasn't for sale. Guess he couldn't take no for an answer."

I gently freed the book from its box and looked at the smooth, unmarked leather cover before flipping it open. The pages inside were of vellum, high quality, and completely blank, yet the book reeked of magic. "Whose diary was this?"

"My friend wasn't sure, but she thought it belonged to some wizard named Simon. I think he might have been grand magus once, but I'm not sure." She took the book back and carefully boxed it up, then glanced at my face and stopped.

"Simon Magus?" I asked. "She thinks that's the diary of Simon Magus?"

"Yes . . ."

"And your friend isn't Arcanum?" Meggy's eyes widened in alarm as I grabbed her shoulders. "You can't sell this," I said in a rush. "Not to her. *Maybe* to Greg Harrison, if you're feeling especially generous, but not to some halfwit witch. If she's right, this thing is almost priceless."

"Colin, I don't—"

"Remember the time I got into a fistfight with a customer? You called the police, and he ran?" She nodded, scared by my urgency. "He was willing to kill you to get Simon's diary. The Arcanum would probably pay millions for it. And your friend—"

"Is my friend. And that's the end of it."

"Just *talk* to her," I pleaded. "See what she's planning, huh?"

Meggy scowled, but she nodded as she put the diary away. "Look, we can discuss this later. Surely Olive has made it around the house by now, right?"

I glanced down at my watch and was surprised to see how far along the afternoon had gone. "Best that we reclaim her," I agreed, heading for the stairs. "She's probably cursing my name." I passed through the failing wards again, then looked back at Meggy. "You know, if you want, I could redo the security for you. No pressure or anything," I hastily added, "but you see how weak this system is . . . after we talk to Olive . . ."

My voice trailed off, and Meggy studied my face for a long moment before nodding. "Yes, that might be nice."

We made it to the top of the stairs before Meggy tugged on my sleeve and said, "Hey, Colin?" As I turned around again, she grabbed my collar, pulled me closer, and kissed me deeply.

She took her time in breaking away, and I stared at her in utter bewilderment as I caught my breath. "What was that for?" I asked.

"For us," she said, smiling sadly, then reeled back

and slapped me full across the face while I was still distracted. "And that was for the last sixteen years, you son of a bitch. Now come on, my baby is waiting," she ordered, dragging me out the front door as I clutched my stinging cheek.

CHAPTER 6

We heard Olive before we saw her. Returning to the house after her fruitless examination—as I'd suspected, the perimeter wards were broken beyond repair—Olive had tripped over a loose brick in the walkway and stumbled. In trying to break her fall, her hands had gone down first, and both her palms and her forearms had made contact with a rusty rake Meggy had forgotten by a flower bed. Cut, burned, and blistering, Olive wailed at the pain, then tried to fight Meggy off when she ran to help her.

Dodging her elbows, I dragged Olive inside, pinned her to a straight-back kitchen chair, and ordered her to stop resisting. "You want an infection, is that it?" I said as Meggy carefully rolled Olive's bunched-up sleeves away. "Those are open sores, kid—you get the wrong kind of bacteria in there, and you'll lose tissue."

"The wrong kind of *what*?" she snapped.

"Bacteria, honey," said Meggy, beginning to press a washcloth against Olive's arm. "They make you sick."

The girl still seemed befuddled, and I moved to stand behind Meggy to distract Olive from the operation. "Here's the truth," I said, waiting until her glance turned away from Meggy's unpleasant work. "You're mostly human. And while there's a chance that you may be immortal, we're not going to risk it. So, you need to sit there, let your mother clean you up, and stop squirming."

"It hurts," she began to complain, then froze and looked at me strangely. "What do you mean, *mostly*? I thought you said I was a changeling!"

Meggy looked up at me over her shoulder. "Is this really the best time for this conversation, Colin?"

"She's not going anywhere for the moment," I replied with a shrug. "Yes, you're a changeling"—Olive winced again at the word—"but not in the strictest traditional sense. You, uh . . ." I paused, trying to find the phrasing least likely to upset either woman in the room, then said, "As it turns out, I'm your father. So, you're actually a quarter fae, which would explain your ability with—"

Her eyes flew open wide as I spoke. "*No!*" she shrieked, yanking her arm out of Meggy's hands. Forgetting that she was in a chair, she pushed backward in an effort to get away and wound up flat on her back on the slate floor.

"Oh, baby, your head!" Meggy cried, scrambling to pick her up. "Is it . . . no, I don't think it's bleeding, but your head, are you okay?"

Olive blinked groggily at her for a moment, stunned by the fall, then groaned as the pain, or maybe the realization, hit. "This isn't happening," she mumbled, shielding her face with her wet arms. "Go *away*, this isn't real . . ."

I flipped her and the chair upright, and gripped her shoulders to steady her. "It is, Olive. I didn't know, but I would have come for you, I wouldn't have let her—"

"*Don't touch me!*" she shouted, slapping at me until I stepped back and let Meggy resume her work. "I'm not yours, I love Mother, I'm no traitor—"

"Olive, please . . ."

"My name is Moyna!" She breathed in furious snorts, as if her chest was straining not to burst with each breath. "And you are a *filthy* traitor, and you're going to take me home *right*—"

Her rant turned into a scream as Meggy cleaned her wounds with antiseptic spray. "I'm sorry, sweetie," she murmured, putting the bottle aside as Olive wailed. "I know it hurts, but it's for the best. Almost finished, just need to wrap everything up . . ."

Olive jerked her arms away again, but managed to stand without knocking the chair over. "You have no right to touch me, you . . . *dog*," she said, wrapping what remained of her sleeves around her wounds. "Coileán, you will take me home this instant."

"I'll do no such thing," I replied, as Meggy, reddening, began to clean up without a word. "And you'll apologize to your mother."

"My mother is the queen!" she yelled, stamping her foot. "And you will take me home!"

"For the last time, she's not your mother!"

"She's her grandmother, though," Meggy muttered.

Olive inclined her head toward Meggy—*See?*—and folded her wounded arms, the picture of pink-clad defiance. "Take. Me. *Home.*"

"You are home," I said, fighting the urge to throttle her. "And I'm not going to drop you off in Faerie and let her kill you, okay? So go upstairs, do whatever you want to do to your arms, and we'll talk about this when you're calmer."

She glowered at us both, then flounced upstairs. "Why don't you both just drop dead!" she shouted down the staircase, and a door slammed.

Falling back into a well-worn groove, Meggy and I ordered Chinese and made camp on the gray futon in her back room, hoping that the smell would draw Olive out. But our daughter showed no sign of emerging—as if to hammer the point home, she'd managed to enchant a lock onto the door of the bedroom she'd appropriated—and so Meggy and I settled in for a long evening vigil.

Around nine, Meggy cocked her head toward

the ceiling and frowned. "Quiet up there. Think she found a way home?"

"Doubt it," I replied. "It takes a little practice to open a gate. If she's still distraught, I doubt she can focus long enough to make one open—*if* she's strong enough to do it in the first place." Seeing Meggy's uncertain frown, I murmured, "I'm not dumping her on you. If you can't handle this—if you don't *want* to handle this—just say the word. I'll take her back to Rigby, try to sort her out, and maybe with time—"

"I can handle it. She's my baby, I can handle it."

I couldn't tell whether she was trying to convince me or herself. "She *does* have some talent," I cautioned. "Like I said, I haven't tested her, but I know she can do more than just glamour. And I . . . uh . . ."

Meggy watched me fret, then finished, "You're worried about me."

"Yeah, I am. I know you want to keep her, but if she's too much . . ."

"She's not some vicious puppy I can just hand off," she replied, rubbing her elbow. "Is there some way to, I don't know, put a damper on her until she grows up? Give us a chance to get to know each other without her trying to kill me in my sleep?"

I hesitated. "There . . . *is* a way to put a bind on her, but it's difficult, risky. Not something I'd attempt. Mother could probably do it, Mab, Oberon . . . but not me. You'd need one of the Three for something like that, or else someone significantly older and more experienced than I am."

"Probably stupid to ask, but—"

"There's no chance of getting help from the Three. I have no idea where Oberon is these days, and there hasn't been a reliable sighting of Mab in fifty years."

Meggy twirled her hair, deep in thought, then ventured, "What about the Arcanum?"

"You want to take a partly fae child to the Arcanum and ask for a bind?" I asked incredulously. "More specifically, you want to take *my* partly fae child to the Arcanum and ask for a bind?"

"We could ask nicely," she said with a little shrug. "Or . . ."

Her voice trailed off, and I waited, fighting the urge to look at her thoughts. "Or?"

Meggy pointed to the floor. "The diary," she whispered. "The one you got all bent out of shape over—what about a trade? I give it to them, they . . . do what they can. Just temporarily, I mean, until she adjusts . . ."

She chewed her lip and watched me mull it over, and I finally said, "Honestly, I hate the idea of doing that to her, but . . ." I sighed. "Binds are possible with spellcraft, and I could ask Greg. He'd at least hear me out."

"*You* know the grand magus?"

"You sound surprised."

"I thought you didn't consort with wizards," she retorted.

"I don't, but it's wise to know your competition. Anyway, I could probably get a word with him within the week. But I can't make any promises. Even for the diary, Greg might not do it. It's . . . *distasteful*, you understand?"

Meggy nodded. "Like shipping your kid off to boot camp."

"Actually, no, it's more like cutting off her arms and saying you'll give them back someday if she's a good girl," I snapped. "It's just about the worst thing I can imagine doing to her, short of actual torture, and this certainly comes close." I paused, wrestling with my temper, and found Meggy watching me with worried, guilty eyes. "But I'll do it," I muttered. "It's either this or she lives with me. You're not safe alone with her, not now."

"Or you could move in."

I jerked, stunned. "Sorry, what did you say?"

"If you wanted to," she mumbled. "For Olive. You could stay here until she's, you know, better. Or whatever. Never mind." Her face burned.

"Why don't we take it a day at a time?" I replied carefully. "I'll do my best to talk to Greg this week, and until then . . ." I glanced around the room and sighed inwardly. "I could camp on the futon, if that's agreeable to you."

"Only if it's no trouble."

"It's not."

Meggy's smile spoke more of relief than happiness. "It's not a bad futon, really. I'll get some blankets from upstairs. There's a guest bedroom, but Olive . . ."

"Don't worry about it." I briefly considered remodeling her back room with a decent mattress, but I decided that Meggy had seen enough magic for one day. "A blanket will be fine."

As she headed out, she paused in the doorway and glanced back. "You can drop it," she said softly. "The glamour, I mean. If you want to. I, uh . . . I don't mind."

I don't sleep much, as a rule. Two or three hours is usually more than sufficient to see me through the day, but the old futon and my guilty mind conspired that night to deprive me of even that short stretch.

Trying not to think about what I had promised Meggy was like telling my tongue not to probe a sore in my mouth. Oh, I had little doubt that Greg would see me, especially if I brought tidings of the long lost diary, but surely he would find my request as repugnant as I did. He was a father, after all, and what father would condemn his child to binding unless said child had set out upon a promising career in supervillainy?

This one, apparently.

The girl—Olive, Moyna, whomever she wanted to

be—would never forgive me if I went through with it, that much was plain. And she wasn't likely to thank her mother for the spell, even if I took full blame for the procedure.

It wasn't a permanent thing, I mused, trying to convince myself that I wasn't the worst parent to walk the earth. Just for a few months, maybe a year or two, long enough for the girl to get to know Meggy. Once she learned to like her mother, once they got along . . .

Fat chance, my head insisted. Olive would never love Meggy, not the way that Meggy loved her baby's memory.

But what if I took Meggy up on her offer and moved in? The idea became sweeter every time my thoughts circled back to it. We wouldn't need the bind if I was around to keep Olive in check. I could change my name, my face, start over here with Meggy. Do what I should have done sixteen years before.

But for how long? my head cut in. *Fifty years? Sixty?*

I could give Meggy the illusion of her youth back, but in the end, it would only be smoke and mirrors. Even if she loved me, even if she wanted to be with me, Meggy would leave me, and there wasn't a damn thing I could do about it. Someday, not too many years away, she would be a fading memory and a face in photographs. And for the rest of my life, I would carry her with me, her eyes and her smile and the un-fillable void she had created in my soul. A few decades of domestic comfort with Meggy would be bliss, but the cost would be dear.

I sat bolt upright to the sound of Meggy screaming my name, scanning the dark room for the source of the muffled noise as I tried to reconcile the sound with reality and calm my racing heart. After a few seconds, I realized that it was coming from downstairs, and I ran through the unfamiliar house, trying to remember how to get to the basement. Two wrong turns later, I found the basement door, half-tripped down the staircase, and found Meggy standing on the edge of the strangest gate I had ever seen, straining to hold on to Olive's arm.

"Help me!" she cried, and I grabbed her around the waist to anchor her to the floor.

On the other side of the gate, my mother stood beside her golden filigreed throne, her perfectly arching eyebrows scrunched together in befuddlement as her guards took up positions around her. Olive, halfway through the gate, reached for Mother as she tried to pull herself through. "I'm coming!" she yelled in Fae as the unsteady gate crackled around her like lightning. "Take me back, don't leave me here, Mother, I love you!"

"Colin, I can't hold her!" Meggy screamed, trying to grip Olive's bandaged arm. "It's too strong, it's sucking her in!"

I dug in my heels against the carpet and fought the strange pull of the gate. This was nothing of the girl's creation, and certainly nothing of Mother's—gates are passive things, but this one threatened to wrench all of us across the border. "We've got to back up!" I said, yelling to be heard over the noise. "Pull back with me!"

"I can't! It's too . . . *no!*" she howled, scrabbling in the air as Olive finally freed herself and raced into Faerie. "No, come back, Olive! *Olive!*"

The girl tumbled out of the gate at Mother's feet, beaming, her pink ensemble once again a black dress. Mother cocked her head and frowned at me in puzzlement. "Coileán?" she called, almost inaudible over the crescendoing noise of the failing gate. "What is this you've done now?"

"Olive, *come back!*" Meggy wailed, and struggled against my grasp. "Let me go, I've got to get her back, I've got to—"

"It's suicide!" I shouted in her ear. "We'll get her back, but you can't go through that gate, there's something wrong about it!"

Desperate and enraged, Meggy ignored me. She fought with a strength I'd never seen in her before, and before I realized it, she had pulled us to the brink. "Let me go!" she shrieked, and then she pivoted and employed the one defense tactic taught to all women.

Her knee aimed true, and I barely managed to keep hold of her wrist as I fought the urge to simultaneously crumple and throw up. "Meggy, no," I groaned, clinging to her against the pull of the gate. "No, not like this, I'll get her back, I promise—"

"Not my baby. Not again," she said, and slipped free.

"No!" I yelled, but by then, it was too late. The gate was pulling Meggy through.

I stood a few inches from the border, buffeted by the wind, and watched helplessly as she was carried away from me, straight to my mother's feet. And when Meggy raised her head and looked back at me, the face I saw wasn't the face I had seen an instant before. It was younger—not that of the woman I had last known, but of a younger version of Meggy, scared and suddenly quite small with the distance between us. "Colin!" she called, and stretched out her hand. "Colin, help me!"

"I'm coming!" I yelled, and sprang for the gate.

I leapt through empty air and plowed into Meggy's folding chairs, then hit my head against the plastic table and sank onto the carpet. When I looked back, dazed, the gate was gone.

As if from a great distance, a voice at the top of the stairs called down in Fae, "Who's the stronger now?" Its owner laughed, and before I could shout a reply, I was alone.

CHAPTER 7

Dawn found me kneeling on the basement floor with a knot on my temple, trying to figure out why the universe had stopped working as I pushed down waves of panic. Opening a gate isn't difficult, not for someone like me, but I couldn't do it. In the past, it had been as simple as pushing on an invisible wall. Now, not only would the door not budge, but the wall itself had disappeared. There was simply nothing to push against, and my efforts to run to Faerie proved futile. And that wasn't the worst of it.

My first clue that something was awry, other than the massive problem of the gate, was when the basement wards collapsed. I felt them go down, like a battery running out of power, then paused and sniffed deeply. The wards hadn't failed purely due to their shoddy construction, I realized. They had failed because the magic that was powering them was ebbing.

As a test, I started a fire in my palm and watched with relief as the flames danced, but they were smaller than usual, paler and colder, and I quickly put the fire out.

What had opened in the basement hadn't been a gate; gates didn't pull, they didn't throw you through ungracefully, and they didn't close that quickly. If the look on Mother's face was to be trusted, whatever it was had been a surprise to her, too. And the fact that no one had come after me in the intervening hours gave weight to my suspicion that the worst had happened.

Faerie was closed off, which meant that the little magic left on this side was fading away.

And something told me that the same wasn't true for the *other* realm, the Gray Lands.

The Arcanum had done its best over the years to plug up the naturally occurring gates into that realm, but those plugs were created with concentrated magic. Once they failed, the gates would reopen, new gates would continue to form, and the strange etheric force of the Gray Lands, known to us as dark magic, would flood across the border—and, in all likelihood, so would that realm's denizens.

There were nightmares in the Gray Lands. Without magic to fight back, I would be a sitting duck. The entire mortal realm would be.

So there I knelt, by halves terrified and despairing, unable to rescue Meggy and Olive, but at a loss for a better move than remaining where the gate had last been. My last glimpse of Meggy wrenched at me, her fear, her eyes . . .

Younger.

It made no sense.

Passing into Faerie strips away illusion. You can't come through and maintain a disguise, and anyone burdened by a bind or aided by a spell or enchantment quickly finds himself unburdened or unaided on the other side, as the case might be. Sure, you can do whatever you want once you're in Faerie, magically speaking, but the process of going through makes you momentarily vulnerable, naked of glamour.

Meggy had changed. But what sort of enchantment could possibly be on her? There was nothing extraordinary to Meggy—I would have sensed it! She felt no different the night before than she had when I'd first known her. But she had *changed* . . .

As my thoughts circled, I distantly heard a door open and slam, and a woman's voice call, "Hello? Megs, you here? *Meg?*"

Footsteps paced above me, and then the stairway creaked. "Meg!" she shouted. "Hey, Meg! Where are you?"

By the time she opened the basement door, my personal fog had lifted enough for me to recognize that I couldn't defend myself well with my back to the stairs. Reluctantly, I stood and watched the intruder make her rapid descent. "She's gone," I said, squinting at her in the gloom. "I can't get to her. They're gone."

She paused at the foot of the steps where the wards used to run, a tanned, spike-haired apparition in a gray Virginia Beach T-shirt and black shorts. Her dark blue eyes, rimmed with a thick smudge of mascara, widened when she caught sight of me, while her right hand darted around to her back and fumbled under her shirt. "Stay where you are!" she ordered, producing a wooden wand. "Nothing funny now, I'm warning you—"

"You must have made the wards," I interrupted, glancing about the room. "Not particularly effective."

Her tough shell showed its first crack as her brow furrowed. "How'd you—"

"Know about the wards? I was down here yesterday, before they failed." I started another weak fire in my hand and held it up, illuminating my face. "Put the stick down, kid."

She breathed in sharply, but she had enough sense to let the wand fall. "What did you do to Meg?" she demanded in an angry rush. "She wasn't hurting anyone."

"I didn't do anything to her," I replied, and let the fire go out. "Gate opened in here in the middle of the night. Olive went back through. Meggy followed her. I tried to stop her, and then I tried to open it again . . ." I shrugged. "Faerie's closed to me. Think you can open it?"

"*Olive?* What do you mean, *Olive?*"

"Her daughter."

"I know that!" she snapped. "How did Meg—"

"Find her?" I slumped against the desk and folded my arms. "Kid was kidnapped and held in Faerie. She was basically dropped in my lap, and so I brought her back to Meggy. And now they're gone because I couldn't hold on against some sort of super-gate, and I haven't the faintest idea of how to get another gate open. Like I said, you want to try?"

Her eyes darted back and forth between her wand and me. "How do you know Meg?"

"We go back. And in the current parlance, I'm her baby daddy. Surprise!" I shook my head and laughed weakly, too weary to think straight. "And now my mother's going to kill them, knowing my luck." I scrubbed my hands over my face. How had this become my life?

The wizard's expression had shifted from cautious defiance toward outright caution. "Your . . . mother?"

"Titania," I muttered, and winced as my fingers ran across the knot on my head. "You mean you don't know me, kid? I got underlined in that little field guide of yours."

"There was a lot to underline. Want to be more specific?"

"I sell books and answer to Colin. Better?"

"*Shit,*" she whispered. Her glances toward the wand increased in tempo. "You . . . and Meg . . ."

"She didn't know. We got kind of drunk, and . . ."

The girl scowled and planted her fists on her skinny hips. "*You're* Phoenix Colin? Seriously? Do you have any idea how long she's been . . . and . . . you . . . you . . ." she sputtered. "Son of a bitch!" she finally managed to shout. "You knocked her up and ran!"

"I didn't know about the knocking up bit!" I yelled back, feeling the first twinges of a headache coming on. "Now, if you don't have anything constructive to add, then get the hell out of here and let me think."

She said nothing, but she remained at the foot of the stairs, watching me. I produced a bottle of gin and took a couple of long swigs, then set it on the table and found her scowling. "Yes?"

"That's not going to help anything," she said. "And I don't know about you, but I think it's pretty damn irresponsible to be wasting a finite resource on Bombay Sapphire."

"Finite?"

One thin black eyebrow rose. "Oh, you hadn't noticed that the general magical levels around here tend to be, you know, *falling*?"

"Of course I noticed," I muttered, taking another drink for good measure. "Got a headache, that's all."

"Then take a damn aspirin, you big sot. And get out of my way." She scooped up her wand, shoved me away from the desk, and sat cross-legged on top. After running her hands back through her dark mop, she extended the stick and slowly exhaled. "I want to see what we're dealing with."

"We?" I replied, but broke off my half-planned retort when the girl muttered and waved her hand, and the room began to glow with green swirls and indecipherable characters. "What are you—"

"Shut up and let me concentrate," she growled through clenched teeth.

The etheric traces began to glow brighter, a web of phosphorescent fog stretching across Meggy's basement. At their center was a vibrant clump of green strands, tangled in a ghostly Gordian knot. The girl had closed her eyes with the strain of the spell and began to sweat, even though she sat perfectly still. "Can you take it?" she finally mumbled, her face tense with exertion.

"What are you talking about? I can't do spellwork!" I protested, still clinging to my liquid breakfast.

Her brows twitched slightly. "The spell is laid, you moron. Just keep feeding it and let me see what we have here, okay? Can you do that much?"

"I'll try, but this isn't my specialty," I muttered, sending the bottle away.

"Don't give me that bullshit. You're a fucking faerie lord, you can manage to keep this going for five lousy minutes."

Fighting down the urge to smack the wizard, I turned my attention to the mess before me. So unaccustomed was I to actually *seeing* magic in action that it took me a few seconds to spot what the girl had done to raise the green work, but I felt her spell soon enough and began to feed it. The process was unwieldy, like trying to power a hair dryer with a car battery and a set of faulty clamps, but the green lines soon glowed like fire, and the girl opened her eyes.

"Keep it steady, I'm going in," she said, then hopped off the table and stepped into the middle of the light show, her wand stretched before her.

"What *is* that?" I asked, fighting to hold the spell together.

"Echoes. Tracers. The runes show me what went into this business. It's like getting a chemical signature from the spell."

My head pounded with the effort. "And that thing in the middle?"

"Enchantment." The green began to flicker, and she glanced back at me with a frown. "Don't wuss out on me, man. I've got to read this mess, and it's *extremely* complicated, so if you don't mind . . ."

"Just hurry," I began, but my complaint was cut off an instant later when something heavy slammed into my side and knocked me to the floor.

"What the hell did you do?" an all-too-familiar voice shouted in Fae. Before I could move, the voice's owner grabbed my shoulders and began to shake me back and forth, up into the air and down against the carpet. When the shock passed, I saw red tangles and furious brown eyes glowing green in the last light of the broken spell, and I shoved my assailant off me.

As he tried to scramble to his feet, I tackled him and wrapped my hands around his neck. "You bring them back and do it now!" I yelled, pressing my thumbs against his windpipe. "Do it! Do it or I'll kill you right here, I swear it!" I shook him, pounding his head against the floor, and barely registered his hands scratching at my arms. "Damn it, bring them *back*!"

The world around us flickered, and suddenly we were across the room and vertical, rolling along the wall. He tried to throw me into one of the bookcases to shrug me off, but I clung to him and dug in deeper. A second later, I had him upstairs, ramming his head against the futon frame's wooden legs, and then I slung us into the backyard, where we tumbled over and over in the brown grass, trying our damnedest to kill each other. His skin heated, mine burned with cold, and I littered the yard with broken glass in time to roll him into a sharp patch. He yelped with what little air he had left before sending us two stories skyward and back to earth. The impact knocked the wind from my chest and made me see stars, giving him a chance to slip free and put a few feet between us, where he crouched and slightly wheezed, waiting for the next round.

By that time, however, the wizard had managed to find us. "Stop it!" she yelled, sprinting into the fray with one fist securely wrapped around her wand. "I'm running out of time down there, we've got to get the spell read—"

He threw himself at her, grabbed the wand from her hand, and cast it across the yard in a shower of splinters. "*What did you do?*" he bellowed, then jumped on top of her and began to throttle her in turn. The girl's face went purple as she kicked and scratched, and her bare arms and legs bled from my broken-glass booby trap in the yard.

I pushed myself to my feet, still woozy from the fall, and thought I was hallucinating when a knight vaulted Meggy's low wooden fence and ripped the arming sword from his back. He ran to the fight, kicked my brother in the side with a steel-toed boot, then pressed the blade hard against his throat. "Yield," he mumbled through his black motorcycle helmet. "Or die. Your choice."

"Yield!" he squealed, holding his burned neck as soon as the point was lifted. "Yield, I yield, get that thing away . . ."

The knight stepped back, then knelt beside the girl and offered her a black-gloved hand. "Are you hurt?" he asked, propping her head against his arm as she sat up and coughed.

He turned just enough, giving me a glimpse of the red cross on his white surcoat—a Templar, then. But no one had seen a legitimate Templar since I was a child . . .

I shook my head, driving the mists aside. That wasn't a Templar, that was a tall, armored lunatic in costume. "Who in blazes are you?" I shouted, running across the yard before he could abduct the wizard.

He held up one hand to stay me, then lifted his visor to reveal worried brown eyes in a young, familiar face. "Father Paul said he had a bad feeling about this," said the seminarian. "Asked me to check in on you on my way. Probably a good thing, huh?" As I goggled, he pulled the girl upright. "So, who's the cretin?" he asked, cocking his head toward his vanquished foe, who by then had crawled out of striking distance and continued to hold his injured throat.

"My asshole half brother. Well, one of them," I replied, keeping my distance. Running straight into a steel bodysuit, I had by then recalled, would only end in tears. "You're about seven months too early to play dress-up, you know."

Joey pulled off his helmet and tossed it into the grass. "Not a lot of trunk space on a Harley. I figured I'd wear my gear down and leave the Kevlar at home. Might work against road rash, I guess." He sheathed his sword and folded his arms, regarding the three of us in turn. We made an ugly scene—my brother in jeans and an oversized yellow polo, the only one actually dressed, struggling to his feet and wincing at the pain from the rising red welt across his throat; the wizard in her T-shirt and bed shorts, bruised and bloodied, still coughing as she recovered; and me, haggard and scratched, wearing sleeping sweats and feeling the chill in bare feet. "So, uh . . . someone want to fill me in?" he said.

The wizard cut her eyes to me. "You pal around with cosplayers?"

"Not knowingly," I muttered.

"It's not cosplay," Joey protested. "I'm supposed to be jousting all next week. This stuff's legit, not that costume nonsense. *Ah*," he barked, seeing my brother step back. "Hold it. We're not finished yet, bub."

He scowled, his burn momentarily forgotten. "You *dare* to give me orders?" he snarled, and dropped to a half crouch.

I jumped between them before the idiot could charge. A quick burst sent him sailing headfirst into the trunk of one of Meggy's shade trees, where he groaned and fell. "Okay, Joey," I said, turning my attention back to the ersatz knight, "how about an explanation that makes sense this time, huh?"

He watched my brother rub his head. "Is he all right?"

"Fine. You mentioned jousting?"

Joey's face reddened under his helmet-plastered hair. "It's just something I've done for a while, you know. My dad did it—he smiths now—and my mom's always been really into the medieval scene, and they tour . . . I sort of picked it up along the way, horses and swords and lances and all of that. We're going on spring break now at school, and there's a fair going on about an hour outside of Raleigh—I'm still plugged into the circuit, uh, and . . . well, I mean, they had an extra slot . . ."

"And the Templar getup?"

"Seemed kind of appropriate," he mumbled. "Look, Father knows about it, I'm not doing anything wrong . . ."

"Can you actually use that thing?" I asked, pointing to the steel-and-leather hilt peeking over his right shoulder.

He nodded. "Decently enough. I won some tournaments in high school."

Although I can create clothing out of nothing, I don't like to take chances with iron-based items. Rather than summon a pair of gloves and hope for the best, I ripped my T-shirt off, wrapped it around my right hand, and gestured with my bare left. Joey took the hint and held out the blade hilt-first, and I carefully gripped it with my covered hand. It wasn't perfect, but the shirt sufficed for the moment. Duly equipped, I appeared at my brother's side and held the sword to his throat. "Okay, Robin," I said as his head began to clear from the blow against the tree, "I'm giving you one chance to tell me what the hell you did to my daughter and my . . . uh . . . to Meggy. *Talk.*"

His glazed eyes tried to focus on mine and settled for my chin. "Move the sword."

"Try me and I'll move it closer."

"They call him 'Ironhand' for a reason," said the wizard, who had jogged over to see the show.

My brother managed to shoot her a contemptuous glare. "Who do you think gave him the name, witch girl?"

"Wizard," she snapped. Joey grabbed her arm before she could lunge at him, and though she slapped him off, she kept her distance.

I moved the point of the blade half an inch closer to Robin's exposed skin. "Stop trying to antagonize the witch."

"*Wizard!*"

"Whatever," I muttered. "Now, you're going to tell me exactly what you did and why I can't get a damn gate open, or you're going to end up just like Áedán. And I liked him a lot more than I like you."

Robin's Adam's apple bobbed just beneath the sword point. "I didn't know it was going to close off Faerie," he said quietly, keeping his dark eyes on the steel. "She never said anything about that."

"Who didn't?" the wizard cut in.

"Let me ask the questions, okay?" I said, sparing her a quick glance. "Guy with the sword talks."

"Screw that. Meg's *my* friend, and I'm not going to—"

"I have an incredibly vested interest in keeping her alive, you understand?" I interrupted. "And don't you have a spell to read or something?"

Her jaw clenched. "Bastard there broke my wand. I can't."

"Okay. Then Robin can just tell us what we're up against and spare you the trouble," I countered.

He looked up, found the three of us ringing him, and swallowed hard. "It was Mab, all right?" he whined. "She gave me that thing, and I—"

"You're working with *Mab*?" I shouted. "What the hell is wrong with you?"

"It was just supposed to pull those two into Faerie! I didn't know it was going to cut off the connection!"

I breathed deeply, trying to regroup my fleeing bits of self-control. "First, where did you find Mab? And secondly, why would she have any interest in sending people over the border?"

"I didn't find her, she found me," he replied in a rush, keeping a nervous eye on Joey's scuffed boots. "She had a plan, she said, she was going to go home, and my father was going to go with her, and getting those two in was the first step. She wouldn't tell me why. Would you *please* get that away?"

I moved the sword closer. "Not yet."

"My neck really hurts!"

"Suck it up," the wizard muttered.

Robin's eyes turned sullen. "I told her I wanted revenge," he mumbled. "She said this would do it. I set it off, I get what I want, she gets what she wants, only you and Mother lose. Happy now?"

Joey's brow scrunched. "What's your beef with Colin?"

"Remember that faerie problem back in Harrow?" I cut in. "He gave the green light. And I slapped his hand, and he doesn't like it—do you, little Puck?"

If I hadn't been armed, my brother would have tried to rip my head off. Instead, he lay there, pinned and seething, and I held my hand steady. "Whatever you did was a combination of enchantment and spellcraft," I continued. "What was it?"

"I don't know. Little black box. She said to put it down and count to ten." He tried to press himself deeper into the grass, away from me. "I think she woke the girl. The other one ran after her, and then you butted in. That's all I know. Can I get up?"

"You realize," I said quietly, "that you're solely responsible for this. Congratulations, genius, we're severed for the moment." I held up my other hand and started a fire, but this one burned even weaker than the last. "The magic's fading, and it's not being renewed."

"So put out the damn fire already," the wizard interrupted.

I closed my hand, and a little tendril of smoke escaped through my fingers. "If we can't open a connection, there isn't going to be any magic left. It's just a matter of time."

"You think I hadn't realized that?" said Robin.

"Why did you think I came back, to spend some quality time with you?"

"Oh, now you've hurt my feelings," I replied with a smirk. "So here's how you're going to make it up to me: you're going to take me to Mab, and we're going to convince her to undo this."

"I have no idea where she is."

The wizard bent and stared at his face, then straightened with a little sigh. "He's not lying."

He looked up at her in agitation. "Would *you* lie with a blade at your throat?"

"Depends on how well I could cover it up, Puck," she shrugged.

"*Shut up!*" Robin shouted, straining as he fought the obvious urge to throw himself at the wizard.

"He's kind of sensitive about that name," I warned her, seeing her flash of malicious delight. "*Homicidally* sensitive. Bear that in mind." I considered the situation for a moment. "The Arcanum might be able to read the spell, but I won't go to them unless it's dire. We're dealing with hybrid work, and Greg's going to want to sit around and analyze this to death before he does anything, I know him. Meanwhile, Meggy and Olive are still on the other side—"

"And Titania's a capricious bitch," said the wizard. "Sorry."

"No offense taken. So . . . I guess . . ."

I didn't want to say it, but she beat me to it with pleasure. "You need me. Get me a new wand, I'll read the spell, and we'll go from there. And we'll need to bring him," she said, nudging Robin's leg with her dirty sneaker. "I don't want him running back to Mab the instant we're gone."

"I told you, I don't even know where she is!" he protested.

"Yeah, he's coming along," I said, "because he wants this gate reopened as much as we do." I turned back to my brother and shook my head. "Your father's not going anywhere until this is righted, you understand."

Robin stared up at me and blinked slowly. "You know, Coileán, I'm not a complete imbecile."

"Prove it." I handed the sword back to Joey, who kept his stoic watch. "All right, you, me, him . . ."

"And me," Joey added. We turned to him as one, and he sheathed his sword. "I mean, all I'm hearing is that there's two people in trouble," he explained. "Father Paul would want me to help you. It's what he would do, right?"

"No, it's not."

The kid was taken aback. "But you two—"

"We work together," I said, "but Paul's experienced enough to know his limits. He wouldn't get involved here."

Joey folded his arms. "Well, I am."

"This isn't a game," I told him, slipping my shirt back on. "If we have to stand against Mab—"

"We die," said the wizard. "I get it."

"*He* doesn't. Get out of here, Joey."

He regarded me for a long moment, then shook his head. "You need me."

"I don't need a kid playing dress-up."

"I told you, I know what I'm doing," he replied.

I never saw his foot coming. In an instant, he had kicked my legs out from under me, and the sword bobbed above my breast. Robin grinned over Joey's shoulder, and even the wizard smirked. "Not bad," I allowed. "But I'm not Mab."

"Father told me what you are," said Joey, keeping the sword steady. "He gave me his notes on you to study on my trip. I read most of them last night."

"He has notes on *me*?"

"They're largely inherited." Joey moved the sword and offered me his hand. "What am I supposed to do, just go off to the festival and pretend I saw nothing? What kind of ass would do that?"

Robin shrugged. "The smart kind."

"Then maybe I'm not that smart." Joey leaned back, pulling me to my feet. "I've got my own wheels, too. Nice little checking account. Knot-tying skills."

"A claymore," the wizard offered.

"Arming sword," he corrected. "A claymore is two handed. So." He looked around at us, then at the empty house. "Where are we going?"

It took Robin nearly ten minutes to find the trap in the basement—admittedly, I had torn the room up after

the gate closed, and our fight hadn't helped matters—
and when he finally located it under a stack of empty
shipping boxes, I sent him and Joey away to prepare.
"Get together whatever you want for the drive," I told
them. "I don't know how long this is going to take.
And Joey, for the love of all that's sacred, lose the
maille. You look like an idiot."

"I left my riding gear at home," he protested. "It's
a safety thing."

"We'll drive slowly."

Robin draped himself across one of Meggy's folding chairs. The other, I saw with a pang of remorse,
had been splintered in the last hour. "What's the point
of packing?" he said. "Need something, get it."

"Until the magic dries up, dolt." The wizard shook
her head and started for the staircase. "Lancelot, why
don't you make a grocery run? Colin, I need your help
with something back at my place."

When she was halfway up the stairs, Robin muttered, "That's not worth the risk."

"Not everything is about sex," I replied, giving the
bookshelves a quick scan.

"Please," he scoffed, "that's the most blatant request I've heard in ages. Why just you, hmm? Why
not all of us?"

I looked over my shoulder in time to catch his las-
civious smirk, then pulled out a small stack of books
and turned for the stairs. "Because Joey's being useful
elsewhere, and you broke her stick. Now pack."

He spread his hands, and a pair of matching purple steamer trunks appeared in the middle of the basement. "Done. What next, O mighty slave driver?"

"Why don't you just guess what I'm thinking?" I replied, and slammed the door on his laughter.

The wizard drove us to her apartment in a sputtering blue panel van that was one bag of candy away from a search warrant. "It was cheap," she explained without preamble upon sliding behind the wheel.

Her home turned out to be half of a weather-worn duplex five miles farther back in the woods from Meggy's house. The other half was clearly uninhabited—the boards over the door and windows made that much apparent—and the wizard hadn't done much to improve the look of her side. She led us up the short, cracked concrete walk, unlocked her peeling front door on the third try, and waited until I was over the threshold before locking the door behind me.

"Okay," she said, once she was sure we were alone, "when are we ditching them?"

I blinked. "Who said anything about ditching them? And for that matter, why are you so certain that I want your help?"

"Yeah, whatever, you don't deal with wizards," she replied, absently running one hand through her stiff hair. "It's not like I want you tagging along on this, either, bucko, but I don't see a better option for the moment. You can't read spells, and I can't do the heavy lifting on my own." She shrugged. "Lancelot and Tinker Bell are superfluous, however."

"You're thinking of Galahad, not Lancelot, and really, you'll want to watch yourself around Robin," I cautioned. "But as far as heavy lifting goes, he's nearly my equal, and Joey—"

"Is a civvy."

"Is a crazy, sword-wielding civvy," I countered, "and let me be the first to say that I'd be happy to have steel on our side if we're going up against Mab. Now, what did you need from me?"

"Just that," she replied. "Though I was hoping for a plan to dump them. Well, you might as well make yourself comfortable," she said, gesturing to a battered green couch that ran the length of one wall. "Let me get my shit together."

While the wizard packed, I carefully maneuvered around her sitting room, examining the items on her cluttered bookshelves. Most of the space was occupied by old volumes, many of which I knew by reputation. Interspersed among them were copies of John Grisham paperbacks and a smattering of VHS tapes with tattered boxes. Her record collection marched along on its own shelf, giving ground to a shorter line of CDs that extended to the end of the wall. I couldn't be certain, but I thought she had arranged her music chronologically, ignoring the conventional categorization by name and genre. There were no photographs, no framed diplomas—not even a poster, I realized, seeing the bare beige walls around me. The wizard had seemingly limited her décor to the couch, which smelled of fast-food grease, a coffee table picked up at someone's grandmother's garage sale, a fat CRT television set with a tiny screen—circa 1990, perhaps—a long strip of flypaper, and half a dozen strategically arranged mousetraps. In short, a dump.

I glanced around her dusty but otherwise spotless kitchen, turned off the dripping faucet, and then noticed a scrap of yellow beside her wall phone, which proved to be a personalized notepad upon inspection. *TOULA* marched across the top in a bright green script, ornamented with curling leaves and vines.

So the wizard had a name, then.

By the time she emerged from her bedroom in jeans and a thin brown sweater, I had resigned myself to the odd-smelling couch and the old television. "All done?" I asked, watching her pad to the kitchen.

I heard the sound of a soda can open, and she returned a moment later with a Tab. "Almost. Did you screw with my stuff?"

"Would I tell you if I had?"

"Probably not," she concluded. "Thirsty?"

"Not for that. So, Toula, is it?"

She nodded and took a long sip of her vile drink.

"Why won't the Arcanum take you?"

She started, swallowed the wrong way, then almost spit her soda across the room. "None of your business," she choked out between coughs. "And who says they won't take me?"

I pushed myself out of the cushion depression and studied her. "You're not Arcanum—you'd have their tchotchkes around if you were. And they tend to conform to a certain mold, which you . . . an iconoclast, perhaps," I offered, seeing her eyes darken.

Toula played with the pop tab on her can. "Why would I want to be in the Arcanum? They suck."

"Now you just sound childish," I countered, propping my elbow on the stained armrest. "I've seen your work. Highly technical." Her expression shifted toward suspicion, and I said, "The wards. I mean, the spellwork was tight."

"Thanks, I guess," she mumbled.

"You've got the craft down. You just don't have the power to keep it intact." She shrugged halfheartedly and turned to the television, which I'd tuned to PBS, one of the three stations she received without cable and the only one not showing a church service. "It's nothing to be ashamed of," I offered. "Not every wizard's born for the big leagues. But I *am* curious as to what you were planning to do with the Magus's diary."

She whipped around, eyes wide. "Who said—"

"Meggy told me. She had the book waiting for you. I assume that's why you dropped by this morning, right?"

She tried to hide her anxiety with nonchalance.

"So what if I ordered it? I collect old books—you might have seen them behind you."

"I did. But come on, kid. Meggy might not have known what she had, but you and I both know the Arcanum would give a fortune for that book. So what's it to you?" I asked, tucking my hands behind my head as I leaned into the couch. "You can't expect anything in that diary to work for you, not if you can't even keep a ward system up. A barter, then? You give it to Greg, he gives you your membership card?" Toula glared back at me, and I shook my head. "I'm not going anywhere with you until I know your game. The last wizard who came to me for that book threatened to kill Meggy over it, and she was just my salesclerk at the time."

She didn't blink for half a minute, but her fist slowly crushed her soda can. "I'm bound, okay?" she muttered. "Harrison did it when I was a baby. I want free."

I tried to ignore the wave of guilt. "You don't *feel* bound . . ."

"Only because it's not complete. He left me a little. How generous. Pay attention and you'll see it."

"I can't see magic. You smell wizard-ish enough."

"You're a nose, eh?" she replied. "Weird. I'd show you the spell, but I'm currently down one wand. Anyway, you can probably smell the bind. And since we're playing twenty questions, now you get to answer something for me," she added, taking a seat on the coffee table, which creaked in warning even with her slight weight.

"Just a minute," I said, leaning toward her across the gap. "Why, exactly, are you bound? What could you possibly have done as an infant to scare the Arcanum?"

Toula pursed her lips. "My last name is Pavli. Clear enough?"

"As in . . . ?"

She nodded, and I made a face. Pavli wasn't an old wizard family name—the only one who came to mind was Apollonios, a Greek wizard who'd turned on the Arcanum in the late seventies and blown up forty-odd of its members at a training session outside Chicago, the single worst act of wizard-on-wizard violence in nearly a millennium. Anyone in the magical community who'd spent time in the mortal realm in recent decades knew about him. Sure, I'd killed more wizards than Pavli had over the years, but I'd acted in self-defense. Mass murder was a different matter entirely, especially when perpetrated by their own kind.

"Understood," I murmured. "Never knew he'd had a daughter."

"Yeah, well," she muttered, "they don't exactly parade me around."

"Your question, then?"

"Who bound Meg, and why?"

I laughed at the absurdity. "What are you talking about? Meggy's never been anything but normal, she's not bound—"

Toula's spikes bounced, cutting short my denial. "It's not visible, and obviously, you didn't pick up on it. But it's there, and it's like nothing I've ever seen."

I stared at her, bewildered.

She slumped toward me, resting her elbows on her knees, and lowered her voice. "Meg and I met ten years ago—she was willing to try anything to find Olive, and I guess magic made as much sense as the psychic she'd been paying. I showed her what I could do—didn't mention the Arcanum—and tried every spell I knew, everything I could find, to locate that child. I've *been* trying," she added, nodding to the bookcase behind me. "I don't have the oomph to do blood traces. But I couldn't even get a hint of Meg's baby, no matter what I did. Of course, if she was in Faerie, that would make a lot of sense.

"Early on, when everything was failing, I thought I'd dig back into Meg's past, see if she remembered anything odd from that night. It's a simple spell—put someone in a trance, then get them to remember. One step up from basic hypnotism," she explained. "Well, I got her into a trance easily enough, but when I tried to work the spell, it blew up on me. Tried again, same thing. And then I had enough sense to do to Meg what I did to the spell in the basement this morning."

I felt my insides roil. "And?"

"She lit up like a Christmas tree. And it sure wasn't spellcraft on her. It was pretty, and it was subtle, but it was definitely enchantment, hidden *deep* in her aura. I'd never have picked it out unless I'd amplified it like that. So tell me," she said, glaring holes into my face, "which one of you bound Meg?"

I had no answer for her. If the wizard had indeed seen an enchantment that extreme on Meggy . . .

. . . and the metal allergy, her contact dermatitis . . .

. . . and her face, how much younger she had seemed at Mother's feet . . .

. . . her hair, those beautiful red curls . . .

"Oh, no," I muttered. "No, no, *shit*, this is bad, this is very bad." I pushed myself out of the couch and began pacing the length of Toula's sitting room, trying to think of a better explanation than the one staring me in the face, but it was the only one that made sense.

Meggy had changed when she passed through the gate. That meant that something had been on her, aging her. But I had felt *nothing*—not a hint, for all of those years!—meaning that whatever was there had been put on her by someone not only stronger than me, but far more practiced. I had learned to make my work more technically precise, but that was the end result of trial over centuries. So whoever had bound Meggy had to be older than me . . .

Three candidates came to mind.

I was almost positive that Mother wasn't involved—

she would have had no cause to torture Meggy until I entered the picture. Mab was a cipher. But then there was Oberon. I knew a little of the man—I'd seen him occasionally as a child, and I saw plenty of him in Robin—but what had always stuck out to me about him was his coloring.

Red hair is even rarer among the fae than among mortals. Oberon had been a bizarre genetic anomaly, and most of the redheaded faeries I've known can trace themselves to him—his children, grandchildren, great-grandchildren *ad infinitum*. Robin bore his hair and our mother's brown eyes, which had never seemed to please her. Little about Robin ever did.

Meggy's eyes were blue, not green like Oberon's, but . . .

Sandra Bellamy's Floridian fling with a bartender . . .

Toula shot out one arm, stopping me in my circuit with a chop to the stomach. "Got a name?"

I nodded reluctantly. "I think she's half fae," I mumbled, trying again to push Meggy's terrified eyes from my mind. "I mean, the skin thing could just be an allergy, but she got younger when she went through the gate."

"If by 'the skin thing' you mean her glaringly evident aversion to iron and silver, then yeah, I'm with you," said Toula. "That's not a normal allergy. Nickel, sure, but iron *and* silver? I'd stake good money on fae blood in that mix."

"Olive's sensitive," I said, "and she's only a quarter . . . oh, wait, no. If Meggy's a half, too, then Olive—"

"Could be more fae than either of you," Toula finished. "If you're right about Meg. And I guess whatever was on her is off now, since she's on the other side. She *did* de-age?"

"A bit." This couldn't be happening.

"Well, at least going through must have taken the bind off," she continued, oblivious to my distress. "I'm sure it'll take some adjustment, but there are worse things than finding out you're half fae . . ."

"She's in the wrong court."

Toula paused and cocked her head. "What do you—"

"I think she's Oberon's. Maybe not *his*, not directly, but no one outside the Three is strong enough to work an undetectable enchantment that strong, and he's the only redhead among them. Meggy's family is all dark," I told her, seeing the realization begin to dawn. "She had to get that hair from *someone*."

"Oh, shit," Toula whispered, then darted into her room, grabbed a black duffel bag and her purse, and ran for the front door.

CHAPTER 8

"**Y**ou think that girl is my *sister*?"

I glanced in the rearview mirror and saw Robin's eyes narrow. "Did you get a good look at her? Plus, there was a heavy bind on her—enchantment, not spellcraft—and I never noticed."

"What a surprise. You're dense, but what else is new?"

I checked the side mirror, saw that our would-be Templar was following closely, and noted with relief that he had packed the armor away. His bike was actually a black-and-chrome trike towing an extra luggage trailer, but Joey seemed unabashed by the situation. Whatever the third wheel detracted in terms of coolness was restored by the arming sword strapped to Joey's back.

"It's not his fault," said Toula. Both of us started—I

thought ours had been a private conversation for linguistic reasons—and she smirked and shook her head. "I can read runeworks, you know. Fae's a walk in the park by comparison."

Robin's lip twitched into a brief snarl. "Your accent's weird."

"And so's your face, but I'm being polite about it. Jackass," she muttered, and gave me a look when I cut my eyes to the passenger seat. "It was definitely enchantment. I know the difference. So tell me, genius," she continued, turning to face Robin, "what are the odds that a redheaded woman from a family of brunettes, a woman with a strong and nearly invisible bind on her, a woman with a serious iron allergy who gets a few years knocked off her face when she runs into Faerie, *isn't* kin to you?" She flopped back into her seat and folded her arms. "We should find Oberon and let him know about this. If Meg's his daughter, then he'd help us save her."

Robin chuckled. "Even if you're right about the woman, which I'm not conceding, why would he trouble himself over her? Do you have any idea how many siblings I've had?"

Toula scowled, then dug in her bag and produced a spiral notebook. After a brief search through the tabs, she said, "Eight hundred seventeen known, possibly up to fourteen hundred. Records get spotty after a certain point."

He rolled his eyes. "Father's had at least one a year

since he came of age, as far as I know. Mother's record is more like one a decade. You might want to update your notes."

"You said you were going to give me directions," I interjected, looking at Toula before she and Robin could start a true fight.

She waved one hand at the windshield. "It's up the road a bit, on the coast. Place called Rigby. You know how to get there?"

"Well, I live there, so yes."

Toula frowned. "Rick never told me that. I would have thought he'd known about you. He keeps track of so many halves and . . . uh . . ."

"Mongrels?" Robin supplied.

"The polite term is *witch-blood*," she snapped. "But if you want to be crass about it, go ahead, you're not hurting my feelings. Just don't try it with Rick, or I'll shove a wand so far up your—"

"Okay, new car rule," I interrupted. "You two can't antagonize each other, no matter how strong the temptation."

Toula glowered back at me. "But—"

"My Honda, my rules. I can't break up fights and keep us on the road at the same time."

"It's not *that* difficult," Robin muttered.

"It is if you're not relying on magic to drive your car for you," I retorted.

"And this drive is completely unnecessary . . ."

I let it go. Convincing my brother that we needed

to drive in order to preserve what little magic was left took nearly twenty minutes. Yes, making an intra-realm gate would have been a much faster way to get to Rigby, but all three of us could sense the levels dropping, even as we stood in Meggy's driveway and argued. In the end, Toula's logic had prevailed. "*You* have no idea how to undo your mess," she told Robin, "but *I* can read the tracers, and to do that, I need a new wand. So you can either sit here and think about what a colossal screwup you've made, or you can come with us, our way."

Her way meant my car—Toula's van had almost overheated on the short drive back to Meggy's house—and my way meant that Robin rode in the back. Toula had mentioned motion sickness, and I wasn't about to let her ruin my semi-clean upholstery.

Despite the empty seat, Joey insisted on taking his trike. He claimed that it couldn't hurt to have another vehicle on standby, but his twitching eyes made it fairly evident that the idea of spending quality time in an enclosed space with two faeries and a wizard gave him pause.

Honestly, I was impressed that he hadn't run off when I gave him the out. I hadn't lied when I told him that Paul wouldn't have come along. The priest wasn't young any longer, and even when he'd had the stamina to stay up for two days at a time, he'd had enough sense to choose his fights. Paul was an excellent associate—calm in times of difficulty, rational in matters outside his faith, and secure enough in himself to ask for assistance when necessary—but beyond the spiritual realm, he had never been a fighter. As I tracked the trike behind us, I wondered about his choice in assistants. Paul was clearly grooming Joey to replace him, but I didn't yet know the boy well enough to decide what Paul had seen in him, other than a willing helper and a sword arm.

At least he hadn't tried to cast any of us into hell yet. Then again, the day was still young.

I pulled into Rigby's deserted downtown square shortly after ten that morning. The public parking lots were full, but the town's old Methodist and Episcopal churches were still in session, and none of the downtown eateries would bother opening for another hour. One didn't have to attend services in Rigby, but one wouldn't find much entertainment in town otherwise, especially on a cool morning with clouds rolling in from the sea. Granted, the breakfast place and the coffee shop by the ragged boardwalk were certain to be at least half full, but they were located a respectful five blocks from the heart of the old town and the disapproving stares of the devout.

As I circled the block, I spotted Mrs. Cooper's rusting green Continental in its usual spot beside the Methodists' front door. She had given up on dragging me along several years ago, but I suspected that she still prayed for me to change my mind.

"Turn right on Third," Toula directed, "and it'll be at the corner of Jefferson."

I followed her blue-nailed finger with skepticism. "There's nothing on this end of Jeff but a bar and some empty storefronts," I told her, making the turn.

"I know. Head for the bar and let me do the talking, okay? Rick's not going to be too happy to see me."

"What, with your winsome disposition and abundant charm?" said Robin. "I can't believe that."

"Bite me, Tink," she muttered, and pointed to the half-occupied line of spaces outside of Slim's. "Park there. Guess the bar opened early . . ."

I did as bid. "No, these are from last night," I explained, pulling in between a familiar pair of pickup trucks. "Slim's decent about taking keys."

Her eyebrow arched. "They *let* him?"

"The alternative is drinking at the beach bar, and no one wants to put up with that tiki bullshit." I slid out of the car and stretched my legs as Joey puttered in two trucks down. "Your guy's hiding around here?"

She didn't answer, but leaned against the car's warm hood and pulled her phone out of her purse. "Hey, Rick, it's Toula," she said after a minute. "Yeah . . . I'm outside . . . yeah, I'm sorry, this is an emergency . . . I know, I'm trying to put it right . . . *No*, of course I didn't do it! Sheesh . . . Yeah, I'm here because this dumbass faerie broke my wand . . ." She glowered at Robin, then stepped away from the car, talking in rapid spurts as she paced away. After a moment, she smiled and headed back toward us. "Aw, Rick, you're the best. Ta." She put the phone away and gestured toward the bar's delivery door. "Give him a minute. He's probably getting dressed."

Five minutes later, the door unlocked, and there stood Slim, baggy eyed and sleep mussed, wearing a tent-like Redskins T-shirt and shorts. He blinked in the morning sunlight, studied the small crowd outside the door, then shook his head and stepped aside. "Motley crew," he muttered. "Y'all might as well come in. Mind the floor, I mopped last night."

"Have I ever told you that you're fabulous?" Toula replied, sweeping past him into the dark bar.

"Only when you need something." He saw my confusion and nodded. "Missed you last night, Colin."

I forced my drooping jaw to rise. "Morning, uh . . . Rick?"

"I answer to a few names," he said, casting a wary eye on my brother as he followed Toula inside. "But you know how that game goes." He waited until Joey crossed the threshold, then leaned closer to me, frowning. "Isn't that the priest's buddy?"

"Seminarian," I replied absently, trying to reconcile my quietly attentive bartender with the witch-blood craftsman Toula had promised.

Slim snorted. "He's cool with all of this?"

"Still a little shocked, I think."

"Hmm. Well," he said, heading for the door, "I usually have a strict limit of one faerie lord at a time in here, but I guess I can make an exception this once."

I smirked and followed him. "Do you, now?"

"Absolutely. The premiums on this place would double otherwise." He closed the door and locked it, then muttered, "Please tell me you have him on some sort of leash."

I cast my eye toward the bar and spotted Robin sitting happily in front of a bottle of Glenfiddich and a pint glass. "I'll make it up to you."

Slim grunted and turned his attention to Toula, who had taken a seat on the splintering lip of the karaoke stage. "Total loss?"

"Total," she replied, glaring at Robin, who was too engrossed with his whisky and a jar of cocktail onions to notice. "There wasn't even a core to salvage. I'm sorry . . ."

He waved her apology aside and, with a weary sigh, headed behind the bar. "It's fine. I've got enough in reserve to make you a sufficient core."

She stood and rubbed the back of her neck. "I, uh . . . I'm a little short on funds at the moment, Rick . . ."

"The installment plan is fine. Colin, come with

me," he ordered, hoisting the trapdoor to the beer cellar.

Toula and I exchanged a quick look. "I beg your pardon?" I said.

Slim beckoned me toward the hole with two doughy fingers. "You and I need to settle your tab before you run off and get yourself killed," he explained. "My ledger's downstairs. Fotoula, you stay here and take care of your, um . . . associates, okay?"

She cringed at the name. "Can't I just—"

"How many times do I have to say *delicate process* before it sinks in, girl?" he interrupted. "Colin's not going to mess up the energy down there. You are. So make yourself useful and . . . you know." He cocked his thumb in Robin's direction. "Keep an eye on my top shelf, yeah?"

Slim descended into the basement without another word, leaving me little choice but to follow him into the darkness. At the foot of the stairs, my loafer touched concrete, and Slim pulled the cord for the bare bulb hanging above us. "Clear off," he instructed, waiting until I had stepped away from the staircase before pressing a button in the wall. With a slight mechanical whine, the trapdoor in the ceiling closed and locked, and the staircase folded upward to bar the exit. "I don't want to be disturbed," he said, heading for a second trapdoor on the far side of the room, directly under the stage.

I stumbled after him, wishing for one of the new-fangled cell phones with their large, glowing screens. Aside from the problem of the rapidly dwindling reserve of magic, I surmised that it would be in poor form to create a fire in a craftsman's workshop.

As if sensing my thoughts, he pulled another cord at the bottom of the second wooden staircase, and the red ceiling bulb revealed the chaos of his office. Heavily laden oak shelves, no two units alike, lined both of the walls and stretched back into the shadows. A long, well-scuffed table occupied the middle of the room, supporting half a hardware store's worth of saws, knives, and instruments I couldn't name. A fat, leather-bound book rose on a low stand over the clutter—probably handwritten, I thought, glancing at the script, and at least a few centuries old—while a black boom box with early nineties bulk and angles squatted silently at the far end of the table. The unventilated room, packed to the ceiling with magic-channeling materials, reeked of citronella so strongly that I coughed.

"Sorry about the light," said Slim, heading for a cluster of wooden rods on the nearest shelf. "Some of the shit down here is photosensitive, and red's the color least likely to set off an explosion. Also good for photography development," he added, pointing to an empty clothesline strung up between the two walls of shelves. "Haven't done much lately, but when I do, this place is great. Ah, here we go." He held a thin rod to the light, squinted, then nodded. "White pine. Not my first choice, but it'll do in a pinch."

I stepped out of his way as he carried the rod toward the one stool pulled up to the table. "So . . . how bad's my damage?"

Slim's bulk overflowed the stool when he sank onto it, but he paid the creaking wood no mind. "About a grand and a half," he said, strapping a magnifier to his head with a Velcro band, then fitted the rod into an angled holster with its fat end raised toward his face. "Don't worry, you haven't beggared me yet."

I reached for my wallet, but hesitated. It would be simple enough to create the money, as I usually did—Slim never made a peep when I paid him in stacks of new twenties and fifties, even if the serial numbers all tended to match—but with the situation, prudence called for me to dip into my bank account. That was well and good, but I hadn't brought a check with me, and I didn't see anything in the workshop that could read my seldom-used bank card. "I don't have the cash today," I began, "but would you take a check? I could run back to my place . . ."

He flipped the magnifying lenses over his eyes and picked up a tiny hand drill. "The money's not important right now," he muttered, applying the drill to the base of the wooden rod—an embryonic wand, I gathered. "We need to have a little chat about your posse upstairs."

I looked around for a stool, found none, and resigned myself to leaning against an almost clean section of the table, far from Slim's metal drills. "Toula explained the situation?"

"Roughly," he replied, raising his voice slightly as the drill did its work. "Didn't need much. I felt it when Faerie closed. Like a silent concussion, you know?" he added, sparing me a quick look. "I take it you were there? How bad was it locally?"

I swiped a bit of sawdust onto the floor. "Honestly, I was too preoccupied to notice much. And I plowed into a chair headfirst at about that moment, so I suppose I overlooked the etheric event."

Slim grunted. "Well, *I* felt it, and I guarantee you that anyone with the slightest sensitivity on the East Coast did, too. Hell, this thing probably registered worldwide. You're going to have the Arcanum up your ass in short order, you know."

"I was planning on avoiding them until we right this."

He paused, blew the dust from the rod, then frowned and recommenced drilling. "And how, pray tell, is that going to go down?"

"Won't know until we get the magic read, will we?"

Slim stopped working and gave me a puzzled stare, his fat lenses glowing red in the naked bulb's light like the eyes of a demonic owl.

"Toula was reading the traces of it before her wand was ruined," I told him. "She said that whatever closed the gates looked like a mixture of spell-craft and enchantment."

"I'd trust that reading," he said, bending back to his task. "Kid's got a solid head on her shoulders—from a technical standpoint, she's fantastic."

"And bound."

He stopped again, but he put the drill aside that time. "She tell you why?"

"Apollonios Pavli?"

Slim whistled softly. "Yeah. Daddy Dearest."

"Who's the mother?"

"One of his assistants, I heard. She dropped the kid and ran once the Arcanum caught him. It was either kill the baby or bind her, and Harrison's not the type to kill without good cause." He plucked the wand from its holster, examined the core he had drilled, then nodded to himself and reached for a little baby food jar across the table. "Toula was a good kid. Arcanum reared her. Never any trouble."

"But the bind stays?"

He unscrewed the jar's top. "A hand-reared wolf is still a wolf, Colin. If you're going to be dealing with her, don't forget that." He produced a tiny metal scoop from the detritus on the table and began to carefully transfer the brown powder in the jar into the hollowed-out wand, one infinitesimal spoon-ful at a time. "I'm the only craftsman authorized to make wands for her, and that's only because Harrison knows I can keep my mouth shut."

"About her?"

"About this." He tapped the scoop against the side of the jar. "Know what's in here?"

I peered at the faded label. "Guessing that's not sweet potatoes."

Slim's lips twitched into a brief smirk, the closest he ever came to a smile. "Close enough. You ever see *Dumbo*?"

It took me a moment to place the name—I've never been a great patron of the cinema, particularly not of those films featuring the Disney brand of magic. "The cartoon with the elephant?"

"Yeah. Little elephant, big ears, holds a magic feather to fly." Slim shook the wand back and forth, making the brown powder settle deeper into the core. "Thing is, he doesn't actually need the feather—he *thinks* he does, but it's all in his head. 'Believe in yourself,' all that bullshit, you get me."

"Sure, sure . . ."

He tamped the powder down with a thin rod, then resumed filling the wand. "Harrison put binds on Pavli and the kid. Pavli, no problem—could have left him alone in a room full of wands, and he'd have been impotent. But the kid—"

"Toula said he made the bind incomplete," I interrupted, but Slim cut me off with a curt headshake.

"Same bind. Same spell, same procedure, and she was only two months old."

I felt a slight chill up my back. "What're you saying?"

"I'm saying that she's stronger than the grand fucking magus," he replied. "He's not *letting* her do magic—he can't *stop* her." Slim tamped down the new layer of brown powder, his mouth a grim line. "I've been crafting since I was fifteen—done pieces for some of the most powerful in the Arcanum, and for some of the weakest. You get a really weak wizard or a witch, you give him rowan filled with dragonscale, yeah?"

"You still have a supply of dragonscale? When did any of you last make the crossing?"

"Believe me, it's recycled," he muttered. "Which was why Toula was apologizing up there—she thinks her wand's a dragonscale."

I watched him seal the end of the wand with dark putty and a lighter. "It's not, I take it."

"Sawdust and brown sugar. Finely ground and mixed, so it should *look* like dragonscale if it ever leaks out. By the way," he said, giving me another red-eyed glance, "if you were ever in the neighborhood of a dragon and wanted to help a guy out . . ."

"I'll keep that in mind, but I haven't been to Faerie in seven hundred years."

"Just think of me if you ever go back, okay?" He pointed to a ceramic pot on the shelf beside me. "Hand me that, if you will. It's just wood stain."

I watched Slim doctor Toula's new wand until it was dark and solid, indistinguishable from many of the wands I'd destroyed over the centuries. "You feel the magic disappearing, don't you?" I finally murmured.

"Mm-hmm."

"Which means that whatever bind is restraining Toula is going to fail eventually."

"Yup." He held the wand in a pair of plastic salad tongs and continued to paint.

"Of course, by the time that happens, there won't be enough magic left for anyone to do anything, let alone her."

"So I hope," said Slim. "But if y'all get the tap open again and she's unbound . . ." He paused, twirled the wand around, then set it in a makeshift drying rack. "What makes you think Harrison will be able to bind her again? All she's been talking about for *years* is figuring out how to make him lift the spell—so when all of this is said and done, assuming whatever you come up with works, we're going to have a little Pavli on our hands, and she may just have some scores to settle. Get it?"

I shrugged. "What are you suggesting, then?"

"I'm not. I can't do jack about it, and I don't know what to tell you. Just trying to warn you, that's all." He took off his magnifier and pushed himself up from his stool. "Wouldn't say we're friends exactly, but a bartender–patron relationship is quite nearly sacred, wouldn't you say?"

I smirked back at him. "I'd say I'm almost touched, Slim. By the way, if Toula knows you as Rick, then where did Slim come from?"

"I've carried that one for a while," he said, and gestured at his gut. "If you make fun of yourself, you beat everyone else to the punch, see?"

Slim began to move items around the table—tidying up, I assumed, but failed to see the logic to his system of organization. After a moment, I turned my attention to the dusty canisters and jars filling the shelf beside me; watching Slim toss bits of metal around made my skin crawl.

"It doesn't hurt, you know. And I promise I'm not going to bean you. Well, not intentionally."

I whipped around, the row of cloudy glass specimen jars I'd been studying forgotten, and found Slim grinning in the bulb's crimson glow. "You—"

"Are slightly sensitive to emotional changes. I put two and two together when you started twitching." He patted a wrench against his palm, then put it safely aside. "We're not all complete duds. *Mostly* duds, but not always complete."

Silently floundering, I struggled to find the right response. *So, you're a mongrel* was rude and unnecessary; the crafters wizards employed were always mongrels, sensitive to magic but unable to manipulate it. Their limitation made them suited to working with delicate magical energies that a wizard could easily knock out of place, while their sensitivity helped them know just how hard they could push before starting an explosion. *You're not a dud* would also be unappreciated. Slim didn't strike me as the sort of fellow craving empty platitudes.

I settled for, "Why didn't you tell me about . . . this?"

"What, my day job?" he replied, swinging one meaty arm around to encompass the sub-basement workshop. "It's on a need-to-know basis. And it's not exactly a secret that you don't like wizards."

"I like tiki bars a hell of a lot less, man."

Slim chuckled softly. "Well, then, if you can bring yourself to make the best of a bad situation, you're still welcome upstairs. Your brother, however, is not." He gave me a pointed glance, then cut his eyes to the ceiling.

"Really, I'll pay you for whatever he drinks . . ."

"It's not the booze that bothers me, Colin—correct me if I'm wrong, but that *is* the Puck, yes?"

"Best watch it with the name."

"If it were my nickname, I wouldn't like it, either." He squinted at me in the red light. "He's the one who closed off Faerie, though? How?"

"Damned if I know," I replied, moving closer to him to keep my voice low. "Some sort of trap—opened a gate, waited until . . ." I paused, not wanting to relive the previous night. "Waited until enough bodies went through, then closed down the whole thing."

"Mm. Not his own creation, then?"

"Mab's, he claims."

Slim hissed, a sudden intake of breath against his clenched teeth. "Yeah, this is one rodeo I want no part of. Hope you understand, but the sooner I see the back of you, the better."

"Understood. Just give the wizard her stick, and we'll see ourselves out." I headed for the staircase, but turned on the first step to meet Slim's eyes. "Just one question: How'd you recognize me?"

He smirked. "Arcanum-reared, and you aren't exactly disguised. I keep tabs on most of the witches and mongrels and duds around here—we've got a little support group, you know."

"I'll pay up when this mess is sorted out. And if something happens to me . . ."

"I've got your bank account on file."

"Good man."

Before I could take two steps, Slim clapped his hand on my wrist and squeezed. "My father was from Mab's court," he said in a low rush. "Raped my mom. And when he came around again to kill me, she cut his fucking head off, *Highlander* style."

I met his eyes and nodded.

"You packing steel?"

"Will be. And the kid is." Slim's brow furrowed, and I explained, "Seminarian with a sword. Don't ask."

"Man," he muttered, releasing me, "your crew's not just motley. That is a *fugly* crew up there."

"Yeah, but it's all I've got," I said, stepping up into the basement.

Slim turned off the red light and followed me. "I know, I know," he said quietly. "Best of luck. Glad this ain't my fight." He suddenly paused with his hand on the switch and stiffened. "Have you given any thought to what *else* happens when the magic's gone?"

"You mean the dark magic situation?" I murmured. Away from Slim's storeroom, I could detect a new scent in the air, a faint odor of gardenia and formaldehyde beneath the citronella smell of magic, and I folded my arms. "Yeah, I know."

"Got a plan?"

"Get Faerie opened again before the border turns into a sieve."

He nodded and pushed the button. We waited while the steps descended, and then I followed Slim back toward the ground floor. As he opened the trap, I heard Toula's voice to my right: "Don't be stupid, there is *no* magical boarding school. I went to public school and dealt with . . . ah, Rick, it's gorgeous!" she exclaimed, reaching across the bar to take the wand he extended to her. "Perfect! Thank you so much!"

"No problem," he grunted, then pointed to the door. "Out, y'all. It's past my bedtime."

Toula led the way, half dragging Joey along as she continued to mock him. Robin fell in behind them, still clutching the now half-empty bottle of whisky. I glanced at Slim, shrugged, then headed out into the morning to the cacophony of competing church bells.

CHAPTER 9

I seldom drove between my place and Slim's. The distance was slightly less than a mile, and when the sea breeze mixed with a decent buzz, the walk home could be quite pleasant. But that morning, I was entirely too sober to enjoy the exertion, and besides, I couldn't very well leave my car parked outside the bar—what would Mrs. Cooper say?

I had expected to pile everyone back in, drive home, and set Toula to work in under five minutes, but she had other plans. "I didn't eat breakfast," she griped, buckling her seat belt, "and this ain't exactly a cakewalk I've got ahead of me, so I'm going to need feeding."

After a pass through a drive-through on the outskirts of town, I drove home smelling charred meat and grease, wondering where the hell the weekend had gone so very wrong. The last time I had seen the inside of my garage had been Saturday morning, and Olive had been slouched beside me, complaining about the hour and my culinary skills.

As Joey puttered in behind me, I lowered the garage door with a button tap, then slid out of the car, careful to touch nothing without my leather buffer. "When you drove in front of my building, up the alley—what did you feel?" I asked him as he pulled off his helmet and strolled over.

His brow furrowed. "Nothing special."

"Shit," I sighed, and slammed the car door.

Toula came around to join us, still clutching her burger. "Wards failed, huh?" she asked, perhaps a touch more enthusiastically than was necessary.

I resisted the urge to slap her lunch out of her hands. "They didn't *fail*, they're intact—"

"Oh, I know, and they're pretty," she replied between bites. "Nice work. I mean, that's like *wizard*-level detail you've got there."

"I'll try to take that as a compliment," I muttered, heading for the garage door. The whole place smelled wrong. I picked up the undertones of dust and mildew, overshadowed by the sharp odors of engine exhaust and fries, but the familiar scent of magic was faint and fading—and the warning hints of dark magic were growing stronger. Palms up, I closed my eyes and tried to feel my carefully built wards. Still there, I sensed with relief, but weakening.

Toula joined me and nodded at the invisible barrier. "Yours are a hell of a lot stronger than mine, man."

"Let's hope so. I've been at this slightly longer than you have."

She snorted. "I'm serious, it's a nice network. Tidy. Just . . . you know . . ."

"Yeah."

We were still staring at the garage door in silence when Joey cleared his throat. "Is someone going to tell me what's up," he asked, "or are we just going to stand around all day and watch paint peel?"

"It's his wards," Robin offered, digging into a paper bag. "Coileán has his little fences, and with the magic fading . . . *poof*." He pulled a burger free, tucked the bag under his arm, and unwrapped his food with one hand.

I scowled at the garage door. "It's worse than that. The enchantment holding the wards together took *work*. Once the wards fail, it'll be history, and I'll get to start from scratch when this is over." I sighed again, then took a bag from Toula and helped myself. "My guess would be that anything dependent on a constant stream of magic is going to go down in the next day or so."

She pursed her lips. "It's dropping faster than I'd thought it would."

"Not if you consider how many of these power-sucking constructions exist. Think about the security network at the Arcanum silo . . ."

"Oh, *right*. That thing's massive." She glanced at Robin and said, "They're going to be so pissed at you when it fails."

My brother merely shrugged. "What do I care? And how would that be any different from the status quo?" He smirked at me and added, "The only wards that matter right now are the ones around this hovel."

I stared him square in the face for a long moment, watching the corners of his mouth twitch. "If anything happens to my stuff," I murmured, unblinking, "and I so much as think it was due to one of your people, I'll kill you. If you need to pass the word along, you can borrow my phone."

Robin sniffed. "What could I possibly want with your *stuff*? I mean, look at this place." He spread his free arm, encompassing a broom, a rusty snow shovel, and six dead roaches. "Please tell me it's bigger on the inside."

"Please *don't*," Toula whined. "Whovian geometry makes me queasy."

I headed for the inner door and pulled my plastic-capped key off its hook. "I'm serious, Robin. Feel free to try my patience if you've tired of life. If not, the phone's upstairs."

He stayed in the kitchen as the rest of us ate, mumbling into the handset in nearly unintelligible Fae. When I had finished picking at my burger, I left Joey and Toula in the living room and slipped back to my bedroom, which was still the pink mess Olive had left the morning before. Before Toula could see it, I returned it to its normal appearance. The reminder of Meggy and Olive hurt, and I wasn't about to sleep on pink sheets.

"**O**kay, people, here's how this goes down."

Toula sat cross-legged in the depression I had worn in my couch, her wand across her lap. Robin had unpacked the trap, an unremarkable black six-inch cube, and Toula had placed it on the coffee table in front of her. The table's normal layer of account books and shipping logs had been relegated to my office nook. We had unplugged every device in the room at Toula's bidding and pulled the shades, and now, leaning against the bare spots on the wall, the three of us stared at her with varying degrees of wariness. Robin maintained his usual look of casual indolence, but Joey's jaws were clenched, and his hand had wrapped around the silver crucifix hanging from his neck.

"I'm going to do what I was doing this morning before we were interrupted," said Toula, sparing a cross look for Robin. "Colin, you're going to feed it, just like before. Galahad, you're going to keep Tink out of my way. Got it?"

"Let's just get this over with," I said, cutting Robin off as he started to speak. "You two, kitchen. Give her some space." I waited until they were behind the half wall, then took a seat in the armchair beside the couch and exhaled slowly. "Whenever you're ready, kid."

She closed her eyes, held her new wand out like a conductor's baton, and began to mutter.

The popular conception of magic is that in order to make something happen, it's necessary to wave a stick and shout a set phrase in bastardized Latin. The stick part is usually true for wizards—wielded properly, a wand is an excellent focusing tool and amplifier—but there are no true magic words. A wizard can yodel his grocery list, for all the difference it makes, so long as it puts him in the right frame of mind.

Toula's preferred mantra sounded suspiciously like *"Lorem ipsum dolor,"* but I decided to confirm this only after the trap stopped glowing.

I felt the spell she wove, sensed the tendrils flowing around and through the box, and tentatively began to feed it, strengthen it, bolster it against the magic protecting the trap. Toula's face reddened, then paled, in her effort to conjure the traces forth from the box, and I tried to ignore the migraine that threatened more forcefully with every passing moment. Pushing power into a spell was difficult enough, but doing so in an environment that was already drained of magic was painful.

"How much longer?" I muttered, risking a glance at the wizard.

Toula sat motionless in the middle of a storm of green swirls, her eyes open and fixed at some point beyond the horizon. "I'm in," she whispered. "Hold it . . . keep it . . ."

Someone rapped thrice on the kitchen door, a loud report in the near silence of the apartment. The sound alone almost broke my concentration, but I knew, even with my focus directed elsewhere, who my caller had to be. No one but Mrs. Cooper ever came up the fire escape.

Unfortunately, my kitchen door was decorated with four quarter-panes of frosted glass—too distorted to show her who was in my house, but clear enough to show her that I wasn't alone. "Mr. Leffee!" she called through the door. "Are you there, dear? It's Mrs. Cooper! Are you all right?"

"Damn it," I muttered, then waved at the kitchen, hoping someone was looking out in time to see me flail. "Robin!" I hissed. "Get in here!"

He wandered in a moment later, keeping well clear of the etheric maelstrom flowing around Toula. "Yeah?"

The rapping at the door increased in tempo. "Take over. I've got to get rid of her."

He cocked his head back toward the kitchen. "Want me to—"

"*No.* Just take over here."

"Please don't tell me you're sleeping with *that*," he sighed, but slipped into my seat as I vacated the chair. He closed his eyes, screwed up his face, and forced power into Toula's spell—not as gracefully as

I had, I noticed with slight satisfaction, but effectively enough to leave the wizard undisturbed in her work.

Even with the connection broken, my body ached. I stumbled into the kitchen, where I found Joey crouched over his luggage, hurriedly slipping into a clean black shirt and clerical collar. "What are you—" I began, but he shook his head to silence me and pointed to the door. A moment later, he tucked his shirt into his jeans, pulled his crucifix necklace into position, took a deep breath, and cracked the door open. "Yes?" he asked.

Mrs. Cooper peeked around him and caught a glimpse of my face. "Gracious, Mr. Leffee, you look *dreadful!*" she cried, covering her well-rouged lips with one hand. "What on earth happened? I saw your car parked downtown this morning, and I . . . well . . . I suppose . . ."

I suppose you had too much to drink, and that bartender made you take a cab was the end of that thought, but my head felt too fuzzy to come up with a convincing story on the fly. Five minutes with Toula had drained my last reserve, and I leaned against the counter for support, trying not to give her cause to come in and drag me to a doctor.

Mercifully, Joey stepped into the breach. "I'm terribly sorry, ma'am, but it's not safe for you to be here right now," he murmured, sliding between Mrs. Cooper and me. "This is an active exorcism. Please, for your own safety, you need to leave the premises."

Mrs. Cooper's pale eyes widened. "An *exorcism?*"

Joey nodded, and I realized he had dropped his voice half an octave when he replied. "I'm Father Joseph Bolin, assistant to Father Paul McGill."

Her brow scrunched, and I added, "Top exorcist in the area. Called in specially."

Joey glanced at me in acknowledgment, then back at my visitor. "This is a very sensitive case. Brother Colin has been assisting us, but as you see"—he inclined his head in my direction—"the strain is almost too great even for him, and he's young and strong. We've taken a quick break, but you really must go."

She stared at us, speechless, and I realized that she was buying it. "The girl," I said. "The one you found? It was worse than I thought. She . . . poor kid, she . . ."

Joey put a steadying hand on my shoulder. "The Evil One is never worse than when he preys upon the innocent."

Mrs. Cooper twisted her purse's thin strap between finger and thumb. "Is she going to be okay?"

"With the Lord's help, yes." Joey reached across the threshold and clasped her hands tightly. "Colin tells me you're strong in the faith. Bless you, sister. The best thing you can do now is pray for her."

"I will, I will," she rushed, her head bobbing like a toy. "Of course. If you need anything . . . I could call Reverend Martin, he's a wonderful man of God . . ."

"We'll let you know," Joey replied, gently but firmly, and with a final squeeze of reassurance, he sent Mrs. Cooper on her way. When she was speed walking back to her building—Eunice Cooper was a lady, and ladies did *not* run—he shut and locked the door, then leaned against it and exhaled. "Close, man. And she's right, you look like shit."

I slumped to the floor, succumbing to the vertigo that had been threatening for the last two minutes. "Tough work in there. Want to check on them? I'd go, but the floor's moving."

"Yeah, sure." He stepped over my legs, then slipped around the cut-out wall into the living room. A moment later, Joey leaned through the window and said, "They're out cold. Were we expecting this?"

"No," I sighed, wishing my building weren't being tossed at sea.

"Want me to try to wake them?"

"Are they breathing?" I mumbled into my palms.

"Breathing, pulses, but no reaction to light. I held their eyes open, but they didn't even flinch."

"They're probably just exhausted."

"I don't know about—"

I forced myself to crane my neck upward and meet his worried eyes. "Big spell. Mediocre wizard. Faerie. Exhausted."

Joey shrugged. "If you say so. Go on, get some rest. I'll take first watch."

When I managed to pull myself out of bed again, Joey was sitting alone at the kitchen table, playing solitaire. Half a cold hamburger sat on a plate to his left, forgotten in his concentration on the spread, and he jumped when I cleared my throat. "Any sign of waking?" I asked, heading for the refrigerator.

"Not a peep. I covered them up, but your brother's still on the floor. Didn't exactly have a place to move him. And are you really making a—"

"Bloody Mary, yes," I finished for him, pulling a bag of celery from the crisper. "This is one of life's great cure-alls, Joey, and you need to respect it." I held out my empty glass in invitation, but he shook his head. "Not much of a drinker, are you?"

"Not a fan of tomato juice," he explained. "But seeing as it's after five, if you're pouring . . ."

I glanced at the microwave clock, then out the kitchen door, where the frosted panes revealed the growing dusk. "Damn. Sorry about that. The spell really took it out of me," I said, rummaging through the liquor cabinet under the counter. "Where the hell is . . . ah. Good." I produced a half bottle of Belvedere and poured generously. "What are you drinking?"

"Guess there's no chance of a Bellini, is there?"

I stopped, put the bottle down, and stared at him. Joey smiled sheepishly. "Worth a shot, right?"

He cracked open the can of beer I handed him as I finished my dinner preparations. "Father said you're a bit of a lush."

"Father probably didn't tell you the half of it. Cheers." I hoisted my glass and chugged it back, then grimaced as the full force hit. While he returned to the sad remnants of his burger, I began to make a second drink. "You're taking this whole situation unexpectedly well."

"Yeah?"

"Yeah. It took Paul two months to look me in the eye. His predecessor got spooked and 'accidentally' spilled a bottle of holy water on me. *His* predecessor carried around an iron bar for the first decade of our acquaintance, just to be safe. I still have it, actually. Handy little memento." I stirred, tasted, then added more vodka. "So what's different about you?"

Joey took a bite of his dinner and chewed slowly before speaking. "No one's tried to kill me yet, I suppose. That goes a long way toward establishing a working rapport."

"Just keep your eye on Robin. Toula seems level enough for now." I pulled out the chair beside him. "Any burgers left?"

"Two in the fridge. I can go for more," he said, pushing himself up, but I waved the offer away, and he sank back into his seat. "Can I ask you something?"

"Sure."

He wiped his hands and began to clean up the cards. "You guys were saying something about two people trapped in Faerie, right? That's what all this is about?"

"Partly." I created a fire in my hand, but the flame was barely larger than a match. "Magic flows into this realm from Faerie. With the realm sealed off, we're running out. That's why those two are still sleeping— we're working with almost nothing, and the strain of it was awful."

"And we . . . want to be connected?"

That gave me pause. "Yes and no," I said after a moment of thought. "While I'm almost positive this realm would be better off without faerie intrusions, it's the price you pay for magic."

"But do we *need* magic?" he asked. "I mean, yeah, I can understand why you three might *want* it, but it's not doing much for the rest of us, you know?"

"And that's where you're wrong." I sighed. "There's the Gray Lands to consider."

"The what?"

"The Gray Lands. It's the third known realm, sort of a dark reflection of Faerie. Each has its own set of unpleasant natives—we're just prettier." Joey smirked at that, and I shrugged. "It doesn't take fangs to kill you. But whatever sealed off Faerie *didn't* seal off the Gray Lands, and as soon as the juice dries up, the Arcanum's safeguards on the gates are going to fail."

Joey grimaced as he stuffed the cards into their

box. "So if we don't get the connection fixed, what happens to you?"

"Not much. I'm not going to shrivel up and die, if that's what you were implying. I'm just going to have to move more often, since, you know . . ." I pointed to my face. "I look pretty damn good for my age."

He nodded. "And who are the two we're trying to rescue?"

I took a long drink. "My daughter," I said quietly. "And her mother. I barely know the one, and I never stopped loving the other. So here I am."

"Meg, right?"

"Yeah. Meg."

"And Toula knows her, too?"

"So she says, yes." I drank again, then wiped the thin film of tomato off my mouth. "Look, Joey, you don't have to do this—"

"Forget it," he interrupted. "I'm in. Damsels in distress and all that, you know. Right thing to do. We've been over this." He began to take a bite of his burger, but paused. "Robin wasn't really planning to wreck your place, was he?"

"Of course he was," I replied, leaning back in my chair. "He's been waiting for the opportunity for *years*. Little bastard's one of the reasons why I built wards in the first place."

"Oh. Then I suppose all of that talk about killing him . . ."

"Never make a threat you don't mean to carry out."

Before Joey could ask another question, Toula slunk into the room. "Got the spell," she muttered, heading for the sink.

I waited while she downed about a quart of water. "Great. How do we break it? Or is it going to fail first?"

"Not going to fail. It's the only thing with a connection to Faerie at the moment." Ignoring my quiet profanity, she put the glass in the sink, belched, then rubbed the sleep from her eyes. "Wake Tink. He's going to *love* this."

Robin slept like the dead that evening, but when a few strong shakes wouldn't rouse him, Joey got creative. "No one push me," he warned, pulling his sword from its scabbard. "I don't want to actually touch him, but if I get close enough . . ."

He held the blade half an inch from Robin's hand, and my brother began to twitch in his sleep. After a moment, his eyes cracked open, and seeing the cause of his discomfort, he jerked his hand away and rolled toward the television. "What the hell are you doing?" he snapped as Joey put the sword up.

"Sorry," I said, stepping between them as Robin scrambled to his feet. "Toula wants to talk to us. You wouldn't wake up."

He stared at me, aghast. "A slap in the face, Coileán. A bucket of water. *Maybe* a light electric jolt. But moon and stars, a damn *sword*?"

"Kid wasn't going to touch you," I replied. "That's why he was holding it instead of Toula. Or me." Smiling, I flopped onto the couch. "But now that you're awake, let's see what we're dealing with, eh?"

Muttering curses in Fae, Robin slunk to the far side of the couch, and Joey pulled up a chair. Toula, who stood by the coffee table, picked up the black box and began passing it from hand to hand. "It took some doing, but I think I was able to dissect the trap."

"Oh, let's hope," said Robin, folding his arms. "Because if I did that for nothing—"

"God, you complain," she huffed. "Here's the sitch, guys. The spellcraft component of that mess was primarily aimed at Faerie—it's like a wall between the realms. A second skin."

"Can you *do* that with a spell?" I asked, frowning.

"Not *a* spell. There's about thirty different ones working in tandem—it's unlike anything I've ever seen, and it's a *massive* construction. Punching through it would take work and a considerable amount of power, and at the rate things are going, we have neither of those, so we have no choice but to try to work on the enchantment component, because they're connected. Don't ask me how the parties responsible for this disaster got that much enchantment and spellcraft working together without turning their workshop into a crater, but they did it. The one feeds the other—the enchantment is the portion drawing power from Faerie, and the spell's siphoning power off the enchantment. Seriously," she added, bouncing the box in her palm, "this thing needs to be studied and *taught*."

"Assuming we live that long," I replied. "Okay, how do we break the enchantment? Can't punch through it either, can we?"

"Not a chance," she agreed. "But there's a lock built into it."

"A lock?" asked Joey.

She nodded. "Think of the fairy tales you know— the spell's broken with true love's kiss, or whatever. Yeah?"

"Yeah . . ."

"That's a lock," Toula explained. "The key is the kiss. Now, ordinarily, we don't build locks into our work—we just use enough power to overload the spell and break it apart. But if you're dealing with a massive spell that you can't easily overpower, you build a lock in as a safety measure. It's like having an emergency shutdown button."

"And what's the key in this case?" I interjected.

"Again, this in the enchantment portion, so I can only *guess* I've read it correctly . . ." She sighed. "It'll take one of you from each court. If we can find someone to stand for each, plus a decent amount of magic, you'll be able to open the lock. Once that happens, the enchantment will fall apart, and the binding spells will go down. Dominoes."

"Right, then, we work quickly," I said. "I can stand

for Titania, and Robin's clearly with Oberon. Slim told me his father was from Mab's court . . ."

But Toula shook her head. "We need three who can control the power it'll take to open the way. Rick's useless on that count. You're going to need at least a half faerie, not a witch-blood."

"Damn it," I muttered. "And even if we do find the third, where are we supposed to get enough magic to unlock this, anyway?"

The wizard smirked and folded her arms. "Want to tell me where you hid the diary?"

CHAPTER 10

When I rummaged through the books I had taken from Meggy's house, I had a moment's fleeting panic that the diary, somehow knowing that I planned to give it to a person who could use it, would hide itself from me. But it sat where I had left it, wedged between two thick bestiaries of creatures that hadn't been seen in that realm since Rome fell. The smell of magic was definite but faint, like an odor more remembered than sensed. Whatever protection had been placed on the diary was failing along with my wards.

And the wizard's bind, the soft voice in the back of my mind insisted, but I pushed it aside and brought Toula her prize.

She sat on the couch, wrapped in a plaid afghan, and took the box from my hands with as much reverence as if I'd just offered her a stone tablet from Sinai. "Do you have gloves?" she asked. "I don't want to get oil all over this."

I pulled a pair of white reading gloves and a set of foam blocks from my desk, and Toula gently unpacked the diary. Joey had pulled my desk chair closer but kept his distance from Toula, while Robin had stalked off to the fire escape to sulk about his rude awakening.

"I've lost days in the Arcanum's library," she said, carefully flipping through the front pages. "This is nice vellum—you can barely see the pores." She ran a gloved finger over the hide. "Whoever made this got all the hair off, too, thank God. I *hate* furry books. Creeps me out."

Joey leaned closer, his curiosity piqued, but my attention was caught by the neat lines of black ink covering the page Toula had revealed. "That was blank the last time I saw it," I murmured.

She glanced up from her work and nodded. "Protective spells are failing. Want a look?"

I slid next to her on the couch and peered at the script. "At least he wrote in Latin. I was afraid he'd have gone with something more exotic for security."

"This was Simon Magus, not da Vinci," she replied. "With the spells on this, he wouldn't have needed to write upside down and backward."

"I'm sorry, *whose* diary is this?" Joey interjected, retreating slightly from the book.

Toula smirked. "Simon Magus the Younger, not the one you're thinking of. He served as grand magus during the Great War."

The boy's brow wrinkled. "Then why was he writing on *vellum*?"

"Wrong Great War," I explained, seeing his confusion. "Not World War I."

"Yeah, sorry," said Toula. "The Great War spanned the first half of the eleventh century. Basically, all of these little arcana had been fighting each other for power until *the* Arcanum started to take over, and so they fought against consolidation for fifty-odd years. The Magus was instrumental in the Arcanum's victory."

Toula cracked her knuckles and turned the page. "The man was a genius. The official version of the story is that the Arcanum won the war because of the nobility of our cause, the rightness of our hearts, et cetera." I snorted at that, but Toula ignored it. "The real reason they won is that the Magus built about a dozen instruments that were capable of containing and releasing magic—not energy, but pure, raw *magic*." Joey cocked his head, so Toula explained, "Say that you have two bands of wizards standing out in a field, throwing lightning at each other. They're going to be set for a time, but eventually, the rate of magic expenditure in that localized area will surpass the flow rate of magic. It's like drawing from a reservoir during a drought—you're taking water faster than you replace it. Get it?"

Joey frowned. "I guess. And these devices . . ."

"Deployed on our side when the levels reached a critical low. When the two sides could no longer fight effectively, the Arcanum brought out the batteries and smoked the opposition. Maybe not the most sporting way of waging a war, but it was pretty damn effective. And this"—she gingerly patted the open diary—"should tell us how to make them."

The boy's frown deepened. "Correct me if I'm wrong, but if the magic . . . reservoir . . . is almost gone as it stands . . ."

"Oh, no, we're not actually going to be *making* any," Toula replied. "No, we'd need all kinds of tools, stuff that probably even Rick doesn't have, and . . . you know." She cut her eyes to me and muttered, "A halfway decent wizard. No, what we're going to do is find the ones the Magus hid. Assuming they're still charged, we might just have enough juice to get the gateway open again—"

"Pretty big assumption," I cut in. "I mean, it's been almost a thousand years, kid."

Toula shrugged. "Got a better idea?"

"No," I admitted. "And we've still got to track down someone from Mab's court, if you're reading the enchantment correctly . . ."

"Let's hope." She ran her hands through her short

hair. "Here's the plan, fellows: I'll stay up tonight and read through this, figure out where the Magus hid his toys. We'll reassess in the morning. Okay?"

I tapped the page in front of me bare-handed, earning a look of reproach from Toula. "My Latin is at least as good as yours, if not better. Let me read it, and you get some rest."

Joey came around Toula's side and squinted down at the diary. "Is that even Latin? The letters—"

"Carolingian miniscule," I replied. "Easy to read once you have the knack." He looked at me doubtfully, and I shrugged. "When you're one of a handful of people in a fifty-mile radius who can read and write, you learn to read and write *everything*. There are at least two manuscripts at the Bodleian with my handiwork in them."

"Seriously?"

I grinned at his expression. "I'd call myself a bit of a Renaissance man, but I predate the Renaissance."

"Cute, Gramps," said Toula, "but I can handle it." She stretched her legs out again and bent over the diary. "Besides, someone has to go handle Tink, right?"

The fire escape remained quiet, and I checked at three that morning to find Robin still outside, smoking a cigarillo. He had dragged a kitchen chair onto the landing, positioning himself so as to catch the sea breeze while avoiding the metal railings. "Nice of you to join us," I said, leaning against the door frame.

My brother exhaled a long, thin stream of smoke, then shifted in his chair to face me. "Everything still hurts. That is the *last* time I fill in for you with spell-craft, understood?"

"Appreciated."

He snorted. "The crone?"

"Across the street," I said, pointing to the darkened windows of Tea for Two. "Nothing to worry about."

"Who's worried?"

I watched the glowing tip of his cigarillo wobble in his hand. "You're twitchy."

"I am not," he muttered, taking a drag.

"You are. You're literally twitching." I grabbed his smoking hand and held it steady. "What's the matter with you?"

Robin's façade of nonchalance couldn't hide the unease in his eyes. "It's almost gone," he said quietly, pulling his hand free. "Can't you feel it?"

"Certainly."

"And you're not concerned?"

"Of course I'm concerned," I said, folding my arms against the night chill. "But fretting about it isn't going to solve the problem, is it?"

He took another long drag. "Where in the bloody hell are we supposed to find one of Mab's people?" he muttered. "They're impossible to track—the only one I've seen in ages is Mab herself, and you see how well that went."

"Oh, yes, blame Mab," I snapped. "This is all her fault."

"Well, it *is*," he replied sulkily. "I just wanted to destroy you, not close off Faerie."

"That makes me feel so much better."

Robin flashed a half grin in the kitchen's glow, then pushed his wind-tousled hair from his eyes. "Seeing as we're not currently working at cross-purposes, Coileán, I'd be amenable to a temporary arrangement. A cease-fire, if you like."

"I'm listening."

He stretched his legs, resting his black boots on the railing. "Here's the situation: I'm willing to do whatever it takes to bring my father back to Faerie. I'm also willing to do whatever it takes to cast Mother out."

I shifted against the door frame and mulled that over. "I'm not fundamentally opposed to the former."

"Yes, you are," he said, pointing his cigarillo at my face. "If my father goes back, even as a co-ruler, then you and I will be on equal footing in the realm. And when that happens, you won't be able to terrorize my people any longer."

"Robin," I said quietly, "no matter who's in power in Faerie, I will always have iron and the stomach to employ it. Tell your people to leave the mortals alone, and you and I will have no quarrel."

He blew concentric smoke rings into the night. "Why should I?"

"You speak of terrorizing, but what do you think your people are doing? Or Mother's people, for that matter? I've convinced most of them to keep their distance, but you're impossible!"

"Keep your voice down," he said, nodding toward Mrs. Cooper's building. "Unless you wanted to see your girlfriend again."

"Look, I understand that you're bored. I understand that your entire *court* is bored. But making life hell for people who wouldn't know how to defend themselves if they even knew what they were fighting? You're shooting fish in a barrel. Where's the sport in that?"

"As you say," he replied, "we're bored."

"I thought you had a place in Hollywood these days."

"I do. Nice little mansion. *Fantastic* parties. As many beautiful would-be actresses as I want."

My eyebrow rose. "And?"

"Still bored."

"So if we get Faerie open again, and if we were to somehow give your court leave to return . . ."

Robin sat up, faintly smirking. "That might alleviate some of your problems."

"I could live with that."

"Mother couldn't."

"Forget her for the time being," I muttered. "Want a drink?"

He shook his head and smoked in silence for a long moment, and we listened to the distant ocean crash upon the sand. "What's the girl to you?" he asked.

"Which one?"

Robin's eyes narrowed. "Which do you think, halfwit? The child's your blood, I understand that. What about her mother?"

"Your half sister, you mean?" I retorted.

"We don't know that for sure . . ."

"It's a fair assumption, is it not?"

Robin shrugged.

"She worked for me when she was starting out. I fell hard," I told him. "If anything happens to her before we get the gate open . . ."

I left the thought unfinished, and Robin knocked his ashes over the railing. "Message received." He sighed, then rested his elbow over the back of the chair and stared up at me. "I suppose I should pity you, shouldn't I? You invested yourself in the life of a girl who you thought to be nothing more than mortal. That's . . . *pathetic*, Coileán."

"It's not pathetic," I mumbled.

"It *is*." He stood, took a long last draw, then stubbed the cigarillo out and threw it toward the street. "You're a high lord of Faerie," he said, clasping my shoulder. "Try to act like it. Right now—and I'm quite serious about this—you're embarrassing me."

Before I could respond, Toula popped into the kitchen, scowling. "Someone is *trying* to work, here, guys. Want to keep it down?"

"I told you," I said, "I'm willing to take over—"

"And I told you I've got it, but it's kind of tricky to figure out what the hell the Magus was going on about when all I can hear is you two fighting." She rubbed at the bags under her eyes. "Look, no one wants to be here, okay? Can we just try to get along until we get Tink's mess cleaned up?"

"It's not entirely my mess," Robin began, but I shut him up with a look.

"We'll be quiet," I told Toula. "Anything hidden close by?"

She began rummaging through the pantry, her voice slightly muffled. "You know that these hiding places are probably out of date, right?"

"That's what I was afraid of."

She emerged with a box of saltines and unwrapped a new sleeve. "Okay. So I know the Arcanum has one—it's their backup generator. I just don't know which one it is. These are stale, man."

I shrugged. "I never promised gourmet cuisine. What else do you have?"

"Well"—she bit into an unusually chewy cracker and made a face—"he gave one to the merrow."

"Meaning that they probably still have it," said Robin, dragging his chair back inside. "They're usually off the Keys this time of year—Father showed me where they come ashore." I turned to stare at him, and he shrugged. "He's been down in the Keys for years. You're not the world's greatest detective, you know."

Toula set the disappointing crackers aside. "I haven't had any dealings with the merrow."

"We have," I replied, and Robin nodded. "They're not impossible to work with if you're polite and amenable to their terms. Though I don't know how to summon them, not with the current conditions . . ."

Robin took up Toula's discarded snack. "I told you, my father knows them. He could help us."

The wizard's visible discomfort intensified. "Dragging one of the Three into this . . ."

"Robin and I will handle it," I told her, trying to sound more confident than I felt. "What about the other devices?"

She sighed wearily. "I've got initial locations, and I think I've got them plotted, but this would all be a lot simpler if *someone* had Wi-Fi." I looked at her blankly, and Toula rolled her eyes. "Internet access, Gramps. I've been cross-referencing on my phone all night, and my data plan's not that generous. And what's the carrier situation here, anyway? I'm barely getting 3G speeds."

I blinked slowly, trying to process the words coming from her mouth, then shook my head. "Moving on. I propose that you reach a stopping point and rest, because we're going to have a long drive tomorrow."

Robin began to protest, then shut his mouth, his

shoulders slumping as the realization hit. "There *is* no faster way, is there?" he mumbled.

"Not unless you have a helicopter on the roof. The atlas is in my car . . ."

But Toula had already headed back toward the living room. "I'll just Google it," she called over her shoulder. "Hey, Tink, where's your dad hang out? Got an address?"

Once she'd routed the trip to her satisfaction, Toula fell into a deep sleep on the couch, curling up until she was nothing but a mess of black spikes poking from beneath the plaid afghan. I packed away the diary and cut the lights, then rejoined Robin in the kitchen. "You're showing remarkable restraint," I whispered, cleaning up the mess.

"In what sense?" he replied.

"The wizard's been nicknaming everyone, and you haven't tried to strangle her yet. Well, at least not in the last few hours," I amended, opening the dishwasher. "I'm almost proud of you."

He leaned back, bemused. "What's the problem? She's been respectful."

"Ti . . . oh, no," I muttered, rubbing my forehead. "Not *Ti'ank*. Tink."

"Hmm?"

"You honestly thought she would call you 'the mighty one'?"

"I don't know," he replied, "her accent's weird. So what is she—"

"It's probably best if you don't know, okay? Just do us all a favor and let it slide."

"But what—"

"*Please*, Robin."

"Fine," he huffed. "For now. But you're going to tell me eventually, or so help me . . ."

I threw a dish towel at his face and wandered back to my bedroom, where Joey lay fast asleep on the bed. Stretching out on the carpet, I locked my hands behind my head and waited in the darkness for morning, wondering just how many hours we could drive before someone mutinied.

And whether Meggy and Olive were still alive to be rescued.

CHAPTER 11

We struck out shortly after sunrise, Toula and Robin riding with me and Joey soloing close behind. By ten that morning, the radio had cycled through six pop stations, and the incessant bass was killing my head. Toula insisted upon playing DJ, while Robin lounged across the entire back bench, periodically giving my seat little kicks. He swore that the jostling was unintentional, but his smirk said otherwise.

By noon, my passengers were shouting at each other over some triviality—the merits of a program I'd never seen due to basic cable and lack of interest—and I called a halt for food at a forlorn McDonald's on the side of I-95 deep in South Carolina. My head was pounding, my eyes were glazing over, and the stress of watching for hidden cops had knotted my back and shoulders. The enchantment protecting my car had finally failed, and I was torn between the need to make good time and my paranoia, which saw headlights peeking out behind every bush in the median.

Joey parked beside me, then slid off his trike on shaky legs and pulled his helmet free. "How much farther?" he asked.

I consulted Toula's handwritten backup directions. "Another eleven hours or so. How's your gas?"

"Nearly empty," he replied, massaging a kink from his leg. "Look, you weren't planning on making this trip in one day, were you?"

Truth be told, I'd been planning just that when we left Rigby, but I wasn't sure how many more hours of chauffeuring I could take before driving myself off a bridge. "We can stop for the night in north Florida," I suggested. "That should put us well within a day of the Keys."

I handed Joey my road atlas and pointed at the route. His shoulders slumped, but he nodded and headed inside.

Robin slipped out of the car and stretched. "If we were going to ditch him—"

"If you give me one more word on the matter," I muttered, "then so help me, you're walking the rest of the way."

I followed Joey into the restaurant, leaving my passengers to continue their bickering in peace. My stomach craved grease, my head craved at least a rum and Coke, and what little sense I still had at that moment warned me that telling Robin his hated freckles were back wouldn't be prudent. As much as I relished the thought of seeing his face when he learned that his personal glamour had fallen, I realized the implications all too well, and I couldn't bear his whining on top of everything else.

Sleep at the hotel in Jacksonville where we'd finally crashed came only in brief bursts, despite the fact that I had booked us into four rooms on different floors, and was completely exhausted.

When I tired of staring at the ceiling and wandered down to the lobby around one in the morning, I spied Joey sitting alone at one of the breakfast tables in a T-shirt and black flannel pants, drinking something from a foam cup and holding a piece of flat plastic a few inches from his face. "Couldn't sleep either?" I asked, crossing the lobby.

He startled, then put the plastic down and nodded. "And my upstairs neighbors are apparently honeymooning. It was getting awkward in there."

"My condolences. I'm going out. Need anything?" He shook his head, and I pointed to the black plastic. "What's that?"

"Just a tablet," he replied, flipping it around to reveal a computer screen. "Cheap model. I wanted a reader and e-mail, and this was the best bargain I could find. Here, take a look," he offered, holding it toward me, but I stepped backward and shook my head.

"No thanks. Doing your homework on vacation, hmm?"

Joey flushed and put the tablet aside. "No. Some personal reading."

"Oh? What?"

He smiled weakly. "Yeats."

I sighed, feeling my headache threaten once more. *The Celtic Twilight?*"

"Yeah?"

"Joey," I muttered, "if you have questions, just ask, yeah? Now come on, I need air."

He began to protest, but I pulled him from his chair and half dragged him out of the hotel and into my car. "I'm not dressed," he mumbled as he buckled his seat belt.

"This is Florida. Shoes are optional. You have pants on, so you're fine." I tore out onto the empty highway. "Think I saw a late-night shop about ten miles down the road, and that seems to be as good a destination as any. Ask away."

Joey fidgeted for a moment, leaning back in the seat and staring out at the potholed asphalt, avoiding my side glance. "Okay . . . *sidhe*."

"Yes?"

"What about them?"

I cranked up the air-conditioning, grateful for the

breeze against my gloves. Humidity and leather were proving to be a poor combination. "First, the current version of the word is pronounced *shee*, not *sid-he*." The boy's sudden embarrassment was almost palpable. "Secondly, the proper term is *aes sidhe*—'people of the mounds.' *Sidhe* just means 'mounds.'"

"So . . . they're a kind of faerie, right?"

"Not exactly." I glanced at him, saw the gooseflesh on his arms, and played with the temperature controls again. "It's an old term for a race of magical, easily annoyed beings gallivanting around Ireland. They don't per se exist."

"Then what—"

"You're seeing the evolution of fact into folklore and mythology, kid. The *aes sidhe* are what happened when faerie encounters reached a critical mass and mortals got creative in the retelling. Magical and easily annoyed, yes; mounds, no."

He nodded. "Seelie and unseelie courts?"

"Pure bullshit. And you can burn your Yeats—if he believed half of what he wrote, the man was delusional."

"Nothing to burn," said Joey. "I downloaded it."

He frowned out at the night, wrestling with his thoughts, and though I hated to waste the magic, I stole a look in his head. "*A Midsummer Night's Dream* is largely Robin's fault," I said, answering the unspoken question.

Joey whipped around as if I had struck him. "How did you—"

"Magic. Anyway, Mother has never cared for Robin, Oberon's not the most attentive parent, and my brother is nothing if not a whore for attention. The way I heard it, he found this young playwright, got staggeringly drunk with him, and then told him all of these details about Faerie—he was aiming for some great tribute to his parents and himself, I suppose. You know how the play turned out."

He whistled softly as I headed through the deserted intersection. "And that's why we don't call him Puck?"

"No, the play's only a part of it." I spotted the comforting neon sign and window bars of the liquor store ahead. "Robin's the only child Mother and Oberon had together. They never meant to have one—crossing court lines only leads to problems—but there he was. Mother pushed him off onto a nurse, as usual, and called him her little *puk'a*—'mistake.' You can see where that might have given rise to some issues."

"Shit, man," Joey muttered.

"Exactly." I pulled into a parking spot in front of the plate-glass window. "Mother rejected him, Oberon tolerated him, and that's why he ended up in his father's court. He tried to make her like him for a while, but I'm fairly certain that he's given up on the exercise by now."

"Oh?"

"Yeah, he tells me he wants her dead. Coming inside?"

Joey pointed to his bare feet and shook his head, and I hurried in, hoping to find something better than moonshine. The store was a pleasant surprise, well stocked and reasonably clean, and I returned to the car with a paper sack and a much better mood. "You don't do tomato juice," I said, starting the ignition. "What are your thoughts on Johnnie?"

The seminarian grinned. "Mr. Walker and I have been introduced."

"Splendid," I replied, and tucked the bag more securely under my seat. "You'll be joining me, then."

Joey and I sat in the lobby until four, drinking scotch out of coffee cups and eating peanut-butter cookies while the disinterested night clerk flipped through a worn paperback with a half-dressed man on the cover. When Joey finally passed out, I slung him over my shoulders in a fireman's hoist and dragged him off to my room for safekeeping. The kid might have made Johnnie's acquaintance, I decided, dropping him onto my spare bed, but he had a long way to go before he could keep pace with me. Once I was sure that he wasn't dying, I returned to the lobby to retrieve his tablet, which I carried back to the room at arm's length in case of combustion.

I fed Joey Advil and half a gallon of water when

he woke hours later, forced him to slink out to the lobby for a biscuit, then rounded up my passengers and headed south.

Our destination was East Rock Key, a mile-long stretch of sand and scraggly palms bisected by a two-lane road. The island offered little in terms of accommodations other than a short strip of purple and green bungalows, but Robin pointed us onward to the end of the road, a weather-cracked parking lot fronting the beach. Tucked away from the shore in a palm grove was an open-front shack, roofed with rusty corrugated iron and illuminated with strings of oversized novelty bulbs: flamingoes and peppers and improbable blue icicles. The roof extended out to the side of the main building, giving shelter to a few mis-matched picnic tables in the sand, where a dozen or so twenty-somethings in bathing suits had gathered with beer cans and plastic glassware.

"This is it?" I asked, killing the ignition.

Robin nodded. "He calls it Red's. Does shrimp boils occasionally."

I shook my head, then climbed out and waited for our biker to join us. Catching a whiff of the breeze coming in past the shack, my first thought was that the place reeked of magic, but my excitement died when I realized that all I was smelling was the citro-nella torches lining the path to the bar. "We're going to go find him," I told Toula and Joey, swallowing my disappointment. "Come along if you like, but if you'd rather not—"

"First round's on you," Toula interrupted, stomping off through the sand.

The search for Oberon was anticlimactically brief, as we found him standing behind the bar with his arms folded, watching our arrival. "You're overdressed," he called with a slight twang, cocking his head toward a wooden placard nailed to the wall behind him: *No Shoes. Strictly Enforced. —Management.*

Toula kicked off her tennis shoes and headed for the bar. "Got anything frozen back there?"

Oberon shrugged. "You paying?"

"He is," she replied, thumbing at me. "Margarita if you've got it, daiquiri if you don't. Kid'll have a Coke," she added, dragging Joey toward a bar stool.

He peered at Joey, taking in the boy's helmet hair and jeans, then smirked. "You're in strange company, young man."

"Tell me something I didn't know," he muttered, rubbing his temples.

The old king chuckled softly, then beckoned to his well-sculpted assistant. "Vinnie, start a tab for these folks and take care of them, okay? I need to step out for a second." With that, he jumped up and pushed himself over the bar, then began striding toward an outbuilding. "My office!" he called after him, and Robin and I jogged through the sand to keep pace.

When the door closed behind me, Oberon turned on the lights, a green-shaded banker's lamp on the desk and a bare bulb poking out of the chrome fixture squatting on the wooden filing cabinet behind him. He wore gloves, I could tell upon closer inspection— plastic and translucent, but thicker than food-service disposables. They clashed with his clothing, dark blue board shorts and a white linen shirt left open to bare his tanned chest, but they seemed to do their job. I hastily stuffed my driving gloves into my back pocket and took the stool he offered, and Robin followed suit.

"So," said Oberon, settling into the swivel chair behind his desk and folding his hands beneath his chin, "who wants to tell me what's going on?"

"Faerie's been closed off," I replied.

He arched a thick ginger eyebrow. "Coileán, your grasp of the obvious never ceases to amaze." Robin laughed, and Oberon turned his attention to his son. "All right, what did you do?"

That sobered him quickly enough, but I interjected before he could protest. "The enchantment at the heart of this has a lock. The wizard out there thinks she knows how to open it."

He nodded slowly. "Interesting. And you're here because . . ."

"Because we need magic if we're going to accomplish that, and the merrow have something that could be of use."

Oberon leaned back in his chair and closed his eyes. "You want me to summon Grivam," he groaned.

"Only if it's no trouble," I retorted. "I mean, we don't really *need* magic ever again . . ."

He sat up and shrugged. "I don't."

Robin began to speak, but I beat him to it. "Bullshit," I said, planting my palms on his desk. "Disregarding for the nonce the little matter of the Gray Lands, what's going to happen to good old Red in ten years, hmm? Twenty? You're going to start selling miracle wrinkle cream with your beer, is that the idea?"

His face remained impassive. "You think you're the only one with a contingency plan, boy? I've sold this bar to myself three times, and the paperwork is already in place—"

"There's not going to be a fourth. People aren't stupid, and they're not blind. Come on," I snorted, "who would ever believe that you're a day over thirty? You can't make yourself age, you can't sell the bar to someone who looks *just like you*, and you're going to have to start over when the questions begin. So yeah, you need magic. *I* need magic. Your idiot *son* needs magic," I added, pointing to my silent brother. "And if that's not enough, this entire realm's going to go to hell if things start to migrate in from the Gray Lands."

Oberon folded his arms and glared at me, his attire giving him the look of a sullen surfer. "I don't like your tone."

"You don't have to like it," I replied, going to my

feet to better stare down at him. "All we ask is that you get Grivam, and then you can go back to your little bar and your jailbait."

"They're legal. I card."

"Sure you do." I folded my arms in mirror of his. "Look, I don't want to be here, and if I knew of a faster way, I wouldn't be dealing with you. But my daughter's trapped in Faerie, and her mother's with her. We think she's one of your children, by the way. I'm trying to get them out of there before Titania does something stupid."

His brow wrinkled. "When did *you* breed?"

"Accident," I said shortly.

"And what makes you so sure the mother is mine?" he continued, drumming his fingers on his bicep.

"Seems to be half fae. Only redhead in the family. Mother had a one-night stand with a bartender in Florida. This would have been about thirty-eight, thirty-nine years ago . . ."

He shook his head. "If she's noticeably half fae, she's not mine."

"She *wasn't*," I replied. "I never suspected until she ran through the gate and lost ten years when her glamour dropped. The wizard says there was some sort of a bind on her."

With a deep sigh, Oberon muttered, "Shit."

I pulled out my wallet, then slipped a folded photograph free of its sleeve. "Here," I said, passing it to him, "her name's Meghan."

He unfolded the picture and glanced at it only a moment before handing it back. "Okay, yes, I suppose she's mine. What do you want me to do about it?"

"Getting Grivam over here would be a good start."

He sighed again, but stood and headed for the door. "Fine. Just this, and then you take your menagerie with you."

"Agreed." I pulled Robin from his seat. "And now we know that *you* shoved your baby sister into Faerie. Think about that one."

He shrugged me off and followed his father out of the building, calling after him to slow down.

"**T**he bind was a kindness," Oberon half shouted above the roar of the outboard motor. "I remember that woman—Candy, right? Tandy? No—"

"Sandra," I said.

"*Sandy*. Knew it was something like that. She was too easy." He glanced at Toula, who perched in the middle of the boat, concentrating on her breathing to quiet her nausea. "Apologies to present company if insulted."

"How far out are we going?" Toula muttered, gritting her teeth every time the boat hit a wave.

"Just around the back side—there's a bit of an inlet, deep, wooded. Old bastard comes up there when he's of a mood." Oberon turned the rudder, steering us around the island, while Joey wrapped his arm around Toula's shoulders, sheltering her from the spray. In light of the chop and her unsettled stomach, she didn't bother shaking him off.

"How could binding her have been a *kindness?*" Robin asked.

His father shrugged. "You know the difficulties with the half fae," he replied, cutting his eyes to me. "Better for her not to know. Sandy insisted on going bareback, so I put the bind on her, just in case. Probably a good thing I did."

"So . . . what then?" I cut in. "She was aging, but . . ."

"The bind would have killed her eventually," he said, his tone as casual as if he were discussing the weather. "She would have seemed to keep aging, maybe to a hundred, hundred and ten, and then the enchantment would have taken care of the cleanup. She'd never have known the difference."

Joey whipped around, shocked. "You'd kill your own *child?*"

Oberon smirked. "Never met the kid, and I've lost track of half the ones I have."

"Easy, Galahad," Toula muttered, gripping the Joey's arm before he could rise from the bench. His eyes blazed, but he stewed in silence.

I glanced back at Oberon. "Any other potentials out there?"

"Nah," he said, bracing as we hopped a crest. "It was too much work to put the bind on. Gave me a terrible ache for the next week. Never again. No," he said, tapping his head, "I came up with a much easier solution."

"Oh?" I muttered, not sure I wanted to know what Oberon's idea of a solution was.

He nodded, nearly smiling. "If there's any chance of pregnancy, I just make her barren. Problem solved. Not nearly as complicated as it sounds, either. I just got tired of all the kids, you know? Ah, here we are," he said, slowing us to a halt in the middle of a natural bay.

I gave Toula and Joey pleading looks, silently begging them not to say anything, while Oberon reached over the side and planted his palm on the surface of the water. He closed his eyes, frowning as he strained, and a white glow appeared below his hand, spreading and descending like an underwater aurora. With that, he sat up, exhaled loudly, then wiped his wet hand on his shorts. "And now we wait," he announced, looking at his passengers. "Did anyone bring entertainment?"

The popular conception of mermaids puzzles me. Take a human female, cut off her legs, and slap on a fishtail—how does that make any sense?

The merrow resemble what might happen if you mated a human with a dolphin—they're gray and smooth of skin, hairless but for short bristles covering their bodies, and sleek but relatively fat. In short, there's nothing particularly sexy about a merrow in his element. There is, however, an abundance of teeth.

Though native to Faerie, most of the merrow crossed into the mortal realm long before my time, because, I can only suppose, they also wearied of putting up with the fae. Unlike us, they can't manipulate magic, though they're sensitive to its presence. But even without magic, they can shape-shift—sort of an emergency measure in case the water dries up.

Grivam surfaced slightly after nine that evening, tugging on the side of the motorboat hard enough to get our attention. Oberon looked over the side, spotted the pair of webbed hands clinging to the hull, then muttered, "Took your time, did you?"

"Your pardon?" Grivam replied, his Fae accented but otherwise impeccable. He pulled himself partway out of the water, and Joey gasped.

"Nothing of importance, my lord," I replied, giving Joey a warning glare as he fought the obvious urge to scramble to the far side of the boat. "Thank you for coming. We have a matter of great urgency to discuss."

The merrow king's inner eyelid retracted as his face began to dry in the breeze. "Young Coileán," he said, bobbing slightly with the waves. "I admit, your presence here is . . . surprising." He glanced around the rest of the boat, then said, "Young Robin, greetings. It's been a time since our last meeting. And . . ."

He cocked his head as he examined green-faced Toula, and Joey, who was doing his best not to panic. "Your companions, my lords?"

"The boy is with me," I replied; Joey had no idea what was being said. "And the girl—"

"Fotoula Pavli is my name," she interrupted, her voice calm. "I've heard much of your people, my lord, but have yet to have the honor."

His black eyes, side-set already, seemed to widen toward the space where his ear canals opened. "Pavli? I've not heard of one bearing that name since—"

"My father is dead and gone, and his daughter is not her sire," she replied. "And she is also not entirely comfortable on the water, if you'll excuse me for not leaving my seat."

Grivam's wide mouth opened in a nightmar-ish approximation of a shark's smile. "Understood, little wizard. Now"—he turned his attention back to Oberon—"your coming has been anticipated. What's happened to Faerie?"

"Nothing of my doing," Oberon replied, flicking his hand toward Robin and me. "Those two seem to think they can fix it."

One of Grivam's eyes swiveled toward me, while the other focused on Robin. "What's the cause of this, then?"

"Spellwork tangled with enchantment," I re-plied, covering for Robin yet again. "A trap of Mab's design."

"You didn't tell me she was behind this," Oberon muttered.

I ignored him. "Breaking the spell will require one faerie from each of the courts working in tandem. We also need a power source, which is difficult, as we seem to be running out of magic."

Grivam nodded. "You have the third?"

"Not yet," I admitted, "but we're working on it. We came to you for assistance for the power source."

"Do you recall Simon Magus?" Toula interjected. "Grand magus of the Arcanum . . ."

"A time ago, yes, a great time," Grivam replied. "He was a mighty man in his season."

"Did he give you a gift?" she pressed. "After the Great War, did he entrust you with an object?"

"Yes, yes, a gift was made." Grivam paused, peering at us more shrewdly. "What importance is this gift to you?"

"We think it can help us open Faerie," said Robin. "Surely that's enough . . ."

But the old merrow shook his head. "Nothing comes without price, young Robin. You must learn this lesson." He looked around the boat, studying our faces in turn. "What is being offered for the Magus's gift?"

"Whatever you desire," I replied before the others could try to dicker. "Within my power to grant, of course."

"Of course. And a generous offer, young Coileán."

He flashed his predatory smile once again. "Because we have a mutual interest in this venture, my price will be low. A trifle in comparison to the gift's true worth."

"What is it?" Robin asked, leaning forward.

Grivam rested his elbows on the edge of the boat. "My youngest, Ilunna, has seen her two hundred fiftieth moon. I would make her a present for the occasion by seeing one of her desires granted."

I ran the numbers. Two hundred fifty moons put the girl at about nineteen. I'd been with worse. "I should be happy to assist you in this endeavor," I replied. "She'd have no cause for complaint."

"My thanks, young Coileán, but no, not you."

By then, Robin had caught up on the math and realized what was at stake. "Then I would be pleased to—"

But Grivam shook his head again. "She is still young, and she would prefer someone closer in age."

Toula's finger popped up, and she said, "I'm willing." Robin and I turned as one to stare at her, and she rolled her eyes.

"Really?" Robin asked, suddenly intrigued.

"Oh, like you two have never slept with men," she retorted.

Grivam nodded to her in acknowledgement. "Your willingness is most appreciated," he said, "but alas, Ilunna is particular in her partners. She wishes a male."

At that, the three of us turned to Joey, who had been watching uncomprehendingly as we negotiated. "Shit," Toula muttered to me, "you want to ask him?"

I sighed and switched tongues. "Joey, buddy, we need you to do us a favor."

"Uh . . . okay." He kept one eye on Grivam, as if waiting to be attacked.

"That fellow right there is king of the merrow," I explained, sliding closer to the boy. "And his little girl is all grown up and looking for new experiences."

Joey's eyes narrowed. "I don't follow."

I tried to choose the most delicate phrasing. "The merrow are kind of a . . . well, a *free-loving* sort of people, if you get me." He nodded slowly, and I said, "Having sex, for them, is kind of like giving an extended hug with a chance of long-term complications. It doesn't have the same sort of baggage for them that it does for . . . you know . . ."

"Yeah . . ."

"Well, there comes a point in most young merrows' lives when they start getting a little, uh . . . *adventurous*, shall we say? I've been with a few"—Joey glanced at Grivam in alarm—"and I'm pretty sure that Robin—"

"Six," he offered.

"This isn't a competition," I muttered, turning back to Joey. "Look, Grivam's daughter really wants to get with a human guy. And she wants someone young—I've already been shot down," I hastened to add. "We all have. You're kind of the last hope for us to get the thing we've been driving for two days to retrieve."

Joey flushed scarlet. "You're not *really* breaking any vows or anything," I hastened to add. "I mean, she's not even your species—"

"That makes it worse!" he managed to shout. "And she . . . I . . . *he* . . ."

"They're shape-shifters," I explained quietly. "Trust me, whatever comes out of the water isn't going to look a damn thing like him, okay? And she's nineteen, so everything's nice and legal. Please, Joey, I hate to ask, but . . ."

He gave me a long, hard stare, then barely nodded. "Okay," he whispered. "But we never speak of this again, understood?"

I clasped his shoulder, then turned back to Grivam. "He's willing, just shy. When should we expect her?"

The old merrow smiled. "She will come ashore at midnight," he replied, then slipped beneath the waves.

"**M**aybe he needs some pointers," Toula said, sipping on the dregs of the third margarita Vinnie had poured her since our return. "Performance anxiety, you know? I've had to walk virgins through it, and trust me, that's no fun for either party . . ."

"Who said he's a virgin?" I replied, knocking back a beer.

Robin chuckled. "If he's not, then surely he's out of practice."

"Well, *I'm* not about to explain anything to him." I glanced around the bar, which had emptied right on schedule. Oberon had driven his regulars away on some pretense, and even the lovely Vinnie had been relieved of duty for the night. "Maybe we should make sure he's not having second thoughts," I began, but then Ilunna appeared in the shallows.

The lights of the bar gave just enough illumination for me to make out a thin, pale face and long, dark hair. Joey stopped pacing a trench into the sand and stared as she swam closer, then began tottering her way up the slope. He ran into the water to help her, and with slow steps, they made their way onto land, Joey sodden, Ilunna naked and clinging to him as she tested her balance on unsteady feet. She turned her eyes up to him and smiled, and the kid smiled back. It was too dark to see whether he was blushing, but I had my suspicions.

Robin whistled beside me. "Not bad."

"Not bad indeed," Toula replied, stretching out her glass. They clinked around me and drank, and I shook my head.

By then, Joey was pointing toward a secluded stretch of beach, and Ilunna nodded. Neither could understand the other, but gesturing seemed to be working for the moment. I watched them stagger off together, pleased with myself for forcing shots upon Joey to build his confidence, then toasted the black horizon. "So, what do we do until they finish?" I asked the others.

"You can start by paying me for the booze," said Oberon, appearing from the storeroom. "After that, I don't care. Watch and learn, if you like." He shrugged. "This might be amusing."

Oberon owned all of the houses on the island, and Robin was able to snag a couch at his father's place. Knowing better than to ask, Toula curled up in my car, and I kept vigil at the bar, finally turning on the cracked coffeepot I found in the storeroom as the sun rose. By the time the drip stopped, Joey was wandering up the beach, still damp and covered in a fine layer of white sand. "Morning," I said, handing him a plastic tumbler full of black coffee. "You want a little Irish in that?" He nodded wordlessly, and I topped his drink off with a generous dose of whisky. "Cheers, kid," I said, lifting my own tumbler, and he tapped his glass against it wearily.

We sat side by side at the bar in silence, watching the sky lighten. As he finished his coffee, Joey began to brush the sand from his arms. "Sorry, little gritty."

"Understandable. We'll check into a hotel in Key West," I offered. "Let you shower and, uh . . . sleep?"

"Haven't yet. She, um . . . uh . . ."

"Didn't stop after round one?"

"Exactly."

I hesitated. "Did everything, uh, work out?"

He began to blush again. "She wasn't . . . *entirely* sure about the mechanics."

"First time in that form, I think."

"Yeah." Joey refilled his cup, and he'd reached for the whisky when we heard the sound of a splash and caught a glimpse of a gray tailfin. Something glinted at the water's edge, and we abandoned our seats to investigate. As I approached, I found the source of the twinkling: a small golden orb, half buried in the sand. I picked it up and felt it thrum in my hands, and Joey stared. "Is that . . . is *that* what we're after?" he asked.

"Yes," I said softly, turning it over and feeling the faint runic lines scratched upon its surface. "And I know where we can find another."

I tried to smile at Joey, but the thought of the journey ahead left me feeling ill. It seemed my past was coming back to haunt me in more ways than one that week. There were too many buried memories from Sligo that I had no desire to exhume.

But what choice did I have?

CHAPTER 12

Oberon opened his front door and leaned against a wooden porch pillar with his tanned arms folded, watching as Joey and I shuffled up the street. My car and Joey's trike had mysteriously disappeared since dawn, and I was unsurprised to find both vehicles blocking Oberon's driveway. "They're in here," he said, cocking his head toward the door, which the sun had bleached to pale lilac. "The witch went down the highway and bought doughnuts."

"That's all it takes to get in your good graces?" I asked, trying not to drop Joey as we crossed the crab-grass lawn. The kid's adrenaline had worn off, and with the whisky in his system, he was little better than dead on his feet.

Oberon chuckled. "Who said anything about that?

I want the lot of you out of here within the hour, understood?"

I grunted, shifting Joey's weight into a slightly less cumbersome position, then dragged him up the porch. "Mind if I drop the body for a minute?" He spread his hands in a mockery of largesse, and I deposited the kid on a stretch of semi-clean planking. "That's generous of you, thanks."

"I've done more than my share already," he replied, and cut his eyes to my bulging pants pocket with a flicker of interest. "Grivam delivered?"

"As promised." I stretched my back, wincing as my spine creaked. "Let me round up the others, and we'll be off."

"Not so fast, Coileán." He quietly closed the front door and nudged Joey's motionless foot with his flip-flop, then nodded to himself and pointed to the empty road. "Walk with me, boy," he said, leading the way down the porch steps, and for lack of a better idea, I followed.

We set off side by side down the road, making our slow way into the dawn. Oberon remained silent until we were several houses away from his, then said, as if an afterthought, "You forgot to mention Mab."

I kept my eyes on the bright horizon. "Didn't want to give you anything else to worry about."

"I'm not bothered," he replied, but his voice was tight, and he cleared his throat. "Did Titania ever tell you why we threw her out?"

"She's never told me much of anything."

"Obviously," he sighed, squinting down the silent street. "It was the three of us for ages, you know, Titania and Mab and me. And it worked."

"What happened?"

He paused on the side of the road and held up his fingers and thumbs in a triangle. "Three sides, all pushing on each other. As long as they push equally, nothing changes. That was us, all of us wanting more of Faerie, none of us strong enough to take it over the others." He moved his thumbs out of the way and arched his eyebrow. "Take one of the three out of the equation, and the whole thing falls apart."

I nodded. "Mab grew too strong?"

"No. I said to hell with it all." He began to walk again, and I jogged a few steps to catch up. "Coileán, do you have any idea how infuriating it is to deal with a court? Everyone wants something, half of them are picking fights with the other half, and you never have a moment's peace. It doesn't *stop*." A little breeze began to pick up from the sea, and Oberon absently pushed his tousled hair from his eyes. "I grew weary of it all. Mab sensed it—she wanted my place—and Titania couldn't have that. If the two of them fought for power, they'd have ripped Faerie apart again, and honestly, I was too old to deal with that shit a second time."

"Why did you side with Titania?"

Oberon shrugged slowly. "The sex was better."

"You . . ." I paused, rubbing my head. "You cast Mab's entire court out of Faerie—"

"For the sex, yes. That was part of it," he replied. "Titania got what she wanted, I dealt with my court for as long as I could, and then I left."

"And took them with you."

"They could have defected to Titania's court."

"Oh, come on," I protested, "you know that wouldn't have worked!"

"Probably not. But they were free to try." His foot sent a beer can careening off in the direction of a dead crab.

I shaded my eyes with one hand, wishing I'd brought my sunglasses along on this stroll. "Robin's desperate to go back, you realize."

"I do." A bleached fast-food cup rolled along to join the can.

"He's doing his damnedest to get you back on the throne," I pressed.

Oberon shook his head. "A persistent fool is still a fool. I'm not going back."

"Then why not give it up?" I tried. "Pass the court to your eldest, let Robin and me work with him, and we'll see if we can't get the court back into Faerie . . ."

I let my voice die when he started laughing. "My eldest?" he chortled, grinning as he cut his eyes to mine. "*Robin* is my eldest still living. If you think I'm giving him the court, you've lost all sense."

I made a face as I tried to imagine a world in which

my brother wielded Oberon's authority. "Understood," I muttered. "But isn't there someone else—"

"Do you have any idea of my power?" he interrupted, pausing in his trek to face me. "Any real sense? That was rhetorical, Coileán, you don't." I closed my mouth, and Oberon rolled his eyes. "Faerie knows me. It knows who and what I am. It knows your mother and Mab in the same way. The realm itself gives us more than enough power to keep the peace. And that power, boy, is something that you cannot *begin* to imagine. Moon and stars," he added with a snort, "why would I surrender *that*?"

For the good of your court was on the tip of my tongue, but I recalled whom I was speaking with and kept my mouth shut.

Oberon's lips twitched as he gave me a quick stare of appraisal. "I've often wondered why Titania hasn't killed you yet," he said, abruptly turning to head back to the house. "She could, you know. You wouldn't be the first of her children to predecease her."

I thought of Áedán, and of Mother's eyes when I stood prisoner before her, how they had flashed like summer thunderheads with the promise of pain to come.

"I suspect that I'm more fun to her alive and provokable," I replied.

He patted my shoulder. "Probably. So, boy, you think you can really get Faerie open again?"

"I'm counting on it," I muttered, feeling the slight

weight in my pocket where the Magus's device rested. It shifted against my leg as I walked, slightly warm to the touch and practically vibrating with magical potential. The impulse to draw from it that second was strong, but I suspected that we'd need every drop if we were to undo Mab's work—especially if she had the power of Faerie itself in her corner.

"Well, good luck," said the old king. "You've got half an hour to vacate the premises."

As I showed the others our prize, I explained that I thought I knew where to find another in Ireland. After a bit of negotiation, we decided that Toula and Robin would stay at my apartment while I took a quick jaunt abroad, Toula to work on the diary and Robin to hold anything unsavory at bay. Since Robin had rummaged through Joey's gear and found a fairly new passport, the kid would come with me— assuming that he didn't run away the moment his hangover wore off, naturally.

With Joey indisposed in the backseat of my car, Robin took over the trike duties, leaving me with Toula for company. As he sped north, she grabbed the keys from my hand and pointed to the passenger side. "You haven't slept in at least twenty-four hours," she reminded me.

"No one drives my car but me," I protested, but she wouldn't hear it.

"*I* drove the damn car halfway to Key West and back for breakfast," she pointed out. "I think I can get us to I-95 in one piece."

She had a point; I was weary and growing wearier by the hour, and so I grudgingly slid into the passenger seat and held my breath as Toula eased us out of Oberon's sand-crusted driveway.

When we reached the Overseas Highway, she glanced over her shoulder and clucked her tongue. "Dead to the world. What did you do to him?"

"Irish coffee," I yawned, leaning against the window.

She gave no reply for a long moment, then mumbled, "I feel really bad about this, you know?"

"How so?"

She looked at me in exasperation. "We asked our priest to pleasure a mermaid. What part of that *don't* you feel bad about?"

"Technically," I said, "he's not a priest yet. He's still a seminarian."

"Yeah, fine," she huffed, "but isn't there something about a vow of celibacy in there?"

"Probably." I shifted in my seat, trying to get comfortable.

Toula remained unappeased. "So what's this going to do to him? I mean, how long's his dry spell been? Is this going to throw a major wrench in his life plan or something?"

"No clue," I mumbled, closing my eyes. "He can probably say some Hail Marys or something—"

"*Colin*," she snapped, slapping me on the arm until I opened my eyes again. "I'm serious! He may have just broken some major vow, and we coerced him into doing it. Please tell me that doesn't sit easily with you, because if it does . . ."

"It doesn't," I admitted. "At all. But it's done, I can't undo it, and he should feel better once he sleeps." I sighed and leaned into the headrest. "Damn picky merrow . . ."

"Tell me about it. What I could see of her was cute."

She fell silent, and I tried in vain to sense her thoughts without magic. Finally, I said, "You gave Grivam your full name last night. Why?"

Toula drummed her fingers on the steering wheel and said nothing. I was about to close my eyes again and attempt to nap when she murmured, "It commands a certain amount of respect. That's all. Whatever else he did, he was a talented wizard. But I'm not my father, okay?"

The tension in her voice spoke volumes. "I never said you were."

"Good." She popped open the gum cup I kept in the console and helped herself to a piece. "What was your dad like?"

"Don't really know," I said quietly. "I only met him once. Why?"

"I saw mine once a year—a two-hour visit on my birthday. That's all Harrison would give me. Guess he didn't want me to get contaminated," she added. "So yeah, I never really knew him, either."

I hesitated, looking for the right words. "I'm, uh . . . sorry . . ."

"Save it," she interrupted, waving her hand as if to push my condolences away. "He was a shitty father, anyway. My fosters would dress me up and take me to his cell, and I'd sit outside the bars and try to talk to this . . . *stranger* . . . and he'd tell me to show him what I could do with my wand, and I'd get flustered and screw up, and he . . ." She stopped the rapid flow and sighed. "He was always disappointed. I mean, I'm bound—what did he expect, miracles?"

"He was Apollonios Pavli," I replied with a shrug. "No offense to you, but I don't think he was the most rational of men. It takes a special kind of crazy to throw bombs at the *Arcanum*."

Toula seemed not to have heard me. "I sent him letters, too, when I was a kid. Drawings, stories, stuff like that. School projects. Harrison let me have his personal effects once they . . . carried out the sentence," she said, drumming faster. "I went through everything."

"He kept your letters, huh?"

"No. Not a one. No drawings, nothing of mine. Not even my school pictures." Her jaw clenched. "Like I said, I was a disappointment. So I packed up the little I wanted and threw the rest away. Not like my mother was coming for it," she muttered.

I played dumb. "Your mother?"

Toula shrugged. "Harrison said she worked for my father, and she was on the lam. Some low-level wizard, maybe just a witch. Had enough sense to keep her head down. Never tried to make contact with me. Of course," she added, glancing at me, "seeing your wonderful relationship with your mother, maybe I lucked out, eh?"

"I'd say so."

She smiled sadly. "Yeah, but you were never fostered. The Arcanum raised me—passed me around to different families living in the bunker, kept me in the little public school out there with all the other Arcanum kids. They used to call me a witch to get me riled up. Then they got old enough to know whose I was, and after that, they just avoided me." Her dark blue eyes darted back to mine again. "My father was the bogeyman to a whole generation of wizard kids. You can imagine how popular that made me." Her fingers tightened around the steering wheel. "It was the talk of the bunker the day they executed him. Nothing like walking down the hall, hearing snippets of an excited conversation around the corner, and then watching everyone shut up the instant they see you."

There just *wasn't* a non-awkward response to that. "I knew he had died, but I didn't know how long ago—"

"My eighteenth birthday. Harrison let him live until I was grown, and they did it that morning. I was going to go down after school, and instead, they gave me a box of his shit to go through." She shook her head as if dispelling the memory. "Hey, mind if I turn on the radio?"

"Go ahead," I replied, looking at Joey over my shoulder. The kid slept on, his brow furrowed, and I curled up against the door, thinking the old refrain for him:

Et dimitte nobis debita nostra, sicut et nos dimittimus debitoribus nostris.

And forgive us our trespasses, as we forgive those who trespass against us.

CHAPTER 13

Night passes slowly over the North Atlantic, especially when one can't sleep and isn't a fan of flying to begin with. As Joey, too, was staring into space, I suggested we retire to the aisle near the toilets, where we might at least be able to help ourselves to the beverage carts. Joey agreed and leaned against the wall, staring out through a porthole at the blackness around us, and I joined him, though I kept my gaze fixed on the glowing switches of the first-class kitchen instead of the abyss outside the plane. "Holding up?" I enquired quietly.

"Yep." He turned from the window and folded his arms against the chill.

Joey had said little during our brief return to Rigby, and in my hurry to pack, I'd neglected to say what needed to be said most of all. "Look," I told him, "I'm sorry about . . . that thing we're not going to discuss. I appreciate it. We all do. She wouldn't have us—"

"It's okay," he interrupted. "I, uh . . ." He struggled for the words, then murmured, "I knew things wouldn't be . . . you know, normal . . . if I started working with Father. My advisors all discouraged me, but there's the spiritual warfare thing and, well . . . Father's pretty damn good at what he does. I know it wasn't going to be like *The Exorcist*," he continued, his color blossoming to full scarlet, "but I was prepared for *weird*. And Father—he told me that sometimes, in his work . . . you've got to cross some lines. You do it quietly, right, but you cross them."

I barely spoke above a whisper. "Let me tell you a little story about Paul when he was just a bit older than you. We did a stint in New Orleans. Somewhere along the way, he made the acquaintance of a . . . well, let's call him a Houngan, I don't know the proper term. Anyway, this fellow told Paul that he had a potion that would allow him to see the invisible. Well, I don't know what possessed him in the end, but he took the man up on his offer, went off with him in the Quarter, and drank the stuff."

Joey's eyes were saucers. "What happened?"

"No permanent damage. He was out of his mind for a few hours—the stuff was mostly hallucinogens and moonshine—and I sat with him until the walls stopped melting. That's actually not the craziest thing I've seen him do," I added, watching Joey's jaw drop, "but he'd be peeved if I shared anything worse. So yes, I know all about Paul's philosophy on crossing lines for the cause. I mean, he works with *me*, right? I'm not exactly kosher."

Joey grinned. "I read his notes, remember?"

"You know, I'm going to need a copy of those at some point."

"We'll see. Question."

"Go for it."

"If we find this—you know—doohickey, is that going to be enough to get the job done?"

I thought for a moment, trying to recall the strength of the magic I'd felt in the merrows' sphere, which I'd left locked in my fire safe in Rigby. "Possibly, but I doubt it. I think it'll take at least three."

Joey nodded slowly. "And we're waiting on Toula for other leads?"

"That we are." I paused, then said, "Look, we'll have you on a plane home in good time for class Monday—"

"Forget it. I spoke to Father before we left this morning, and he's making my excuses for me. I'm in this to the bitter end, got it?"

I shifted against the wall, feeling the twinge of guilt return. "Thanks, Joey."

He glanced around, then darted into the kitchen and extracted a Coke from the docked cart. "So how're we coming on the second part of the problem?" he asked as he cracked it open.

"Second part?"

He took a long sip. "Two courts down, one to go. Any leads on the third?"

I shook my head. "The only person connected with that court I've seen in decades is Slim, and he's useless in this case."

The kid's forehead creased. "That Rick guy? He's *fae*?"

"Witch-blooded fae," I corrected. "Wizard mother, faerie father. When we mix, it's like we cancel each other out." Joey's confusion deepened, and I leaned toward him to be better heard over the drone of the engines. "We work with magic in different ways— enchantment and spellcraft don't play nicely together. Most of the time, if you find a mongrel, he's sensitive to magic and unaffected by iron and silver, but he's mortal, and he couldn't cast a spell or create a simple glamour to save his life. They don't have an easy time of it. There's no place for them in Faerie—hell, I've known of faeries killing their mongrel kids to avoid dealing with them. If they have a place among the wizards at all, it's as crafters. Slim's one of the lucky ones."

Joey frowned. "You said 'most of the time.' What about—"

"Occasionally," I allowed, "you'll find a mongrel who can pass for a witch—a kid with minimal magical ability," I explained. "If you find a creepy old woman with seventeen cats who's oddly good at the tarot and sells love potions, that's a witch."

He nodded. "So that's why we don't call Toula a witch?"

"Wizards take that term *very* personally."

Joey sipped his soda and stared into space for a long moment, then glanced back my way as the flicker of an idea crossed his face. "A locating spell."

"What about it?"

"Do they exist?"

I shrugged. "Sure. Might work, might not. Depends on the wizard casting it. And that really is a wizard thing—I'm terrible at finding people, and I doubt Robin's any better. He just stalks."

"But a *good* wizard could cast a functional locating spell?"

"Yeah, why?"

Joey bit his lip. "I was thinking . . . look, I know you've got a problem with the Arcanum," he said quickly, "but what if we asked them to help out? To find the third faerie we need?"

"Assuming, for the moment, that an Arcanum wizard would be willing to help us, he wouldn't be able to do anything without magic," I replied.

"But we *have* magic," Joey pointed out, lowering his voice. "The doohickey. You just said that we're probably going to need at least a third—let's get a spare, let the wizard use it enough to find Mab's people, and then work on convincing one of them to pitch in. Hmm?"

"That . . . *might* work," I grudgingly admitted.

"But I want to avoid getting the Arcanum involved if at all possible, understood?"

He finished his Coke and tossed it into the drink cart's waste bag. "I understand avoiding bureaucracy in a time crunch, but I don't see why you hate them so badly. Toula's all right, isn't she?"

"She's not really Arcanum. They hunted me for a few hundred years," I muttered. "I find it rather difficult to trust them now."

His expression was inscrutable. "Would you trust them for your daughter's sake?"

"No," I said, and sneaked a glance out at the night. "But I might have to for Meggy's."

We made it to Dublin midmorning Friday. As will come as no surprise to anyone who's spent more than a week in Britain or Ireland, it was drizzling as we taxied to the terminal.

I sent Joey ahead of me through passport control. "You're here on pleasure. Tourist," I whispered as we deplaned. "You're traveling alone. If there's trouble, better for one of us to slip through solo."

"Paranoid much?" he replied, but did as instructed.

In truth, I *was* paranoid—I've never been a fan of anonymous crowds, and without magic to warn me of potential troublemakers among the throng, I felt half blind in the groggy press.

I followed several passengers behind Joey, pressing my best American accent into service when questioned and fighting off the urge to copy the middle-aged border guard's lilt. The language had changed since I'd first come to the island, but I still heard hints of familiarity in his voice and was trying to place it regionally even as he asked, "You're *forty?*"

"Baby face," I replied, going for nonchalance in my shrug. "I get carded all the time—it's such a pain . . ."

"Enjoy it while you can," he muttered, and stamped me through. I smiled and hurried on, kicking myself for going so long between passports and grateful for the advent of plastic surgery, which had made my lies plausible on more than one occasion in the past.

Joey and I rendezvoused beside the baggage carousel once I was certain that we weren't followed—I couldn't shake the feeling of being watched, though I chalked it up to nerves after the plane ride—and I surprised him by stopping at a phone kiosk on the way to retrieve our rental car. "I'll pay for this one while we're here," I explained, watching him inspect the wares. "Call Toula every so often and see how the work is progressing. If she finds anything promising in Europe, it would be simpler to extend our trip here than to go back and forth."

His eyebrow arched. "Or I could just text her and tell her to get in touch whenever she comes up for air. She seems to get a little twitchy when disturbed."

"Whatever you think best. And once you have it

working, try to find a hardware store, okay? I'll feel better if you're carrying something iron based."

Joey purchased a phone, and within ten minutes, he had contacted Toula and pulled up an address for supplies. A short time later, the rental agent handed me the keys to a sporty little Fiat that most self-respecting Americans would dismiss as a clown car, and I slid behind the wheel, silently cursing the man for giving me a car with a manual transmission. "Where to?" I asked as Joey squeezed in and buckled up.

"Hang on," he said, reaching toward the GPS.

"Can't we do without the machine? Just read the directions and tell me where we're going."

He scowled at his telephone. "We could try. But I can't pronounce half of this."

"Give me that," I said, pulling the phone out of his hand, and glanced at the screen. "Those aren't so difficult . . ."

"I couldn't pronounce *sidhe*, remember?"

"You still can't," I muttered, then headed out into the rainy morning.

The hardware store Joey located was little more than a mom-and-pop establishment, and I remained in the car. I told him I needed to adjust to left-hand shifting—I was relying on muscle memory forty years unused, and my muscles had apparently developed amnesia in the intervening decades—but truthfully, hardware stores, with all of their exposed iron-bearing wares, creep me out.

He emerged twenty minutes later with a large paper sack, which he stowed behind him before resuming his seat. "And what did we buy?" I asked, looking up from the road atlas the rental company had left in the door pocket. "Hammer? Rebar?"

Joey smiled and wiped the rainwater from his face. "Nail gun."

"A *what?*"

"Nail gun," he repeated, evidently pleased with himself. "Great for construction, but if you employ a few, uh . . . modifications"—his eyebrows waggled—"that I may or may not have tried with some like-minded friends one boring summer, you can bypass all of the safeties and actually shoot nails."

I looked over my shoulder at the seemingly innocent bag. "How far?"

"They're short-range weapons, but I could hit a target consistently at twenty yards. Aiming's a little tricky. But since *someone* wouldn't let me bring my sword on this trip . . ."

"Kid," I muttered, "you're brilliant. And concerning, but I can work with that."

"Good to know. She's not fully operational yet," he cautioned as I started the car. "I'm going to need a few hours of quiet time."

"Understood. You're navigating for now," I said,

thrusting the atlas into his lap. "We're heading toward Sligo. I think I have the route down, but shout out if I'm about to miss a turn."

His eyes drifted across the map. "We're just going to pretend this is all pronounced phonetically, okay?"

I pulled onto the road, pleased that I had yet to stall out. "Do you have any idea what a tricky bastard English is by comparison?"

"I've been told." He pushed his damp hair back and settled into his seat. "Why Sligo?"

"The county includes the ruins of several monasteries," I replied. "The sphere is hidden in one of them. We'll retrieve it tonight."

Joey nodded slowly. "So . . . the plan is to break into a historical site after hours and remove an artifact? That sounds only slightly felonious."

"It's only felonious if we get caught, remember. And since I put it there in the first place, I have no reservations about taking it out again."

He snorted. "Oh, yeah, I can see that conversation going well—'I swear, Officer, I was coming right back for it! Just got delayed for a few years, you know how it goes . . .'"

"Precisely." I chuckled.

"What were you doing at a monastery, anyway? Just passing through?"

"Something like that," I said quietly, and Joey had enough sense to drop the matter. I stared out at the road as he scanned the radio dial, letting the rhythmic swish of the wipers calm my nerves, and tried to see the land I remembered through the rain.

Once we'd checked into a hotel, I left Joey to tinker with his nail gun in peace, then slid into the rental car and drove out of town, heading for the countryside and whatever wilderness might be left. I couldn't see the old terrain, but I could *feel* it, and with each bend in the road, the pieces of the landscape began to slot back into my mental map. But as I focused on my bearings, I let down my guard, and the memories started to float to the surface, until I heard from the recesses of my mind a much-loved voice, long silenced: *I knew you would come.*

Defeated, I pulled the car off the road, cut the ignition, and sat alone while the rain pounded down, allowing myself to hear Étaín once again.

CHAPTER 14

She was my world when I was young. Soft of face, with hair so blonde it was nearly white and eyes like glacial pools; she was my provider, my nurturer, my protector, and my tutor. We lived alone, the two of us, in a cozy one-room thatched-roof cottage in the middle of a grassy meadow that stretched for leagues and never went to straw. Ten running steps out the door was our lake, a glorified pond stocked with all manner of fish and graced with the occasional swan. The sun might rise and set for a fortnight without our receiving a guest, and I never paid it any mind—I had Étaín, she loved me, and that was all the mattered.

By the time I was three, I realized that I could do things she could not—I could make fish leap onto the shore, for instance, or I could take our roof apart and scatter it across the meadow. My tiny body contained all the power of a god, and the only thing standing between me and chaos was Étaín, whose smile could charm me into obedience. Her brief melancholic spells terrified me—perhaps, I reasoned, she might stop loving me and leave if I displeased her—and I did anything I could to make her happy.

As I grew, I began to catch more frequent glimpses of Étaín's sadness, brief flickers of despair and resignation when she thought I wasn't looking, and I tried all the harder to make her happy—an acre of thornless roses just for her, a little boat of gold for our fishing trips, a bed so soft that she could sink into it and nearly disappear. She smiled and called me her little angel, and taught me words from a language I had never heard. She tried to teach me the stars, but ours moved unpredictably, and the exercise was always a failure. But I didn't care—why would I need to navigate when I would never, ever leave our cottage by the lake?

And then, when I was seven, Mother summoned me for the first time.

Étaín explained to me what a mother was, and she warned me that I must be on my best behavior and not wiggle around when I visited. Fearful of this unknown mother, I clung to Étaín's skirt and refused to go when the air parted in two and the messenger stepped into the meadow. She pried me loose, kissed my forehead, and sent me on my reluctant way.

When I first saw Mother's throne room and spied

her seated on the crystal dais in the middle, my heart leapt. She was younger than Étaín, it seemed, her hair like honey, her eyes dark as old wood, her face and form slender, her movements graceful when she rose to receive me. But her smile was thin and cold, almost predatory, and I shrank away in fear. Her laugh was as beautiful as her face and as sharp as her smile, and she dismissed me without a second look.

The gate opened behind me, and I ran toward Étaín and home, resolute in my decision to never again leave.

For ten years, I never did. Instead, the outside world invaded our sanctuary, first in the form of tutors, and then in visiting members of the court, Mother's friends, her sycophants, and occasionally, her other children. I learned to read and multiply, to recite history and poetry, to shape my world to my will. I learned what I was, and what Étaín was, and finally, when I was on the cusp of manhood, one of my tutors let slip that I might have a father elsewhere, and that he probably looked like me; I barely resembled Mother, after all, and my coloring had to come from someone.

One of my sisters suggested that he lived close to Étaín's old home—Mother, with an odd compulsion, tended to steal potential nurses living near her children's fathers when she coupled with mortals. I knew little of the place, but with years of prodding, Étaín gradually told me bits and pieces about her tiny village, the sun rising over the mountain, the dark sea to the west, the endless sprawl of stars at night, the rains and the fogs and the pungent smoke of peat fires. Not until I was twenty-five did she speak of her husband and her three strong sons, boys with flaxen hair and their father's dark eyes.

My heart broke for Étaín even as I clung to her. I knew I had the power to free her, to send her back across the gulf between the realms to her good, strong man and her boys—now men, surely, with wives and children of their own—who must have missed her. I simply couldn't bring myself to do it. I tried to rationalize my decision to keep her with me—perhaps Mother would be angry, I thought, if I sent one of her pets away—but my heart knew the lie even as my mind insisted it was the truth.

Even as I tried to push thoughts of Étaín's lost family from my mind, thoughts of my own began to encroach with greater persistence. Étaín had explained to me the limitations of the mortal life span, and by the time I reached my forties, I had to face the fact that my father, whoever he was, was quite possibly dead. I wondered if he had left other children behind, if I had siblings who looked like me—or *had* looked like me at one point, I reasoned, unsure of their potential ages. My curiosity grew, and finally, a few days before my fiftieth birthday—at least by Faerie's reckoning, which didn't necessarily align with that of the mortal realm—I resolved to search for my family while there might still be a trail to follow. Étaín's village would be a logical starting point, I mused, but grudgingly admitted to myself that if anyone knew where to find my father, it would be Mother.

And so, with Étaín by my side in encouragement, I presented myself to Mother on my birthday, explained my proposed errand in the mortal realm, and asked for her assistance. To my surprise, she favored me with a smile—still as cold as ever—and replied that she would give me three gifts. First, from the throne room, she opened a gate to reveal a tantalizing sliver of rolling green country. Next, she beckoned me to her side, then took my face in her hands. I felt a quick, disorienting buzz, and when it subsided, she explained that she had given me the locals' tongue. Mother then stepped out of the room and instructed me to wait. An hour later, after I'd sneaked a thousand glances at the open gate, she returned with a strand of wooden beads in her hands. "He gave this to me," she said with a smile. "Perhaps you can ask for its owner." She would give me no other hint.

With the beads clutched in my fist, I thanked Mother and bid her farewell. The last thing I did before beginning my first foray out of Faerie was kiss Étaín's cheek and promise I'd return soon. She nodded, then quickly cut her eyes to Mother before stretching on tiptoe to whisper in my ear, "If you find my Rónán, give him my love."

The clouds overhead threatened a hard spring rain, but I didn't know that at the time, having never before seen precipitation. What I sensed as the gate closed behind me was that this realm seemed darker somehow—in retrospect, that was the thick cloud cover—and colder, and it smelled . . . well, *fresher*. I sniffed deeply, trying to pinpoint the change, then realized that I was smelling the land itself, the vegetation and the smoke of distant fires (and, as I would soon discover, the livestock and their leavings). The overpowering scent of magic, so omnipresent in Faerie that my nose had long since tuned it out, was far weaker here, and I stuck my face in the first bush I saw just to experience the difference. Unfortunately, that bush had thorns hidden beneath its leaves, and I pulled back in alarm, bleeding from a dozen shallow scratches and slightly disenchanted with the realm. I cleaned myself up and repaired my injuries, and then I heard two male voices in conversation approaching down the dirt track on which I found myself standing.

In hindsight, I should have asked Mother to open a gate a few days in advance and allow me to observe the locals without attempting to interact with them. As it was, however, I was clueless about mortal societal niceties, and so I stood by the thorn bush in my golden cape and matching suit and waited for the travelers to come within hailing range. When the men rounded the bend and spotted me, they froze, and I quickly took stock of their dress: short, belted, off-white tunics and brown leggings, all crafted from a rough cloth and dirt stained. Their heads were bare, and each had tied back his auburn hair with a leather thong. I stepped forward, smiled, and displayed to them my beads. "Gentlemen, good day," I began, trying not to trip over the foreign syllables. "I search for the man who once owned these. Do you know him?"

They continued to stare in silence, blanching slightly, and then the braver of the two pointed behind him toward a stone tower in the distance.

"My thanks," I replied, sensing that I would get nothing further from them, and walked past them to be on my way. The men slid to one side of the road, giving me a wide berth, and I felt their eyes on my back until I rounded the bend and walked out of their sight.

The stone tower was farther away than I had imagined due to the winding road, and I soon grew impatient to reach my destination. Still, prudence counseled me to walk, as any fellow traveler I came upon might have information about my father.

If they did, I never knew it; the few souls I passed on my way either ran or pressed themselves to the far edge of the road and stared in unabashed silence, and I hurried on so as not to frighten them. I tried to determine what was giving them such cause for alarm, but not knowing the region, I was at a loss as to how to remedy the situation.

Thunder was beginning to rumble in the distance when I finally reached the tower, which resolved itself from the hedges and low stone buildings into a modest but well-kept complex. A neat field stretched behind it, away from the road, and a pair of beasts I would later recognize as cows grazed at a slight distance, fenced off from the partly tilled earth. I hesitated, uncertain of the best approach, and studied the complex for a long moment, trying to decide between two wooden doors. As I pondered, the first drops of rain fell on my face. I glanced up in alarm, looking for the source, and heard deep laughter across the road. Snapping my attention back to the complex, I spotted a queer figure standing just inside the smaller door. It took several seconds before I realized the figure was a man, albeit an ancient one, his face deeply creviced and his little remaining hair gray. He wore a long dark hooded robe and had slipped a strand of beads not unlike mine through the rope around his waist.

"Were you planning on drowning in the rain, then?" he said with a smile, stepping back from the door. "If not, come in."

I joined him inside just as the heavens opened up, and he nodded at the deluge. "Good for the fields. Now," he said, closing the door on the storm, "I just had word of a young man all in gold wandering in this direction. What say you to that?"

then saw the window behind me, which was nothing more than a bare hole in the wall.

The old man cleared his throat. "Your father, you said?"

I nodded. "My mother won't tell me anything about him."

He sighed softly, then put his cup down on the hearth. "If he's the man I think he is, then he lives not far from here. I . . ." He paused, frowning into space. "I can help you find him."

My heart lightened, and I resisted the impulse to embrace the old man. "I am Coileán, of the queen's court," I said in a rush. "If I can repay you—"

He shook his head. "Eoin. Father Eoin, I am called, and I need nothing of you." He pulled his chair closer to the fire, then stared into its glow. "Spend the night here, I have room," he offered. "In the morning, I'll send you on your way." He glanced at me, then shook his head. "Those clothes will not suffice."

I wrapped what was left of my cloak around my shoulders, suddenly self-conscious. "Wrong color?"

"Wrong everything. I've never seen anything so strange. And with the weather, you'll want wool— like this," he said, pinching a fold of his sleeve.

I studied him for a few seconds, then shifted my attire into a copy of his. "Like so?"

"Not exactly—you're not of the clergy," he replied. "But that's close enough for the moment." He leaned back in his chair and closed his eyes. "Your father, if

A boy who had run the other way without bothering to speak was his source, I reasoned, but decided not to mention him. "I mean no ill," I replied, and held out my beads. "I'm searching for the man who owns these . . . or owned them once, I suppose. I . . . I know not if he still lives . . ."

My host took the beads from me, studied their markings for a brief time, then handed them back with a tight mouth. "I might have an idea," he said, then motioned for me to follow him. "But first, to warm and dry you. Come with me."

The smaller door, as it happened, led into a sort of apartment set off from the larger complex. Around a corner, I spied a low fire burning in a stone hearth and a pair of wooden chairs clustered before it. "You're most kind." I sighed, sinking into one of the chairs— the day had turned unpleasantly cold—and the old man smiled.

"I'll fix a drink," he said, then ducked out of the room for a short time. When he returned, he carried two cups in his hands. The first, made of a rough sort of pottery, he set beside the empty chair for himself. The other was made of a gray metal and finely decorated, and this he extended toward me. "My best for visitors," he explained. "This should warm you, my son."

Something about the drink made my hair stand on end, but I didn't want to insult him, and so I simply smiled back. "Thank you," I said, and reached for the cup.

The instant my fingers touched it, they began to smoke and blister. I yelped and retracted my wounded hand, and as I sucked on my fingers to ease the burn, I thought that perhaps the drink was just overly hot, that my host had been careless with his fire. But the look on his face told me otherwise; though watery with age, his eyes had hardened, and he watched dispassionately as I suffered.

"You've never seen silver before, have you?" he asked after a long moment, once I had ripped a long section from my cloak to wrap around my burned hand.

I shook my head, beginning to worry, as the simple enchantment that healed my cuts and scrapes seemed to be working far more slowly than usual. "I meant you no harm—"

"I don't believe you, I'm afraid." He pulled his beads loose, and I noticed a large T-shaped piece dangling from one end. "Behold and tremble!" he cried, holding it close to my face. I didn't flinch, however, and he stepped back, perplexed. "You . . . have no fear of the cross?"

I assumed he meant the dangling bit. "Should I?"

The old man frowned and put his beads away. "You are of the *aes sidhe*, are you not?"

The term was a mystery, and I gave up and peered into his thoughts, too bothered by the pain to play guessing games all afternoon. What I found there confused me, but it was close enough to work for the moment. "More or less, yes," I replied, perplexed at his reaction. "Is that a problem?"

He sat in the empty chair and drank deeply from his clay cup, staring at me all the while. "My mother told me of the *aes sidhe*," he said quietly when the cup was dry. "Iron and silver can protect. I had thought the cross might as well, but I see I was mistaken."

I frowned, still befuddled. "Iron?"

He pointed to a blackened metal stand beside the fireplace, which carried a set of long tools. "I wouldn't touch that, were I you."

"Noted," I mumbled, wondering if he would be upset if I created a bowl of ice for my hand. When I had spoken to her of my intent, Étaín had cautioned me that magic frightened mortals, but my fingers were beginning to throb. Throwing manners aside, I produced the bowl and shoved my hand deep inside, numbing the pain until I could deal with my injuries.

My host's bushy eyebrows rose, but he kept his composure. "Now, why do you trouble poor Christian men?"

"I meant no trouble, I swear it," I protested, and held out the beads again. "The man who owned these was my father. I wish to know his name."

"Only his name?"

I hesitated. "And if he lives yet, then to meet him. That's all. Please, can you help me?"

We sat in silence for a moment, listening to the rain pelt the roof. I shivered in a draft and turned,

I'm correct, hasn't spoken a word in almost fifty-one years. He won't until he has his rosary back," he explained, pointing to my beads. "The way I heard it told, he gave his rosary to a lover, and he's done penance ever since."

I ran the beads through my unburned fingers, feeling their smooth forms. "Penance?"

"For his sin," said Eoin. "He's a monastic brother—they vow to remain chaste, just as I did."

My nose wrinkled. "Whatever *for*?"

"I don't presume to question the will of God. But you must realize that Finnén . . . he was never supposed to have a child."

Finnén. For the first time, I had a name, but my excitement was tempered by the blow the old man had just dealt. "He won't want to see me, then," I replied, mentally dismissing my imagined siblings.

Eoin shrugged. "Perhaps, perhaps not. You will need to be cautious and, uh . . ." He gave my modified clothes another look. "It would be best not to let our little secret slip, understood?"

The ice bowl disappeared, and I carefully unwrapped my fingers to check on their slow progress. "Understood. Nothing about the, uh . . . *aes sídhe*, correct?"

He gave me a flicker of a smile. "Wise boy."

Night fell, though with the storm, I couldn't be certain of when the transition had finally come. Eoin busied himself in the largest room in the complex—a church, though I had no clue as to its use at the time—and I lurked in the back, shivering against the stone wall as I tried to avoid the spray coming through the open windows. At the priest's direction, I had modified my dress in half a dozen ways, but even the wool that he suggested did little to warm me in the open room. Still, something told me that artificially raising the temperature would be frowned upon, and so I tried to tough it out in silence as Eoin went about his business, lighting a few candles and spending the better part of an hour on his knees before a wooden altar.

When his prayers were completed for the moment, he led me back into his apartment, which was significantly warmer and smelled of stew. "It's just me here," he said almost apologetically as he removed a covered iron pot from the fire. "My cooking would shame my mother, rest her soul, but then she's not here to complain, is she?"

I couldn't, either; the soup tasted strongly of brine, but I craved its warmth. I huddled by the fire, wrapped in a well-worn blanket, and drank straight from the clay bowl Eoin had given me. He watched me shake for a moment, then frowned and prodded at the fire until the peat bricks spat. "Constitution's a bit weak?" he asked.

I shook my head. "It's never this cold at home. Or wet," I muttered, glancing toward the noisy roof.

"You'll survive," he replied, putting the poker away.

"And you can sleep by the fire, if you like—I've only the one pallet for myself, but there's blankets enough to soften the floor . . ."

A soft rapping at the door caused us both to whip around in surprise, and Eoin scowled as he rose. "Evil night to be abroad. Come with me—and not a word, now," he cautioned, then took up a candle and headed out of the room. I followed close at his heels, tossing off the blanket in an effort to give the visitor no cause for a second glance, and waited a few paces behind the priest as he threw back the bolt and opened the door. "Yes?" he asked the night, glancing about him, then cast his eyes on the soaking wretch at his feet. "Saints defend us," he murmured, crouching to throw the visitor's face into candlelight, "and what might you be doing out on a night like this? Come in, my daughter, come in. Coileán," he called over his shoulder, "help me carry her!"

I joined him at the threshold, where I found a wizened, white-haired creature huddled against the wall, her eyes pale blue and clouded. I couldn't tell the color of the rags she wore—the night and the weather made everything beyond Eoin's candle a dark mess—but she trembled with cold and stared up at me imploringly. "Here, it's warm inside," I began, reaching to scoop her up, but froze when I finally saw what the lines of age had momentarily masked.

"Coileán," Étaín croaked, then doubled over with a spasm of coughing.

My body moved, though my mind was elsewhere, screaming. I gathered her into my arms and ran past Eoin toward the hearth, then put her in my chair and began to remove her dripping wrappings. The fabric, ancient and sodden, tore like wet paper in my hands, and I pulled back, panicking as her clothing seemingly dissolved at my touch.

She groped for my hand with her gnarled fingers and tried to squeeze. "It's all right, sweet boy," she murmured, and her head lolled against the back of the chair. "Let me rest."

I knelt before her, too stunned to move. "Étaín," I whispered, "what . . . why . . ."

Her eyes drifted in the direction of my voice, and I realized that she couldn't see me.

"Threw me out," she said softly, and coughed again. "Said I . . . I was no longer—"

I grabbed my cast-off blanket and wrapped it around her while she hacked and wheezed. "Who said?" I demanded, though I feared I already knew the answer.

Her fingertips grazed the rough wool, and her body shook again with her deep and rattling cough. "The queen said I was no longer needed. Time to go home. She . . . opened the gate on the road, where you had gone. I tried to . . . to find you . . ."

By then, Eoin had joined us, and his knees creaked as he dropped into a crouch beside Étaín's chair. "Where did you come from, my daughter?" he asked.

She turned toward his voice, then reached out and

touched his cheek. "Faerie," she whispered. "I was fifty years away . . . Coileán?" she called, sensing my movement as I ran across the room for more blankets.

"He's here," he soothed, wiping what was left of her hair from her face. "You're safe, my dear, you're safe."

I hurried back to her side to replace the dampened blanket with dry ones. "Here," I said, wrapping her up, "don't worry, I'll fix it . . ."

In an instant, Étaín's wrinkles smoothed into the cheeks I knew so well, her hair thickened and regained its pale luster, and her beautiful eyes unclouded. But something was still wrong—her now youthful hand continued to grope for me, and her grip when she caught my wrist was weak. "Sweet boy," she murmured, smiling sadly, "you can't undo what time has done. The years . . ." She paused to cough, then spat a red stain onto the corner of the blanket. "The years caught up with me." Étaín reached up until she found me, then patted my cheek. "I thank you for the gift, but I want my own face now."

I nodded, willing myself not to weep, and removed the glamour.

She patted my face again, then turned to Eoin, who watched with obvious concern. "You . . . you're a priest?" she asked.

He took her free hand. "I am. Daughter, will you make your confession?"

"I will," she said, then coughed again. I held her up,

trying to keep her from tumbling from the chair, and she panted when the fit subsided. "Father, please," she rasped, "my Rónán . . . the blacksmith, my Rónán . . . and my boys, my sons . . ."

He gently stroked her arm through the blanket. "Of course, my dear, I'll send someone right away. Wait here, and I'll return to hear your confession."

Eoin caught up with me when I was halfway to the door. "Through the church, son. My men are this way," he said, catching my sleeve, and pulled me into the cold room. When the thick door closed behind us, he lowered his voice and shook his head. "We'll wait here for a few minutes, then return to her."

"What about your men?" I cried, looking around the dark church for the door.

He grabbed my shoulders and shook his head again. "There are no men," he said softly. "And you're not going on a fool's errand."

"But . . . but Rónán—"

"Is long dead." The priest released me and sighed. "I knew the blacksmith Rónán when I was a boy. I played with his sons, and my aunt helped keep his house when his wife disappeared." He pointed to the closed door and raised his eyebrow. "She was in Faerie all the while?"

I nodded miserably.

"Fifty years," he murmured, folding his arms. "And perhaps it was a blessing. Raiders burned our village when I was fifteen. I was away, then—I was being trained for the priesthood," he explained absently, "but they killed every man and boy, and they took the women they wanted. Rónán and his sons are long dead. *She* might be, too, had she been there. They even put a torch to the church." His mouth tightened as he glanced at the door again. "I'll tell her I've sent word. There's no need to grieve her now. She'll be with them again soon enough."

My stomach clenched. "With them . . ."

Eoin must have sensed my distress, as he gripped my shoulders again and squeezed. "She has to be eighty, at least," he said, "feeble, soaked, exhausted, and from the sound of it, sick. She's coughing up blood." His grip tightened as he stared me in the eyes. "I doubt she sees the dawn. Be strong for her."

He had me carry Étaín to his bed, and then he bundled her up, produced a small box and vessel, and sent me out of the room. They were alone together for nearly an hour, and when Eoin came for me again, I had moved close to the front of the church, where there was shelter from the wet wind and a bit of candlelight. "She's resting," he told me, and ran one hand through his thin hair. "And she's made her peace with the Lord. I gave her something for the pain, but it's not going to delay the inevitable." I said nothing, and he nodded toward his apartment. "She told me about you. You should be there with her now, in case she wakes."

And so I kept vigil that long night, wrapped in

a blanket beside Étaín's deathbed. She woke for a few minutes every hour or so, muttered a word or two, and fell back into her fitful sleep. Her thin skin burned, even in the chill of the priest's quarters.

As dawn began to break through the window over the bed, Étaín's unseeing eyes opened, and she looked past me to an empty place in the room. "Rónán," she whispered, and beamed. "Oh, Rónán, I knew you would come . . ."

I never knew, and I suppose I'll never know, whether Étaín's last words were the ravings of a fevered mind or something more. All I know is that she died with a look of happiness on her face, and that I held her hand long after it had gone cold.

"The sun will rise tomorrow, God willing." Eoin handed me another bowl of stew and put the lid back on the pot. "And she's in a far better place, my son. Remember that."

I stared into the bowl, wondering what the point of eating was. "How do you know?"

"I don't. But I have faith." He took his seat again and sighed. "Coileán, she lived her span, maybe more. That's all anyone can ask."

"I should have sent her home—"

"To what? To this?" He put his bowl on the floor and pointed to the road beyond the apartment. "Her family was killed when you were a child. She *had* nothing here."

"It should have been her choice."

"Perhaps." He shrugged weakly. "She did love you, you know. That much she made abundantly clear to me. Asked me to help you. I promised I would."

I stared at the fire. "I promised her I'd be home soon."

"You can't blame yourself."

"If I hadn't left . . ."

"It was her time. She knew it, and she made her peace." He picked up his bowl again, but paused before tucking in. "I know what it's like to lose a mother. Mine died trying to birth my sister when I was twelve. My father died the next summer, and then my family was lost to the raiders." He reached across the space between us and planted his hand on my arm. "I *know*, Coileán. The pain fades. The sun rises. Life goes on."

"Étaín wasn't my mother," I mumbled.

Eoin patted my shoulder. "Not all family is bound by blood, and not all mothers bear children." His voice softened as he added, "There's no shame in mourning her. Carry her with you, let her guide you. Remember what you learned at her knee." He paused. "You've never known a death, have you?" I shook my head, and he patted my shoulder again. "Unfortunately, it's the cost of living."

I spent a largely sleepless night on Eoin's floor, staring at the ceiling and trying to ignore the scuffling sounds within the walls. Around dawn, as the fire was dying, I rose and tried to prod it back to life. After a moment's experimentation, I managed to wrap my hand well enough to keep the iron poker from burning it, and with that success, I was emboldened to put the iron pot back on to reheat the last of the fish stew.

Eoin rose soon thereafter, grunted with approval, and sat to break his fast. "I have a plan to get you to your father," he explained as he ate. "I'll write a letter to the abbot—he and I have been corresponding on matters of theology for years," he said offhandedly, "so this will be nothing unusual. You can ride out, deliver the letter, and ask about the rosary. Agreed?"

The plan sounded solid to me, and I stood by and watched as Eoin scratched out his note. Seeing me observing him, he asked, "Do you read?" I nodded, and he grunted again.

After a final inspection of my clothes, he led me to his tiny barn, which housed an old skinny mare. "She's gentle as a lamb," he promised as I eyed the beast with caution. "I'll saddle her, and you can be on your way."

This was far easier said than done. As I quickly discovered that morning, animals—which are far more sensitive to unseen forces than most humans will ever be—don't like me. The horse shied away and reared when I came within striking distance, and Eoin frantically tried to calm her before she broke a wall down. When that failed, however, I screwed up my courage, grabbed the horse's reins, and stared at her nose. She fought the enchantment I threw at her, but with sufficient effort, I managed to drag her under my control. "She'll be fine," I insisted as I awkwardly climbed on top of her.

"Just bring her back in one piece," Eoin replied, unconvinced, and watched until we disappeared around the bend.

The monastery was located on the far side of the little mountain, a relatively brief trip made intolerable by the bouncing of the bony horse, who wanted nothing more than to trample my corpse into the dirt. I managed to hold her steady until I reached my destination, another stone-walled compound, then turned her over to a confused novice who couldn't understand why the mare was in such a hurry to escape me.

The abbot received me in his cell and accepted the letter from Eoin with a smile. "My old friend is going to think himself into trouble one of these days," he laughed when he finished reading, "but would you mind waiting until I write a response?"

"It's no trouble," I replied, then pulled out my beads before the abbot could begin drafting. "Please— Father Eoin said you might know who owns these."

The old monk took the beads from me, peered at them, and then nodded slowly. "Yes," he murmured, giving me a more studied look, "I think I might." He beckoned to the novice at the door, then quietly said, "Please bring Brother Finnén."

The abbot, at least, had the decency not to ask about the beads' provenance, instead limiting our conversation to the weather and his hopes for a pleasant summer. Soon enough, I heard returning footsteps, and as I rose from my chair and turned, I saw the novice shepherd an old man into the room. He had been tall at one point, I surmised, but the years had bent him, and his dark robe hung loosely off his shoulders. He was bald but for a gray ring around his temples, but his eyes were still bright and green.

"Brother Finnén," the abbot said, gesturing to me, "this young man has brought me something that I believe might be yours."

He frowned, but then the abbot pressed the beads into his hands, and he began to tremble. He stared at me in shock, and the abbot cleared his throat. "Finnén, perhaps you could show our guest around while I write this letter."

"Yes," he whispered, and the abbot smiled.

I said nothing as we slowly walked down the stone hallway, letting him set the pace. He turned the beads over and over in his shaking fingers, then held them to his lips, kissed them, and slipped them into his pocket. Before I could inquire, he stopped at the door to another cell, then stepped aside and beckoned me in.

The room was bare but for a straw pallet, a stool, and a few unknown items I assumed to be of religious significance. Something about the room perplexed me—I thought I could sense more magic than I had elsewhere in that realm—but I tried not to let on.

"Water?" he asked, his voice creaking with disuse, and pointed to a pitcher across the cell. I shook my head, and he helped himself to three glasses in rapid succession before returning to me.

I could only stare back at him, into a face that could well have been mine if I suffered time's ravages.

He took my hands and bent close to me. "Did Amadeus send you?" he whispered.

"Amadeus?" I echoed, confused.

He nodded. "Does he live yet?"

I peered into his mind for a clue, and suddenly, I realized the extent of what Mother had done to the poor man.

An inn some miles away, one wild night and decades before. A beautiful young man with honey-colored hair and flashing dark eyes, Amadeus, beloved of God. Finnén, a handsome youth of twenty-three, waylaid on his return to the monastery, smitten with the sort of lust he had tried for years to tame. Amadeus flirted and cajoled, and his smile, though enticing, had a frozen core.

They rutted in secret in a dark corner of the barn, the young monk and the beautiful stranger, watched only by a pair of sleepy horses and the innkeeper's mutt, an old cur he unimaginatively called Coileán—*pup.* Amadeus took Finnén's rosary as a prize when he slipped away the next morning, never to be seen again. Finnén was left with broken vows, years of guilt, and a nagging suspicion that there was something otherworldly about his lover.

Seeing my father's hopeful face and knowing what Mother had done, I wanted to throw up. Instead, I squeezed his hands and took a deep breath. "Amadeus lives."

His smile lit up his craggy face. "Is he still beautiful?"

"He is."

My father's smile faltered. "He was too beautiful— I've never seen his like, not in all these years. I always supposed that he was of the *aes sídhe,*" he added, laughing hesitantly as if worried that I wouldn't believe him.

I nodded.

"He *is?*"

I nodded again, struggling for words.

He sighed. "And you, sir . . . you are come from him?"

His eyes—*my* eyes—showed a spark of fear, but I had to press on. "Finnén," I said softly, keeping my grip on his hands, "the man you knew as Amadeus . . . he is no man."

"Yes, I understand," he replied. "He comes from the *aes sídhe*—"

"Besides that," I interrupted. "He is, uh . . . a

woman." My father's face clouded, and I hurriedly explained, "Whatever you saw, whatever you . . . did, she masked her true nature. She can do that. I . . . I'm terribly sorry for the deception, I didn't know until . . ."

His eyes widened, and he freed himself from my grip. Raising my chin with two fingers, he whispered, "Amadeus . . . is she—"

I saw the thought before he could finish it. "My mother."

He stared at me anew, finally seeing the years peeled away from his own reflection, and with a wordless cry, he pulled me to his breast.

We spoke in his cell until nightfall, when the novice finally sought him out for prayers. My father sent him away with a promise to hurry, then embraced me one last time. "I have one request," he whispered. "Something I found in the field, it . . . makes me feel odd. Would you look at it?"

"Of course," I replied, and waited while he dug a wrapped bundle out of his mattress. When he removed the cloths, I saw a golden ball in his palms and realized where the smell of magic was coming from. I took it from him, turned it over, and frowned. "It's magical, but I don't know its provenance," I admitted. "I've never seen anything like it."

"Do you want it?" he asked.

I shook my head. "No, I've no need of it. But . . ." I hesitated, considering the ball again. "This shouldn't be left in the wrong hands."

"Agreed. Perhaps you could . . . hide it for me? I don't want the abbot to know about it," he confessed in a rush. "He knows about Amadeus, and if this were to come to his attention . . ."

"It won't." I thought for a moment, then produced a crystal cube slightly larger than the ball. The ball went inside, and I filled the cube with water before I sealed it shut. "The water will dampen the magic, and the crystal should block the rest," I explained; the scent had faded already. With a flick of two fingers, a large stone flew out of the cell wall, and I slipped the cube inside and repaired the hole. Within seconds, the wall was unmarred, and I grinned. "Problem solved."

My father's face showed his relief. "I wish I could offer you something," he said. "What you see around you, this is all I have."

"I want for nothing," I replied, smiling again for him. "And I'll trouble you no more . . ."

He squeezed my shoulder in silent thanks, then reached up and pressed his palm against my head. "All I can give you is a father's blessing," he said. "Be strong. Grow in wisdom. Walk with God." He released me and smiled sadly, and I offered him my arm for the walk back to the abbot's cell.

We parted company outside the abbot's door, and the novice led him off toward the voices in the distant chapel. The abbot's letter had been left for me, long dried and sealed, and I took my leave by starlight.

Eoin seemed surprised to see me that night with both the letter and the horse. "A success?" he inquired as I jumped away from the irate mare, which would have run for the hills had he not grabbed it.

"A success," I replied, and waited outside the barn as he tended to the beast.

When he emerged again, Eoin dusted off his hands and stared up at the cloudless heavens. "So, young man . . . where do you go from here?"

I followed his eyes to the unfamiliar constellations. "I can't go back."

"Oh?"

"No. Not yet."

"Something's keeping you here?"

"No. But if I go home, I'll probably try to kill my mother."

Eoin nodded. "Matricide is seldom a wise idea, Coileán." He cleared his throat and looked away from the stars. "Any experience in the field?"

"None," I replied.

"Can you cook?"

"No."

"Willing to learn?"

I looked at him inquisitively, and the priest shrugged. "I'm not as spry as I once was. You want to think things over, find your path—I could use a bit of help around the place, I suppose."

I nodded, considering this. "No magic, I assume."

He made a face. "Nothing *big*."

I nodded again, watching the moon rise. "I accept."

My father died three days later. I never saw him again.

CHAPTER 15

I was grateful for the little car's heater against the wet chill as I passed endless fields and modest houses around Benbulbin and Truskmore, drove down streets I'd never seen, and eventually gave up and headed for the coast in an effort to orient myself with the Atlantic to my back. After spending half an hour on the side of the road with my jacket hood up, triangulating points on my now water-spotted map, I managed to zero in on the old monastery's location and turned my car back toward the interior.

An hour, a cup of coffee, and half a dozen wrong turns later, I idled on a dirt road that abutted a large farm and tried to find the ruins in the mist. Halfway up a hill, I spotted a pile of stone that seemed only vaguely familiar, but when I stepped out of the car for a better look, I sniffed the air and caught the faintest scent of magic.

I had protected the sphere with water and crystal and stone, making it blend into the background magic of the area. With that magic gone, however, I could pick the sphere's signature out of the air—I could have followed the smell in a beeline to the stone pile—and I glanced about, looking for interlopers similarly drawn by the only hint of magic for miles. We had to move in quickly and grab the sphere, but I couldn't do it by daylight—not with a farmer lurking nearby, and not with the sturdy wire fence separating his property from the road.

I glared at the ruin and tried to formulate a plan. We would come by night, but we'd need wire cutters—and if the fence had an alarm, we'd certainly trigger it. And once we were on the property, could we safely use flashlights without attracting attention? What about dogs, didn't farmers always have those skulking about? And I still needed a tool to get the sphere out of its hiding place in the wall . . .

As I mulled over my options, a lone ewe wandered close, looked up sharply at me, and ran for the safety of the flock.

In this ever mutable world, it's nice to see that some things never change.

I returned to the hotel around six with takeaway curry and found Joey still tinkering at the room's table, which was littered with bits of metal and discarded plastic clamshells. He had procured a pair of safety goggles, I noticed, and with his hair and clothing in disarray from travel, he looked rather like the sort of scientist who should only be trusted with safety scissors.

"Find it?" he asked, watching me through a thick layer of plastic.

"Yeah. Food?" I lifted the plastic bag in offering, and he cleared half the table with the sweep of his arm.

Joey pushed his goggles up on his forehead, squinted at the green sauce in the first foam box he opened, then shrugged and started unwrapping a fork. "Almost finished here," he said between bites. "Seems to be working, but I can't really test it, you know?"

"So how do you know it's working?"

He pointed to the curtained window. "Alley out back. I might have shot a few nails into the hotel's dumpster for range-gauging purposes."

"I know nothing," I replied, opening another container of rice. "How are you with fences?"

Joey leaned back in his thinly padded chair and cracked his knuckles. "What kind of fence are we talking about?"

"Wire. The property owner has sheep."

His mouth twitched. "Sheepdog?"

"I didn't see one, but—"

"But that doesn't mean anything," he finished,

taking his turn with the rice. "Okay, so a multi-strand wire fence, right? Barbed wire?"

"No barbs. It might be electric."

"*Might?*"

"I didn't exactly test it," I mumbled into my dinner.

"Right . . ." He pushed his curry around for a moment, frowning, then nodded. "So, the first problem to get around is the fence. They all have control boxes, but I'm betting the owner keeps his protected. We'll just go over." My eyebrow rose, and Joey grinned. "Yet another boring summer, this one with a tempting pond in a field inside an electric wire. A bunch of us kids used to sneak in at night until the owner caught us, and then I spent the rest of the summer in my parents' RV. Lesson learned, eh?"

"How?" I asked skeptically.

His grin widened. "Rubber gloves and galoshes. If you're careful, you can make it over without shocking yourself." He glanced at our luggage, then said, "I suppose we'd better go find some before the stores close."

"The ones near us already have," I muttered. "We'll be halfway back to Dublin before we find something open."

Joey put down his fork, grabbed his nail gun, stuffed his tools into his paper bag, and headed for the door. "Let's move, then. You can fill me in on the rest on the way."

It was nearly two thirty on Saturday morning before we made it back to the dirt road and the ruins. I parked the car in the weeds half a mile away and led Joey back up the road, feeling slightly foolish to be out in rain boots after the rain had ceased. He had picked out a hammer and chisel at the store as well, plus black gloves that reached to our elbows. "Heading north tomorrow," he told the weary clerk. "*Far* north. Little fishing trip with an old friend—he warned us that ice is still a problem this time of year."

"Very far north," the clerk had mumbled, but took my bank card without protest.

Now appropriately suited and armed—Joey had fashioned a quick holster for his nail gun out of duct tape on the way—we approached the fence and surveyed the dark field. "See anything?" he whispered.

I shook my head and tapped the penlight in my pocket. "No lights. Farmer's probably asleep."

"How close are we?"

"The ruin's halfway up the hill," I replied, then gingerly reached out for the top wire. When I didn't receive a shock, I slowly let out my breath. "Okay, so how do we do this?"

"Watch and learn," Joey whispered, then pulled on the top wire just enough to give himself room to maneuver. In a matter of seconds, he had vaulted the fence without electrocution, and he flipped on his flashlight to show me the shaking wires. "Want help?"

Though embarrassed to ask, I let him guide me over into the field, and I shifted my tool pack when I was clear of the fence. "I thought you were supposed to be a priest," I muttered. "Since when has breaking and entering been part of the job?"

He chuckled. "Technically, I'm still on vacation. Where's the doohickey hiding?"

I clicked on my light for a moment and showed him the ruins in the distance. "Hike's not bad. I'd watch for sheep droppings."

"Mm. What's that?" he asked, quickly flicking his light toward a modest outbuilding near the ruins.

"Storage shed?" I guessed. "I have no idea."

Joey grunted, then cut his light and began to trudge up the hill. I followed a pace behind, keeping an eye out for unfriendly lights, but the night was still and quiet. "It's in there," I murmured. "I can smell it."

"Do you have any idea how weird that sounds?" he replied.

"Not really," I admitted. "Paul's grown accustomed to it."

"He's got a head start on me, you know?" Joey's breathing had begun to grow more labored, but he marched on. "I mean, this week has kind of been a crash introduction to weirdness. No offense."

"You're handling it well," I said, grateful for the rubber boots with each squelching step.

Joey paused, then took a long sniff. "Horses. *Definitely* horses."

"You can tell that from here? Do you have any idea how weird that sounds?" I couldn't resist mocking him.

"I was on a horse before I could walk," he replied, pointing to the outbuilding. "Must be a barn. I spent enough summers mucking out stables to know what horse shit smells like," he explained.

"I wouldn't really know. Don't do well with animals," I said. "Avoid them when I can."

"Bad encounter?"

"It's a faerie thing. I freak them out." I glanced over my shoulder at the dark bulk of the barn and hoped whatever was in there kept on sleeping. "I bought one of the first Fords. You have no idea how nice it is to get into a vehicle and not worry that your propulsion system is going to bolt on you." My boot hit the first fallen stone. "Ah. Light, please."

Joey turned on his flashlight again, and I surveyed the few remaining walls, trying to orient myself in a building I'd seen exactly once. That proved futile, however, and so I resorted to walking the perimeter and sniffing. In a few moments, I centered in on the strongest smell, and I pulled the hammer and chisel from my pack. "Here goes," I muttered, and began my work. "Keep watch, yeah?"

He disappeared around the corner, taking the light with him, and I worked by touch, feeling the edges of the loosened stone through my thick gloves. Ten minutes later, I had chipped the mortar free and pulled the stone from the wall, revealing the hiding place I had casually created centuries before. I reached into the hole and pulled the crystal box out, then flipped on my light to examine my prize.

Before I could try to get the cube open, footsteps ran down the former hall, and Joey panted, "Someone's coming!"

"What?" I hissed, wheeling away from the hole.

His head bobbed in my flashlight's beam. "Six guys. There's a couple down by our car—I saw them from the top of the wall," he said, glancing toward the missing ceiling, "and the other four are heading this way. What do we do?"

"You stay here," I ordered, pushing him against the wall before darting out of the ruins. Joey was right, I noted with a tightening stomach; four lights bobbed through the wet grass, heading our way. "Who's there?" I called, scrambling to think up a plausible lie if the newcomers were the farmer's family.

The nearest of the lights flashed into my eyes and back to the ground. "Just a friend, my lord," its owner called back in Fae, and I slipped behind the wall once more.

I found Joey waiting where I had left him, and I thrust my pack in his face. "Doohickey's in there. Get out of here, now."

"But I—"

"*Go.* I'll be along shortly. Just keep it safe."

"Who's coming?" he pressed, slipping my bag over his shoulders.

"Friends of Robin's. Don't let them get the sphere," I said, and headed back to meet them as Joey ran the other way.

The lights were still coming as I hoisted myself onto the wall, and I spotted the two down at our rental car, blocking our escape. An ambush, then, I decided, trying to judge my attackers' positions by their lights. "How did you find me?" I called, hoping their voices might provide me with insight as to their identities.

The lead light called back, "Lord Robin told us where to look!"

Shit. If Robin had planned this, then his goons knew what I was after. "I warn you, I'm armed!" I yelled—but that, I realized as soon as I had let it slip, was a lie. The hammer and chisel were in the pack I had given Joey, and I had exactly one small, plastic flashlight with which to defend myself. Still, bluffing seemed like the best option. "You know what I'm capable of!"

"We do," said another light. "But this is a contest of muscle now, isn't it? The magic's gone."

"There are four of us," the third added. "And . . . two of you?"

They were right, of course, but I had to stall and

give Joey time to flee. "My associate's stronger than he looks. You won't like him when he's angry."

"Is that so?" the leader asked. "Shall we test him and prove you a liar *and* a coward, Ironhand?"

I ground my teeth but forced myself to remain still. There was nothing to be gained by engaging them sooner. "My brother put you up to this, you said?"

The leader hesitated. "Not in so many words."

"But he said you'd be here," the fourth chimed in.

"And we have affairs to settle," the leader continued, back on firm footing. "Now, what brings the likes of you here—"

His words were cut off by a shrill neighing, and then a giant blur came thundering around the mountain. The lingering clouds broke for just a moment, and I caught a glimpse in the moonlight of Joey astride an enormous black horse, his head bare, his pack bouncing on his back, his dirty rubber boots clinging to the beast's sides. The horse sensed what was around him and reared, but Joey held on and coaxed it back to the ground. "Freeze, motherfuckers," he snapped, aiming his flashlight at the approaching faeries.

Something seemed odd about the flashlight's position, and then I saw what Joey had quickly taped it to.

The leader began to run at him, but fell an instant later, shrieking at the nail embedded in his thigh. The others stopped in their tracks, giving Joey time to turn around and reach for me on the wall. "Get on!" he shouted. "What are you waiting for?"

The horse was barely in check, and I couldn't see this ending well. "I can't! Without enchantment, I can't control—"

"Damn it, don't be difficult!" he snapped, then grabbed my wrist and yanked me forward. Even with the horse's back nearly level with the broken wall, mounting the terrified beast was still a tricky proposition without the aid of a saddle, and I only kept my seat by clinging to Joey like a barnacle. The beast reared again as I swung my legs into place, and Joey kicked it back to earth as he sighted down the remaining three faeries. "We're getting out of here. Hang on, Blücher," he muttered.

The horse screamed and reared once more, but Joey drove it onward down the mountain, firing nails at every shadow. The cries told me when he fired true, but soon we were past the faeries and racing for the road. "They're in our car!" I yelled, holding on to Joey for dear life.

"And theirs is blocking the road!" he yelled back, pointing his gun at the dark van I had missed. Without slowing, he took aim at the rental car and fired, driving nails through the windows and into the tires. The van received the same treatment, and then Joey kicked the horse into high gear and cleared the electric fence. We raced away through the night, the sphere safe between us and half a dozen angry faeries at our back.

Joey finally slowed several miles away, then pulled the lathered horse to a halt and slid down. As soon as I was off its back, the frantic creature bolted, and Joey sighed. "Well, I honestly didn't think I'd be adding horse theft to my spring break plans," he muttered, "but I'm sure he'll find his way home."

I breathed deeply, trying to steady my nerves, then leaned against an ancient stone wall and closed my eyes.

"You okay?" he asked.

"Adrenaline," I mumbled, willing myself not to be sick, then reached into my pocket and found the car keys, which I dropped into the tall grass. "Car was stolen at knifepoint. We went out to a club and got jacked. Got it?"

"Works for me."

"Good." I stood up slowly, testing myself for vertigo, then opened my eyes. "Kid?"

"Yeah?"

"Thanks."

"Sure," he grunted, and then we started our long walk home.

Ten steps up the road, I asked, "So, how many Hail Marys does horse theft earn these days?"

Joey sighed. "This little escapade is between you, me, and the Almighty, right?"

I patted his shoulder. "Was there a minibar in the hotel room, by chance? Felonies make me thirsty."

"I think there might have been a bar in the lobby," he replied. "Hey, does this mean Robin's dead?"

"Maybe." I shrugged. "I'll think about it in the morning."

CHAPTER 16

We ditched our rubber gloves and boots in separate bins. Though he was loath to part with it, I insisted that Joey dump his nail gun as well, and he tossed it into the Garvoge in pieces. The makeshift holster went into a public can several blocks away, tucked under a greasy pizza box for extra safety, and then, divested of anything incriminating, we made our way to the police station on aching feet to report our rental stolen.

"We were on our way back from Dublin," Joey lied, putting on his best choirboy face. "Met up with some friends for a few hours. We stopped for gas and got carjacked by two guys. They had these big knives . . ."

The officer's face was weary with the hour. "What was the name of the petrol station?"

He consulted the ceiling. "I think it was a Topaz . . . some sort of gemstone . . ."

The scribbling intensified, but the officer was nodding. "Remember where?"

"No, I'm sorry, it's all kind of a blur . . ." Joey swallowed hard, then mumbled, "We'd been out clubbing, see, and it was late . . ."

The officer held up his empty hand. "Say no more. Get a good look at them?"

"Maybe six feet tall, little less. Skinny. Black track suits, black ski masks."

"We were at the far end of the pumps, too," I added. "I didn't see a security camera . . ."

"Clever bastards," the officer muttered, and snapped his notebook closed. I couldn't see his thoughts without magic, but something told me we were off the hook for the time being.

We left Joey's cell phone number and our hotel address, promised to stay in town through the weekend in case the police collared anyone, and shook the officer's hand as he assured us that he'd straighten everything out with the rental company. With that, we walked home to the hotel through the dawn's first light, both of us stiff after sitting at the station and blistered from our night's exertion. "Made up your mind yet?" Joey asked as we turned onto the final stretch of sidewalk.

I glanced at him, but he had shoved his hands into his jacket pockets and was staring straight ahead, giving me no indication of his thoughts on the matter. "I suppose I should call Robin before putting a bounty on his head, shouldn't I?"

"Seems wise."

"Fine," I sighed. "But once I get answers out of him, I'm having a drink or three. Think we've earned it, don't you?"

When the elevator doors closed and we began our slow trip up, Joey murmured, "There are six pissed-off faeries in the area, and I assume all of them know what you look like. We're unarmed. I can take on one, maybe two, but not a whole pack. So I need you focused and sober, okay? At least until we're safe."

"We lost them back—"

"*They knew where to find us,*" he interrupted. "And if it's one cheap hotel door versus six faeries, I really don't like the odds."

The elevator opened again, and we turned for our room. "They're powerless right now," I replied, trying to reassure him. "They're licking whatever wounds you gave them last night, and even if they were to find us, it's not like they have access to any source of magic. The sphere's protected, and if it comes down to it, I can tap it before they know what hit them."

He slid his plastic key into the lock and depressed the steel handle. "Magic or no, man, those guys weren't exactly puny. I told you before, I'm not a brawler."

"You're the next best thing to a knight," I protested, stepping aside to let him slide the chain latch on.

"I didn't bring a sword with me, remember?"

I frowned at the floral curtain. "There's probably a gift shop around here with—"

"Cheap replicas. Europe's lousy with them. The steel's weak, and it bends and snaps." Joey tossed himself onto his bed and groaned into his palms. "Maybe I should have checked a bag and chanced it."

I sat on the edge of the other bed and shrugged. "You know, the sharpness and strength aren't as important as the fact that you're waving around a big iron stick. Hell," I said, plucking Joey's new phone off the nightstand and tossing it at him, "we'll find another hardware store, and you can get yourself a nice length of iron pipe if it'll make you feel better. Now call Toula."

He rolled up onto his elbow and squinted at the bedside clock. "It's two A.M. in Virginia. You sure about this?"

"She's not the one who got ambushed last night. Dial."

He made a face but did as I bid, and after a few seconds, I heard a sleepy voice mumbling incoherently on the other end.

"Hey, Toula, it's Joey. How're . . . Yeah, it's Galahad. I'm sorry to call so late . . . No, we're fine, everything's fine, but is Robin there?"

I pried the phone from his hand and held it to my ear. "Toula, it's Colin. Put him on."

Joey began to make turning motions beside his

head, and I realized the phone was upside down. It didn't seem to make much difference, however, as I heard springs creak and a door open, and then Toula's muffled voice said, "Tink? Hey, Tink, come on, wake up, phone call."

"Kick him if you have to," I offered.

"No need, he's stirring," she replied. "Did you find it?"

"Yes. It's safe," I murmured, tracing a crack in the wall with my eyes. "Hey, does this phone have one of those speaker things?"

There was a pause on the other end, and then Toula said, "I have no idea what *you're* using, but *I'm* on an iPhone. You want it on speaker?"

"I want you both to hear this," I replied, and waited while she made the necessary adjustments. When I heard Robin grumble near the phone, I lowered my voice and tried to push down my sleep-and alcohol-deprivation-fueled anger. "Who are your friends, Puck?" I began, waiting for the explosion on the other end.

None came. "What friends?" he yawned. "And it's two in the goddamned morning, Coileán—"

"The six goons you sent after us!" I shouted.

"*What?*"

"Don't play dumb with me, you sick bastard—"

"What goons? I have no idea what you're talking about!"

I heard a moment's shuffling on the other end, and

then Toula said, "I'm pretty sure he's telling the truth. What happened?"

I breathed hard, surprised at my own rage, and Joey took the phone back and pressed the necessary buttons. "Toula? You still there?"

"We both are," she replied, sounding worried. "Is he okay?"

"Been a long night," he said as I slunk off to the bathroom to calm down. "We went after the sphere thing, and six faeries sneaked up on us."

"Damn," she muttered.

"And they said Robin told them I was coming!" I called, turning on the tap.

"Give me that," Robin snapped, and yelled, "Are you there? You're breaking up!"

"He's just getting a drink," Joey replied, and I popped out of the bathroom with a tumbler of water in my hand.

"Of course he is," Robin sighed, then said, "Yeah, Coileán, I called the necessary parties and told them you were heading over, but I told them to leave you alone. I was trying to avoid surprises."

I knocked back my drink in two quick sips, giving myself a moment to calm down. Unfortunately, the water tasted vaguely of lemon furniture polish. "There were six of them, all your people."

"Look, I told them to leave you be, but I can't help it if the entire court wants you dead. You know how it is." He paused, then asked, "You all right?"

"Only because Joey's a horse whisperer."

Robin whistled softly. "That so?"

"And handy with a nail gun."

There came a moment's silence, and then Robin asked, "Kid, did you, uh . . . you didn't shoot my people with a *nail gun*, did you?"

Joey's face was expressionless. "Self-defense."

"*Shit*," he grunted. "That's . . . not the kind of thing that's easily forgiven, you know."

"Understandable. So can you call off your dogs or what?"

"I didn't loose them in the first place," Robin replied testily. "Like I said, I warned them you two were coming and told them to keep away. Whatever's going on isn't my doing—and no, Coileán," he said as I reached for the phone, "I can't stop them from here. What am I supposed to do, threaten them long distance? My father isn't going to punish them, so what can I do?"

I took the phone from Joey and held it between us. "Just try to be persuasive," I said. "We'll be out of here soon. The sphere's been shipped to a safe location for now." I met Joey's eyes and winked, and he nodded. "Toula, any potential locations?"

Her voice grew on the other end—I assumed Robin had handed the phone over. "Not yet," she muttered. "Everything I've been able to trace has dead-ended in Arcanum hands. I can't believe I'm saying this, but it might just be faster to ask Harrison."

"*You* want to ask Harrison?" I goggled.

Toula growled through her nose. "You have no idea how frustrating this diary is."

"We'll talk about it," I said. "Kid and I will be back as soon as we can."

I kept watch with the television during the day as Joey slept, and while I rested in turn that evening, he set off for Mass. "You're on vacation," I reminded him as he slipped into his jacket.

"No excuse. Vigil's at five, if you're interested. Just down the block. I think it's casual, but at least it's in English."

"Thanks, but I'll pass. I'm going to try to sleep for a while, all right?"

"Sure," Joey nodded, watching as I rolled over to face the wall. "Hey, Colin?"

"Yeah?" I mumbled.

"We're going to find them," he said quietly. "Keep the faith."

The door closed behind him, and I buried my face in the flat pillow and closed my eyes, willing myself not to get attached to the kid. Priests, after all, had an unfortunate tendency to grow old and die.

Left to my own devices, I drifted off, only to be pulled from chaotic dreams into darkness by a tinny fugue theme. I sat up and blinked groggily at the room until I saw Joey's phone illuminated on the nightstand beside me. Of Joey there was no sign, but I caught a glimpse of the bedside clock, saw that it was seven, and wondered just how late Mass went around there. I picked up the trumpeting phone, stared at the smooth screen for a moment in confusion, then touched the most likely button and said, "Hello?"

"Missing something?" a familiar voice asked in Fae.

I rubbed my eyes for a second before I placed it as the leader of the goon squad. "What do you want, Setile?"

"Why, *you*, my lord," he replied with a smirk in his tone. "We have the boy. If you want him back, you'll have to fight for him."

I stood and opened the drapes to stare out onto the alley. "Robin told you to leave me be, did he not?"

"Perhaps," Setile allowed, "but Lord Robin isn't here to stop us, now is he?"

"Put the kid on. I want proof that he's still alive."

"As you like."

I heard shuffling and muffled voices on the other end, and then Joey said, "Hey, Colin? You there?"

"What the hell happened?" I muttered, rubbing my forehead.

"Ambushed after Mass," he said apologetically. "Threw me in the back of the van and everything. Guess they fixed their tires after last night . . ."

"Are you hurt?"

"Little banged up, nothing major," he said, keeping his voice light. "But, uh . . . these guys would really like a word with you . . ."

Joey's voice cut off. "We'll kill him if you don't come to claim him," Setile resumed, and I heard Joey yelp in time with the sound of flesh striking flesh in the background.

I took a deep breath and stared at my dark reflection in the dresser mirror. "Go ahead."

Setile hesitated. "You think this is some sort of game?"

"I think this is a blatant attempt on my life," I snapped, "and I'm not about to walk into whatever you've set up."

"But the boy—"

"He knew the risk of running around with me. One less mortal—why should I care?"

The kidnapper seemed momentarily stumped, then muttered, "Try us, Ironhand. The empty warehouse on the south bank. If we don't see you by midnight, the kid's dead." He held the phone slightly away from his face, then yelled in English, "Hey, boy! He says he doesn't care if you live or die! Here, my lord," he continued, lowering his voice, "why don't you tell him yourself?"

Joey's voice returned to the line. "Colin?"

I tried to keep the cold edge in my tone. "Sorry, kid. Too risky." Before he could protest, I pushed buttons until the call ended, then stared at Joey's empty bed.

Joey was presumably immobilized, so the fight would be six on one. Under ordinary circumstances, this would have been a cinch; Setile was the strongest of the lot, and he wasn't more than a few centuries old. I had beaten him plenty of times before, and I hadn't had to resort to iron to do it—a faerie's skill in magic continues to grow over time, and I had a considerable age advantage. Without magic, however, the fight was lopsided in the other direction, and I didn't like the look of things. Surely, I surmised, they were expecting me to come armed, and they had probably prepared for it.

In short, I wasn't going to win that fight. I had no court to call on for assistance—most of Titania's tolerated me only because they had to—but I couldn't just leave Joey behind, and for all of my posturing on the phone, I had a feeling that Setile knew a bluff when he heard one.

So I did the one thing the six of them would never expect, considering our history: I went to the lobby and called the police.

"The riot gear was a nice touch."

Joey looked up from the Styrofoam cup of tea the medic had pressed into his hands and pulled the gray blanket more tightly around his shoulders. I gingerly sat beside him on the back of the ambulance, trying to avoid making contact with the steel all around me. "Anything broken?" I asked.

"Nah. Like I said, just a little banged up." His black eye crinkled when he smiled. "I've taken worse. You don't become a seasoned jouster without getting to know the ground."

I took up the cold pack he had dropped between us and held it toward him. "Go on, you're swelling."

He touched the pack back to his face, wincing with the temperature shift, and took a sip of tea. "They were so *surprised*," he said, grinning again despite his discomfort. "I mean, all they'd been doing for the half hour after they called you was stand by me and bicker, and then the doors flew open and the cops stormed the place. It was pretty sweet."

"What were they arguing about?"

"Damned if I know," he shrugged. "I don't speak Irish, remember?"

"You were probably hearing Fae."

"Same difference to me." He sipped his tea again, grimacing at the taste. "Anyway, you should have heard the screams when the cuffs came out."

"I think I would have liked that," I replied, smiling back at him. "Got them all?"

"Yep. What do you think will happen to them?"

I consulted the van's ceiling. "Well, I doubt any of them has an identity card," I said, keeping my voice low while the officers on clean-up finished their work.

"We tend to play outside the law. They may not have legal identities at all," I explained, and smiled again. "But that doesn't mean that they didn't leave finger-prints all over our rental car."

Joey's teeth flashed in the ambulance's light. "You're set if questioned, then?"

My eyebrow rose. "I'm Colin Leffee of Rigby, Virginia, forty-year-old purveyor of secondhand books, and I've got the doctored papers to prove it."

"*Forty?*"

"Forgot to get my passport changed," I muttered. "But play along, okay?"

"No problem there," said Joey, forcing another sip of tea down. "Seeing as the truth would get me locked up and sedated, right?"

I patted his shoulder. "You're learning, kid."

As soon as the medics cleared Joey, I walked him back to the hotel, then slipped out to the off-license down the street for a bottle of Johnnie Black. By the time I returned, Joey had called down to the lobby bar to send up a sandwich and fries, which he ate from a tray incongruously decorated with a porcelain bud vase holding a pink rose and a spray of baby's breath. "Got your dinner?" he asked as I locked the door.

I held up the bottle and smiled tightly. "I'm set."

He shook his head and turned back to his food. "Ever think about cutting back?"

"I'll tell you the same thing I told Paul," I replied,

taking one of the water tumblers from the dresser. "It serves a purpose, and I don't want to hear about it."

Joey chewed a fry slowly, watching me pour. "What are you trying to forget?"

My hand clenched around the bottle, but I put the whisky aside and met his gaze. Contrary to my expectations, his expression bore no reproach, but it was otherwise inscrutable. "Too much, kid. Cheers."

"Whatever's in that glass isn't going to make it go away," he murmured, returning to his sandwich.

I put my drink down and stared at him until he grew uncomfortable enough to look up. "Maybe not," I said quietly, "but it makes the memories a little duller for a time, and that's really all I can ask for."

"That and cirrhosis."

"Fortunately enough, I seem to be immune," I replied, and drank again, watching him watch me. "Let me guess, alcoholic in the family?"

He nodded. "My granddad drank himself to death after Grandma died. Got wasted and drove into a tree when I was eight."

"I'm sorry. Is he the only person you've lost?"

Joey mulled it over for a moment. "Yeah. Only one I remember, at least."

"You're fortunate, then," I replied, and stared into my glass. "Everyone I have ever loved has died on me. That's something you don't just get over, you know— there's no therapy for someone like me, there's no grief counseling. You deal with it the best you can, and you go on, knowing full well that the hole that person left behind is never going to close. By rights, I should have drunk myself to death a hundred times by now, but I keep waking up, and I keep pressing on. And when the memories come back too quickly, I drink them down again."

"I understand—"

"You don't. You *can't*." I realized I was descending into self-pity, but I was too tired to drag myself back from the brink. "I mean, look at you," I said, gesturing at him with the half-emptied glass. "Sure, you lose people along the way, but you blindly trust that in another seventy-five years or so, you're going to meet up with everyone again in this beautiful wonderland of harps and fluffy clouds. I don't have that luxury."

Joey pushed his tray aside and folded his arms on the table. "You don't believe in an afterlife?"

"Never really saw the point. And if you're right, then whatever's coming to me is fairly depressing." I put my glass down and mirrored his posture. "Going to try to convert me to the One True Faith now? I warn you, I've heard most of the pitches."

He slowly shook his head. "Nope. Just going to remind you that Meg and your daughter aren't dead yet."

"Might be," I mumbled.

"Live in hope," he replied, picking up a fry. "So what's your daughter's name, anyway?"

"Her mother named her Olive Marie. My mother called her Moyna."

"Well, that's confusing. What does she go by?"

"Moyna," I sighed, recognizing Joey's attempt at a diversion. "I'm not sure what she hates more, the fact that she's partly human or that she's related to me." He remained silent, and I filled the space. "She's sixteen. Little younger than you. Thinks she's the queen of the universe, from the sound of it."

He bit off the top of his fry. "A lot of that could have to do with being sixteen, man. I mean, I was *this* close to a juvenile record a few times as a teenager, and I turned out fine."

I stared at him as he ate. "This is fine? You, me, merrow, horse theft—*this* is fine?"

The corner of his mouth twitched. "Still on vacation, Colin."

"You're going to make one hell of a priest, kid," I replied with a snort, and rose. "I'm going for a walk. Get some rest, eh?"

Leaving Joey secure in the room, I wandered off down the street, listening to the town slow around me. A group of teenagers laughed as they walked, and I saw the warm lights of a pub up the road. But as my feet instinctively headed in that direction, I stopped myself and took another street. The memories were going to come that night, no matter how much I tried to drown them, and so I headed for the river alone.

CHAPTER 17

Eoin had occasional letters from the southeast, warning of skirmishes with the invaders from over the narrow sea, but the conquest didn't hurt us greatly in those early years. While the invading Normans settled down and built up Sligo, the surrounding farmers tilled the soil and protected their flocks, fishermen went to sea and sometimes never returned, and the faithful trooped into Eoin's church on a regular basis, leaving him gifts of food. The local lordling, a pinched-faced third son of little account whose name I've long since forgotten, demanded a more substantial share of his people's harvest, but even he contributed to Eoin in his turn.

"The Lord asks for a tithe," Eoin explained as I helped him carry vegetables to the root cellar. "He gives us all we have—surely we can give that little back."

The theology that flowed so readily from the old priest was unfamiliar and perplexing to me, but Eoin insisted that I learn it. "If you're to pass as my novice, or even a lay brother," he said, "you must know these things by heart. Even the unlearned know the stories," he added with a hint of reproach. "How do you propose to walk among them if you don't even know the Blessed Mother's name?"

"Margarita?" I guessed.

"Maria. *Muire.*" He sighed, and shook his head.

The key to all of this knowledge was Eoin's prized possession, a large book filled with tiny, neat, indecipherable black characters. It was a Bible, he told me, and I must learn to read it. "I won't ask you to profess the faith," he said, "but I'll ask you to render a fair impression."

And so, every night, once the chores were completed and the prayers were said, I hunched over the massive tome and squinted at the letters in the firelight, trying to make slow sense of their meaning. There was no need for the exercise—though I had come to Eoin without a word of Latin, I could have pulled it from him, just as Mother had given me his tongue—but Eoin seemed to enjoy teaching, and so I plodded on as a child might. The priest proved a patient and apt tutor, explaining the characters and their sounds, turning sounds into concepts, and weaving those concepts into the fuller story he so fervently believed. Sometimes, in his excitement for us to relate passages to each other, he would forgo the Latin lesson entirely for a moment and translate the text himself, looking up periodically to make sure I understood.

Within the year, I had committed the basics of Eoin's faith to memory, and I could hold my own when he tested me with questions. Knowledge didn't equate to belief, however—at least not in my case—but I kept my thoughts to myself; faith gave Eoin comfort, especially as he saw his life beginning to draw to its close, and I didn't want to grieve him. "I'll be sixty-two this summer," he told me one afternoon as we tended his garden. He rested with his foot on his spade and grimaced as he unkinked his back. "I don't know how many more years the Lord will see fit to give me."

Even after spending months among Eoin's people, I found it almost inconceivable that he could be a mere eleven years my senior. His body was already failing him. Eoin had seen nothing more than blurs in the distance since childhood, but his near vision had begun to dim, too, making his reading all the more challenging. His joints ached with every change in the weather, and his hands often rested on his lower back, as if he were attempting to buttress his weak scaffolding. A few of his teeth had fallen out; the rest were yellowed and crooked. "I'll be deaf and blind before they bury me, if I'm lucky," he joked, and I heard the resignation he tried to mask with laughter.

But Eoin showed me a rough sort of kindness, and I did what I could to ease his burden. I cleaned and polished, taking precautions with his few iron and silver things, and kept his fire going. On his orders, I avoided the village girls, even the plump young woman who flashed come-hither looks at me during Mass. Eoin didn't need to tell me to avoid the village boys; a quick mental scan of the Sunday crowd had made it clear to me that such advances wouldn't be welcomed. And so I labored on in unplanned celibacy, wondering to myself what sort of deity would demand that life of his faithful.

I had been surprised at first when Mother didn't trouble herself with bringing me back to Faerie. True, she had other matters to address and children she liked better than me, but surely, I reasoned, she would miss me eventually. Christmas came and went with no sign of her, however, and then Easter and the summer warmth, and I ceased worrying about the matter. I still hated her for what she had done to Étaín, but with time and thought, my rage had cooled from suicidal to merely simmering. Simply put, I couldn't beat her, and so I turned my energy to Eoin's garden and tried to forget her. And aside from the occasional birth, death, storm, or escaped horse, each day rolled on like the one before in pleasant monotony.

The best things always end too soon, however,

and this end came with a pounding on the door in the middle of the night.

I rose first from my bed by the hearth—even at midsummer, I appreciated the warmth—and, wrapping my hand in my sleeve for protection, drew back the bolt. A young man stood outside, waiting a few feet away from a tethered horse, which nervously stamped as soon as I appeared in the doorway. "What's wrong?" I asked, trying to discern the time from the position of the setting moon.

His face was drawn, and he tripped over his tongue in his rush to get the words out. "Something's attacking my lady, something invisible. Could Father—"

Eoin shuffled up beside me and held his candle aloft. "Niall? What troubles you, my son?"

The man cast his glance back at the horse, obviously eager to be off. "It's my lady, Father—she's under attack by something unseen—"

That was enough for the priest. "I'll gather my things and join you shortly," he interrupted, and pushed me toward the door. "Coileán will accompany you now."

I turned back to Eoin, wide-eyed. "*Me?*"

"Get the others away from her," he muttered. "If she's under attack by the Evil One, they're all in danger."

I nodded and followed Niall toward his gelding. "He's not usually like this," he said, puzzled by the horse's fear.

"Let me try something," I offered, then grabbed the leather reins and pulled the horse's face level with mine. I'd had ample opportunity to practice the enchantment that forced the beasts into submission, but it grew no easier, and this horse in particular wanted to murder me. Still, even he faltered after a moment, and I swung up onto his bare back behind the servant. "Just a trick I learned to calm them," I lied, anticipating the question. Niall was too worried to press me further, and we rode off toward the small stone tower near the shore where the lordling had brought his young lady wife, a particularly beautiful redhead named Ita. The girl couldn't be more than sixteen, at least half her husband's age, but she carried herself well, smiled demurely, and always had a kind word for Eoin. I couldn't imagine what the trouble was.

We rode up to the gate, and I slid off the horse and headed inside, cringing as the freed beast sprinted for the fields with Niall still clinging to his back. A servant half dragged me to the bedchamber, which rang with muffled cries even through the stone walls and heavy wooden door. As her terrified husband and household watched from the safety of the hall, I cursed under my breath, pushed up my sleeves, and let the servant fling the door open so I could face the alleged demon head-on.

What I saw in the firelit bedchamber threw me for an instant. The room was a disaster, strewn with bits of clothing and items evidently tossed from the dressing table. Ita herself was pinned to the bed by an unseen force, which held her arms above her head and spread her legs wide. Her nightgown was torn and hiked up to her hips, and she sobbed and begged her assailant to stop.

The room stank of magic, and when I applied it properly, I found the source.

"Get off her!" I shouted in Fae, throwing myself at the bed.

My older half brother, who was still invisible to the mortals around us, fell to the floor with the force of my blow. He rose slowly, clutching his head where it had struck the wooden bed, and glared at me. *"Coileán?"*

"Áedán," I growled. "Leave her be."

His forehead wrinkled. "You weren't using her—"

"She's not to be used!" I slid over the bed as Ita curled against the headboard, sobbing, and stood between them. "You can't just . . . just *rape* her!"

"Why not?" he asked, perplexed and annoyed at the interruption, and clutched at his trousers. "What does it matter to you?"

"It just does," I said, stepping toward him. "Go home."

He sighed, then tossed me into the wall with a burst of energy. "I'm not finished yet, stupid," he replied, and began to crawl back onto Ita, who shrieked when his fingers grabbed her ankles.

I picked myself up and closed my eyes until the room ceased spinning, then looked about for a weapon.

The girl's cries crescendoed, and distantly, I heard her plead with me for help.

And then I saw the lordling's dagger on the dressing table.

Wrapping my hand in my sleeve, I pulled the steel hilt free of its ornate leather sheath. The blade caught the firelight, reflecting red flashes into my eyes, and I seized the opening.

Before Áedán knew what hit him, I leapt onto the bed, flipped him onto his back, and plunged the dagger into his throat. He gasped and gurgled, staring at me in shock, and I pulled the blade free. "I told you to leave her alone," I said, waiting for the healing to begin.

I was still waiting five minutes later when Eoin arrived and closed the door behind him. "What happened here?" he asked, bending over Áedán's now visible body.

Ita's husband had carried her off some moments before, but I had barely noticed her leave. I stood by the bed, the dripping dagger in my hand. "It wasn't supposed to kill him," I mumbled, staring at the corpse. "Just hurt him. It . . . he should have healed . . ."

Eoin pried the dagger from my fist and peered at his prize. "Steel," he said softly. "You know how long it takes you, son." He put the blade on the bed and gently pulled me away. "What happened?"

"He raped her. Ita. I . . . he hid himself, but I . . . I saw . . ."

At that moment, the touch of Eoin's hand on my shoulder was the only thing tethering me to reality. "You know him?" he asked.

I nodded. "Áedán. My brother."

The priest sighed and tightened his grip on me. "Be strong, Coileán. I'll take care of this," he murmured, and led me out of the room, past the staring throng.

They burned Áedán's body that night and scattered the ashes on the sea. The next morning, Niall brought me the bloody dagger. "My lord wanted you to have it," he explained. "He sends his thanks."

I carefully took it from him, and Eoin moved between us so Niall wouldn't see my reaction. "And your lady?" he asked.

"Resting," the servant replied, then hesitated before asking, "Father . . . why would a demon take such a . . . a form?"

Eoin covered the young man's hands with his own and stared into his eyes. "Never underestimate the Evil One, my son. Not for a moment."

When the door closed, he turned back to find me with my bare hand wrapped around the hilt, my teeth gritted against the pain, my flesh smoking.

I bore those deep scars for many years. In the right light, I can still see them.

Ita returned to her husband's bed, but it was obvious that the first son she bore him wasn't his. The baby was beautiful, fat and red-cheeked and topped with his mother's red hair, but his eyes were Titania's in a smaller face, dark against his parents' blue. Though unaware of his father's name, they called him Áed. The villagers whispered about the demon child, but Eoin chided them, baptized the boy, and then quietly asked me what was to be done with him.

"He's half fae," I told Eoin. "Like me. Áedán was full-blooded."

Eoin's brows knit in thought. "So, the boy will be like you in . . . *all* respects?"

"Probably. And he's my nephew, after all . . . I should look after him, shouldn't I?"

"That would be wise," he said, but lowered his voice. "Coileán, for his sake—"

"I know, I know," I interrupted. "I won't tell him the truth. Not now."

Eoin frowned. "Not *ever*. The boy's future depends upon him carrying his father's name."

I pointed to my ever youthful face. "He's going to know something's wrong eventually," I reminded him, and the priest slowly shook his head.

Ita's husband may have been nothing more than an ignorant Norman, but she was a local girl, well versed in the land's lore. More important, she was clever beyond her years, and so I wasn't surprised when I realized that she knew there was something odd about me. I *was* initially surprised that she kept the matter quiet, but then there was the matter of her baby.

When Áed was a few months old, Ita came to me in the middle of the night with him bundled against her chest. "Strange things happen around him," she whispered in the stillness of the empty church. "Objects move. Things appear, disappear. I . . . I don't know what to do," she said, rocking the sleeping child. "Please, Brother, is there anything . . ."

I tried to concoct a reassuring lie, but something told me the girl was strong enough for a form of the truth. "Strange things will always happen around him," I murmured, stroking his fine hair as he slept in her arms. "He can't help it right now. When he's older, when he . . . well, when he understands what he's doing," I said, struggling for just enough of an explanation, "be kind with him, but be firm. And if that fails, bring him to me, and I . . . I'll see what I can do."

She nodded in the darkness. "Is he a danger to us?"

"Yes," I admitted, "but he'll be less so if he knows you love him."

"I do," she softly replied, glancing down at his face, then met my eyes. "Brother Coileán," she began, but hesitated.

I could hear the unspoken thought: *The thing that did this to me, the thing that fathered my Áed—you knew it, didn't you? How? What was it? And what are you?*

I shook my head. "You don't want to ask me those things."

Ita nodded again, resigned. "If something should go wrong . . . will you promise to take care of my son?"

I did, and she slipped back into the night, carrying her uncanny child with her.

As the years passed, I took it upon myself to look after the boy. When he reached the age of four, Ita sent him to Eoin once a week under the guise of improving his religious education. In truth, the priest passed him to me, and I tried to stress to him the importance of keeping his talents secret. Poor Áed was young and impulsive, but he meant well, and he dearly loved his parents and his baby brother. Still, I found myself explaining to him that he shouldn't make the unsavory parts of his dinner vanish, that toys shouldn't move of their own accord, and that even though his mother missed the summer flowers, the climbing roses weren't meant to bloom in the snow.

Sligo burned, the skirmishes came and went, and Áed continued his weekly visits. "You're very special," I told him one day when he was a solemn nine-year-old, his baby face beginning to sharpen into contours I recognized all too well. His mother had caught him eating fresh apples long out of season. "Not everyone will think that's a good thing. You must be cautious."

He sat beside me on the stone altar steps that morning with his chin in his palms, frowning at the distant door, and I studied him in silence for a moment. "What's troubling you, Áed?"

When he faced me, his eyes threatened to brim over. "I heard the cook talking yesterday when she didn't know I was there. She said I wasn't my father's son."

I kept my face still. "Is that so?"

Áed nodded miserably. "And I looked later, like you told me, and the other servants think so, too. And . . ." He sniffed, fighting back tears. "I didn't want to ask Father, but . . . but I . . ."

I glanced away, giving him his privacy while he wiped his face dry, and wished for his sake that he'd been born with wisdom enough to override his curiosity. "Áed," I said quietly when the worst of the sniffing had subsided, "if I tell you a secret, will you swear to me that you'll never repeat it?"

"I swear," he mumbled, watching me with red eyes.

I took a moment to choose my words, then murmured, "Your father—your true father—did a very bad thing to your mother. You were born from that. Do you understand?" He nodded, though his lip quivered. "That doesn't make *you* bad," I continued, lifting his chin. "But you should know that your father was . . . special, and that's why you are, too."

"Do you know him?" he whispered.

"I did."

Áed's brow began to wrinkle. "He's dead, then?"

"Yes," I replied after a moment's pause, trying not to upset the boy. "He was hurting your mother. I tried to help her." I released him and waited for the inevitable next question, but then I felt the faint sensation of Áed clumsily searching my thoughts for the answer. His eyes widened, and I looked away. "I didn't mean to kill him," I said. "But in truth, Áed, the man you call your father is a far better father than Áedán would ever have been."

"Áedán," he mumbled, and my gut wrenched.

"He was my brother," I said, and Áed looked up in surprise. "I promised your mother I'd keep you safe, and I will. But Áed," I added, reaching over to muss his hair, "for the love of all that's holy, *think* before you act! Ripe apples, boy? With the fields just now blooming? What were you thinking?"

He flashed a mischievous half smile. "That I was hungry?"

I couldn't stay cross with Áed for long, but his father's patience was growing thin, and Ita knew it. She had given him three more sons and a daughter since Áed's birth, but the fact remained that he was her first child and the lordling's presumptive heir, despite his dubious origins. To make matters worse, Áed shared few of his father's interests. His brothers, like their father, were the martial type—budding swordsmen from a young age, trained on horseback from earliest childhood—but Áed had a queerly painful reaction to iron, and no horse in his father's stable would suffer him for more than a moment. He read and studied voraciously and had a pleasant enough voice, and his mother dropped hints that perhaps the boy should be trained for the priesthood. But her husband, who grew more concerned by the season for the well-being of his true sons, feared even then that Áed might find a way to return and steal an inheritance.

Ita told me all of this through tears. As she had done ten years before, she and Áed rode to me one night after the moon was down, but this time, the boy's arm was in a sling, and his face bore fading traces of bruises. "He tried to make it look like an accident," she said, holding her son close. "The old well in the courtyard . . . Áed caught himself halfway down, but if he had landed . . ."

I took the shaken boy from her and rested my hand on his broken arm, dulling his pain. "He will heal," I began, but Ita cut me off.

"Can you take him somewhere safe?" she begged. "Please? He's in danger if he stays here, and I can't . . . I *can't* . . . just until—"

Until my husband dies, she tried to say, but I saved her the effort. "Yes, of course."

By then, Eoin had joined us, and he watched Ita weep with a grave face. "What do we tell your husband?" he asked. "That the boy ran away?"

She wrung her hands. "If he thinks Áed is still alive, he'll come after him, I know it, he'll hunt him down . . ."

I gripped her cloaked shoulders to calm her hysterics. "I'll give you a body," I murmured, holding on to her until her breathing calmed. "Bury it. He'll never know the difference."

Her eyes were wide and wet, but she nodded her assent.

There was a rotten piece of timber in Eoin's field, the remains of a lightning-blasted stump of about Áed's weight. I threw a glamour over it, giving it the boy's face and form, and added deep gashes to his body. "He ran away, and a wild animal found him," I told Ita, presenting her with the double. She paled and backed away, but I said, "It's harmless, and no one will ever know the lie."

"I'll conduct the service on the morrow," Eoin assured her. "Your boy will be safe." He turned to me and asked, "You'll go with him, Coileán?"

"Yes, of course." Áed looked up at me with frightened eyes, and I patted his uninjured shoulder.

The old priest grunted. "Then I've sent you down south with a message, and I'll look for your return." He pointed to Ita's horse and added, "Time's wasting. Let's get it lashed on."

I did as he asked, holding the horse in check one last time, then waited while Ita embraced her son.

"Be good," she whispered, pushing his unruly hair from his eyes. "Do as Brother Coileán says. I love you, my Áed."

I waited until she had ridden out of sight before taking the boy in hand. "I'll come back when I can and see if it's safe," I told Eoin.

He nodded curtly and said, "Don't be away too long, now." With that, he squeezed my shoulder, then stepped into his house and closed the door.

I looked down at Áed and tried to smile. "We'll have to see your grandmother, I'm afraid," I explained, "but after that, there's a lovely little house by a lake. You'll be safe there. And here," I said, placing a hand on his temple until he looked up in bewilderment. "You'll need the tongue," I said in Fae. "Understand?" Áed nodded and smiled back at me, and with that, I opened a gate to Faerie in the middle of the road and pulled my nephew through.

I had aimed for an area slightly outside Mother's throne room, but to my dismay, we stepped out into the middle of the cavernous space—which had become a pink crystal construction in my absence, I noted—and found her holding court. She paused mid-sentence, rose, and marched off the rose-colored dais toward us. "*Coileán*," she snarled, and the hair on my arms stood on end with the force of the magic building around her.

I quickly pushed Áed behind my back. "Mother. It's been a time."

She stood on tiptoe and grabbed the front of my tunic, pulling my face to a level with her flashing dark eyes. "What have you done?" she murmured, her voice soft but frigid.

Resistance seemed like a bad idea at that moment. "I brought you your grandson," I replied, trying to keep my voice steady. "Áedán's boy. Áed," I said, gently pulling him forward, "this is your grandmother."

There was terror in his eyes, but he bowed clumsily and held his tongue.

Mother released me for the moment and turned her attention to the boy. "He has Áedán's look," she said, taking Áed's face in her delicate hands. "Not his hair, not at all, but the look . . . yes, I see it." She pulled back slightly and stooped to look into Áed's eyes. "Are you a good boy?" she asked.

He nodded after a moment's pause. "Yes, my lady," he whispered, "I . . . I try."

"Hmm. And this?" she inquired, touching his sling.

"I fell and broke my arm, my lady."

Mother smiled again, then looked back at me, all pretense gone. "I know you killed Áedán."

"I won't deny it," I told her, "but it was an accident. He was raping the boy's mother, and I tried—"

She held up her hand to silence me. "Rape, you say?"

The room continued to hold its breath, watching our reunion play out. "He came at her invisibly and took her against her will," I replied. "She was frightened and in pain. I tried to stop him."

"You did, obviously." Mother smiled down at Áed again and stroked his hair. "So, Coileán, you think what Áedán did was . . . wrong?"

"Yes, Mother."

She weighed this for a moment, then patted Áed's cheek. "Well, it's said that sons are like their fathers, and we can't take the chance of displeasing you again, can we?"

She snapped, and little Áed fell lifeless at her feet.

Before I could lunge at her, Mother's guards were on me, and she took my chin in her hand. "Oh, Coileán," she sighed, "I have so much planned for you."

I should have known better than to return to Faerie. I should have grabbed Áed and fled with him to the ends of the earth, and we could have passed the years in relative peace. I should have known that Mother would know of Áedán's death and my hand in it, and that she wouldn't forgive me for killing a child she preferred. I should have anticipated that she had been planning my punishment for the best part of a decade.

For fifty years, I sat in a gray-walled room with only a skylight to let me mark the days. I could produce food and water, but the bind Mother placed around my prison kept me from escaping. I saw no one, spoke to no one, and heard nothing but my own thoughts and the voices of the dead. To stave off madness, I produced vellum, ink, and a quill, and I began to write down what I remembered of Eoin's precious book, over and over and over again.

When she finally released me from my hell, the piles of vellum reached the ceiling, and she incinerated them all with the flick of a finger. "Go where you will, I have no use for you," was all she said, and then I was left to my own devices.

I made my way back to the meadow of my youth, hoping to find solace in the familiar, but all I found was a fire-charred shell where my home had been. The lake was choked with weeds, the birds had vanished, and a cold wind blew through the high grass. I wrapped my cloak around me against the chill and surveyed the ruins of my childhood one last time, then changed my clothing and turned my back on my homeland.

Eoin's church remained, but I knew without asking that Eoin was long gone.

I wandered through the little village, which had grown larger in my absence, then made the hike to a new monastery a few miles away to seek information about the priest's end. My father's monastery, an old farmer told me through suspicious eyes, had burned years ago.

The abbot, old, bald, and rust-bearded, welcomed

me into his cell and listened to the story I invented about living in the village as a boy and coming home for the first time in years. He nodded along, and when I ceased talking, he smiled and said, "Father Eoin died when *I* was a boy, my son. You would never have known him." One thin eyebrow rose fractionally. "Unless, that is, you're the man who took my brother away."

I kept my expression neutral. "Your brother?"

"My eldest brother, Áed," the abbot replied, and I traced Ita's features in his lined face. "I was five when we buried him," he said quietly, "but Mother told us the truth when Father died. Are you the man?"

I nodded silently, seeing Áed's open, unseeing eyes.

The abbot's face creased into a warm smile. "And my brother, how does he fare abroad?"

"He fares well," I heard myself say in a passing impression of the truth. "He fares well, and he sends his love."

The lie was, I decided, a kindness.

The abbot—Kevin was his name—was gracious enough to show me to a cell for the night. The room was drafty, and the bedding stank, but after my imprisonment, hearing voices in the corridor and rats in the walls was heavenly. "If you need help, we might be in need of an assistant," the abbot offered. "We've produced several beautiful Bibles—do you write, by chance?"

I thanked him and told him I would consider the matter, then settled down to sleep.

For three months, I shared the brothers' food, ground their inks, and sharpened their quills. I prepared vellum—in truth, I'd take a hide over a horse any day—and tended the garden, and I sat quietly in the back of their chapel at prayers, contemplating the candlelight and remembering Eoin's voice as it rose and fell when he read. Eventually, I was given some practice pages and instructed to copy, and when the brothers were satisfied with my hand, I joined them at their painstaking labor, copying thick books one cramped letter at a time. The work was largely mindless, but I craved companionship after so many years of solitude.

Half a year passed before the bishop sent a messenger requesting my presence. "His Grace wishes to meet you outside the town tonight," the abbot told me, frowning as he rolled the note in his hands. "He didn't state the cause, but he knew your name."

I didn't like the summons, but one did not simply ignore a bishop, and so I found myself standing in a field east of Sligo that night, watching warily as a man in a dark hooded robe walked up the path to join me.

"Your Grace?" I asked when he drew within hailing distance, puzzled at his appearance. I had anticipated more ornate apparel befitting his station, but the man I presumed to be the bishop had dressed like the poorest monk.

He paused a few feet away from me and pushed back his hood, revealing a well-lined face in the moonlight. I could make out pale, bushy eyebrows and a fat nose, but his eyes were deep pits of shadow, and his voice was unfamiliar. "Are you the one called Coileán?" he asked.

"I am."

"Of the king's court or the queen's?"

I froze, considering my options, then settled for the truth. "The queen's, though she and I aren't speaking for the foreseeable future. How did you know—" I began, but before I could finish the thought, the old bishop pulled a long stick from within his sleeve and pointed it at my face.

"Die, devil," he whispered to the night, and I smelled the unmistakable odor of magic.

I dodged the lightning that exploded from the stick, then ducked and appeared behind him. Wrapping my arm around his throat, I pulled the bishop to the ground and set fire to the stick in his hand, which fell into the wet grass and began to smolder. "Who are you?" I hissed, tightening my chokehold. "What do you want? Did she send you?"

"Arcanum," he gasped. "To protect—"

I saw his hand reaching for a backup stick in his other sleeve, and I snapped his neck before he could pull it free. When he was dead, I burned his body and let the wind take the leavings, and then I made my way back to my cell.

The abbot must have seen my face the next morning, as he was wise enough not to ask.

About a week later, I was heading into the garden when I heard a weak cry for help. Rounding the corner of the barn, I found a wizened old man huddled against the stone, dew soaked and shaking. "What's wrong?" I asked, crouching beside him. "Are you hurt? Wait here, I'll get the abbot . . ."

The man feebly pulled on my robe until I ceased my attempt to rise. "She sent me away," he croaked, panting as if exhausted by the declaration. "Told me to . . ."—he gasped, straining for air—"to seek Coileán for help. Please . . . please, I don't want to die . . ."

I took the changeling's ancient face in my hands and smiled sadly. "You don't want to live like this," I murmured, and stopped his heart.

The next morning, four of the bishop's associates arrived, reporting him missing and seeking his last known whereabouts. They asked the abbot if they might speak with me.

I smelled the faint odor of their hidden wands, calculated the odds, and slipped out the back of the chapel.

For the next three centuries, I ran from wizards and changelings alike, but somehow, they continued to catch up with me. Some nights, I see their faces when I close my eyes, the ones I killed in self-preservation and the ones I killed in mercy.

Sometimes, I forget which are which.

CHAPTER 18

Hearing nothing more from the police in Ireland, Joey and I caught a flight home in short order. Night had fallen, clear and chilly, when I finally drove past the weather-worn *Welcome to Rigby, Home of the Buccaneers!* sign and shook Joey awake. By the time he'd cleared the sleep from his eyes and patted his hair flat, I was pulling in front of my place—only to see a line of unfamiliar sports cars parked in the street. Without slowing, I rounded the corner, then turned onto the street behind Mrs. Cooper's building and parked at the back of her shop.

"Were you expecting company?" Joey asked as the car ticked through its cooldown.

"No." I opened the door and stepped out onto the cracked driveway, listening for clues. The night was silent but for the sea, however, and I pointed to Mrs.

Cooper's fire escape. "She might have seen something," I whispered to Joey. "Let's go."

I led the way up the staircase, weaving around the haphazardly scattered pots of daffodils that would surely have been Mrs. Cooper's death in the event of an actual fire, and rapped on her back door. A moment later, her silhouette shuffled into view through the lace curtains, and she drew back the bolt. "Oh, Mr. Leffee, *there* you are!" she whispered, stepping aside and beckoning me into her laundry room. "I was so worried, dear—there are *hoodlums* in your apartment, did you know that? Oh, hello, Father," she added, catching sight of Joey, but had the grace not to mention his black eye. "Come in, come in, close the door."

I picked my way past her line-drying undergarments and headed for the front windows. "What's been going on, Mrs. Cooper?" I asked, scanning the windowsill for her binoculars. "Father Joseph and I were out of town on business. We just got back—"

"*They* got here last night," she said, pulling the binoculars from her pink housecoat's pocket. "I hadn't seen your car for a few days, but I knew you had company . . ."

"A friend and my brother," I muttered, taking the binoculars from her and drawing back a corner of the curtain.

She clasped her hands together, momentarily distracted from our surveillance. "You didn't tell me you had a brother!"

"They're not close," Joey offered, holding the curtain so I could focus on spying. "What have you seen, ma'am?"

"Well, first of all, they don't close the blinds properly," she replied. I could practically hear her lips tightening in disapproval. "And I was only checking because I was worried about you, mind."

"Of course," I mumbled, looking around my living room. I could make out two of Robin's men in front of the television—I'd run into them before, a pair of nuisances lately based out of Los Angeles—and spotted what appeared to be a trussed bundle on the couch.

"There's a young lady over there," Mrs. Cooper continued, joining me at the window. "Dark hair, quite short, but I don't think we've been introduced . . ."

I heard the hopeful query in her tone. "Toula. Friend of mine."

"Ah. Well, I almost called the police a dozen times since last night—they've got her tied up with clothesline in there!"

Shit. I saw the bundle squirm and recognized Toula's spikes, and I ground my teeth.

"You haven't called them yet?" Joey pressed.

Mrs. Cooper hesitated. "Well, um . . . you see, Father, before Mr. Leffee moved in . . . there was this young couple living over that shop, and I . . . uh . . . *saw* something one night, and I called the police, and as it turned out, it was all a terrible misunderstanding . . ."

"This isn't that kind of bondage," I broke in, saving

her the embarrassment of further description. "How many have you seen in total?"

"Besides the young lady?" She took the binoculars from me and had a peek, then said, "Those two men, a pair of ladies, and another two men. Seven all told, then."

"All about my age?" I asked, taking the binoculars back.

"From what I can tell. I haven't seen any up close outside the building—well, no, I take that back, I saw one of the men come out when the others drove up. Their engines were so *loud*! My windows started rattling like you wouldn't believe—"

"The man who came out, what did he look like?" I asked, cutting her off.

"Him? Maybe a little taller than you, a bit stockier, messy red hair . . ."

"Robin," Joey muttered. "Damn it."

Mrs. Cooper gave him a sharp look but held her tongue. "Is that your brother?" she asked me.

"Half brother, actually," I replied, putting the binoculars back on the windowsill. "And I need to have a little talk with him."

Joey gripped my arm as I turned from the window. "Come on, man, don't do something stupid. They've got you outnumbered. Let's just call the cops and let them—"

"This is personal," I said, brushing him off. "They're in *my* house."

"And it's still six on two," he insisted. "You don't know what sort of weapons they might have. They must have threatened Toula with *something*. She doesn't strike me as a pushover, and if she couldn't get to"—he lowered his voice—"you know, the *doohickey . . .*"

"It's in my fire safe," I replied. "Hidden in the master closet." I stared at Mrs. Cooper's chintz-covered recliner for a moment, mulling over my options, then nodded. "Okay, here's the plan. Joey, go out to the car and get our bags. You stay here. Mrs. Cooper, will you do me a favor?"

"Of course, dear," she said, putting the curtains back to rights.

"Thank you. I've got an antique that I need to hide for a bit while I take care of this mess," I said, cocking my head toward the window. "Just a little thing. Could you keep it here for me?"

"Yes, certainly." She peered at me through her bifocals. "This isn't anything illegal, is it?"

I shook my head. "No. A gift from my father, actually." I waited until the door closed behind Joey, then took her hands and led her to the love seat. "Mrs. Cooper, there's a lot going on right now that isn't safe to talk about, but I need you to trust me. Can you do that?" Her head bobbed, and I continued, "Those people in my house aren't good people. I'm going to try to get them out of there, but it might take a while. If you don't hear from me by morning, please call the police. Deal?"

She tightened her grip on my gloves. "I'd feel so much better if you'd let me call them now, Mr. Leffee."

"I know, and I'm sorry, but this is one of those things I can't talk about." The door slammed open and shut again, and Joey marched into the sitting room with our gear. "All right, Father," I said, standing to reclaim my bag, "you stay here and keep Mrs. Cooper safe. *No buts*," I insisted, seeing his mouth open. I took the sphere from my bag and handed it to my neighbor. "That's my little antique. Thank you. Father, *sit down*, and you two call the police if I don't report back by morning."

Joey scowled, then muttered, "Can I speak with you for a minute?" Before I could answer, he dragged me into the laundry room, then whispered, "You've lost it, Colin. The odds were bad enough when I was going with you, but six on one? Are you out of your mind?"

"I've got to try—"

"*Bullshit*. You're not Superman, you're not taking the one functional magical object in your possession with you, and if those guys are anything like their buddies in Ireland, you're not going to make much headway by yourself. Call the damn cops."

I took a deep breath to keep my voice level. "Joey, if I call the cops and they arrest everyone in my apartment, we're screwed. Toula's going to be interviewed, Robin's going to be in a holding cell, and then we're going to have to find *two* faeries instead of just one. I don't like this plan, but I've got to try *something.*"

He must have seen the desperation in my eyes because he took a step back. "Then let me come with you, at least. My sword's in the garage. If you can distract them, I can sneak in and get it . . ."

"Your job is to keep the doohickey safe," I told him, and gave his shoulder a squeeze. "Stay here and keep Mrs. Cooper company. If she offers you tuna salad, just say no."

Before he could protest again, I shouldered my bag and stepped out into the night. As I closed the door, I heard her ask, "Father, *what* is going on?" but I trusted that Joey had slept enough on the journey to come up with a convincing lie.

I drove my car back around the block and parked in the alley, opting not to fool with the garage. Luggage in tow, I walked into my shop—unsurprisingly, Robin had neglected to lock up—and marched upstairs to my apartment. I could hear voices rising on the other side of the door as I climbed the steps, and as I approached the top, the door was thrown open by a familiar blond. "Welcome home, Ironhand," he said with a smirk, then grabbed my bag and pulled me into the living room.

I pushed him off and looked around, doing a quick body count. There was Toula, one ball gag away from a porn movie, looking at me like I'd taken leave of my senses, and there was my welcoming committee, the blond—sporting a fauxhawk, I noted with distaste—and his buddy, a black-haired faerie I'd last tangled with in Phoenix. Jiren was short by fae standards, maybe only five and a half feet tall, but he made up for it in muscle. I hoped he wouldn't break my nose.

Before I could decide whether to go for Toula or the boys first, Robin sauntered down the hall with the rest of his entourage. "Coileán!" he said, spreading his hands. "You're back! Where's the kid?"

"School starts tomorrow," I told him, resisting the urge to drop into a fighting crouch. "And your friends messed up his face pretty badly. I can't say I blame him for wanting out."

Robin grinned. "Smarter than I thought. Where's the sphere?"

"I shipped it," I lied. "Not here. You didn't think I actually trusted you, did you?"

His smile soured. "That wasn't smart at all."

"Well, considering the company you kept in my absence, I don't know if I can agree with you on that." I pointed to the couch. "Why's the wizard tied up?"

"Security," he shrugged, then glanced at his posse. "Have you met everyone?" he asked, and pointed to them in turn. "Seena and Delilah"—he indicated the blondes to his right—"I think you know Jiren and Aro, and this," he concluded, clapping a redheaded teen on the shoulder, "is my great-great-add-a-few-grandson, Tony. Tony, say hi to your uncle."

The kid barely lifted his chin. "'Sup?"

"Charmed." I sighed. "Why are they here?"

Robin stepped away from the boy and wrapped his arm around my tight shoulders. "We need to have a little talk. Let's go into the bedroom for a minute and sort some things out, yeah?" He nodded to the others, and they clustered in the living room, keeping silent Toula company as the television flashed a weather report.

Robin led me back into my room, then closed the door and motioned for me to keep quiet. "I didn't do it," he whispered. "They just showed up last night, and one thing sort of led to another."

I scowled. "Get them out of here. We've got work to do."

"See, that's the issue," he replied, rubbing the back of his neck. "I can't just tell them to go—I mean, if they knew I was working *with* you . . . you see the problem?"

I did—I had beaten all of them but young Tony at some point in the last century—but Robin's shit-eating grin was doing nothing to help matters. "You outrank them, moron. Tell them you're working with me at your father's direction and under protest, and that should let you save face."

"Maybe, maybe not," he shrugged. "But I was thinking, you know, since they're here now—why don't I call the shots for a while? I'll make sure they don't hurt you and the witch, we'll find the other devices—"

"Right, because Toula looks so pleased with the situation as it stands," I snapped. "She wants to go to the Arcanum. They're going to have a tough enough time dealing with me, especially if you're tagging along. And now *you* want to try to negotiate with Greg?"

"Who?"

"Exactly. At least the grand magus knows and tolerates me."

"There's no reason we *have* to go that route," he began, but before I could counter, we heard a loud rapping at the kitchen door.

A moment later, Tony cracked the bedroom door open and mumbled, "Someone's out there, my lord. Want us to handle it?"

"Who is it?" Robin asked.

The kid's slumped shoulders rose and fell. "Some old broad."

Robin glanced at me, then at the ceiling. "Moon and stars, I don't need this right now. Coileán, go get rid of your girlfriend and I'll let her live, okay?"

"That's so very generous of you," I muttered, and pushed past the boy.

I found the pack huddled around my dinette, casting suspicious glances at the frosted panes of my kitchen door. "Back off and let me handle this," I growled, then unlatched the door to find Mrs. Cooper standing on the landing in a bulky pink sweater and coordinating stretch pants, holding a steel teakettle.

"Oh, Mr. Leffee, I'm *so* sorry to bother you," she said, all grandmotherly sweetness, "but a few of my girlfriends are coming over tonight for tea, and my water tastes odd right now—you remember the fish in the main last year, don't you?—and I was wondering if you'd be so kind as to let me fill up."

I stared at her pale gray eyes through her glasses, trying in vain to communicate that now had not suddenly become a good time.

She winked.

"Uh . . . sure, help yourself," I said, stepping aside to clear a path to the kitchen sink. "I think my water's still good."

"Bless you," she replied, shuffling past me, then looked up and noticed the small crowd watching her in silence. "Oh, I didn't know you had company! I am *so* sorry, dear, I'll just—"

"No, no, you go right ahead," I said, ushering her to the sink. "Do you need anything else? Sugar, maybe? I've got that fancy colored stuff you like . . ."

She left the kettle under the spigot and followed me to the pantry closet, then made a show of examining my half-empty shelves. "Where did I put it?" I said, then bent closer to her ear and muttered, "Get out of here, Eunice. Whatever you're thinking, it's not a good idea."

"That's all right, dear," she said, "I can do without it. I've got petit fours in the fridge, anyway." She retrieved her kettle and turned off the tap, then smiled at Robin's minions. "Hello, there. Are you Colin's friends?"

They looked at each other uneasily, and I stepped to her side. "My brother's friends, actually," I said, pointing to Robin as he walked into the room. "Mrs. Cooper, this is Robin."

"So nice to make your acquaintance," she said, beaming as she extended her free hand toward him. He took it and smiled weakly, but before he could release her, she swung up and slammed the teakettle into his face.

Robin howled and staggered back, holding his burned cheek, and Mrs. Cooper wheeled on the others. "Who wants a piece of this?" she yelled, holding the kettle at the ready. "Come on, you little hoodlums, who wants to try me?"

I could only gape as she advanced on the crowd, moving with surprising speed for her age, and began whipping the kettle around like an oversized pocketbook. Robin's people shrieked at her blows, but I saw stocky Jiren rise and recover. "Mrs. Cooper, eight o'clock!" I cried, just as he grabbed her arm and wrenched her to the ground.

I yanked open my cutlery drawer and produced a ceramic knife. "Get away from her!" I bellowed, but before I could jump on him, the front door slammed open and a tall, thin figure stepped into the living room, maille gleaming, sword strapped in place, and Desert Eagle outstretched.

"Freeze, mother*fuckers*," Joey snapped, and fired a warning shot at the ceiling.

Robin's crew dropped to the ground, and Joey stomped over in a shower of plaster. "All right, anyone who doesn't want a new piercing should get the hell out of here. Hey!" he yelled, seeing Jiren on top of Mrs. Cooper, "get off her! That's right, back away, you son of a bitch." He waited until Jiren had slid against the wall before crouching and offering Mrs. Cooper his hand. "Did he hurt you?"

"Nothing aspirin won't cure, dear," she replied, letting him pull her to her feet.

Joey beckoned me over with a twitch of his head. "Want the Mag or the blade?"

"I'll take the gun," I replied, and held it on the cowering crowd as Joey unsheathed his weapon. "Now, you heard the nice man," I said, pointing the barrel at each in turn. "You've got one minute to get the hell off of my property before I let Galahad use you as practice dummies. He's pretty good, I hear."

"The fucking *best*," he spat. Mrs. Cooper cleared her throat in disapproval, and he mumbled a quick apology.

"Robin," I continued, cutting my eyes in his direction, "why don't you tell your friends to be on their way?"

"Go," he croaked, suddenly finding Joey's sword at his throat by way of encouragement. "I'll handle this. *Go!*" he screamed as the blade edged closer.

The others needed no further encouragement to scramble for the open door. A few seconds later, I heard the last of their footsteps run out of my shop, and then a chorus of engines and squealing tires pierced the night.

I lowered the handgun and exhaled. "Robin, you stupid bastard," I muttered, slamming the door. "Joey, cut Toula free. I've got the situation under control here."

"First time all night," he replied with a snort, but headed for the living room to free the wizard.

I took a closer look at the gun in my hand, then at Mrs. Cooper, who stood by with her kettle ready. "Is this yours?"

She nodded. "Mr. Cooper wanted me to be safe."

"Mr. Cooper bought you a .44 Magnum?"

"He thought it looked impressive," she explained, and put the kettle on the table. "I hate the recoil on that thing. My real gun's a Colt .22."

"This one seems real enough to me," I replied, glancing at the blackened hole in my ceiling, and handed the gun back to her. "I, uh . . . I don't know what Joey told you . . ."

"The quick-and-dirty version," she said, giving me a little smile. "That poor girl I found is *yours*?"

I nodded. "Surprise, huh?"

"Messy business," she said, and headed around the table as Joey led Toula into the room. "I'm so sorry, I should have called the police hours ago . . ."

"It's fine, I'm here," she said, rubbing her chafed wrists. "Uh . . . hi. Thank you."

"Don't mention it, dear." She glanced down at Robin, who still crouched against the hallway wall, watching us for signs of attack. "So, what are you going to do with him?"

Toula glowered as she cracked her fingers. "I'm thinking castration with a rusty knife."

"Will ceramic do?" I asked, pulling my improvised weapon from the back of my pants.

She rolled her eyes. "It's not the same if it's not good and *dull*. Useless faeries," she muttered, and headed for the bathroom.

"Relax," I said, kicking Robin's foot, "no one's getting castrated until we get the gate open." He blinked, and I added, "You try anything this stupid again, and I'll let Joey shoot your balls off, got it?"

"Ooh, can I use the Mag?" Joey asked, sheathing his sword.

"Now, boys," Mrs. Cooper interrupted, "isn't this all a little drastic?"

I gently took her by the shoulders. "Drastic is sometimes the only smart option in these sorts of cases. Did Joey tell you what you were dealing with?"

"I did," he confirmed as Mrs. Cooper nodded.

"You *believed* him?" I asked her.

"Well, he's a priest, isn't he?" she replied.

"Mostly." I gave Joey a look, and he shrugged.

"Didn't see the point in getting creative tonight," he explained. "Since you were off playing Rambo and all."

"No, you just let a little old lady attack six faeries with a teakettle."

Mrs. Cooper pointedly cleared her throat, and I said, "I know, 'old' is a relative term."

"*He's* ancient," Joey offered.

"Keep it up," I muttered, "and you're never going to see old age, period." I released Mrs. Cooper and folded my arms. "Got to say I'm impressed with your moves."

Her little smile returned. "Played my share of tennis in my day, dear, and I carry these kettles around often enough—I've got at least a little muscle left." She hefted her kettle again and frowned at a new dent in the side.

"I'll get you a replacement."

"Oh, don't go to any trouble, it was a Target special." She put it down and studied my face for a long moment, then said, "You know, I lived on books of myths and legends as a child."

"Did you?"

"Yes." Her lips pursed. "You're not what I expected, Mr. Leffee."

"I'm . . . probably not the most impressive example of the race," I replied, smiling apologetically.

"He's not," Robin offered, then yelped as Joey kicked him.

"Surely that's not priest-like behavior, young man," Mrs. Cooper clucked.

Joey's maille jingled as he shrugged. "Technically, ma'am, I'm still on vacation."

CHAPTER 19

Having run out of good ideas, we were left with little choice but to head for the Arcanum's headquarters and hope for the best. I'd have preferred to drive—being confined in an airplane, thousands of feet in the air, surrounded by metal, and hoping the engines don't get cranky has never been my idea of a good time—but alas, the Arcanum, in its wisdom, had set up shop in an abandoned missile silo in Montana. Time was precious, so as I griped about the many disadvantages of air travel, Joey made the arrangements and suggested that I suck it up.

Even with the threat of a nine-o'clock flight out of an airport two hours away the next morning, no one cared to sleep. While Robin hid in the bedroom and licked his wounds, Toula sat with Mrs. Cooper at the kitchen table, answering her questions over tea and slightly stale petit fours. As midnight came and bled into Monday, Mrs. Cooper began to lace her tea with gin, but I couldn't blame her. For a lady dealing with the sudden knowledge that her neighbor was a magically gifted octocentenarian with a long list of enemies, she was being perfectly pleasant.

When I went down to the shop to check on our resident Templar, I found Joey pacing in front of the plate-glass window with his sword drawn. Having recovered his gear from its storage place in my garage, he appeared to be in no hurry to relinquish it again. He covered a yawn with the back of his hand, and I pointed to the dusty pendulum clock ticking on the wall. "It's almost one, kid. Get some sleep."

"Nah," he replied, jingling as he leaned against the counter. "They might come back. Someone should keep an eye out, right?"

"And if they do, you'll what, skewer them?"

"If I have to."

I started to grip his shoulder, but reconsidered; Joey was still wearing his maille, and that much steel gave me pause, even with gloves on. "Listen to me," I said quietly. "Listen to *yourself*. I know this has been one hell of a week for you, but kid—try to remember who you are. Joseph Bolin, priest-in-training, not Sir Galahad, Slayer of the Unseelie."

His face twisted briefly into a half smile. "Am I?"

"Are you what?"

He met my eyes, but his expression was inscrutable. "Am I Joseph, masquerading as Galahad, or Galahad, masquerading as Joseph? Quite honestly, I don't know right now."

"That's an easy one . . ."

"You'd think," he muttered. "But you know, I'm not really certain anymore. I've been wrestling with this for a while . . ."

I gritted my teeth and grabbed his arm, hoping the leather would suffice for protection. "You've had one bad week, kid. Let's not be hasty."

"I'm not," he replied, shrugging me off. "I've always had doubts, right . . . concerns, questions. And I've been doing a lot of soul-searching over the last few years. I mean, you have to with this sort of calling." Joey paused and straightened his scabbard's strap as he stared out at the empty, night-dark sidewalk. "I thought working with Father was going to be what I needed," he continued softly, folding his arms. "Maybe it was, for a little while." He glanced at me over his shoulder. "But I have *never* felt more alive than I have this week, and . . . I don't know," he sighed, almost hugging himself. "I don't know what that means."

"It means you're coming down off an overdose of adrenaline, exacerbated by a lack of sleep. Go back to school, get a week or two of classes under your belt, and you'll be back to normal—"

"Will I?" he snapped. "And do I even *want* normal?"

"Trust me," I murmured, "it's better than the alternative."

"Is it?"

I would have given almost anything at that moment to see what was swirling behind his dark eyes. "I've had my nose pressed to the glass for a long time," I replied. "After a while, you get tired of looking in." I paused, trying to judge his mood, then said, "You need to go home. Not because I don't want you here—and I do, kid, you're great," I hastened to add, "but for your own sake. This business isn't . . . *good* for you, Joey."

He began to protest, but I silenced him with a raised hand. "Let me finish. This isn't just me trying to assuage my conscience about all the shit I've asked you to do. This is . . ." I struggled for the best explanation, then settled on, "If we want to find one of Mab's people, we may have to do some unsavory things. *Truly* unsavory. Toula would probably call it black magic."

Joey's forehead crinkled. "A locator spell's that bad?"

"No—it's where the spell will point that worries me." I stepped toward him and lowered my voice. "Rumor has it that Mab may have been camping over in the Gray Lands of late. If her court is there, then I may need to make the trip, and opening a gate to the Gray Lands . . ." I shook my head. "If it comes to that, I don't want you anywhere near me. Get it?"

His jaw tightened. "I can take care of myself."

"Not against some of the things that come out of there, you can't. Iron doesn't faze them, and they'll use that nice little necklace of yours as a toothpick."

Joey's hand went to the silver crucifix under his maille.

"And it's not just the Gray Lands I'm worried about," I continued. "Assume we get one of Mab's people to cooperate and find enough spheres to open the gate—you're just planning to stroll into Faerie?"

"I'll go armed—"

"Which will be useless if Mother electrocutes you from across the room." I closed my eyes and rubbed my forehead, trying to make Áed's face recede into my memory. "Joey . . . I can defend myself against magic to a point, but I'm not Mother's equal. Neither is Robin. Even if I tried to protect you, I couldn't promise that you'd walk out alive."

"You think she'll try to kill you?"

"Probably not, she prefers to make my life hell. But you're superfluous, and if you walk in dressed like *that*, you're going to be a superfluous annoyance, understand?"

Joey was silent for a long moment, and then he murmured, "She can really shoot lightning?"

"She doesn't need to."

"Shit." He sighed, but then he frowned and nodded to himself. "I'm still in, Colin."

"*Joseph*—"

"You can't even work the e-ticket consoles," he said with disdain. "If you're planning to go to Montana tomorrow—"

"Today, actually."

"Whatever. You need me."

"We have Toula to push the buttons, remember?" He crossed his arms and glared at me, and I threw up my hands. "You want to come along? Fine. But as soon as this gets ugly, I'm going to sic a pack of wizards on you for your own good, got it?"

He smirked in victory. "Didn't know you cared, man."

"Yeah, well," I said, turning toward the staircase back to my apartment, "I'm just trying to keep you alive."

"Likewise," he called after me.

I paused at the foot of the stairs, then glanced back at Joey. "Think you can build another of those nail guns?"

"Sure, but why? They're wizards, iron doesn't bother them."

"A nail to the chest is a nail to the chest," I said, heading upstairs.

By three, I had packed and finished the gin, Toula was asleep on the couch, and Joey had ended his self-imposed watch and shoved his armor and weapon into my largest spare suitcase. Robin was awake—I could smell the telltale smoke wafting from my bedroom—but only Mrs. Cooper and I remained in the kitchen, she with her endless tea and me with my thoughts. I had long given up on convincing her to return home that evening; she claimed she was worried about Toula after her ordeal, but the tight-lipped looks she gave the kitchen door pointed to a deeper fear, and I wasn't about to kick her out. She had brought up a badly dog-eared paperback romance from my bargain bin around two and sat across from me in companionable silence, reading as I brooded.

So lost was I in my thoughts that I jumped when her hand landed on my wrist. "You can't let yourself despair, dear," she murmured, flipping the book over on the table to save her spot.

"I'm not—"

"I know that place," she continued, overlooking my aborted protestation. "It's dark and it's lonely, and once you're in, you wander around for ages until you find your way out again."

Her eyes were soft but haunted.

"I almost killed myself when I lost Mr. Cooper," she said, her voice low and monotonic. "He was my only close family, you know—we never had any children, and my parents are long deceased. My only brother was dead, as was my only niece. He was my everything, and then he was gone."

She swirled the last dregs of her most recent mug of tea, then set it aside. "I didn't leave my apartment for three months after I buried him. Some of the girls at church came by to look in on me, and when that didn't work, Reverend Martin insisted on driving me to counseling until I opened the curtains again."

Her grip on my wrist tightened. "It was *despair*, and it almost killed me. And I see you heading in the same direction," she continued, cocking her head. "You've given up."

I shook my head. "You don't know my mother—"

"No, but I can hope. Maybe that's all I can do," she admitted, releasing me with a pat, "but someone needs to. Now, why don't you try to sleep?" she said, pointing to the empty patch on the rug beside Joey. "I don't like the thought of you driving after an all-nighter, dear. It's not safe, and you've had an awful lot to drink."

"So have you," I replied with a little grin, tapping the side of her mug.

"Oh, honey," she scoffed, "I've been spiking my tea for *years*. Go on, now, get some shut-eye."

There was no arguing with her logic, and I rose to retrieve a blanket from the hall closet. When I returned, she had already resumed reading with a fresh cup of tea beside her, and I shook my head as I passed. "Good night, Eunice. That one's on the house."

"I figured you wouldn't miss it," she replied without looking up. "Good night, Colin. I'll rally the troops at dawn."

CHAPTER 20

The snow I had feared we'd find in Billings proved to be nothing but my own catastrophizing, a few fifty-times-refrozen gray hillocks on the side of the highway, long since plowed out of the way and forgotten. The north wind nipped through my jacket, however, and I hurried across the parking lot to the red Yukon I had selected out of an abundance of caution. To me, the vehicle spoke more of over-quaffed soccer moms than of serious business, but the clerk promised four-wheel drive and new tires, and I decided that Joey could take the third-row bench and keep Robin in line as we made the trek into the wilderness.

If my brother had thoughts about the SUV, he kept them to himself, but then Robin had said virtually nothing to any of us that morning. I suspected that the burn stretching across half his face accounted for some of his unwillingness to speak, but a large part of his reticence was surely due to the threats Toula and Joey silently communicated with every glare. I could have told them that the vigilance was unnecessary— knowing Robin, I believed his explanation that the temporary takeover had been a decision born of a moment's impulse—but I held my tongue. Watching him squirm had given me something to do on the flight.

Even though I was reasonably comfortable that Robin wouldn't try anything requiring an air marshal, I still had to reassure Mrs. Cooper before she let us leave for the airport. "He's never really been a long-term thinker," I had confided as I escorted her and her kettle back across the street. "If something halfway promising pops up, he takes it, and damn the consequences. That's why we're in this mess right now—Mab dangled something shiny in front of him, and he didn't stop to ponder the ramifications."

She had still seemed uneasy when I left her, but she promised to keep an eye on my place until I returned. "If *they* come back," she told me, pocketing her binoculars, "I'll have the police out in a jiffy. Don't you worry about a thing here, dear."

"Just keep the kettle close," I said, and took my leave. I could feel her watching through her lace curtains as we drove out of Rigby.

Eight hours later, as we finished loading the Yukon,

I pulled my atlas out of my suitcase and flipped to the Montana spread. "Okay, we're here," I said, pointing to the city's dot as Toula looked on. "Now, what's the fastest way to the silo?"

"Head to Glasgow and veer north."

I frowned at the map. "So . . . 87 north, and then . . ."

She cleared her throat and held up her telephone, which displayed a list of directions. "Try to remember that GPS isn't the enemy," she said, elbowing me for good measure, then hopped into the shotgun seat.

As I closed my atlas and tried to hold on to my dignity, Joey walked up with his phone poised and ready. "Found a Home Depot on the way. Here, I've got the directions . . ."

"Talk to Toula," I muttered, and glanced at the cloudless sky. The spring sun was still weak that far north, and with the afternoon already upon us, I doubted we'd reach the Arcanum's hideout before nightfall.

Joey was in and out of the hardware store in twenty minutes, his arms loaded down with plastic bags, and he set to work in the backseat as Robin edged forward, distancing himself from stray metal shards. Toula landed on a station playing nothing but overprocessed pop, but I didn't have the fight in me to protest. The gates had been closed for eight days. Try as I did to keep Mrs. Cooper's warnings in focus, thoughts of Meggy's tortured corpse kept flashing across my mind. I could barely recall the details of the dream from which Mrs. Cooper had shaken me awake that morning, but from the drawn look on her face, I knew they couldn't have been good.

I desperately wanted to believe that Meggy and Olive weren't dead, but nothing about the situation inspired my confidence. And so I silently drove north to the sound of synthesizers and the clanking of metal tools, staring out at the still-brown grasslands as the sun made its slow descent out my window.

Nearly five hours later, long after Toula's phone ceased to be of navigational assistance along the back roads, I located the hamlet of Wright's Mill, pulled up in front of a split-rail fence, and surveyed the ramshackle trailer park on the other side. The circular drive's gravel glinted in the white light of the security lamps, though it didn't extend as far as any resident's driveway. Ringing the road, set back more or less into the weeds at odd intervals, were single wides in various states of disrepair, their paint peeling, their skirts mildewed and rotting away. A few sickly daffodils made a brave stand beside the nearest, growing up in the shadow of a plastic flamingo and what appeared to be an oversized ceramic squirrel. One resident had put a rusty pickup on cement blocks in his yard, while another had pinned a Confederate flag in his window. It glowed as it filtered the light from inside the trailer onto the scraggly grass, a warning to the unwary.

I suspected that the locals didn't ask too many questions of their neighbors.

"This is it?" Joey asked from the back seat. "*Seriously*? You've got the top wizards in the world, and this is the absolute best you can do?"

Toula swiveled in her seat. "Ever hear of a decoy, Galahad? The silo's underground—most of those trailers are covering air-exchange equipment." She rolled down the window and closed her eyes, then nodded. "Security's still strong, I feel it. Guys?"

"Yeah," Robin murmured, moving closer to the door. "The wards must still be operational."

The night breeze carried with it the unmistakably sharp odor of not-citronella, and I realized how badly I'd missed it. But the longer I smelled the active magic, the angrier I became. We were in a crisis, the Arcanum had obviously found a few of the spheres, and they were *wasting* them on wards? How long had they been running on battery power? More important, was there still enough in reserve to get us into Faerie? I gripped the steering wheel harder as I tried to wrestle my temper under control.

"We can get into the complex," Toula said, rolling the window back up. "The school bus sometimes turned around in there when I was living here. But to get underground, we're going to need permission." She pointed to the faux manager's office, a slightly nicer trailer at the far end of the circle. "Park there. I'll try to sweet-talk us downstairs."

I inched the SUV around the crunching drive, keeping an eye out for sentries, but the complex seemed abandoned. At Toula's direction, I parked in front of the weather-grayed *Sorry, No Vacancy* sign, then stepped out into the night and waited as my passengers disembarked. Robin came empty-handed, but Joey had slung his sword over his shoulder and slipped his new nail gun in its duct-tape holster.

"That's subtle," I remarked, grabbing my backpack.

Joey shrugged. "Hey, this place looks like it's home to mutant redneck cannibals. I'm not taking any chances."

"Suit yourself," I replied, noting the telltale bulge in the back of Toula's shirt from the wand stuffed into her jeans. "Right, then, where's the welcoming party?"

"Here," said a familiar baritone from the shack's porch, and I squinted as the building's lights suddenly flicked on. I spotted the grand magus standing on the steps in a red fleece jacket, his arms folded against the chill, and a small phalanx of armed wizards lurking behind him. He leaned against a rotting porch pillar and surveyed the scene. *"You're* a long way from home."

Toula stepped into the light and held up her empty hands. "We need to talk to you. I know how to break the spell, but I need juice to do it."

Greg's white eyebrows met above his glasses. "Do you, now, Ms. Pavli?"

A few of the guards began to mutter, having recognized Toula, but she kept her cool. "I studied the trap that set it off. It's a hybrid construction, and there's a lot of enchantment to work around, but there's a way to unlock it. Mind if we come in out of the cold?"

The nearest guard stepped forward, wand at the ready, and I snorted. "You can put the sticks away, kids," I said. "The only magic in this place is running the wards."

The guard still held his position, and Greg pulled a familiar golden sphere from his jacket pocket. "That's not quite accurate," he replied, "though I'd rather not use this. We've only got a few in reserve, and the one powering the wards isn't going to last another twenty-four hours."

"*Sir,*" the guard protested, but Greg shook his head and gestured toward me with the sphere.

"Lord Coileán wouldn't darken my door without good cause," he continued, "and the company he's keeping makes me believe that cause must be *excellent.*" He straightened and tucked his sphere away. "Well, this isn't getting it done. Have y'all eaten?"

"Doritos," Joey offered, moving into the light with his sword drawn.

Greg gave him a slow once-over, studied Robin's burns, then flicked his eyes back to mine. "Shit, old timer," he muttered, his accent deepening with every syllable, "you're traveling with all of *that*? What the hell happened?"

"**I**f I'm going to live like a rat," said Greg, locking the five of us into his well-stocked study, "I'm going to be a happy rat. Knock yourselves out," he offered, gesturing toward the mahogany bar. He bent to the mini-fridge in the wall and pulled out a bottle of water, then settled onto one of the two green leather sofas and crossed his legs. "I'll send over for dinner in a bit," he said as I poured a neat triple of Macallan. "No tricks. Now, what do you know, and what can we do to get the magic flowing again?"

I passed the bottle off to Robin, sat on the sofa facing Greg, and dropped my bag at my feet. "My thanks," I began, raising my glass in quick salute before downing half of its contents. "Toula knows the spell better than I do, naturally," I explained as she sat beside me with a G&T, "but my understanding is that all we need is one of us from each court and sufficient power to get the gates open again. That's why we're here."

"We've got the diary," Toula added. "Simon Magus's diary, you know?"

Greg's dark eyes widened. "Good Lord, where did you find—"

"My, um . . . well . . . she's kind of . . ." I began, and floundered.

Fortunately, Toula knew where I was heading. "I got Meg, his baby mama, into the dealing circuit. Didn't know about the baby-mama bit. She tracked it down for me."

"And now she's trapped in Faerie with the afore-mentioned baby," I cut in. "Who's actually sixteen—"

"And as it turns out, Meg's one of Oberon's kids," she interrupted, "so you see how that could be a slight problem, right?"

Greg turned to look at Robin, who remained at the bar with the bottle and a newly emptied highball glass. "What?" Robin muttered, pouring a refill. "Her court affiliation isn't my fault."

The grand magus looked back at us with confusion. "And . . . *he's* here because he's of Oberon's court?"

We hesitated. "Yes and no," I said after a moment. "I mean, yes, Robin's covering that court, but he—"

"I triggered the damn thing, all right?" he snapped, slamming his glass down on the bar. "Happy? Can we all just move on and stop dwelling on it?"

"Mab kind of set him up," Toula explained. "And he got attacked by a nice little old lady with a tea-kettle last night, so he's cranky."

"I'm not cranky, I'm in *pain*," he growled, pouring for a third time.

"We've probably got some morphine around here somewhere," Greg replied, "but not if you drink yourself unconscious first." He looked at Toula and me, then asked, "What do you need from me?"

I reached into my bag and pulled out the wrapped spheres. "We have two," I said, unwrapping one to give him a peek. "It's not going to be enough. Toula thought you had at least a third . . ."

Greg frowned, then pulled his reserve sphere from his pocket and put it on the table between us. "Records say that Simon Magus made twelve, and he distributed them widely at the end of his life. We've been able to track down ten over the years, and I knew Grivam had the eleventh—"

"I hid the twelfth," I interrupted. "So, you have ten? That should be more than enough."

But Greg shook his head. "Six of them are just curiosities, long since drained. Two, we've drained keeping the wards together, and the third one should be empty by this time tomorrow."

"Which leaves that," Toula muttered, looking at Greg's sphere.

"Moon and stars." I sighed, pushing myself off the couch, and glowered at the wall behind Greg. "Toula, was there anything in the diary about recharging them?"

"Not that I've found. It looks like he ripped some pages out."

"Then our only hope of breaking this thing is . . . *that*," I snapped, jutting my finger at the three spheres on the coffee table. "I guess we'll see if that's enough, because if it isn't, we're well and truly fucked. But hey, Greg, at least you kept your wards going for another few days—"

"How were we supposed to know?" he protested. "Security first, that's always been the Arcanum protocol—"

"*Damn* the protocol! This isn't covered by any protocol, you bleeding idiots!" I yelled, then snatched up my glass and drained it to keep from throttling the grand magus.

The others gave me a moment to regain my composure. When my breathing slowed, Greg pointedly cleared his throat. "Putting aside for a moment the power situation, who's standing for Mab?"

I could feel Joey's eyes on me as I took my seat. "I've heard rumors that she's kept her court in the Gray Lands . . ."

"I'd heard that, too."

"Yes. Well, unless you know of one of her people in this realm who's suicidal enough to break an enchantment Mab set up . . . I may need to cross the border. I was going to try to make a gate, but since we're down to three spheres, if you could point me to the nearest natural gate . . ."

Greg's lined face was still for a long moment, and I assumed that he was thinking of a way to throw us out before he murmured, "I know of one."

"A gate?"

"Better. One of Mab's people."

My heart leapt. "*Where?*"

"Right beside you," he said quietly, and pointed to Toula.

She stared at him for a moment, caught off guard, then laughed uncertainly. "Seriously, do you have someone? The sooner we can get across—"

"You. Toula, honey, I was hoping to avoid this . . ."

She stood and held up her palms as if warding him off, but the couch blocked her retreat. "No. Unh-uh, no, *stop it*. I'm a *Pavli*, I've been carrying that curse long enough. You're not going to put another one on me . . ."

Greg sighed and closed his eyes as Toula continued her rant of denial, then held up one hand until she wound down. "You *are* a Pavli," he said softly. "That's no lie—and I knew Apollonios well enough to see him in your face." He paused, but kept his eyes fixed on Toula. "Your mother—"

"You said she worked for him," she interrupted, her voice shaking as her finger shot toward him. "You said—"

"I said what I did to protect you, girl. Your mother—"

Before he could finish, Toula marched across the room and beckoned to Joey. After a moment's hesitation, he slid his blade out and handed it to her, and she patted the naked steel against her palm. "I believe you're mistaken, Grand Magus," she said with a smug little smile. "If I were . . . *fae* . . ."

Greg watched her as he might have stared down a toddler in a tantrum. "You know as well as I do that witch-bloods usually aren't susceptible."

"And they usually can't do spellwork, either," she

retorted, thrusting the sword back into Joey's arms as she pulled her wand from its hiding place. "So explain *this*."

He stood and took the wand from her, then snapped it over his knee before she could cry out. "A decoy, child," he said over her yelps, and showed her the hollow cross-section. "Pine, not rowan. Do you see?"

Toula took the pieces from him and stared at what the break had revealed: a layer of stain atop a lighter wood. "I . . . I don't . . ."

"And that's not dragonscale," he continued, nodding to the pile of brown debris on his rug. "Taste it if you don't believe me."

"Or don't," I interjected before Toula could sample it. "It's mostly sawdust. Slim told me."

She whipped on me, eyes blazing. "What the hell did Rick—"

"Rick doesn't know the full truth," Greg said, stepping between us in placation. "Toula . . ."

But she was having none of it. "Rick said he made them for me! Rowan and dragonscale! I have to have something that powerful to work with the little magic you let me use!"

"I don't *let* you use anything," Greg murmured, and Toula fell back into flushed silence. "I tried for three weeks to bind you," he continued. "It took the Inner Council twenty minutes of work to render your father powerless. The best we could do on you was imperfect, and child, you have no idea how hard we tried." He shook his head and pursed his lips. "I lied, Toula. The fact that you've been able to use spellcraft to this point is proof of your own power. Don't you see?" he asked, resting his hands on her tight shoulders. "You're stronger than the best the Council could throw at you. I firmly believe that the only reason the bind didn't fail years ago is because you never tried to throw it off."

Toula's eyes had begun to fill. "I thought . . . you know, if I was good . . . if I didn't give you any reason . . ." She sniffed and swiped at her face furiously. "I'm *not* my father, you know that . . ."

"I know, I know," he soothed. "Toula, the bind was never about your father. Evil isn't hereditary." Greg stooped slightly to look her in the eye. "We bound you because you were the most terrifying little bundle to ever land on our doorstep."

Her voice hitched when she tried to speak. "I . . . I don't understand."

"Honey," he said, pressing on in spite of her tears, "you are the one in a million. The perfect witchblood."

"That's not . . . that's just a theory . . ."

"It's more than a theory—it's a simple matter of numbers." Greg released her and fumbled in his pocket for a handkerchief. "No two witch-bloods are exactly alike in terms of power. It was only a matter of time before the right combination happened." He handed Toula the handkerchief, and she dabbed her mascara into black tracks. "To hear your father tell it, your mother had been trying for a long time before she had you. I've got the tape if you want to hear the interview," he offered. "It's a little grainy, but he—"

"Wait, I'm confused." I pointed my glass at Toula. "You're telling me *she's* a mongrel? I saw her do some incredibly technical spellwork—that doesn't make sense."

"Most of the *witch-bloods*"—Greg gave me a stern look for my slip—"that we've known are the result of a minor wizard and a weaker faerie. Neither parent was particularly strong to begin with, and in combination, their strains of magic cancel each other out. But there's variation. We've recorded instances of outliers through the years—witch-blooded fae with metal sensitivity, with varying degrees of longevity, and with skill in spellcraft or enchantment. Occasionally *both*." He folded his arms. "Toula's father wasn't some minor wizard—Apollonios was incredibly gifted. And her mother—"

I held up a finger to pause the explanation and studied Toula's makeup-streaked face. "How old are you?" I asked her.

"Whatever happened to never asking a lady her age?" she muttered. I gave her a look, and she rolled her eyes. "Thirty-five. Why?"

"You're *thirty-five*?" Joey repeated incredulously.

Toula rubbed at her eyes again. "Good genes. Use lots of moisturizer. Nothing wrong with that."

Joey cocked an eyebrow. "Wow. Ever heard of denial?"

I exchanged a look with Greg, who nodded. "All this time, I thought you were Joey's age," I said. "You don't look thirty-five. Hell, you don't look any older than Robin and me."

She began to tense again. "That doesn't mean anything . . ."

We stood in silence for a long moment as Toula wrestled with the information Greg had thrust upon her. Finally, arms folded and brows lowered, she whispered, "My mother?"

Greg took a deep breath. "Mab."

The video was indeed grainy, but the image was clear enough to show Apollonios Pavli's scarred left cheek and broken nose beyond doubt. The video also showed two black eyes, an arm in a sling, and half his hair burned away, silent testament to the struggle it had taken to bring him down. I hadn't appreciated just how much he resembled an oft-beaten pugilist until I saw him shackled, bound, and wearing the Arcanum's prison yellow.

Greg had fast-forwarded through the early part of the interrogation, then paused a few minutes before the end of the tape as a much younger version of himself asked, "The child, Apollonios—whose is she?"

Pavli smiled, revealing broken teeth. "Mine, of course," he replied, his Greek accent barely noticeable.

"And her mother?"

His smile widened. "Wouldn't you like to know, boy?"

I watched young Greg's dark fist clench at the bottom of the screen. "We know she's fae. Who?"

Pavli's smile dimmed with his trump gone, but he still maintained his bravura. "Stronger than you, isn't she? Little thing's something else when she's upset."

"Rest assured that we'll bind her," Greg replied. "And if that fails . . ."

He let the thought hang, unspoken, and Pavli shook his head. "You hurt a hair on her head, and her mother will destroy you."

Greg paused and shuffled the papers on the table, their contents obscured by the low quality of the tape. "We've checked her aura," he said quietly, "and we know she's a mongrel."

Live Greg flinched at his younger self.

"You weren't just coerced into this . . . transaction," young Greg continued. "So what's in it for you? Donate sperm and get . . . what?"

Pavli's smile returned. "Why don't you wait a few years and find out?"

"How about enlightening me now before I knock your goddamn teeth down your throat?"

Live Greg flinched again, and Joey glanced at me with a question on his face. "The Arcanum's gotten a bit better about employing torture in interviews," I whispered.

"Pavli was a special case," Greg muttered in the boy's other ear.

The prisoner just smiled for a few seconds, letting his inquisitor stew. Finally, he said, "You want the truth? Okay, tough guy. The brat's Mab's and mine. She's going to think kindly of me when she gets her kingdom back. And I guarantee you that if *anything* should happen to that child, Mama is going to be unhappy."

"Jesus, what were you *thinking*, you fool?" young Greg shouted. "That's a fully powered mongrel! The power that thing can wield . . . and *Mab*? You want to give *that* power, too?"

"I don't care who rules Faerie," Pavli replied, "so long as she's in my debt. Now, where's my precious baby girl, hmm?"

Greg paused the tape and stood in front of the TV, blocking Pavli's eternal smile. "He thought that once Toula grew into her power, Mab would come and claim her, and would then spring him from our custody. But the bind held well enough," he continued, looking apologetically at Toula, "and thank God, she never showed. He . . ." Greg hesitated, considering Toula's expressionless face, then said, "He went to his execution screaming for her to remember their deal. Guess she didn't hear him."

"Or, you know, you don't make deals with the Three," I muttered.

"I could have told him that, had he the sense to listen," Greg replied. "Toula, dear," he continued, stiffly dropping to one knee before her and taking her limp hands, "I'm sorry. I did what I had to do. I don't know why they created you . . ."

"I do," she murmured, and turned to the far end of the couch, where Robin was sitting. "She knew my father would go down eventually—the Arcanum was too strong in the end. The trap—the black box—he must have made that with her. He had the spellcraft, and she added the oomph. *That* must have been part of the bargain."

Toula turned to me. "This was never about Meg and Olive. This isn't about you. She wants me." She pried herself free from Greg, stood, and began to pace across the office, running her hands through her dark spikes as she thought. "She *knew* the Arcanum would bind me—you had to, I get it. But she had to get that bind off eventually. Cutting the magic would do it . . ."

"So would pulling you into Faerie," I pointed out.

"Right, yes . . ." Toula stopped and stared back at me. "Don't you see it?" she said, her eyes wide. "She wants Titania gone, right? She's going to need allies who can stand against her. Robin's an easy pick because he's got the planning skills of a damn *mayfly*. You're a good pick because you hate your mother's guts. And me, if I'm at all what she's expecting. Get us in, create a distraction, maybe we take out Titania—and poof, one vacant throne. *Shit*," she muttered, resuming her march. "She's playing us, guys . . ."

"We don't know that," Robin began, but Toula wheeled on him and vehemently shook her head.

"Where else would she have gotten a hybrid trap like that? What wizard would be demented enough to work with *her*? My delusional father, apparently! And she had every contingency covered." Toula's face was a mask of disbelief. "We're going to rescue them, whatever it takes. What if that means killing Titania? There's her entry—"

"Not quite," I interrupted. "If Mother dies, the throne is mine."

Toula paused in her pacing and folded her arms. "You think you're strong enough to hold it against Mab? Fuck." She sighed, and headed for Greg's bar. "If she's really been in the Gray Lands, I don't want to know what she's got planned when she gets Faerie back . . ."

Robin frowned for a moment as Toula opened a bottle of tequila, then said, "So we can legitimately call you a witch now, right?"

She slammed her still-empty glass down against the mahogany and bared her teeth.

A moment later, I joined Joey and Greg behind the safety of the bar as Toula sat on Robin and bloodied his face to the tune of her howled, incomprehensible curses. "You want me to break this up?" Joey muttered.

"Nope," I replied, helping myself to the abandoned tequila. "Just let her get it out of her system." I cringed as something in Robin's face crunched. "Sorry about the rug, Greg."

The grand magus looked at me over his glasses. "You *do* remember that I'm a wizard, right? Hell, I can get blood out of just about anything." He sighed and sipped his water. "I was hoping I'd never have to be the one to tell her. She didn't have an easy time of it here, and that was just with her name."

"Joey! Nail gun!" Toula bellowed from the floor.

I held Joey back and shook my head. "Rule one regarding intervention when two faeries are fighting," I told him, "is don't."

He reholstered his weapon. "I'm guessing I should never call *her* Tink, huh?"

"Yeah, I wouldn't go there," I replied, and drank.

CHAPTER 21

"**Y**ou don't sleep, either?"

Greg looked up from his desk as I closed the door behind me. He had put us up for the night, but as the guest rooms came unsupplied with any libations, I had found my way back to his office, ignoring the pair of guards stationed in the hallway near our rooms.

"You get to be my age, and sleep's the first thing to go, right before hearing and hair." He gestured toward the bar, and I nodded my thanks. "Seventy-eight might not sound like much, but when all those years start weighing down on you, you realize how heavy they are."

I lifted a bottle of scotch. "You're preaching to the choir. Join me?"

"Can't," he replied, patting the purple mug beside

his laptop. "Missy's orders. I sleep even less if I get that gunk in my system."

"So you're drinking coffee instead?" I retorted.

"Decaf," he said mournfully. "She's going to keep me healthy if it kills me."

I glanced at the bridal portrait on the wall, then chuckled as I poured a double. "You're lucky to have her, you know."

"I keep telling myself that," he muttered, and closed his computer's lid. "She's none too pleased that you're here, Coileán."

"She has a healthy sense of self-preservation. It's commendable. Cheers." I clenched my eyes shut against the burn, then put the empty glass back on the bar. "Tell Missy we'll be gone in the morning, assuming that Robin's not dead and Toula's not in the middle of a crippling existential crisis."

"I make no promises concerning Toula, but your brother is good as new, more or less. We've got a few down here who specialize in healing magic—he's going to be a little shiny for a while around that burn, but the fractures knit well. They pulled a little power off the sphere running the wards," he added before I could protest. "No one's touched the other three. Anyway, they gave him a shot of morphine and put him to bed about an hour ago." His face tightened. "I'd offer you backup if I could," he said quietly, "but my hands are tied, you've got to understand that. I've got to think about my people, and getting involved in an inter-court conflict—"

"And the best you could offer would still be little better than cannon fodder," I interrupted.

"You said it, not me." He forced another sip of coffee down, then glanced at the ceiling. "Toula's been out there awhile. Want to check on her?"

"Out where?" I asked, following his eyes upward.

"She's got a place. Head out the main door and hang a right—it's the trailer with the big marijuana flag in the window. She'll be on the roof." He paused, then swung his mug toward the little coffeepot on the filing cabinet. "Maybe she'd like something warm?"

Greg's prediction had been spot-on, and I found Toula sitting on the tar-papered edge of a dilapidated single wide, kicking the wall as she stared out at the stars. "Coffee?" I called to her, holding up a plastic travel mug, and she shrugged.

"Roof access is through the trapdoor," she said.

I made my way through the dark shell of a trailer and out onto its top, then handed Toula the mug. "It's decaf."

"Pity," she replied, but drank anyway.

We sat in silence for a few minutes, shivering in the clear night while she sipped. Finally, I asked, "Are you okay?"

"Hands are sore."

I glanced down and saw in the security lamp's glow that her bare knuckles had turned bluish. "Someone downstairs could fix that for you—"

"Nah."

The silence rolled out over the prairie.

"You want to talk?" I tried.

She shook her head.

"Fine." I pushed back from the edge of the roof and stood. "Might want to sleep. I thought we could make the attempt in the morning, if you're all right—"

"Why didn't she come for me?"

Toula's voice was so soft that I almost thought I'd imagined it. "What was that?"

"Why didn't she come for me?" she repeated, still staring into the night. "The Arcanum raised me. If she's really my mother . . ."

The thought ended unspoken, and I returned to my spot beside her. "It's nothing personal. I doubt any of the Three has ever raised a child. Mother had surrogates for all of us, and I'm sure Oberon did, too. They can't be bothered."

"That's supposed to make me feel better?"

"That's the truth." I hesitated, at a loss for words of comfort. "Toula, this . . . this isn't the end of the world. I mean, you said it yourself, there are worse things than learning you're half-fae. And besides," I said, trying to sound brighter, "with the bind off, there's no reason that you couldn't petition the Arcanum for membership—"

She snorted. "Are you kidding? I'm witch-blooded *fae*. There's no way in hell they'd take me." She sighed and cradled her cooling coffee, then muttered, "What am I going to do?"

"You focus on today, and then you focus on tomorrow, and the tomorrow after that, and you find something that makes the tomorrows worthwhile."

Her eyes cut to mine. "And what is that?"

"You'll be the first to know if I figure it out."

I rose again to give Toula her privacy, but her voice stopped me before I could reach the trapdoor. "Promise me something, Colin."

"Yes?" I asked.

Toula didn't look at me. "If we get Olive out of there . . . you'd better damn well be there for her, okay?"

"I'll do my best," I said, and slipped away.

I stepped out of the elevator and headed for my guest room, intent on at least giving the bed a try, when I heard a familiar tenor drawl behind me, "Not so brave now, are you?"

Turning, I spotted Steve Brownfield, alias Drago, standing a few yards down the corridor. He still sported his black duster and boots, but he held no wand. "Go to bed, kid," I said. "I'm not dealing with you tonight."

"Not your choice," he replied, taking a few slow steps toward me. His boot chains jingled, and as he fisted his hands, I saw the dark piece of metal stretched across his fingers.

"They actually let you underground, did they? I'm surprised. Thought the Arcanum kicks its witches out."

Steve's eyes narrowed. "Who're you calling a witch?"

"Well, it doesn't really matter, does it? You've got no wand, no power to draw on—"

"Got these," he interrupted, holding up his fists. The metal pieces were topped with short spikes, and the color suggested that he wasn't wielding brass.

"Come on," I sighed, folding my arms, *"really*? You want to rumble here, now?"

"Scared, faerie?"

"No. But once I finish with you, Greg's going to kick whatever's left of your ass because I'm his guest, and last I checked, hospitality means something to him. So try me if you like," I offered with a shrug. "If you didn't get enough back in Virginia, I'll be happy to give you more."

"You've got a big mouth," he retorted, then charged at me, arms pumping and steel spikes glinting in the dimmed overhead lights.

Without magic at my disposal, I was reduced to fighting like a mortal, which was far from ideal. But few make it to my age without learning at least a little about unarmed combat, and I'd been in more than my share of skirmishes. As Steve ran at me like a murderous bull, I held my ground and raised my fists, then pivoted when it was too late for him to change course. He stumbled past me, thrown off kilter, and one of his spikes ripped a gash in my sleeve but missed my arm. While he tried to recover, I grabbed the collar of his duster and yanked with all my might, and Steve flew backward. His head bounced off the thin carpet, and as his world spun, I stomped on his wrists until he screamed.

After giving him a solid kick in the ribs for good measure, I stepped back, inspected my loafers, and watched the punk try to pull himself off the floor. "All right, Stevie, that's me besting you with *and* without magic. Had enough?"

Footsteps behind me heralded the late arrival of the guards, and I glanced over my shoulder as they slowed. "Can someone tell me why this kid has a death wish?" I asked them.

One of the guards had pulled a knife, but his comrade stepped forward before he could do something stupid. "Lord Coileán—"

"I just want to go to bed," I griped. "Drago, Dark Lord of the Storm here rushed me with spiked knuckles. Where the hell were you two?"

The lead guard paused, considered the boy writhing on the floor, then stifled a laugh. "Sorry—*Drago*?"

"That's what he called himself. Steve, right?"

The guard shook his head and chuckled. "He's Magus Brownfield's nephew. Don't know where he came up with the title, but his mom didn't like living underground, so God knows what sort of instruction he's had."

"Shit," the other guard muttered, pulling a small phone from his belt. "We've got to call the magus, don't we?"

I loitered against the wall until Greg and a gray-haired woman in a fluffy blue bathrobe stepped off the elevator. "Oh, for heaven's sake," she muttered, catching sight of the casualty. "Get up, Stevie. Your mama's on the way."

Greg gave me a long, weary look, and I walked closer. "He attacked me a few days ago at Meggy's place, and then he came at me just now. What would you have had me do?" I asked.

The woman—Magus Brownfield, I assumed—just shook her head. "Sorry. My nephew doesn't visit often."

"We'll take it from here," said Greg.

I nodded to the guards and started on my way, but before I could go more than a few steps, the elevator chimed again, and I heard a woman scream. Looking back at the newcomer kneeling beside Steve, I surmised that his mother had arrived and decided that my presence could improve nothing about the situation.

Still, the hallways echoed, and I heard her when

she screeched, "That *monster* could have killed my son, and you're letting him walk away?"

I flipped the lock and flopped onto the bed, willing morning to come. The door seemed strong, but it's difficult to sleep in a bunker full of irate wizards who'd prefer to see you dead.

"**U**nless someone has a better idea, here's the plan," I said, settling into the fourth chair at the round table.

We had gathered in a sitting room near Greg's office, where his staff had left us breakfast, but no one looked particularly hungry—or rested. Toula's spikes drooped, a testament to the time she'd gone without a shower, and her under-eyes were dark and swollen. Robin seemed clean, but half of his face was still an ugly red, smooth and shiny with the burn. Even Joey sagged, though he had come to the table with his sword and improvised firearm strapped on and ready.

"We get the spheres, get over there, and try to reason with Mother," I continued. "No sudden moves, no heroics unless it's a last resort."

Robin's unsinged eyebrow lifted. "That's your master plan? Diplomacy? When has that ever worked?"

"There's always a first time," Joey offered.

My brother rolled his eyes. "And with what are you proposing that we barter? Galahad?"

"Me."

Toula and Joey began to protest, but I raised my

hands. "For whatever reason, and I'm sure it's not going to be pleasant, she wants me back under her thumb. I can take care of myself. The goal is to get Meggy and Olive out unharmed, understood?"

"And what about *my* goal, hmm?" Robin retorted. "What's in this for me?"

I glared at him across the table. "You're not seriously suggesting that we kill Mother, are you?"

"That's *exactly* what I'm suggesting!"

I sighed. "We're not even strong enough together. We could give her guard some trouble, but as far as Mother's concerned, it's suicidal to think—"

"We have *her*," Robin interrupted, jabbing his finger at Toula. "She could be enough—"

"She's untested."

"I'll do it for Meg," Toula murmured, pushing her half-eaten banana aside. "But only if I have to. I'd really rather not kill anyone, you know?"

"Weakling," Robin muttered.

"Psycho," she snapped. "Priorities, okay? We get them out, and then you can plan world domination when we're safely the hell away from there." She bit the inside of her lip and glowered at the table. "Mab's going to know once the realm's open again. Whatever she has planned . . ."

"Could help us," Robin finished.

"Could *kill* us," Toula retorted.

"Children," I muttered, rubbing my forehead,

"focus. Toula, if I get stuck over there, I'm trusting you to keep them safe, all right?"

"Yeah, of course," she replied, "but I still think this plan sucks. I'm not agreeing with Tink, but a show of force might help . . ."

"Or it might just piss her off. No. We get them to safety, I do what I have to, and if you think of a way to spring me once they're safe, I'll be grateful."

"Still sucks," Joey mumbled.

I turned to him and shook my head. "Your job is to stay here and wait for us to get back."

"Aw, come on," said Robin before Joey could complain, "if he wants to kill himself, let him go out in a blaze of glory."

"No one is going out in a blaze of glory," I snapped.

"Great, then we're agreed," Joey said smartly.

Toula lifted her finger. "I like backup plans. Galahad comes along."

I could feel my blood pressure mounting. "In what universe is that a better plan than mine?"

"He can fight, he's willing, he goes. End of discussion."

"He's defenseless!"

Toula remained calm. "Once we've got magic back, I can shield him with a spell. We keep him safe, he gets to slash things."

I fought for patience. "And what if she turns on you first? If I have to engage, I can't guarantee that I can keep him protected, too. And you've never been unbound, Toula—"

"Exactly! I'll be at full strength!"

"Or you'll be completely overwhelmed! It isn't safe—"

"I'll take that chance," Joey interrupted, pushing back from the table. "I said I'm with you guys, and I meant it. Now, are you going to reopen Faerie, or are you going to sit around all day arguing about it?"

I stood to look him in the eye. "You don't have to do this, kid."

"Stop." He grabbed my shoulders and shook his head. "I want to." He glanced at the door as Greg walked in with the last of the Arcanum's precious spheres. "And I guess it's go time, huh?"

CHAPTER 22

The problem with the spheres and the spell was that neither had come with clear instructions.

"I just think I should be the one to tap them," Toula explained as the three of us stared down at the spheres on the cleared breakfast table. "I mean, these were spellcraft creations, right? I'm the only one here who can handle that properly."

"But you've never opened a gate before, have you?" Robin countered. "What if you can't manage the surge?"

I cut my eyes to Joey, who stood behind Toula, armored, armed, and ready. He pantomimed little circles with one hand—*Hurry it up*—and I nodded. But before I could approach the spheres, I heard voices rising in the corridor, and Greg ducked back into the room.

"Problem," he said, interrupting Robin and Toula's bickering.

Pointing to the door and the growing chorus beyond, I muttered, "I'd gathered. What's the trouble now?"

"You, more or less." He locked the door but continued to lean against it. "Dotty Brownfield's been complaining to the Council from the moment that she was sure her boy was going to live. And word's spread that I'm giving you the last of the spheres, so, uh . . ." He winced as someone in the hall shouted his name. "Y'all should get out of here posthaste."

"Guard the door," I told him. "Joey, if they break through, hold them off. We're only going to get one shot. Toula, do it."

"But—" Robin began.

"Get out of her way," I snapped, dragging him back from the table. "Toula!"

"Patience," she mumbled, holding her hand over the spheres, and closed her eyes. "I can draw, but I need to be judicious with this. It's going to take me a few minutes to bring the visualization up."

Fists pounded against the door, and the voices outside were swelling into the angry roar of a mob. While Toula's fingers twitched, knitting together the spell that would allow us to see the lock, Greg and I traded worried glances, and even Robin kept his eyes on the door. The grand magus grimaced as the voices of individual Council magi called to him from the crowd, and I saw his gaze drop to the doorknob.

"Come on, Toula," I muttered.

Her face had begun to glisten with the effort it took to simultaneously draw power and weave the spell. "I need time."

"We don't *have* time. This doesn't have to be pretty."

"Just another minute . . ."

"*Now*, Glinda!"

Her eyes snapped open long enough for her to shoot a death glare my way, and with a final flick of her wrist, the green tendrils of the visualization blazed to life above the table. "Call me that again, and—"

"The lock," Robin interrupted. "How do we open it?"

She pointed to the chaos at the heart of the construction, a swirling knot that pulsed half a second ahead of the more orderly spell around it. "That's the enchantment. It's in there somewhere."

"You don't *know*?" he cried.

Toula gestured to it again, exasperated. "It's enchantment! Reading the contours of that crap is hard enough. I couldn't get every detail! If you think you can do better—"

The pounding on the door intensified, followed by the thud of a heavy shoulder. "Guys, do *something*," said Joey, drawing his sword. "I can't hold them all back if they break through."

Greg looked more conflicted by the moment, and I realized his resolve was about to break. "Grab the knot, both of you," I ordered, and reached for the throbbing heart.

At first, I felt nothing but the slight warmth of the visualization, but then my fingertips brushed against my brother's, and a jolt passed between us. Before we could withdraw or reconsider, Toula thrust her hand into the center, and a charge like bluish lightning flew among us, growing as we drew power from the rapidly depleting spheres.

Someone slammed into the door again, then a third time, and the voices set up a muffled chant of encouragement. "Come *on*, guys!" Joey yelled, taking up a defensive stance. "Break it!"

The lightning had quickly become unbearable, fire that burned without leaving a trace, and I clung to the table against the pain. "Almost . . ." I whispered.

Suddenly, I *felt* a sound deep in my body, a rumble far too low to be heard, and the web of lightning exploded like a bomb. The three of us were blasted across the room with the force, and the spheres, now well and truly empty, went flying. Joey ducked and cried out as one clipped his shoulder, but I barely noticed as I rose.

A gate had opened above the table, a gently pulsing circle of darkness framed with a flicker of electricity. From the little I could see through it, I made out the contours of Mother's throne room, but as the sun had yet to rise in Faerie, the throne room was likely to be deserted. Not for long, of course—an alarm would sound as soon as we crossed—but at least we wouldn't be running into an ambush.

Well, this is my reconstruction of my thoughts on later reflection. At that moment, I recognized only two things: the overwhelming sensation of magic flowing out of that gate like a torrent from a ruptured dam, and the rush of adrenaline that propelled me onto the table and through the hole in space.

Robin followed an instant later and cried out as he barked his shin against a crystal pillar. I summoned my blue flame and almost wept with relief when it burst into life in my palm. I was immersed in pure magic, plunged into the ocean at the desert's edge, and momentarily reveled in the potential I felt once again well up inside of me.

I turned to see that Toula had followed us through, but she was staring into space and nearly hyperventilating. Joey stood beside her, tense and ready, but he quickly realized that something was wrong. "Hey, Toula, you okay?" he asked, and reached out his hand.

I doused my fire and tackled him before he could make contact. "Don't touch her!" I yelped, and glanced back at her in time to see the pale lightning begin to dance over her skin. "She's overwhelmed, and she's not in control yet."

He let me pull him back to his feet, but his eyes

never left Toula's startled gaze. "How long is this going to take?"

"Don't know," I muttered, and threw a quick shield around him as I touched his head. When I released him and he blinked the fog away, I asked in Fae, "Understand?"

"Understand wha . . . *oh*," he replied in kind. "Hey, neat! Any chance you could you do that with Koine Greek, too?"

"Focus," I ordered, and waited while Robin joined our clump. "Keep an eye on the doors," I told them, then stooped and stared into Toula's eyes until I saw a flicker of awareness return. "Come back, Glinda," I murmured. "We don't have much time. Get it together—"

Before I could finish my pep talk, her body burst into white flame, and all three of us jumped back in alarm. Safe in the middle of her corona, Toula folded her arms and glared at me. "I *told* you not to call me that, asshole. Don't make me get medieval on your face, too."

I straightened my shirt and tried to project nonchalance at the fact that she had turned into a torch. "Want to dim your highs?"

"What do you . . ." she began, then finally noticed her glow. "Huh. Cool," she declared, and the light show ended as suddenly as it had begun. "Well, that'll be useful should I ever get a s'mores craving . . ."

I began to reply, but I hesitated at the sound of

rapid footfalls, and the four of us bunched up. "Good alarm system," Robin muttered. "What's the plan?"

"Just stay calm and nonthreatening," I said, and squinted as the throne room's sconces and chandeliers blazed to life. When I could see straight again, I spotted two of Mother's guards by the door, both noticeably uncomfortable with our presence. "I've come to see Mother," I announced, holding my empty hands out as I stepped away from the protection of our knot. My voice echoed around the room.

One of the guards stepped forward, befuddled. "Lord Coileán? How did you—"

"I'll explain when I see her. We need to speak."

His mouth flapped for a few seconds, and then he motioned to his companion, who darted back into the corridors from which they had come. "My lady has been most distressed," he cautioned when they had departed. "Whatever you did—"

"I did nothing," I interrupted. "Lady Moyna and . . . the other, where are they?"

Before he could answer, space ripped over the dais, and Mother stepped into the room with Olive on her heels. "*Coileán!*" she shouted, her cry ringing around the cavernous chamber. "*What* is the meaning of this . . . this . . ."

Her face had begun to turn pink with anger. Olive hung back toward the throne, glaring at me with her arms folded over her twinkling bodice.

I held up my hands as if to block her outburst.

"This isn't my fault," I said, trying to keep my voice low. "I've been working on the solution for the last ten days. We just managed to break the spell."

"What spell?" she snapped.

I cut my eyes to my brother, choosing my words carefully. "Something of Mab's design. She, uh . . . used Robin to trigger it. He's been helping me. Look, I've come about Moyna and—"

But Mother was already stomping off the dais and down the long blue runner toward us, her silver gown rippling with the speed of her progress. "Come *here*!" she demanded, pointing at Robin, and then she paused a few feet from us, waiting.

He glanced back at me, questioning with his eyes, and I nodded. Though he strode toward Mother with his head high, I saw him swallow hard as he waited for her to speak.

When she did so after a minute's pause, her voice was calm and soft. "Did you do this, boy?" she murmured, reaching up to cup his cheek in her palm. "Did you cut us off?"

He tolerated her touch with surprising stoicism. "I never intended to sever the realms, Mother," he replied. "Mab deceived me. Father knows the truth."

She looked at his scarred face for a long moment, and then she sighed and shook her head. "Oh, my silly little *puk'a*," she said, almost smiling.

Before I could come to his aid, Robin was engulfed in fire.

He shrieked and flailed, running blindly around the room in search of relief, but Mother's flames refused to be quenched. "Do something," Toula whispered behind me, but I stood frozen and helpless, knowing even as my brother's skin melted that I could do nothing to save him.

Robin fixed his eyes on me, pleading in the second before they burned, and I steeled my will. "I'm so sorry," I muttered, and pulled Joey's sword from its sheath as I ran toward my brother. One slice of the blade ended Robin's screams of agony, and I forced myself not to vomit as his headless corpse crumpled to the floor and blackened.

"You do so love to thwart me," Mother said, and clucked her tongue. "Coileán, what am I to do with you?"

I clenched my fist around the leather-wrapped hilt and stared at her, feeling the warning tingle in my arm at the proximity of so much steel. "Send my daughter and her mother home," I heard myself say, "and you can do whatever you like."

Mother cocked her head, and a blonde lock spilled over one dark eye. "Your daughter?" she asked sweetly.

I pointed the sword at Olive, who visibly struggled to control her revulsion over Robin's end. "Olive. Send her home."

Sighing, Mother turned and smiled at the girl. "Moyna, dear, he wants to take you away from me. What should we do about that?"

Her face hardened in an instant, and her eyes, momentarily uncertain, grew cold. "Kill him, Mother."

The old bitch looked back at me, all smiles. "It seems she doesn't wish to go," she said with an exaggerated shrug, then took a single step toward me.

Before she could take a second, she screamed, and I distantly registered the distinctive *thunk* of Joey's gun firing. I looked back to find him in a shooter's stance, both hands locked around the nail gun, sighting down the short barrel. His finger squeezed the trigger again, and Mother shrieked as the nail drove through her thigh. "What are you doing?" I yelled at him. "Get out of here, go!"

But Joey shot yet again, and Mother fell to the floor of her throne room, howling with the blinding pain of the steel embedded in her flesh. He whirled and fired off a rapid volley as the few guards on the scene rushed toward him, but every bolt they threw at him bounced harmlessly away, as if blocked by an invisible bubble.

I knew *that* wasn't my doing.

Toula's face still betrayed her shock, but her lips moved soundlessly, powering the thick, complex shield that was keeping our marksman alive. She cut her eyes to me for a split second, and I reached out and felt the spell she had woven.

Take it, she mouthed.

I felt her slip away as I fed the spell—much easier to do in a place so saturated with magic—and then, even as I focused on keeping Joey safe, I felt her pry the sword from my hand.

I didn't see my mother die. I felt it.

Afterward, I pieced together what must have happened. Mother, too distracted by the blinding pain of the nails that Joey continued to shoot into her, failed to fight back. Instead, she cowered on the floor, trying to protect herself from the onslaught as the iron projectiles ripped through her shield and trusting her guards to come to her rescue.

She didn't see Toula approach. Given the speed of what happened next, I don't think she suffered long.

Toula bellowed a wordless war cry. Olive screamed. And then a supernova went off behind my eyes.

Fortunately for Joey's continued existence, Toula had enough presence of mind to notice the effects of killing my mother. Even as I collapsed, she slipped back into control of the shield, and Joey continued to harry the guards, who were now torn between destroying him and going to Titania's side. Toula told me later that she extended the shield over me as well, but I wasn't aware of it. I don't doubt her version of events, but I was cognizant of only two thoughts at that moment: *Mother is dead*, followed quickly by *Shit, I can't handle this*.

Faerie knew that Mother had died, and the realm itself—an alien consciousness, the likes of which I had never before known—now turned its attention to me.

The queen is dead. Long live the king.

Oberon was right, I realized, as I fought the impulse to simply explode with the power I felt coursing through me. I couldn't begin to imagine what Mother had wielded, what the land itself had given her.

And now it was going to rip me apart.

I don't know how long I knelt on the marble, holding my head and rocking. I don't know when Toula shot a blast of energy at Olive, throwing her against the throne and knocking her out before she could make a nuisance of herself. All I know is that by the time I could again hear what was going on around me, the realm was wordlessly warning me that something was wrong. I gathered what strength I could spare, looked over my shoulder, and found that a second gate had opened since I'd been indisposed.

I had never before seen Mab, but as the woman smiling at the chaos could have been Toula's sister, I assumed that the third of the Three had finally made herself known. Her black hair fell in a long curtain around her bare shoulders, while her eyes, so blue they were almost violet, surveyed the scene and crinkled.

"*This* is interesting," she said.

The guards and Joey declared an unspoken cease-fire as they turned to the newcomer and readied themselves for a fresh attack. Toula balled her free hand into a fist, which flamed to life as she took her stance. I tried to get up, but I was too overwhelmed to remember how my legs worked. All the while, the realm kept repeating its warning—*danger unwelcome danger foreign danger.*

Mab slowly clapped as the guards regrouped around Joey. "Well *done*," she said, beaming proudly. "Oh, well done, my darling! You were *marvelous!*"

Toula's fiery fist didn't dim. "Mab?" she asked uncertainly.

Her mother nodded and clasped her hands together. "My dear, you have no idea how long I've waited for this moment," she said, sweeping across the floor in a trailing purple gown. She paused long enough to kick me onto my side, and then, ignoring the flame and the sword, she grasped Toula's stiff shoulders and smiled anew. "You are so beautiful," she whispered, staring into Toula's eyes. "So perfect. I would have come for you long ago, but the Arcanum . . ." Her voice drifted off. "Well, that's all a bad dream now. You're home, precious. *We're* home."

Danger, the realm insisted more vehemently, and I felt my strength begin to seep back.

I glanced up in time to see Toula's fire die. "You . . . you wanted me?"

"More than anything," Mab insisted, all tenderness. "Your father was a brute, but you, child . . ." She ran her hand through Toula's messy spikes and shook her head. "I would never have left you, but they bound you so terribly, and I knew they would have killed you had I tried to reclaim you. Oh, my dearest, can you ever forgive me?"

Toula's jaw began to tremble, and then Mab wrapped her arms around her, pulling her close while she cried. "It's all over," Mab soothed. "You did wonderfully, little one. Slaying Titania—my dear, I didn't know you had it in you!" She pulled back and cupped Toula's face in her hands. "Thank you for returning my throne to me. I'll bring the rest of the court home in a short while, and then you will sit at my side, my most favored daughter."

As Mab continued to gush over Toula, Joey backed away, his gun still drawn, and fell behind the equally perplexed guards' shield.

Help me, I thought at the unfamiliar voice in my head. *I can't fight her alone, I'm too young, I'm weak—*

The realm didn't sigh—not precisely—but I could almost feel its impatience as it wordlessly revealed what I had overlooked.

Oberon had left Faerie, but he hadn't abdicated. The realm knew him and would welcome him back. But Mab had been cast out, vanquished. She didn't have the strength to stand up to the others on her own, not without the realm behind her.

Mab was ancient, yes, and incredibly strong due to her years alone. In a fair fight, I couldn't have touched her. But the reason I was a useless wreck on the floor was that Faerie had transferred to me the extra power she had given Mother and Oberon, and then some, making me close to Oberon's equal despite my relative youth.

Breathe, the realm suggested. *You are acclimating.*

Not quickly enough, I thought, looking up at Toula. Flush with power and churning with adrenaline, she faintly glowed as magic flowed freely through her for the first time. She was a titan, I realized, a natural giant, far stronger than her few years should have made her.

And her mother was holding her, murmuring words of comfort and love. No enchantment I could have crafted would have been more powerful than the effect Mab was having on her daughter, the despised, outcast orphan who'd suddenly been freed from captivity and united with a mother who wanted her. Robin was gone, and when Toula joined forces with Mab, what chance would I have?

As if sensing my thoughts, Toula finally glanced down at me and frowned. "I think Colin needs help."

Mab's voice hardened. "That's the enemy, child. Strike him down now, while he can't fight you, and we will rule together."

"But . . . wait, no, that's not right," she replied. "Olive would rule if something happened to Colin, wouldn't she? The courts go through bloodlines, isn't that the deal?"

Mab shrugged. "Then kill her, too. Kill all of Titania's spawn, be done with them. This is your *destiny*, dear, the power that's waiting for you—"

Toula pulled away from her grasp. "I'm not killing Colin."

Her mother frowned down at me as I lay helpless on the marble. "Why not? What is he to you?"

"I don't know, my friend? Maybe?" Briefly, she mulled the question over, then looked back at Mab and shook her head. "Whatever he is, I'm not killing him."

Again, Mab gripped her shoulders. "My dearest," she said, her voice almost seductive in its honeyed gentleness, "he is nothing but an impediment. Don't you know he would keep you from me if he could? Lock me in the Gray Lands for another thousand years, away from my home and"—she leaned closer to Toula's face—"my *family*? Don't you want us to be a family?"

"I . . . I mean . . ." Toula stuttered, "yes, but—"

"Go on, do this one little task for me," she cajoled, giving Toula another smile.

Her daughter stared at her for a long moment. "If you want him dead so badly, why don't you do it yourself?"

She is afraid, the realm whispered to me. *Almost, Coileán . . .*

"I know what's best for us, dear," said Mab. "Listen to your mother."

Toula's voice was low when she spoke. "My *mother*? My mother who abandoned me, who couldn't even bother to find me once I left the silo, who never gave me the slightest indication that she was even alive?" Her face worked as she stared at Mab. "Do you even know my name?"

Mab paused, momentarily flummoxed, then said, "Child of my body, I love you—"

Toula pulled away again and walked to my side, sword in hand. She nudged me until I was on my back, staring up at her. I saw her mouth tighten, and she sighed as she looked back at Mab. "The fae can't love," she murmured, dropping Joey's sword. "Everyone knows that. And I *did* get an Arcanum education."

Mab's voice became shrill. "Listen to me, you silly child—"

But Toula crouched and offered me her hand. "Time to get up, Gramps," she said, and pulled me to my unsteady feet. I tottered for a moment, seeking my balance, but then, as quickly as it had come, the wave of weakness passed. I was in control of myself again—and everything that entailed.

I stared at Mab. "What was that about killing me?" I croaked.

The old queen's eyes blazed, but I couldn't be sure whether the rage I saw in them was aimed at Toula or me. An instant later, she flung a bolt of lightning in our direction—a decent bit of enchantment, certainly, but nothing near what she had been able to do at her peak. Toula threw a shield in front of us both, and I risked a glance at her face. Her expression was terrible—a mélange of anger, betrayal, and hurt—and I reached for her hand. She returned my grip, hard enough to make me wince, and glared at her mother.

"I am many things," Toula murmured, holding on to me as if clinging to a lifeline, "but I will *not* be a pawn."

Mab's motherly act dropped like a mask. "You're a mongrel, nothing more," she bellowed, hurling a volley of fireballs our way, but they bounced harmlessly off Toula's shield. "A little mongrel who seems to have outlived her usefulness. Join me now, or I'll destroy you both."

"*Hey!*"

The three of us wheeled in the direction of the shout to find Joey glaring from behind the guards' shield. "The term is 'witch-blood,' bitch," he said, then fired.

Mab tried, she really did, but there's nothing as excruciating as an iron burn, and Joey was relentless. All of his shots seemed to find her, and as she collapsed in torment and tried to crawl for the safety of the open gate, he calmly reloaded and walked forward, flanked by wary guards.

Toula watched impassively as her mother cried out and dragged herself away from us, smoking and blistering in a dozen places. Fear drove Mab on in spite of the pain—palpable fear, intoxicating fear. The realm knew it and fed on it—and showed me what to do.

I turned to Toula and squeezed her hand to draw her attention. "There are cells here, ones she wouldn't be able to escape. I could lock her away, if you'd like."

"All of this is because of her," she muttered. "Robin's dead. Your mother's dead. I exist." She shook her head as another nail struck Mab's thigh. "Did she tell my father to do what he did? Was that part of her plan? Get me into Arcanum custody, make me hate them, use me to get what she wanted? And how many rejected witch-bloods have been born because she wanted to play genetic roulette? How many did she destroy?"

I flicked a finger, and the gate that had been Mab's salvation shrank to a pinhole and disappeared. "I'll do it if you want. Say the word."

"She tried to kill me," she whispered. "Tried to kill us both." Her eyes—Mab's eyes—met mine and held them for a long moment, even as Joey continued to advance on the queen.

With a nod of understanding, I released Toula, took a deep breath to center myself, then felt the power welling up within me. The realm whispered its approval as the enchantment in my mind coalesced into a white-hot flame. I narrowed its focus, reducing it to an impossibly strong bolt, then exhaled and let it fly.

As if feeling a premonition of her death, Mab tried to throw up a shield at the last moment, but she was too distracted by the burning nails to concentrate, and the shield shattered before my bolt. It pierced her back and embedded itself in her heart, and she collapsed as she breathed her last.

Toula and I shared a look—we were now bound by assisted matricide, if nothing else—and I turned my attention from Mab's smoking corpse in time to see Mother's guards drop to their knees. "Get up," I ordered, and watched as they stood on shaking legs. "If you want to live, then take me to the prisoner."

There was no door to Meggy's prison, just as there had been none on mine. I simply dissolved the wall as my nervous entourage stood around, then climbed through the hole into the stinking, pitch-black cell. "Meggy!" I called, and listened for her voice.

She didn't speak, but I heard her stertorous breathing in the corner of the room.

I summoned a flame in my hand and held it high, trying to assess her condition. "Aw, *shit*," Toula muttered behind me, and she took up the task of lighting the room as I ran to Meggy's side.

There was no food in the room, no water, no sign that she had been given any sustenance whatsoever in the last ten days except a small, dry jug overturned in the middle of the floor. It didn't take a genius to see that Mother had given her perhaps that jug of water and left her to starve.

I scooped her into my arms and held her to my chest, willing her eyes to open. "Hang on, Meggy," I whispered into her curls. "Hang on. Please, hang on."

CHAPTER 23

Greg had refused to send backup with us, but when Toula appeared in his office and demanded medics, he had been willing to play Red Cross. Five minutes after I carried Meggy into Mother's palatial suite and located a suitable bed, Toula was back with a pair of wide-eyed wizards, and I let them take over. The realm protested, but I pushed the little voice to the back of my head; apparently, the realm wasn't a fan at all of new encounters, and I didn't have time to try to reason with it.

As it turned out, the short answer to the question of how one reasons with the soul of Faerie itself is that one doesn't. The realm broke everything into black and white, acceptable and unacceptable. I tried logic—the wizards were my guests, I insisted, and the realm seemed to like me well enough—but my reasoning fell on deaf ears. Faerie wasn't going to be happy until they were gone, and I would simply have to deal with its periodic nagging in the interim.

It also didn't like the thought of my leaving, but there was no way around *that*. Hoping that I hadn't just inherited a homicidally clingy incorporeal entity, I half dragged Joey through a gate into Paul's rectory and caught the old priest in his study, still in his threadbare red bathrobe. "Well, now," he said, pushing back from his desk, "nice of you to call before stopping by . . ." He paused, giving us a closer inspection, then pushed his glasses down his nose and frowned. "Okay, someone want to tell me what on God's green earth is going on?"

"Can't talk," I said as Joey sank onto the study's well-worn couch, weapons and all. "Meggy's hurt, I've got to make sure the wizards aren't killing her, I think my daughter's still unconscious—"

Paul's brow furrowed. "You have a daughter?"

"Technically. And Joey probably needs a sedative."

He turned to his seminarian, who was staring at the wall. "What happened?"

"Shot some faeries," Joey muttered. "I'm okay."

Paul looked back at me, scowling. "All right, Colin, what did you do to him? And why are you glowing?"

I pulled off one glove, inspected my hand, and consciously tamped down the power. "Sorry, tell you later. Kid's bike is in my garage, I'll have the Arcanum send his bag along—"

"*Colin.*"

"I've *really* got to go," I apologized. "Get Galahad a Valium or something."

Before he could protest, I slipped back through the gate and shut it behind me, but found Meggy's sickroom changed from Mother's brocaded opulence to white walls and a well-cushioned, if institutional, bed. "I thought it would be easier on her when she wakes," Toula said, intercepting me before I could question the wizards waving their sticks at Meggy's side. "Everyone knows what a hospital looks like, right? Maybe she won't freak out if she realizes she's safe."

I glanced at the IV stand behind her bed. "What—"

"Just a saline drip," Toula soothed, pulling me toward the door. "And they even worked up some non-steel needles. She's in good hands. They said casting had never been this easy," she added, smirking as she closed the door behind us.

I stared at the ornately carved wood, so different from the featureless gray plastic on the other side. "How is she?"

"Severely dehydrated," Toula murmured, steering me down the hall. "No obvious bruising or breaks, so I don't think she was beaten or anything. The medics are trying to keep her electrolytes regulated and her heart steady, and they keep muttering about kidney issues, but they seem upbeat, all things considered."

I clenched my fists. "And Olive?"

"I took the liberty of keeping her unconscious.

Figured you'd want to put out one fire at a time." She knocked on a door as we passed and added, "I placed her in here for safekeeping. Lets me keep an eye on both of them."

"You were comfortable sedating her?"

"Eh, the blow knocked her out. I've got a rudimentary sleep spell going in there . . ." She saw my expression and shrugged. "Go with what you know, right? I could probably have done something a little flashier, but the spell does the trick." Toula paused at the end of the hall and cocked her head back toward Meggy's room. "Look, unless we've got explosions, I'm going to stay here and supervise. I don't want anyone stumbling down here by mistake and attacking the medics, you know?"

"Best not to provoke the Arcanum," I agreed. "You'll call me as soon as she wakes?"

"Sure, uh . . ." She folded her arms. "How do I find you, exactly?"

"Here," I said, and produced a pair of phones in my hand. "Just call me."

She took one and rolled her eyes. "Flip phones? This is the best you can do?"

"Deal with it," I muttered, and headed back to the throne room.

I never wanted to be a king. Hell, I'd never really contemplated the notion of my mother's death beyond an academic exercise. Yes, *technically*, I'd been her heir, but it wasn't as if anything would ever happen to one of the Three.

And then it had—to two of them in one day.

There was nothing I could do about Mab's court—I assumed they were somewhere in the Gray Lands, but I had nothing solid. In any case, they would never have accepted me as their leader, just as Oberon's people would never follow me. I was an outsider to their courts, Titania's blood—and, lest it be forgotten, the notorious Ironhand. Given my history, I wasn't even sure that Mother's court would accept me.

I suggested to the realm that it might be wiser to choose someone else. I had half siblings in Faerie, and surely one of them would have been more palatable. I could go on my way, I told the little voice, go back to my bookstore in Rigby, do what I'd been doing to keep the more troublesome of my kind in line. Go back to my *life*.

But the realm was firm. Titania was dead, so I was king, whether I liked it or not. This was my circus, these were my monkeys, and it was up to me to deal with them now. *Besides*, thought the voice, *do you honestly believe that any of your siblings would allow you to continue to harass Oberon's people? Titania found you entertaining. Her children have no such reason to permit you to act as you have.*

It had a point. As king, I could order my court to remain in Faerie, thus cutting down on at least a few of the problems back in the mortal realm. And nothing was stopping me from slipping back across to help Paul on occasion, right? If Oberon had a problem with it . . . well, we knew where to find each other. In any case, it was comforting to finally know that my mother wasn't going to come after me in my sleep—and even if the court didn't like me, how many of them would be willing to take me on now?

Still, seeing my unplanned new career as asylum warden stretch out before me, I asked if there was some way that I might abdicate. The realm gave me only one out: Olive would inherit the court on my death. But since I had no desire to pursue suicide, I took a deep breath, made myself presentable, and returned to the throne room to see just what sort of mess I'd gotten myself into.

Word spread quickly, though I wasn't sure how. By dawn, the throne room was packed to the walls with guards, Mother's lackeys, and assorted hangers-on. I spotted a few of my siblings from the dais but waited until the distant doors finally slammed to take Mother's vacated seat. "So," I began, cringing inwardly as my voice echoed around the unnaturally quiet room, "I suppose you've heard the news."

The room erupted in waves of silent nodding, and I waited for the court to still. "Yes. Well. To those of you who don't know of me, I'm Coileán. To those who do . . . you may be able to guess why I'm sitting here."

"What did you do to the queen?" a female voice called out, and I spotted one of Mother's intimates in the middle of the press.

"Defended myself," I replied, trying to keep calm. "She killed my brother unprovoked. She would have killed me. My associates dispatched her before she had the chance." I pointed to a clump of guards standing in the crowd to my right. "If you want to know what happened to Robin, that black smudge on the floor might give you some idea."

The guards spread apart, bumping each other and their neighbors in their haste to get off of the stain.

I looked around the room—the crystal walls, the extravagant pillars, the cloud-scraping ceiling—and grimaced. In an instant, the walls changed to stone, pierced by jewel-toned glass windows, the pillars took on bulk and twisted into carvings of vines and branches, and the entire room widened by a third, giving the assembled room to breathe. "Anyone want a chair?" I asked. "Be my guest."

A few seats of various sizes popped into existence around the modified throne room, and I waited until the crowd shifted and spread. "Right, then," I continued, glancing at the nearest worried faces, "here's how this is going to work. You don't have to like me, but you're not going to touch me or mine. I'll take suggestions, but I don't want a lot of back talk. Bend the knee, and you can stay. Refuse, and you can see if Oberon will take you. I don't know who's running Mab's court at the moment, but I don't think you'll like that option any better." I sat back against the throne—*my* throne now, an intricately carved wooden chair—and waited.

Guards, lackeys, lords and ladies—all knelt in a cacophony of rustling fabric and creaking furniture.

They didn't like me, I knew in my gut, but they didn't have to. The one thing a faerie fears above all else is a stronger opponent, and I had just undone Titania's creation around them.

I didn't know if I would keep the pseudo-Gothic architecture, I mused as the throng went to its knees. But for the moment, it did the trick.

Magic. You've got to love it when it works.

I spent the next two days seeing various would-be dignitaries in my office—I had modified Mother's into a rough copy of Greg's for the sake of convenience—and sneaked away between every few visitors to check on Meggy. Toula's report was always the same, however, and she suggested that I catch some sleep. Instead, I did shots by myself to steady my worn nerves and fought the urge to scare off the unending line of visitors with lightning bolts.

I had shooed the last of my staff off shortly after midnight when my phone began to ring. Pushing the bottle aside, I pulled the phone from my pocket and flipped it open. "And?"

"She's awake," said Toula. "Scared out of her mind, but awake."

I didn't bother with the walk, but instead opened a short gate between our rooms and stepped through to Meggy's bedside, still clutching my phone. "Meggy," I whispered, and almost laughed with relief to see her eyes open. "Welcome back . . ." I reached for her hand, but she pulled away, wide-eyed and trembling, and I paused. "It's me. It's just me," I soothed, backing up a few paces until she relaxed. "Everything's going to be fine. She can't hurt you again."

"Hey, Megs," said Toula, coming around the other side of the bed, "it's okay. No one's going to hurt you, babe."

Meggy stared down at the IV taped in her arm.

"The Arcanum sent some folks to help you," Toula continued, interpreting her gaze. "See? Over by the wall?" The two wizards waved, their sticks safely tucked out of sight, but Meggy continued to cower in silence. "I know you've been through hell," Toula pressed on, "but it's all over. Titania's dead. She can't hurt you, and Olive—"

Meggy's eyes shot up at the name. "Where is she?"

"Next door, sleeping. She's safe, too."

She relaxed fractionally, but then she turned back to me, and I saw anger and terror competing in her eyes. "What did you do to me?" she demanded.

I held up my hands—ungloved for once, as there was no need for precautions in a land singularly devoid of offensive metals—and shook my head. "Nothing, Meggy. What are you—"

She yanked a handheld mirror off the bedside table and held it in front of her face. "To me! What did you *do to me?*"

The age shift, I realized, and deduced that she must have just become aware of her face's missing decade. I met Toula's eyes across the bed, and Meggy watched us silently weigh our options.

"Is someone going to tell me what the hell is going on?" she snapped.

Toula touched the side of her nose and stepped back from the bed, and I sighed. "Meggy," I said quietly, waiting until her eyes flipped back to mine, "I don't really know how to tell you this, but, uh . . . we found your father. Your actual father, not Charlie."

She crossed her arms with care, avoiding the IV line, and waited.

"He's, uh . . . Oberon. You're half fae."

"Welcome to the club," Toula muttered. "I think we need T-shirts. Or therapy. No, *and* therapy . . ."

Meggy stared up at me in confusion, and I hurriedly explained, "He bound you before you were even born. Like . . . you know, what we were talking about. For Olive." Toula grunted her disapproval, but I carried on. "You've got the talent, just like I do—"

"More or less," Toula added.

I glared at her in exasperation, and she held up her hands, surrendering. "You obviously don't know how to use it right now," I said to Meggy, "but I could teach you, it'd be easy. And you could stay here," I continued, letting the words spill out. "I don't think I can go back to Rigby, not on a full-time basis, but you and Olive could stay here, be safe . . . anything you want, just name it." Before she could pull away again, I took her hand in mine and smiled. "Don't you see, Meggy? We *can* be a family—you, me, and Olive. We can be together—"

"I want to go home," she whispered.

My grip tightened as the first tendrils of desperation crept into my mind. "Anything you want, anything at all," I tried again, "just name it, Meggy, and it's yours. *Anything*."

She blinked slowly, but those pale blue eyes I loved showed only fear as she murmured, "I want my life back. I don't want this . . . I don't . . . don't want . . ."

When she broke down in hysterical sobs, I finally released her and let Toula push me into the hallway. "I'll talk to her," she promised, but the door closed in my face, and I listened to Meggy weep as I stood there, more alone than I had ever been.

True to her word, Toula tried, but Meggy would have none of it. Once the Arcanum medics cleared her and departed, she moved next door into Olive's room and took up a vigil by the sleeping girl's bed. She would speak to Toula, but no one else.

"Meg's just scared," Toula insisted in private, "and traumatized, and everything at once . . ." She leaned against the high back of one of the leather couches I'd copied and closed her eyes. "She'll get over it. Just give her time, a little space, room to come to terms with . . . *this*."

But I only lasted two days before I again ventured into that wing of the palace.

Meggy, who was holding Olive's hand as she slept, watched warily as I latched the door. "Hi," I mumbled.

"Hi."

"Just, uh . . ." I rubbed the back of my neck, wishing there were softness in her stare. "Just checking in. Do you need anything?"

She stood and stroked Olive's limp hair. "When is she going to wake up?"

"When Toula lifts the spell on her. She'll be fine."

"And then we can go?"

I racked my brain for an answer unlikely to upset Meggy, but none came to mind. "I'm sorry," I said slowly, "but I can't let you take her."

Her eyes flashed, and her voice, already cold, turned to ice. "My child is coming home with me."

"She's dangerous."

"She's *sixteen!*"

"That doesn't matter! Meggy . . ." I took a deep breath, fighting my temper before it could flare. "The last thing she saw before Toula knocked her out was

Titania die. She'd asked for my head a few minutes before that. When she wakes, the kid's going to have scores to settle."

"Not with me."

"With *all* of us. You're guilty by association, at the very least." I sighed and searched her face, but there was no chink in Meggy's armor. "If I sent her back with you now, you'd probably be dead in a day or two."

"Toula says I have talent—"

"Which you have no idea how to use. Sure, you'll intuit some of it as you go," I allowed, "but you need training before you snap and accidentally burn your house down. It's happened," I added as she began to protest. "Olive's had that training already. Meggy, you can't defend yourself against her. Not yet."

Risking a punch in the face, I crossed the room and took her hands. "Look," I murmured, "if nothing else, you'll have to learn how to use a glamour before you go back, unless you want to tell your friends and family that you've had a revolutionary face-lift. Stay here for now, learn what you need to get by, and let me deal with Olive."

Meggy's eyes bored into mine. "*Deal* with her? How? Lock her up?"

"Probably," I replied, speeding up before she could interject, "but just for a time, until she comes around—"

"No." She pulled free of my grip and folded her

arms. "Absolutely not. If you lock my baby away, it'll be over my dead body."

"Meggy—"

"*No.*"

I didn't have to bargain with her, as the realm hastened to remind me. Meggy didn't have a prayer of besting me, and as Olive had encouraged Mother to kill me, I could by right do whatever I chose with the girl. Still, I heard myself ask Meggy, "What would you have me do?"

"Well," she shrugged, "for starters, you could bind her."

"*Bind*—how can you say that?" I sputtered. "Look at Toula, look in the *mirror*—"

"I think I've done all right," she stiffly replied.

"It would have killed you if it hadn't been broken," I retorted. "You want to put Olive through that?"

"You don't have to copy the one that was on me. Just keep her from using her power for now. How is that any worse than locking her away?" I didn't have a ready answer, and Meggy seized the opportunity. "Toula told me it's possible to make false memories. Bind Olive, take all traces of this place away, and let me give her a chance at the life she should have had with a mother who loves her." Her eyes began to well, and she swiped at her tears before they could fall. "*You're* the reason I lost her to begin with, Colin. If you love me, then give me back my little girl."

I tried one last time, knowing even as I did that I'd lost. "Stay for a while. Let me show you what you can do."

"You've shown me quite enough," she replied as her face shifted to match her age. "Toula showed me how to do that with a spell, and we figured out the other way together. She said that she'll give me pointers when I go home."

The realm wasn't keen on the plan, but I pushed the odd voice to the back of my mind and conceded the victory. "All right," I murmured. "If that's what you want. But you'll have to start fresh," I cautioned. "False memories aren't perfect, and if your neighbors start asking questions about where Olive came from, her real memories might break through. I could put you in my place in Rigby. There's a decent apartment above my bookstore, and you could have my car . . ."

She considered the offer. "And what will Olive think?"

"As far as she'll know, you two will have never been apart."

"Good." She paused, then stuck out her hand. "Thank you."

Our handshake was awkward, but under the circumstances, it was the best I could hope for. "I'll send you back tonight, then. Let me make the preparations."

I had lost track of the days, and so when I stepped through to Rigby, it was quarter of eleven that night. My apartment was dark, but when I flipped on the switches, I found the place spotless and smelling of lemon Pledge, and I suspected that Mrs. Cooper was to thank. The décor simply wouldn't do, however, and so I set about changing the furniture to something more befitting Meggy and Olive, trying to replicate Meggy's house on a smaller scale. My personal books and papers I sent back to my office in Faerie, but I set up a modest office nook for Meggy where my desk had been, reupholstered the couch and chairs, replaced the blinds, and converted my catch-all storage room into a proper bedroom for Olive, heavy on the pink.

As I considered window treatments, I happened to glance across the street and spotted lights on in Mrs. Cooper's apartment. Even with the hour, her silhouette moved behind the sheers—she was nothing if not vigilant—and so I slipped out and up her cluttered fire escape.

My neighbor beamed at me when the kitchen door opened. "Hello, dear, welcome back! How are you? Is everything okay now?"

"Just fine, Mrs. Cooper, thank you," I lied, and followed her to the living-room sofa. "But I can't stay long."

Her brows knit. "Oh?"

"Unfortunately, I'm going to have to get out of the book business. I, uh . . . I'm needed elsewhere."

"Oh, dear," she murmured, patting my gloves. She gave me a critical look, then added, "You haven't been sleeping, have you?"

"Not much," I admitted. "And I need to ask a favor of you."

"What sort of favor?"

"Long story short, I'm moving my daughter and her mother into my building. Meggy's going to take over the bookstore."

Her wrinkled face brightened. "Splendid! Let me know when, and I'll bring over tea and some sandwiches—"

"But," I interrupted before she could start planning a menu, "there's a catch. My daughter isn't going to remember me. *Nothing* about me. It's for a good reason," I explained, seeing her eyes cloud, then muttered, "And I'm fairly certain that Meggy isn't going to want to think about me ever again. Could you . . . you know, look after them? They're going to be new to the neighborhood, and—"

"Of course, dear," she replied, giving my hands a squeeze. "I won't say a word. And . . . about the bookstore, uh . . . ."

"Gift from an eccentric distant cousin," I supplied, wishing Joey were there to come up with something better. "If anyone asks, I've gone to Europe for a while."

Mrs. Cooper smiled tightly. "I'm going to miss you, Mr. Leffee. Good neighbors are hard to come by these days."

I grinned and stood. "Then let's hope you finally get some—oh, almost forgot." A blue ceramic teakettle appeared on top of her coffee table's stack of magazines. "Haven't been out to Target, but will that do?"

"That's lovely, dear."

"Different color?"

Mrs. Cooper stroked her chin in contemplation. "Well, I don't want to put you to any trouble . . ."

I saw her idea at the top of her thoughts, and the kettle morphed from blue to a tiny floral chintz. "Oh, that's perfect!" she exclaimed. "But you didn't have to—"

"Anytime," I said, and took my leave.

That night, I put Olive in a deep trance and wove into her memory the best life I could give her.

Olive's father—her mother's childhood sweetheart—had died of a heart attack just after her third birthday. Her only memories of him were fuzzy but full of love. She and her mother, who had been both orphaned and widowed young, had traveled together around the country, hopping between rare book events and estate sales in a lucrative scouting and reselling business. Now, thanks to a cousin with a wild hair who had abandoned his bookstore to go backpacking in Europe, Olive's mother had a storefront of her own and a place to raise her. She had been homeschooling the girl, but with the stability of the store, perhaps she might consider sending Olive out among her peers. Mother and daughter doted on each other—they were all the family they had left—but even still, both knew that it would be good for Olive to make friends her own age.

I bound her to the best of my inexperienced ability, trying to hide the faintest traces of magic, and crafted the enchantment to age her appropriately when the time came. After all, there was no telling how long the bind would need to remain in place—or, I reminded myself, how Olive would react once it was broken. The best I could hope was that after spending a few years with her real mother, Olive would see the truth of what Titania had done and embrace Meggy without magical prodding.

With that accomplished, I delivered them to my renovated apartment and watched from the doorway as Meggy tucked our daughter into her new bed. "She'll wake in the morning, right?" she whispered.

I nodded and stepped aside so that Meggy could close the door to Olive's room. "Toula said it would come off around seven. She won't remember a thing." I headed for the den and the gate I'd left open, but turned back to hand Meggy another small telephone. "If anything happens, if this doesn't work out, if you think the bind's weakening—"

"We'll be fine," she said, putting the phone on an end table.

The message was clear. Satisfied that the building was secure, I nodded and gave her a tight smile. "Good-bye, Meggy," I murmured, and closed the gate without looking back.

CHAPTER 24

"Hiya, Gramps, miss me?"

The lightning flash in the middle of my office had caught my eye an instant before the gate began to open. Pushing my breakfast plate aside, I smirked as Toula flopped onto one of the couches. "It's called a door. You can knock on them and everything."

"Don't be tedious," she replied, and straightened up. "And this is official business, anyway, so don't give me a hard time."

My eyebrow rose. "How official?"

"Arcanum official."

"They took you?"

"Not exactly," she explained. "But Harrison thought that since wizard-fae relations are still kind of rocky, I have no idea why"—she rolled her eyes in mock exasperation—"that a sort of ambassador might be a good thing to have on hand. Apparently, I was the only candidate."

"Mm. He didn't run this by me."

"No, but he said he thought you wouldn't mind. So here I am," she concluded, spreading her arms.

I took in her ratty Broncos T-shirt and black leggings. "You dress to impress, as always."

"Absolutely. Anyway, your priest buddy got hold of Harrison somehow, and he says he needs to talk to you. Something about Joey . . ."

I was already out of my chair. "On my way," I said, and pointed to my desk as a new gate opened and the realm began to complain at my imminent departure. "Don't touch my bagel."

A fresh one appeared in her hand. "Got any Nutella stashed around here, or do I have to make that, too?"

I managed to catch up with Joey as he was cramming the last of his clothes into his trike's trunk in the dormitory parking lot. "What's going on, kid?" I asked, and he turned and grinned.

"Hey! Come to see me off?" he said, and gave his recalcitrant trunk lid another shove.

I joined him as he struggled against physics. "Paul said you'd quit. What's going on?"

Joey smiled sadly. "I don't feel it anymore. This

isn't where I'm supposed to be. I'm not sure *where* that is, exactly, but it's not here."

I watched in silence as he began body-slamming the lid in an effort to make it latch. "Joey, I . . . I'm sorry . . ."

"I'm not," he interrupted, puffing slightly with the exertion. "Just need . . . to figure out . . . what I'm doing," he added, punctuating his words with repeated blows against the trike.

Pushing him out of the way, I opened the lid, surveyed the mess inside, then snapped my fingers. The contents rolled and folded themselves into neat bundles, and I lowered the lid. "Packing is an art, you know."

"Thanks," he mumbled, somewhat chastened, and picked up his helmet. "So yeah, I'm off for a while. Might go out west for a bit if my cash holds up, see what there is to see."

"Any idea of what comes after?"

Joey shrugged. "Still working on my résumé. So far, I've got down skills in exegesis and swordplay. Suggestions?"

I studied his young face for a moment, then nodded. "Maybe," I said as a fat stack of bills appeared in my hand. "Ten grand. Go figure yourself out. Get in touch with Toula if you need more."

His dark eyes widened. "I can't—"

"It's nothing, and I owe you a hell of a lot more than that. Please."

He unlatched his trunk again and carefully hid the money in his shoes. "Thanks, Colin. Hey, question."

"Shoot," I replied, leaning against a lamppost.

"You remember Ilunna?"

"Sure, why?"

His face began to color. "You, uh . . . you don't think that she . . ."

I sensed where he was going and headed him off. "They're not monogamous, kid. I don't see that ending well . . . but I could be wrong," I hastened to add as his expression changed. "You know the way down there, and you'd be able to understand her this time." I tapped the side of his head and grinned. "Can't hurt to try, eh?"

"Maybe not." He shoved his helmet on and straddled his trike. "How're Olive and Meggy?"

"Just fine," I said, hoping that he wouldn't press the issue.

To my relief, he merely nodded and lifted his visor. "So what was that idea you had, anyway?"

"Go travel first," I told him. "And when you're finished, if you don't have a better plan . . . come see me. I could use a guy like you, kid."

"Yeah?"

"Yeah."

He pondered for a moment: "401k and insurance?"

"Not exactly."

"I'll think about it," he said with a smile as his trike roared to life.

For the first months, I stayed so busy with court affairs that I seldom had a moment to myself. The mess was as wearying as Oberon had promised, an endless parade of grievances and petty squabbles blown up beyond all sense, plus the added joys of determining which of Mother's former aides and guards were willing to work for me. I vetted, mediated, arbitrated, and punished accordingly, and every so often, I got to sleep. Unfortunately, I never had time to cross the border. Toula popped by occasionally with updates from the Arcanum, but she offered me nothing about Meggy's doings, and I knew better than to inquire. Meggy's life was her own, and she'd made it obvious that I was to have no further part in it. And why would I? She was Oberon's, after all, and to that court, I was nothing but a spoilsport specializing in metallurgic torture.

But one Saturday evening in July, as I sat on my office's window ledge, enjoying the breeze and the scent of the eternally blooming roses in the garden below, my homemade phone began to ring. Surprised by the unanticipated call—when Toula wanted something, she simply came over, to my guards' dismay—I opened the phone expecting to hear Joey's voice. "Having a good trip?" I asked.

The other end was silent for a few seconds, and then I heard Meggy say, "Staycation, actually. Olive's off at cheer camp, so I'm here in case she needs something."

"*Meggy?*" I cried, and cleared my throat, forcing myself to calm down. "Uh . . . hi. How are you?"

"Honestly?" She paused again. "I could do with some company. You busy?"

"Not at all," I replied, ignoring the stack of papers on my desk. "Are you home? I'll open a gate—"

"No, I'm out. Meet me at Slim's in a few, okay?"

I didn't have to be told twice. Making myself presentable and aging myself to match Meggy's disguise, I slipped into the alley by the bar, braced myself, then hurried inside.

The night was muggy, and Slim had cranked his air-conditioning high for the benefit of the modest crowd drawn by karaoke night. Ignoring the caterwauling from the microphone, I looked around for Meggy, but as I seemed to have arrived first, I gave in to habit and took my old seat at the bar. Slim walked up, drying a glass with a frayed towel, and grunted. "Evening, stranger."

I nodded. "Slim."

"Drinking?"

"No, I came for the world-class entertainment," I retorted, and smiled as he brought over a bottle of Johnnie Black and a semi-clean glass. "Waiting for someone."

"Mm. Heard you got a new job out of town."

"Something like that," I replied, pouring. "Fumbling my way through it for now."

"Eh, sounds about right." He put the bottle back on the shelf and leaned on the bar, keeping his voice low. "And while you're here, you still owe me, you know."

"Check your register," I said, and he shuffled over for an inspection. He closed the drawer again quickly—I had stuffed it with cash—and I saluted him with my glass. "Greg told you, did he?"

"Toula, actually. After she chewed me out over her sticks." He wandered off for a moment to slake a few of his other patrons' thirst, then returned to my end of the bar and bent close again. "Incidentally, is it Colin or Coileán these days?"

I finished my drink in one long shot and slid the empty glass back across the bar. "Depends on who's asking. Don't go getting fancy on me, man."

"Never," he agreed as he hid my glass away in the wash rack. "You take it easy, hear?"

"Likewise."

He glanced over my shoulder at the sound of the opening door, then cut his eyes back to me. "I think your friend just walked in."

I turned to find Meggy standing in the doorway, a touch on the windblown and frizzy side from the weather, but my foolish heart still leapt at the sight of her. We locked eyes across the room, then winced as the next karaoke hero slurred his way through the first bars of "Bohemian Rhapsody." "Later, Slim," I muttered, and followed Meggy into the night.

"He always does that on Saturday nights," I told her once we were safe on the quiet street. "Trivia can get loud, but when the singers come out . . ." My voice trailed off, and I shoved my hands into my pockets. "So."

"So." She gave me a small smile. "Take a walk?"

At first, neither of us had anything to say, and I didn't know what destination she might have in mind. Her footsteps wound in the general direction of the beach, but she seemed to be meandering. I was in no hurry—just seeing Meggy again was an unexpected boon, even with the silence. But after a time, when the muffled, off-key yowling of Slim's had long since faded, I ventured, "How are things with Olive? Is the bind—"

"Good. We're good." Meggy tucked her hair behind one ear, but the wind tugged it free an instant later. "Seems to be holding."

"But you two—"

"I mean, she's sixteen. *Headstrong.* But we're making it. She's starting as a junior this fall. Even got a spot on the cheerleading squad—they were nice enough to let her try out at the end of the year." She looked at me curiously. "You know, for a kid who's spent her whole life abroad, she has an excellent grasp of American history."

"I . . . may have imparted a bit of that when I bound her."

Her lips twitched in a knowing smile. "What else?"

"Let's just say enough basic knowledge to keep her from playing in traffic and maybe get her through high school."

"Except computers. Never imagined I'd have to explain e-mail to a teenager."

"No one's perfect," I muttered.

We walked on, once more at a loss for conversation, until we reached the wooden shelter at the edge of the beach, a weathered pavilion dotted with picnic tables. The place was deserted, and Meggy picked a spot on a bench with a seaside view. Granted, there wasn't much to see at that time of night, but the stars were out, and the crash and hiss of the waves was as soothing as always.

"Meggy," I said, staring out at the Atlantic, "why did you call me?"

She made no reply for a long moment, and when she spoke again, her voice was low. "Because I thought I was over you."

"Oh." Deflated, I kept my eyes on the horizon.

"Yeah." One hand tightened on her purse strap. "I was crushed when you ran off back then, and you never called, and then I got *angry*. And somewhere along the way, once I'd almost resigned myself to the fact that I'd never see my baby again, I realized I didn't feel that rage toward you anymore, or that hurt, or . . . anything, really. I was numb about you. And then you showed up on my doorstep with Olive, and . . ."

"I'm sorry. About everything. I should have done things better—"

"Yeah, well, too late now." She sighed and shifted on the bench beside me. "But when you came around, the numbness went away, and everything I'd felt about you . . . it all bubbled up at once. I was still furious and so hurt, but . . ." Her voice trailed off.

"But what?" I prodded.

Meggy ignored the question. "Do you remember my birthday, when we went out to the middle of nowhere to drink champagne and watch the stars? We were in the back of your truck on a blanket, and we started getting cold from lying there, and you turned on the radio and danced with me to warm up. Remember that?"

"Yes," I murmured, "I remember."

"Well, as much as I've tried to deny it since then, I fell in love with that man," she softly replied. "And now . . . I guess I called because I need to know if he exists."

Feeling the pressure of her stare on me, I turned and tried to trace her features in the shadows. "He does. And he fell in love with you, too." She said nothing while my searching fingers found hers on the bench. "I'm sorry for the lies, Meggy. I'm sorry for leaving. If you're done with me . . . I understand,"

I forced myself to say. "But I will never stop loving you."

She nodded once, slowly, and her fingers twisted to interlace with mine. "I still . . . *sometimes* . . . I think about the three of us being a family. Maybe someday."

Though my heart began to pound, I tried to keep my cool. "I'd like that."

"But I'd want to get to know you first," said Meggy. "The *real* you, warts and all."

"I want you to know the real me." I realized I was squeezing her hand and relaxed my grip. "Let me make it up to you."

She thought for a moment, then said, "If you wanted to take me on a date some night . . . that might be okay. When Olive's not around, naturally."

"Of course." I hesitated, trying to anticipate her reaction, then said, "I know you didn't see much of Faerie when you were there, but if you'd ever like a tour, maybe while Olive's away—"

"No," she interrupted, "I'm not going over there. If you want to do this, it'll be on my turf."

I had no room to negotiate—Meggy held all the cards—but I was overjoyed to surrender to her. "Deal. Come on," I said, rising from the bench. "I don't want to a waste a minute of this night."

We set off together toward the tiki bar on the shore and the dunes beyond it, hand in hand, Meggy and me. There were no fireworks that night, no music, nothing but the endless black sea and the touch of Meggy's skin on mine.

I could smell magic in the air, untapped potential flowing all around us. Then Meggy's smiling eyes caught the moonlight, and in that perfect moment, that was enough.

ACKNOWLEDGMENTS

Writing may be a solitary endeavor, but books don't happen without significant help along the way.

My talented editor, Priyanka Krishan, improves everything she touches. Thanks to her and to the team at Harper Voyager for making this possible.

Part of the writing process involves getting chummy with the voices in your head, and finding a support network of folks who don't classify that sort of behavior as insanity is invaluable. A big thank-you goes to the Novel Chicks, who welcomed me into the fold five years ago and have been putting up with me ever since. You're the best, ladies! Thanks are also due to Adam Domby and Tina Hammonds for their assistance as early readers.

When I was nineteen, clueless, and in desperate need of a mentor, Eytan Halaban took me under his wing. I'm so grateful to him for gamely slogging through my college writings and for encouraging me in the years since.

Here's to you, Mom and Dad. I can't thank you enough.

And finally, to you, the reader—thanks for coming along for the ride.

ABOUT THE AUTHOR

When not writing fiction, **ASH FITZSIMMONS** is an appellate attorney and an unrepentant car singer. Visit her at www.ashfitzsimmons.com.

www.harpervoyagerbooks.com

Discover great authors, exclusive offers, and more at hc.com.